INTERDICTION

INTERDICTION

MATT HARDMAN

DOUBLE‡DAGGER

Library and Archives Canada Cataloguing in Publication
Hardman, Matt. author
Interdiction / Matt Hardman

Issued in print and electronic formats.
ISBN: 978-1-990644-08-5 (soft cover)
ISBN: 978-1-990644-09-2 (e-book)

Editor: Matt Lennox
Cover design: Pablo Javier Herrera

Double Dagger Books Inc.
Toronto, Ontario, Canada
www.doubledagger.ca

For my wife, kids, and family
who supported me during
twenty years of deployments
and missed time.

1

GOMEZ

HECTOR JULIAN GOMEZ, Captain, United States Navy, strode through the aluminum-framed double doors of the facility with his aide in tow. Both men flashed their identification cards at the quarterdeck watch and Gomez wondered if the N95 masks required in government facilities hindered the identification process.

The offices of Commander, Carrier Strike Group Ten, tucked away in an undistinguished building across from piers eleven and twelve of Naval Station Norfolk, are fairly spartan affairs. Consisting of an uncluttered quarterdeck and two floors of sparsely furnished rooms in a small, mid-century building, the offices are decorated with the same government-chic furniture found in the mid-rise barracks just a few blocks away.

Carrier Strike Group Ten had little in the way of history despite tracing its ancestry back to the First World War, a period when it was known as Destroyer Flotilla Two and the commander's collection of small, thin-hulled tin cans sailed out of Newport, Rhode Island. From inception, the command had experienced all of the heartbreak and happiness of an on-again, off-again relationship with the United States Navy. She'd been activated and deactivated repeatedly during her lengthy history, undergoing several overhauls in name and composition. In 1973 she'd become Cruiser Destroyer Group Two. Twenty years later, she'd been rechristened as the USS George Washington Battle Group, finally becoming a permanent fixture in America's order of battle.

Gomez had little time for history. His appearance at the building's entrance was a simple matter. Commander, Carrier Strike Group Ten was his boss and he'd been summoned by an early morning phone call. His mind was fixed firmly on the present and immediate future.

Gomez watched the young petty officer examine his identification card. The bespectacled sailor saluted crisply and picked up a nearby microphone. Gomez turned away and stepped off down the passageway, making it a full eight paces before a nervous voice rang over the building's announcing system.

"Commander, Destroyer Squadron Two Six. Arriving."

He reached the outer offices of Commander, Carrier Strike Group Ten and was immediately escorted into an inner sanctum. A harried man sat behind a large oak desk amid a mountain of paperwork that kept over fifteen-thousand sailors and their gear fed, paid, maintained, and deployed.

Gomez watched as Rear Admiral Davis Raymond Gray scribbled notes in the margin of some report; writing, erasing, and re-writing before grunting with approval. Gray, he remembered, was a graduate of the United States Naval Academy. Gomez had turned down that appointment in favor of an NROTC scholarship at the University of Notre Dame. The decision had been the source of some good-natured ribbing during his career, but Gomez frequently had the last laugh. Especially during football season.

When the admiral was satisfied with his notes, he raised his eyes from a manila folder. Gray blinked, then grinned. The strike group commander stood and jogged around the desk with his hand extended.

"Hector, Congrats. Just heard," the admiral announced.

Gomez flashed a look at his aide as he took the admiral's offered handshake. A blank face and barely perceptible shrug told him he wasn't alone in his confusion.

"Thank you, Admiral, but congrats for what?"

Gray stood for a second before turning. Gomez and his staffer looked on as the admiral leaned across his desk, shuffling through an array of pens, pencils and highlighters. After a few moments, Gray's hands seized a piece of paper and he turned back, still grinning.

"Here," Gray said, handing over the scrap of paper. "Read that."

Gomez glanced at his aide. His eyes lowered to the paper.

He read the missive once. Then twice. Then a third time.

Well, I'll be damned.

He looked up at the admiral.

Rear Admiral Gray was beaming. "Congratulations, Rear Admiral-select Gomez. Well done."

"Thank you, sir." Gomez wasn't sure what to say. His mind raced.

This would change things. He'd be replaced at his current command. New orders would follow this. Pentagon duty seemed likely. He shook off the horror of that idea. That was something to be dealt with later and he was certain that a promotion wasn't the reason he'd been summoned.

"Admiral, what's this all about? You didn't order me here for this." Gomez held up the message.

"True. Take a seat gentlemen. You can lose the masks if you like." Gray waved the commander of Destroyer Squadron Two-Six to one of two comfortable leather seats opposite the desk. Gomez's aide took the other chair, waiting until everyone else was seated as decorum mandated.

"Not gonna beat around the bush, Hector. I need the Williams." Gray said.

Gomez cocked his head. "The Williams?"

The USS James E. Williams, hull number DDG 95, was a guided missile destroyer that had just returned from wargames with Her Majesty's Royal Navy in the North Sea. She'd gone there short-handed and in need of repairs. She'd performed well during the two month-long exercise and that was a tribute to the crew more than anything else. The ship had gone to the North Sea days after finishing a mini-deployment. Williams had skipped maintenance periods to go on both assignments. Rear Admiral-select Gomez knew that the Williams had issues stemming from two decades of neglect. "Admiral. That ship, and her crew, have a lot of problems. And they're supposed to be heading into the yards."

Gray nodded. "I know. Turning over most of the chain of command and losing part of the Chief's Mess is a big problem. But we need her to go to bat."

Gomez's mind raced. The Williams had just gotten new commanding and executive officers as well as a new Command Master

Chief—men who'd expected to take the ship through an extensive overhaul. Replacing all three positions over a two-week period was not normal. He'd made several phone calls to the detailers at the Navy's Bureau of Personnel. His pleas to spread the transfers out had been ignored. The outgoing men were necessary elsewhere. Needs of the Navy. He'd fumed and turned his attention to other issues.

The Williams had lost a sizable portion of the Chief's Mess, most notably seven of the eight Chief Petty Officers assigned to the Williams' Engineering Department. Planned retirements, a hardship transfer, and a slew of injuries had depleted the ship's senior enlisted ranks. That none of these individuals had been replaced yet was problematic, even with the understanding that the ship was heading to dry dock. Gomez had spent weeks calling detailers, trying to fill the empty billets.

"Where to?" Gomez asked.

"Horn of Africa. Somalia. Maritime interdiction."

Anti-piracy. Independent duty. She'd be alone with no supporting cast. Gomez shook his head. "Admiral."

Gray smiled. The image of the man, in his rumpled uniform, with that grin, reminded Gomez of old black and white war movie officers. "The name is Davis. You're gonna put on a star soon."

Gomez shifted in his seat and nodded.

"Davis, that's a ten-month deployment for a ship that still doesn't have a full crew. The captain and executive officer are both in their second month. They have one engineering chief left onboard. He's not qualified to be the Top Snipe."

"I know all that Hector. But she has to go."

Gomez tried shifting tactics. "It's not just the personnel problems, sir. She's in rough shape. She's not been in drydock since she left the building yards in 2002. She's skipped her last four maintenance periods. In the last five-hundred days, she's spent four-hundred and eight at sea."

Gomez saw a pained expression flash across his boss' face before the man turned to Gomez's own staffer. The Lieutenant Commander hadn't said a word so far. He'd just sat there, stress-testing the buttons on his khaki shirt and keeping a neutral expression on his face. Gray addressed the junior officer. "Excuse me, Commander. Can you step outside?"

The staffer nodded before standing and leaving the room. After the door shut, Gray spoke again. "That boy any good?"

Gomez smiled. "Havner?" A shrug. "Depends on what you mean by that. The man is the best admin guy I've ever seen. Hands down. He never forgets anything and nothing ever needs to be reworked."

Gray snorted. "Bullshit."

"I'm serious. He's got this system that would put the project management industry out of business. If he'd gone into the priesthood, he'd already be organizing the Vatican Archives."

"I hear a 'but' coming, Hector." Gray smiled.

Gomez took a breath. "Let's just say he's not what you'd call tactically adept. Or strategically adept." A pause. "Or capable of leading much more than two or three people at the same time."

"Ah." Gray nodded. "And how'd you find him?"

"A recommendation from an old master chief on the McCain. Mr. Havner has gotten this far by sticking to what he's good at and trusting his chiefs to do their job."

Gray grunted. "Not a bad way to run a Navy. I'm assuming Mr. Havner never screened for command?"

Gomez shook his head. "Not even close. Rumor from the master chief is that he begged his last captain to not endorse him."

Gray's bushy eyebrows went up. "Really?"

The look on Gray's face was clear. This man, the commander of an entire fleet, could not fathom the idea that a naval officer would willingly turn down a chance to have his or her own warship.

Gomez shrugged. "I asked him about that. He was never comfortable being in charge of the ship. His last captain said that the only way he could get through a watch on the bridge was rote memory. If X happens, do Y. That kind of thing. But whenever he was presented with a tactical scenario that required him to think on the fly and make command decisions, he froze. Badly." Another shrug. "What can I say? He's a man who very clearly knows his strengths and weaknesses. He knows his limitations, accepts them, and does what he is capable of doing so damn well that booting him really would hurt the service. He might never promote again, but I think he's made his peace with that. Frankly, with him on the staff, I rarely have to deal with admin headaches."

"Rarely?" Gray cocked one eyebrow up this time. "Not never?"

Gomez smiled, a sheepish grin. "Well. I can't delegate everything."

Gray barked with laughter. "Hector, you figure a legal way to do that, I'll personally get you a second star to go with the one you're already getting."

"Deal." Gomez smiled and leaned forward in the chair, resting his forearms on his knees. "Admiral."

"Davis."

Hector nodded. "That's gonna take some getting used to. Davis, the Williams. She isn't ready. I was down on the pier last week, right after she got back. She looks like the Caine when Willie Keith first shows up. Every system she has is either at, or barely above, red line."

Gomez knew that James E. Williams had been hovering at that line for nearly a year. It was a delicate dance that was, again, more a tribute to the sailors who operated and maintained the ship than it was to the leadership tasked with getting the ship into a steady maintenance and upkeep routine.

Yeah. Folks like me.

Gomez brushed that thought aside. Now wasn't the time to kick his own ass.

"I know all of that, Hector. I really do," the Admiral conceded. "I know she's had a raw deal. I know crew morale is in the shitter. I know the gear is either wearing out or already done for. But she is, literally, the last working destroyer on this coast capable of deploying independently." The Admiral held up two folders. "These are reports from the two ships that should be deploying before the Williams." He tossed the folders across the desk.

Gomez picked them up and leafed through them. His heart sank as he scanned the documents. It took less than sixty seconds of reading for the inevitability of the situation to crash in on him.

This was a losing battle.

Gomez looked up at the admiral.

"When did these come in?"

"Fresh off the printer." The admiral said.

"Shit," Gomez mumbled. He looked up, startled. "Apologies, Admiral."

Gray smiled and waved it off. "Name's Davis. You've got your own flag now. Get used to it. In private anyway." Gomez nodded and Gray continued. "Besides, sailors are supposed to swear." The strike group commander leaned over his desk and pointed at the folders. "As you can see, Oscar Austin has a damaged main reduction gear. She's out of commission for five months, minimum. Burke had a fuel leak and fire in shaft alley. She's done for at least six months. Headed to dry dock next week."

Gomez read through both reports. He had a couple more cards to play, but he suspected how this would end. The James E. Williams, a rusted, battered hulk of a ship so overdue for upgrades to her engineering and combat systems suites that she was analog compared to the ships just coming out of the building yards, would sail halfway around the world on his orders. She would do so with a decapitated crew that had performed well in spite of everything. That was something, he knew. But he also knew that every ship and every sailor had a breaking point. He wondered just how close the Williams and her crew might be to that line.

Gomez leaned back and thought. The mechanical risks associated with sending the Williams out were easy to quantify. Somewhere on the DC beltway, there were groups of engineers—probably men and women who still used slide rules for fun—that could tell him, down to the minute, when a piece of gear would break. What he worried about were the risks to his people. They'd been at sea too long. Away from family for too long. And while every person in uniform accepted that as part of the job, acceptance didn't make it suck any less.

This crew had been away for the better part of two years, picking up slack as other ships suffered endless breakdowns. They'd missed birthdays and Christmases, graduations and anniversaries. At least eight sailors on the Williams had missed the births of their children and two had missed the passing of a parent.

"What about Bainbridge or Mason? They've been back for a few months." Gomez had vague ideas about each ship's status. They weren't under his command so he didn't bother getting into the weeds. His squadron of destroyers had problems sufficient to keep a commander busy for a lifetime.

Gray shook his head. "Neither is available. Mason has a helo hangar door that won't budge. Forty thousand pounds of steel trapping a reserve Seahawk chopper in the hangar."

Gomez looked up. "What happened?"

A shrug from the old admiral. "Lots of stuff. Air motor died. Brakes failed. Retainer pins broke. Weight of the door shifting broke some rollers and such." Gray shuffled through the piles of folders on his desk. He selected one and handed it over.

Gomez opened the folder and blinked. The picture showed the forty-thousand-pound hangar door sitting like a massive accordion on the deck of the ship—no longer attached to the top of the hangar's frame. Gomez flipped through the report and looked up. "No one got hurt?"

Gray shook his head. "Nah. They were paying attention and following safety regs. Maybe a couple folks need new boxer shorts. Only person really hurt is a commander over at the air station. He's pretty hot about having one of his birds trapped in one of my ships and he's right pissed about not getting it back anytime soon. It's gonna take a couple cranes and a few welders with cutting torches to get that door off. After that, well, you know the issues with getting obsolete parts for an obsolete door as well as anyone. Could be a six-month lead time. Probably more."

Gomez looked at the pictures again. Forty thousand pounds of steel breaking free and screeching to a heap ten feet from you was bound to loosen the bowels a bit. He was also aware of the parts issues for the doors. He'd had trouble getting one of these massive doors replaced on a ship of his own. "What about Bainbridge?"

Gray leaned back, his well-worn chair squeaking on a pair of old hinges. "This stays in this room. Understand?"

Gomez nodded. "Understood."

"Bainbridge is about to go through some things. Captain, Executive Officer, Command Master Chief and a few others involved are gonna lose their jobs."

"Frat?" Gomez asked. He'd heard the rumors. He'd not believed them, but he'd heard them. Big as it was, the Navy was too small to keep secrets like that.

Gray nodded. "And a few other issues."

Gomez looked at all of the documents in his hands before giving them back. Those two ships represented the last cards he had to play. A smirk appeared on his lips. This was one hell of a way to run a railroad.

"When does she need to leave?"

The cheap government sedan carrying Gomez was, after an identification check, admitted past the guard shack and barrier at the base of pier six, near the point on the Naval Station Norfolk waterfront where Decatur Avenue made the gentle turn towards gate two on Admiral Taussig Boulevard. Lieutenant Commander Havner navigated the length of the pier to the lone ship at the far end. He avoided sailors, water hoses, supplies, and all manner of equipment necessary to support a ship and prepare her for sea. Gomez sat in the passenger seat and stared out the window.

"Tough decision, sir?" Havner's low voice broke the silence.

Gomez shook his head, the gesture lost on the man driving. "Not really. I have my orders. Williams will have hers this afternoon."

"Permission to speak?" Havner glanced in the rearview mirror.

Gomez nodded. "Of course."

"This is a bad idea, sir. From an admin standpoint, she can't do this. She's undermanned, especially in engineering, and most of her gear is shot. Ten months isn't the issue. She won't last two."

Gomez looked out of his window as the car continued up the pier at a snail's pace. Havner was right. Gomez had made that exact argument less than an hour before. That the argument made sense did not matter all that much. Broke as she was, the Williams did meet all of the standards required for a ship to sail.

"Commander?"

"Yes, sir?"

"When we get to the ship, let's keep those doubts to ourselves."

"Understood, sir. I was just..." Gomez saw the man's ears redden a bit.

"You're not wrong, Havner. But that ship can sail, so she will sail. We're gonna walk onboard and find out what we can do to help and then you and I are gonna spend the rest of the week pulling every string we can for them. Personnel, parts, stores. Anything they need."

Gomez saw Havner grin in the rearview mirror as the man

maneuvered the vehicle into the appropriate parking space.

"I can do that, sir."

Gomez put his cover on and stepped out of the car, not waiting for Havner to pull open the door. A few sailors nearby, surprised to see a full-bird officer suddenly standing in their midst, stopped what they were doing. Each came to attention, saluting as tradition and regulation dictated. Gomez and Havner returned the salutes and headed for the brow, a narrow, steel walkway spanning distance between the ship and the pier.

Gomez stopped to examine the ship and decided that she really did look like Herman Wouk's Caine. Her once haze grey hull was pinstriped with rust streaks which several sailors in harnesses were attacking with needle guns and scrub brushes. Aft, the flight deck was covered with all sorts of items—pallets of gear waiting to be installed, pallets of broken gear waiting to be craned off, sailors on phones, sailors working, trash and the detritus of shipboard life. Her superstructure was streaked just like the rest of her, with patches of rust visible to the naked eye. Everywhere he looked, Gomez saw the chaos that constitutes a normal day in the life of a Navy warship.

While it was true and obvious to even the greenest of sailors that the James E. Williams had seen better days, it was also true that the ship, in her almost twentieth year of service, had never suffered a major casualty. No fires. No flooding. No collisions.

She'd come out of the yards at Pascagoula in 2002 and had been a workhorse for the Atlantic Fleet ever since. The Williams had been worked hard and had always responded. She'd never missed an assignment and she'd answered the bell when other ships could not put to sea.

And therein was the problem. While she'd been out doing her job and covering for everyone else, the USS James E. Williams had skipped more programmed maintenance periods than any other ship in service. The result was inevitable. In building a reputation as the ship that could take a licking and keep on ticking, the USS James E. Williams had caused irreversible damage to her systems—like a boxer refusing to throw in the towel. Now, each new lick hurt a bit more, dug a little deeper. Each new issue became that much harder for the crew to overcome.

Gomez stood there at the end of the brow, looking at the ship and her crew and considering his options, as if he really had any.

He could walk onboard and deliver the news with as little compassion as he could muster, but he wasn't—had never been—that kind of cold-hearted bastard. He could walk on the ship, meet with the ship's commanding officer, and then head back to Admiral Gray's office and let the strike group commander know what he'd seen.

He could do that, but that wouldn't change the fact that there wasn't another destroyer that was ready and capable.

Capable? Ready?

Those words chased around in Gomez's mind for a moment.

Was this ship, or the crew, either of those things? Only one way to find out.

Gomez placed a foot on the brow and started marching towards the quarterdeck.

Chief Petty Officer Brian Thompson had just stepped onto the ferry's short brow when his cellphone began ringing, the iconic sounds of an eighties-era hair band audible over the sound of shrieking and laughing children. He helped usher his wife and kids ashore before answering, smiling at the collection of mouse ears and face paint.

"Hello?" Brian's voice was light. It was hard to be angry after a full day at Disney World.

"Chief Thompson?"

Brian placed the voice. It was Commander Dave Gallardo, his boss at Naval Recruiting District Michigan.

"Sir?"

"Got a minute, Chief?"

Brian stopped walking, on guard. "Sure, sir. What can I do for you?"

"Listen, Chief, there's no easy way to put this, so I'll be blunt. We just got orders for you."

It took a second for Brian's brain to process the words. He knew he had eighteen months left on shore duty. He pointed out that fact to Commander Gallardo.

"I know, Chief. We tried to find out what's going on."

"And?"

Brian could almost hear the man at the other end of the call shake his head. "Nothing. Just some info that there's a destroyer in need of a Top Snipe. That's it."

Brian closed his eyes. "She's going on deployment, isn't she, sir?"

"Yes, Chief. Leaving Norfolk for the Horn of Africa. She's apparently short-handed. Needs a department chief and someone who knows auxiliaries."

And I'm the only sonofabitch on shore duty that can do both? Dammit.

Brian started to ask that question, but the commander cut him off. "Apparently, Chief, you meet three of the ship's needs. That, and being on shore duty, made you the only choice."

"Uh, sir. You mentioned two reqs. What's the third?"

"Vessel boarding."

Brian closed his eyes. He didn't have many options. Which was a nice way of saying he had zero options. The decision had been made and the orders signed. As he thought about how to explain this to his wife and kids, he asked his last question.

"Shit, sir. What ship?"

The phone crackled. "USS James E. Williams."

2

EVANS

PRESIDENT-ELECT OF THE UNITED STATES Daniel Alexander Evans shivered as an icy wind ripped down the steps of the Capitol building's west front. It whipped and snapped countless rows of American flags and tore through the tens of thousands of people gathered there.

Television cameras from every major network trained their lenses on an elevated platform in the center of the neo-classical steps as the crowd, a mixture of frozen bodies, gathered to hear the opening speech of a new presidency. The clamor of thousands of conversations, muffled by a combination of facemasks and scarves, contended with the howling, late-January wind.

Evans had snuck up to an out-of-the-way alcove to take a peek at the gathering. He had to admit that the crowd was an odd sight. He'd watched this ceremony before and the stark contrast between what he saw now and what he'd seen on television commanded his attention.

Instead of the hundreds of thousands of people expected to attend the inauguration of a new administration, a mere thirty thousand people lined the steps and the National Mall. They were gathered in small groups—families and friends, probably—each of which was situated a few feet from the next collection of bodies. The spacing between each group was a nod to the concept of social distancing, something that had become part of everyday life over the previous year.

The president-elect noted that everyone in view was wearing some sort of face covering. That, he thought, was remarkable. Mask-wearing had been a point of contention during the election cycle, an argument and exercise in civil liberty and public health that had become heated over the previous fourteen months—sometimes violently so.

While the president-elect suspected that the masks were driving the Secret Service crazy— inhibiting the agents' ability to match faces to pictures of possible persons-of-interest—he also knew that those masks were part of the reason he was standing here, in this alcove, just minutes away from being sworn in as the forty-sixth President of the United States.

Evans turned away from the scene and began walking back to the conference room set aside for his family, thinking about the months ahead and the challenges waiting for him.

It was, he decided, quite the mood-killer.

Evans was inheriting a mess. He knew it. His staff knew it. Most of the public—regardless of political persuasion—knew it. In addition to a pandemic that was into its fourteenth month of existence, he was jumping feet-first into a slew of other issues, problems with no apparent bi-partisan solutions.

The Evans Administration was inheriting an unstable economy. A delicate organism under the best of days, the American economy had tanked over the past year as the coronavirus pandemic added a few extra degrees of irrationality to a world financial system that no one understood in the first place. Fewer Americans were working. Unemployment numbers were at an all-time high. Taxpayers were hesitant to spend, hedging against the possibility of unemployment. The resulting stagnation was something no incentive had been able to shake.

The pandemic was another problem. Coronavirus had killed more than one million people world-wide, including more than three-hundred-thousand United States citizens. That was bad enough, Evans thought. But the numbers weren't abating. The data coming from Johns Hopkins and the Centers for Disease Control and Prevention were terrifying, predicting another three-hundred-thousand dead by August. That data had kicked off a new round of arguments everywhere from Congress down to the family level about whether the practices of mask-wearing and social distancing were working, in addition to the ongoing debates about whether mandating either was even constitutional.

Social justice reform was still looming. Massive unrest on this particular point had reached Civil Rights-era proportions over the past decade. No one in Washington seemed to have enough political capital to wade into that particular pool and do anything other than drown in a very public manner.

Congress remained as divided as the voters who put them in office. Tribalism outstripped cross-aisle diplomacy. The individuals elected to govern had, at last count, discovered more than three hundred pieces of legislation that they could not come together to pass, reject, or even discuss—relegating such proposals to the constitutional purgatory of the majority leaders' respective bottom drawers.

The War on Terror was the only subject capable of generating massive bi-partisan support. Evans had ridden that issue to the Oval Office, making it a centerpiece of his campaign. It had just been common sense. The American public, nearly eighty-nine percent according to Gallup polls, wanted out of the War on Terror. For good reason.

For almost twenty years, the United States had been involved in a multi-front war with the impossible goal of eliminating terrorism. No bell-ringing was required to keep this problem at the forefront of public knowledge. Americans in the twenty-first century tended to be as aware of the events of this war as their antecedents had of the events in Vietnam. There were similarities between the two conflicts that didn't sit well with a majority of America. To some, the conflicts in the Middle East were nightmarish repeats of the Vietnam-era, right down to the evening news reports that had eroded support for the Vietnam War by providing a thorough accounting of US casualties— a disturbing mixture of young kids on their first deployment and grizzled vets nearing, or past, retirement-age.

In an era defined by partisan politics, this became one of the few issues everyone seemed to agree on. Over the course of a few mid-term cycles, voters had made it clear that small drawdowns were not acceptable. The public wanted a full and complete withdrawal of every soldier, sailor, airman and marine deployed in the Middle East. Almost every politician who failed to understand and acknowledge this reality was removed from office by citizens who were tired of watching flag-draped coffins roll off the tarmac at Dover.

Evans had toed the party line on almost every single issue except this. He'd come out on day one of his campaign with a promise to execute the full withdrawal that the voters wanted. In speech after speech on the campaign trail, he'd re-iterated that promise, noting each time that Americans would never have permitted foreign 'peace-keepers' to occupy even a single town had the situations been reversed. Afghanistan, Iraq and the rest of the region, he said, should look after themselves. The United States owed it to them to step out of the way. That none of the other candidates had adopted similar stances still baffled the pundits and talking heads and op-ed writers whose job it was to second-guess everything.

The general election had been close and Evans' proposal to end the War on Terror swayed just enough voters in just the right places to carry him into the Oval Office as the forty-sixth President of the United States.

Evans looked in the mirror one last time, checking the knot of a deep maroon tie. He turned around, facing his wife, Alicia. She'd been sitting with their children on a small couch in the middle of the room. His voice shook. "How do I look?"

"You look fine. Stop worrying."

Evans frowned. "It's an important day."

A knock on the door cut off his wife's retort.

The door opened just far enough for a frumpy-looking man to squeeze through. Leslie Barnes, the incoming White House Chief of Staff, grinned behind his mask. "It's time Mr. President. You ready?"

"He is," answered Alicia. "He just won't admit it."

Barnes nodded. "Yeah. He's like that."

"You guys know I can hear you. Right?" Evans asked, feigning exasperation.

"You know what Leslie?" Alicia smiled.

"Ma'am?"

"If nothing else goes right during the next four years, at least he learned to knot his ties properly."

Evans turned, a crooked grin on his face. "You see what I have to deal with Leslie?"

The Chief of Staff stiffened and held his hands up in mock surrender. "Mr. President, I did not live to be my age by getting involved in disputes like this."

"Aren't you supposed to help me?"

Barnes grinned. "My duties stop at that front sir. You hired me. You married her."

"Some Chief of Staff you are," the president-elect grumbled, smoothing his lapels one more time.

Leslie Barnes shrugged. "I try. You ready?"

"Almost," Evans acknowledged, still worrying about his tie. A thought popped into his head. "Leslie, how many people out there had to get tested?"

"Hell, Mr. President. Most of the folks on the dais. Me. Everyone you'll be in contact with today. Why?"

"That's a hell of a thing, isn't it?" The president-elect asked. His nose still bothered him from his own test that day. "Some of those people work here and, well, getting a cotton swab shoved hilt-deep up your nose is part of the job. But some of those folks volunteered to be here. Requested invites."

"Masochists," Alicia pointed out. "They want to be here in D.C. to listen to you ramble. Something has to be wrong with them."

Barnes grinned. "Doesn't say much for your husband ma'am."

The future FLOTUS shrugged. "Sailors are a weird breed. What can I say?"

Evans rolled his eyes again. "Are you two finished?" Leslie and Alicia looked at each other. The president-elect sighed. "I've got four years of this, don't I?"

"Eight if I have my way," Barnes pointed out.

"I'd say at least forty more years of this from me," Alicia grinned.

Evans smiled at his wife before turning to Barnes. He took a deep breath and blew it out. "Well? Shall we?"

Leslie headed out through the door to let the Secret Service detail know it was time. Alicia stood and walked to her husband. She wrapped her arms around him.

"Daniel. Relax. You'll be fine."

"I know. Thanks."

"You're welcome. I love you."

"I love you too."

Evans gave his wife a quick kiss and turned to his kids, both of whom were engrossed in cartoons on a handheld tablet. He knelt in front of them.

"You guys ready to go?"

"Where are we going," asked Elizabeth, looking up from the screen.

"Daddy has to give a little speech."

"Another one?" A dramatic eye roll accompanied the question.

The president-to-be smiled and patted his daughter on the arm. "Do you know what comes after the speech?"

"Another speech?"

He fought not to laugh. Already a cynic. Great. "Nope. Parties and ice cream."

Elizabeth looked at her father suspiciously, eyes darting to her mother and back, clearly convinced this had to be some sort of trap. "Really?"

Elizabeth turned her face towards her mother, who nodded. She turned back to her father. "No brussels sprouts?"

"Well. Maybe a few sprouts."

"Daddy!" She glared at him, and crossed her arms.

"I'm kidding. I'm kidding. Just ice cream."

Elizabeth hopped off the couch and held her hand out for her dad.

As he waited just above the capitol steps, Evans noticed just how much the wind had picked up, its icy fingers probing his clothes for an opening. How in the hell did people stand out here for hours? Why did they stand out here? To watch you run your trap for forty minutes?

He chuckled at that idea, gazing at the crowd gathered around and below the dais. Somewhere below him the United States Marine Band belted out an upbeat march he didn't recognize, the big, brassy notes echoing off of the building and carrying off toward the horizon.

The president-elect stood in an alcove, watching as the master of ceremonies introduced his family and marveling at the fact that he was here.

He'd started life as the runt of the litter, the youngest and smallest of six children born to a pair of Indiana farmers. A pair of trips to the state championships, combined with a perfect high school grade point average, landed him at Purdue University as Mechanical Engineering major and walk-on wrestler.

At Purdue, he'd flown through his coursework, finishing his bachelor's and master's degrees in four and a half years, a feat made easier after he'd abandoned his lackluster wrestling career. He'd listened to a pitch by a Navy recruiter during his junior year and had submitted an application for Officer Candidate School out of a sense of curiosity during his senior year. The acceptance notification had come less than a month later. Figuring that anything was better than working on the family farm, Evans had signed on with the Navy two days later.

That had been almost thirty-five years ago. He'd served twenty-four years in uniform, retiring as a captain after commanding a destroyer and two cruisers.

After retirement, he'd been convinced to run for public office. First time out, he'd gotten blown away in a landslide. Second time at bat, he'd beaten the incumbent state representative. From there, he'd jumped the ranks quickly, eventually running a successful campaign for one of Virginia's open seats in the United States Senate before a new acquaintance named Leslie Barnes had pitched him on the idea of a presidential run. Evans had been hesitant at first, agreeing only to the requisite first step of a campaign. They'd formed an exploratory committee and, since the numbers weren't abysmal, he entered the 2020 presidential race figuring there was nothing to lose.

Now he was standing at the top of the capitol steps—watching his daughter curtsy to the crowd—just minutes away from taking the oath of office as the President of the United States.

"Jesus."

"What's that, sir," a nearby aide enquired.

"Oh. Nothing," Evans replied, shaking his head.

The aide nodded. "You're up. Knock 'em dead Mr. President."

"Thanks, Albert."

The march ended, the last notes trailing off on the wind. A brief moment of silence ensued before the Marine Band blasted out Ruffles and Flourishes. Another short silence followed, eventually broken by a serious and steady voice.

"Ladies and gentlemen. The President-elect of the United States—Daniel Alexander Evans."

A deafening cheer rose from the crowd as the Marine Band struck up again—an enthusiastic Hail to the Chief sounding from the instruments. Evans affixed his mask and turned to Albert, flashing a smile that his aide couldn't see before turning and marching down the carpet-covered stairs.

★ ★ ★ ★ ★

Chief Justice Harold Simmons waved to the cheering crowd and turned to the president-elect. The eighty-four-year-old former prosecutor's eyes glinted. "Mr. Evans. Are you ready?"

"Yes, sir." Under the mask, a grin spread across Evans' face. He couldn't help it. Not bad for a farm-boy.

"Then, sir, if you will please raise your right hand and repeat after me."

Evans did as he was told, facing the Chief Justice. Simmons led off. "I, Daniel Alexander Evans, do solemnly swear."

The president-elect repeated the words, slowly, confidently. Simmons continued.

"That I will faithfully execute the office of President of the United States."

The murmur in the crowd started growing again as Evans repeated the line, his voice even, strong. Simmons kept going. "And that I will, to the best of my ability, preserve, protect, and defend the Constitution of the United States. So, help me God."

Evans repeated the last words, smiling as he did so. The Chief Justice's eyes flashed as he stuck out his hand. "Congratulations Mr. President."

3

DEGUERRA

THE EXECUTIVE BOARDROOM OF TITANX security was everything that a visitor would expect of the world's largest private security enterprise. A pair of extravagantly stocked sideboards ran down each side of the room, providing snacks, drinks, and—for special occasions—a collection of top-shelf wines, spirits, and liquors that would put even the most high-end bars to shame. A teak table, its thick legs resting on hand-crafted parquet, was surrounded on three sides by custom-built, tufted leather chairs, each one of which had set the company back over five thousand dollars.

The three men and one woman gathered there should have been comfortable beyond measure—but they weren't and the reason for their discomfort was being broadcast, larger-than-life, on an immense high-definition television affixed to one of the chamber's expansive, claret-painted walls.

The newly sworn president had just finished his inauguration speech to the delighted approval of the thousands of people in attendance and the network was displaying a split screen image—President Evans shaking hands next to a wide-view shot broadcasting tens of thousands of voters cheering on the minutes-old administration.

The man seated at the head of the table reached forward and muted the television. He sat quietly for a few seconds, watching the nation's new Commander-in-Chief.

Nicholas DeGuerra was furious. As the President and Chief Executive Officer of TitanX Security, he viewed his primary responsibility simply. It was his job to take care of the employees of

TitanX. It was their hard work and services he sold. But there was more to it than that. He'd literally built this company from the ground up. Time and time again, he'd put his own money up to expand TitanX into the colossus it was today. He was invested, financially and emotionally, in the success of this organization.

Not just this organization, Nicholas. Everything else too. All of those other contracts.

Nick kept glaring.

But this asshole. This new president with his plan to end the War on Terror. Acquiescing to these bleeding-heart amateurs who didn't understand what it took to keep America safe.

Nick growled under his breath. "Goddamnit."

Nick's mind raged. He told himself that this was insane. It had been four-hundred-years since the pilgrims had landed at Plymouth and America had progressed exponentially while folks in Afghanistan and Iraq and Syria still lived like cavemen and battled each other in useless little tribal pissing contests. Those places needed America; Nick knew. And, by default, that meant that they needed TitanX Security.

But this glad-handing asshole on the television was going to flush all of that down the toilet. He was a career military man. He should damn well know better.

Yes, Nick admitted, the new POTUS was a Navy puke and, therefore, suspect when it came to real strategy and tactics, but he was—had been—an officer charged with the security of an entire nation.

But the bastard had just stated his position. Again. Same as he did during the debates. America was leaving the region. Which meant TitanX was leaving.

America could survive the transition. TitanX could not.

"You smug son of a bitch," Nick muttered.

"What's that," one of the executives seated at the table asked.

Nick waved her off and kept staring at the screen.

★ ★ ★ ★ ★

DeGuerra was the grandson of a pair of Italian immigrants who'd fled hardship and poverty in the old country to only marginally better conditions in New York. The family name, a derivation of the word for a belligerent or soldier, had come courtesy of an official on Ellis Island who'd probably not cared to look up the meaning.

Nick had been born in Brooklyn to parents who had worked themselves to death just to put one meal a day on the table. Never a stellar student—a moderate case of undiagnosed dyslexia had seen to that—he'd managed to do just enough in high school to graduate but not enough to make attending college a viable or attractive choice. His youth had been punctuated by periodic run-ins with the law, usually little more than failed snatch-and-grabs from the random corner bodega or after-school fist fights that earned him a ride home in the back of a squad car and a beating from his old man.

After escaping high school, he'd mooched off his parents for a few months while he and his gang of young toughs roamed the streets and caused low-level mischief. There'd never been any serious blowback for Nick or his rag-tag group of petty criminals—especially after he'd learned to have the cops drop him off at a friend's house whose father, for the low price of a few cans of beer, would pretend to be Nick's dad. Nick's life was stuck in neutral on the day when he and three of his friends picked a fight with another gang in the next neighborhood over. After Nick and his friends considered the fight over, one guy Nick had put on the ground had gotten up and sucker-punched him. The result was predictable. A fair fight was one thing, but Nick's ego and fiery temper couldn't accept getting his nose cracked by a cheater. Nick had beaten the kid to within an inch of his life, which was bad enough. The situation was made worse when Nick, still pummeling the unconscious teen, had attacked the New York Police sergeant who'd tried to break up the fight. Nick was arrested and spent the night in the tank. The next morning, he was perp-walked in front of a judge who presented him with two options—cool his heels in jail for a bit or talk to the nice gentleman from the United States Army waiting outside the courtroom. DeGuerra didn't have to think twice. He chose the Army and, within a week, he was face down, doing twenty in the muck at Fort Benning under the watchful eyes of the biggest human being he'd ever laid eyes on.

After weeks of physical training and a single, behind-the-barracks beat down at the massive hands of Sergeant Jerome Peters, Nick had learned to stow his temper. He'd finished boot camp and his follow-on training as an infantryman just in time to get a first-hand glimpse of the complete and utter destruction that General Norman Schwarzkopf's troops had waged on the Iraqi Army—the world's sixth largest standing military at the time. To no one's surprise, the young soldier re-enlisted at the first opportunity. An appointment to Ranger School was eventually followed by selection to Delta and, shortly after training was complete, Staff Sergeant DeGuerra deployed to Afghanistan in the wake of the September 11, 2001 attacks.

His first tour in Afghanistan started rough. DeGuerra had been one of a handful of operators inserted in and around the Shah-i-Kot Valley before the ill-fated Operation Anaconda. He'd been watching as his fellow soldiers walked into a trap that he and the rest of the Joint Special Operations Command teams had tried to warn everyone about. Nick came through the ordeal, shaken, but determined to stay the course. He'd deployed to the region four more times after earning a commission, surviving a slew of engagements and two near-misses before retiring as a major.

Most people with Nick's experiences would have called it quits after over two decades in combat, content to kick their feet up between occasional rounds of bad golf. That just wasn't Nick. He'd never been the type of guy to sit on the sidelines and his decision to leave the military had nothing to do with needing a break from the life. It had everything to do with the realization that he could make a much better living outside of the United States Army.

During his last decade in uniform, Nick had noted the sheer volume of civilian contracted security throughout the Middle East and Afghanistan. He'd spent innumerable off-duty hours cultivating contacts in the private security world and, when he thought the timing was right, he jumped ship.

He was financially secure long before he retired. With no wife, kids, or parents—they'd passed shortly after he'd joined the Army—to care for, he'd spent almost his entire military career sending his paychecks to a money manager with a knack for managing medium-risk portfolios.

By the time Nick had exchanged his fatigues for a set of three-piece suits from Saks Fifth Avenue, he was a millionaire three times over.

Nick liquidated half of his assets and purchased a pre-existing security firm, taking over a set of mildly-lucrative government contracts. For the first two years after the takeover, Nick did nothing but solidify the firm's reputation. By the end of the second year, Nick and his small company were ready to make a move. With the wealth he'd accumulated over the first two years as a CEO, he acquired three other pre-existing security firms and rebranded the organization.

As the years passed, TitanX grew exponentially. At Nick's direction, the company recruited heavily from the ranks of United States Special Forces. Nick found he was able to use the expertise leaving the service to build his own training cadre—he was, in effect, selling government training and services right back to the manufacturer.

By the end of 2019, TitanX had become a multi-million-dollar empire, a Forbes-listed private army of special operations personnel that subsisted on hundreds of millions of dollars in United States Government contracts.

But Nick's empire was threatened now. He had been forced to acknowledge the existence of a vulnerability. His organization was a one-trick pony. Nick and his executives had bet heavily on the continued need for American involvement in the War on Terror, raking in the cash as TitanX provided training, consulting services, and physical security for nearly every American installation in the region. It was simple. For most of his adult life, America had been chasing terrorists around the Middle East and Asia. The very idea that America would, could, leave it all behind was nothing short of absurd. But it was happening. That formula, the region's demand for, and his supply of, military and security expertise, was at risk. With little more than the flick of a pen on a one-page executive order, the new president could burn everything to the ground.

Each executive in the room knew what that meant. The faucet of government money that fed TitanX would be turned off permanently and there was little or nothing that Nick's friends in Congress, what few had kept their jobs, could do about it.

As Nick's mind worked over the threat facing his company, he could feel his blood boil. He reminded himself to calm down, working to keep his fiery temper in check in front of staff—a task that was requiring a gargantuan effort right now as the newly inaugurated president smiled on the television. Keep grinning asshole.

"Bev, where does this put us?" Nick laid his mask to the side. Everyone else did the same.

Beverly Smith-Walker, was a serious woman with a wicked sense of humor who'd lost her husband to cancer the previous spring. While Nick knew that the loss had to have hit her hard—she'd known her late husband since grade school—he also knew her to be a strong, fiercely independent woman who spent her free time doting on her seven grandchildren. Had Nick ever considered retirement, he would have tabbed Bev Walker as a worthy and capable replacement. Like her boss, Smith-Walker was a military veteran. She'd graduated from West Point with a degree in economics and served six years in uniform before leaving the Army as a captain to head back to school. She held a PhD in Economics and, more important to Nick, was TitanX's Chief Financial Officer. "Short term? We can weather this for a bit. Any sort of withdrawal will take anywhere from six months to two years."

"And the long term?" The question, predictably, came from Paul Burkhart, the Chief Operating Officer for the firm. His voice was edgy already, a bit of anger evident.

"Paul, let her finish." Nick directed, nodding at Bev to continue.

"As I was saying. Short term. We're fine. Two years won't hurt us. It won't be fun, and we'll stay in the red most of the time, but the company could survive. There's always a chance that friends of ours take their seats back in the midterms, but we can't count on that. Long term? TitanX won't be around at the end of this presidency. Four years is too long without new contracts. If he wins a second term, well." She shrugged.

Nick nodded and finished the statement. "If President Evans wins a second term, there is no way in hell we can recover. Four years puts us out of business temporarily, with the hope that we could recover with a new administration. Eight years and we're bankrupt. Correct?"

Bev nodded.

Paul chipped in again, hopeful. "Listen, I'm not on the financial side of things. That's never been my particular ball of yarn. We have foreign contracts. Can't we rely on those to hold us over?"

Bev shook her head and started to answer, but the man across from her, TitanX's Vice President, Daniel Turner, beat her to the punch. "It's true that we have foreign contracts, but we only provide services to customers that are approved by the United States government. It's part of an agreement we have regarding conflicts of interest. We don't provide services to two sides of any issue. Expanding foreign contracts to hold us over would, probably, cut us out of new US contracts if the administration changed its mind or needed our services in the future."

"Dan," interjected Paul. "Are you saying that the US government dictates the rest of our client list to us?"

"In effect, yes. That's exactly how it is." Dan replied evenly.

"How in the hell does that work?"

"Think of it like golf, Paul. Would you use the same caddy as your opponent? In a big money match? Could you be sure a shared caddy has your best interests in mind?"

"That's crazy." Paul snapped. Nick stepped in again.

"It's how it is, Paul. We're an American corporation with no holdings outside of the United States. No one trusts us to serve competing interests. We get what, ninety percent of our business from the United States government?" He looked at Bev for confirmation.

"Ninety-one percent."

Nick turned to Turner.

"And how much of that business goes away permanently if we expand foreign contracts?"

Turner, sixty-seven, the only non-veteran in the room, checked his notes. "Not quite sure. Most of it. I'd have to look up the exact figure, but I'd bet upwards of ninety-five percent of our federal contracts could never be renewed if we take that step. Of course, it would depend on who we expand to. We might find some new contracts that the government would either be agreeable to or at least not openly object to."

Bev spoke up again. "Nick, it's worth mentioning that expanding to foreign governments wouldn't come close to covering what we stand to lose if Evans turns this faucet off. We have one-hundred-and-forty-two active contracts right now. Based on the average amount we make off of the few foreign sales we have, we'd need close to four-hundred new deals to close this gap."

Nick chewed on that for a minute. He hadn't considered that. Pushing for new US government contracts simply meant pushing against other American-run private security firms. Expanding foreign contracts in the numbers Bev was talking about meant competing against foreign companies and, possibly, their parent governments.

"Folks, we're not going to solve this problem in the next thirty minutes." Nick saw a couple of nods. "We do not have the models or data with us today to answer any of the questions facing us with any degree of specificity. We sure as shit don't have enough here to plan our way out of this. So, here's what I want. In two weeks, we're going to meet back here and discuss any viable options you three can come up with. Pull every string to get the information you need to present me with solutions. Every damn string. You have favors you can call in—you call 'em. You have contacts that can help—contact 'em. We are going to keep TitanX from going under and each one of you is going to be a huge part of that."

They were all watching him intently.

"Any questions?" Nick looked each executive squarely in the eye. Three heads shook in unison. "Good. Let's get to work."

Twenty minutes later, Nick was seated at his own desk with the phone in his hand, dialing through his own list of contacts. In a relatively short period of time, he'd left over forty messages. Satisfied that the ball was rolling, he replaced the phone in the cradle and opened the bottom, left drawer on his desk, withdrawing a large expandable folder and placing it on the desk.

While Nick had no problems relying on—or investing in—the newest and most innovative technologies available to the military and security worlds, he did tend to be slightly old-fashioned in a few areas. This was one of those things. The folder, updated weekly for him by a team of three accountants, contained the paper version of his investment portfolio. In a world dominated by electronic ones and zeros, Nick preferred the feel of paper in his hands.

Nick sorted through the statements, making notes as he went. He sorted through every dollar represented on every page and calculated what he stood to lose. He knew that the final sum would be a rough number—a very rough number—but he went through the process anyway. In two hours, he had an estimate that he'd pay the accountants a little extra to confirm.

Nick was as aggressive in the business world as he'd been on the battlefield. He'd committed, against the advice of investment counselors and accountants, significant portions of his personal fortune as venture capital for businesses he saw as up and coming stars in the world of defense technology. Time and conflict would have propelled Nick's personal fortune into the stratosphere. That, Nick realized, wouldn't happen. A full military withdrawal would hurt every one of his investments. Supply and demand. If you were fighting a shooting war, you needed things. New things. Tanks. Guns. Missiles. Ships. Troops. You didn't need quite as many new toys to fight off boredom. Conflict was good for industry. Peace wasn't.

Nick looked at the number he'd written on the final page of notes and swore. Paul, Daniel, and Bev were at their desks trying to come up with ways to save TitanX and none of their work would mean a damn thing if he went down in flames. Nick knew that. TitanX existed because of him. A nasty voice in his head reminded Nick that if the company went down, that would also be because of him. He could almost hear the chorus of "I told you so's" from his advisors and accountants. They'd never say such things to his face, but Nick knew they'd be thinking it. That thought didn't help his temper.

Nick sat at his desk. He tried to breathe and forced his brain to work on the issue. This was a battlefield problem and he was a soldier. His staff was working on the tactical solution, planning the tiny battles that would stop the bleeding. Nick needed to work on the strategic issue.

4

THOMPSON

THE WEATHER MATCHED BRIAN'S MOOD. It was typical late-January weather for Norfolk. A drizzling mist, a twenty-knot wind, and a wind chill of thirty combined to make USS James E. Williams' new Top Snipe shiver. His dark blue coveralls and several layers of woolen undergarments, already soaking wet, clung to his hundred-and-fifty-pound frame.

"Hey, Chief. You ready?"

Brian turned to see Boatswain's Mate Second Class Ethan Coleman waiting, a pair of dirty orange life vests in one hand, hard hats in the other, and a shit-eating grin plastered across his face.

"Coleman?"

"Yeah?"

"Wipe that grin off your face. People might think you like this shit."

Coleman laughed. "I do like this shit, Chief. Beats standing lookout for the next three hours. Besides, we ain't gotta wear masks out here."

Brian rolled his eyes. The mist was getting heavier, blown around by a swirling, gusty wind. "Give me the jacket, Coleman."

Coleman held out one vest and a single, plain white, plastic hard hat. Brian took both items and put them on, resigning himself to the inevitable—three hours in one of the ship's rigid-hull inflatable boats.

"Coleman, you see Ensign Strater or Lieutenant Eckersley?"

"Not yet, Chief."

Brian glanced at his watch. "Give 'em a call. Almost time."

"Roger that, Chief."

As Coleman shuffled off, Brian looked around at the ship. He'd been here less than a week and everything was moving too fast. Two weeks ago, he'd been in Orlando with his wife and kids, on shore duty with the prospect of eighteen more months of easy living ahead. Now, after a couple admirals had made phone calls and his orders had been changed, he was deploying, heading to the Horn of Africa. Brian and his new ship were heading to the Somali coast to conduct maritime interdiction operations. Pirate hunting. He shook his head. He knew the history. The United States Navy had earned its sea legs dealing with pirates. Men like Edward Preble and Stephen Decatur had sailed ships across the Atlantic to attack the North African port city of Tripoli and the corsairs along the Barbary Coast.

Brian continued scanning the weather decks. Clusters of sailors, in dress-blue wool uniforms that offered little protection from the icy gale, were huddled together with family—a last chance for teary goodbyes and hugs before the ship left for ten months.

His family wasn't present. They were in Maryland, near the Naval Air Station at Patuxent River. His wife, April, was pregnant with a surrogate baby and was far enough along that her doctor had put her foot down on travel. The family trip to Disney had been pushing the issue.

"Chief?" Coleman had returned.

"Yeah?"

"They're on their way up."

Brian stretched. The cold was hell on his battered back and neck. "Good. Wouldn't do to leave the swimmer and boat officer behind."

Coleman smiled, adjusting the chinstrap on his hard hat. "Chief, I don't think they'd mind today."

"You're probably right. Let's get the boat ready."

"Roger that."

The two of them left the clusters of sailors and families in their wake and walked around the corner to the stowage cradles. The ship's small boats sat, stacked and slightly offset, on USS James E. Williams' starboard side. Coleman climbed into the lower boat, opened an access panel on the console, and started flipping the toggle switches that routed power from the marine-grade batteries to the boat's controls. Brian walked a few steps aft, following a thick, yellow charging cable to an outlet. He unplugged the cable, severing the boat's power supply from the ship, and called to Coleman.

"Coleman. Unhook the power cable and toss it down."

"On the way."

The blocky, heavier end of the cable came into view over the smooth rubber side of the boat, a ballistic object which Brian caught easily. He coiled the cable and stowed it in a nearby locker before starting his inspection of the boat.

"Everything looks good up here, Chief. Batteries are good. GPS is up and running. No warning lights."

"Sounds good. Check the seacocks and bilge plugs for me."

"Will do."

Brian could hear the popping of the metal latches holding the console in place as Coleman began checking the various plugs and openings that were meant to keep water out of the boat. He'd just finished inspecting the boat's underside when he heard footsteps approaching.

"Morning, Chief. How's the boat?" Lieutenant Eckersley, the boat officer, sounded chipper.

Brian stood, wiping his hands on his soaked coveralls. "We're good. You gentlemen get to say goodbye?"

Ensign Strater nodded. It was his first deployment since graduating from the United States Naval Academy the previous summer. "I did. Dad thinks this is great. Mom's freaking out. Keeps asking about pirates. She's barely standing."

Brian smiled. "Well, moms can be like that. Back in ninety-nine, I forgot to call home for a week before deployment. Mom managed to find the captain's number and I got called to his stateroom and told, in no uncertain terms, just how painful life would become if she called again."

Ensign Strater laughed. "She's seen that one movie too many times. The one with the Somali pirates taking over the tanker."

Brian nodded. He'd seen the movie too. "Alright, gents. It's almost time. Mr. Eckersley, you wanna help our swimmer here get suited up? We're gonna warm up the engines."

The young lieutenant nodded and led the new ensign off to the gear locker. Brian turned and climbed aboard the boat just in time to see Coleman securing the console's final latch.

"She ready, Coleman?"

"Ready as she'll ever be, Chief."

"Alright. Get on the radio and get permission to warm her up."

Coleman did that, the scratchy static of the radio conversation filling the air. Brian looked around at his new ship.

USS James E. Williams was a fifteen-year-old Arleigh Burke-class destroyer currently moored to the piers at Naval Station Norfolk, Virginia. She was five-hundred and ten feet long and tipped the scales at just under ten thousand tons—roughly one-tenth of the displacement of a new Ford-class aircraft carrier. The ship wasn't intimidating. The placement of a single destroyer off the coast of a nation with less than stellar comportment didn't exactly tell the local government to "behave yourself or else". The Williams was versatile. She was the blue-collar, Swiss army knife of the United States Navy. She could hunt down submarines, chase pirates, shoot down ballistic inbounds, send weapons downrange, conduct search and rescue operations, and look good doing all of it.

Brian turned to starboard and peered over the side. USS James E. Williams crouched in the water; a freshly painted, steel-grey lioness straining at her restraints, ready to slip her lines and head out to sea. The Williams had a graceful beauty to her. Low-slung, sleek, and quick, she had the appearance of a sports car. It was, Brian decided, a stark contrast to the boxy, dump-truck design of the amphibious assault ship that had moored on the pier's opposite side the previous evening.

It was a facade. In the few days he'd been onboard, he'd been the recipient of an unending parade of briefings about problems with the gear and issues with the crew.

A few sailors had some legal issues pending—and those were the result of their inability to blow off steam. They'd been cooped up together for most of the last two years. Three-hundred sailors packed together with little personal space. It was a condition which, when you added a lack of sleep and a great deal of stress, was bound to result in lots of fights and quite a bit of drinking. And that was just the beginning.

The ship was broken. Brian already had an entire notebook devoted to the mechanical and electrical issues that plagued the Williams. Two of the air conditioning units were unable to reach designed capacity and a third had some lingering control system problems. The refrigerators seemed okay, but the ship's steering systems had a few hiccups—not the least of which was a glitch that prevented one of the units from shifting remotely. All of the ship's engines—those for propulsion and those for electrical power—were overdue for replacement. A few of the switchboards had breaker issues and one of the shore power connections—an array normally capable of handling more than four-hundred amps—was fried after catching fire the day before his arrival. Every system had leaks and breakage and faults, including the boat he was sitting on. The ship had two of them and Brian had a full four pages in his notebook dedicated to each.

"Chief. Captain's coming."

Brian climbed down from the boat as Ensign Strater, partially dressed in a wetsuit, waddled over, fidgeting with a zipper. Lieutenant Eckersley trailed behind.

USS James E. Williams' captain, Commander Derrick Allen, was a big man, well over six feet tall. Not a graduate of the Naval Academy, he'd started his career as an enlisted sailor, working his way through the ranks as a seaman before earning a trip to Virginia Military Institute and a commission. He'd spent more than a quarter-century of his life to earn command of a sea-going warship and Brian got the impression that he was one of those commanders who hadn't forgotten where he'd come from.

As Commander Allen neared the boat, he pocketed his facemask and spoke. His voice, Brian thought, was quiet for a man of his size. "Chief, we ready?"

"Just about, Cap'n. Getting ready to warm up the engine."

The captain nodded, looked around at the rest of the boat crew. "I suppose you're wondering why we're using our own boat for security on the way out."

It was more of a statement than an actual question, but Brian responded anyway. "That might have come up."

"That's fair. Well, it's pretty simple. When the deployment date shifted to Sunday, no one thought about paying overtime to the folks who do harbor security."

Brian finished the thought. "And there isn't a spare crew to follow us out, right? We provide our own crew to the buoy, crank the boat back onboard, and then haul ass into the Atlantic."

The captain nodded. "Pretty much sums it up." He looked down at his own sodden uniform. "Beautiful weather for it though. Chief, a word?"

Brian followed Commander Allen a few feet forward to the starboard break. "Sir?"

"How's the turnover going?"

"It's going. Chief Guillory and the rest of the folks have a lot to say."

Commander Allen nodded. "Bet they do. Gone through the CSMP yet?"

The CSMP, current ship's maintenance project, was a listing of every repair job for the ship. In this case, the printed version contained more than five hundred active entries, a full third of which were major issues. "I'm about halfway through."

Commander Allen shook his head. "Listen. We didn't get to talk much when you checked in, but I need you to understand a couple things. I made some calls. Turns out I served with a couple of your old department heads. They say you're the hands-on type."

Brian nodded.

"You have to know that that can't possibly work in this situation. There's just too much shit wrong for you to be in the weeds like that. I need you at the top, taking care of the department. Won't do anyone much good if you work yourself to death turnin' wrenches. Follow?"

Brian smiled. "I follow."

"Good. I'm not trying to tell you how to do your job, just pointing out the obvious. You and Guillory got a lot of shit to do. Let the division officers and first classes worry about the trees. You two keep an eye on the forest. Which brings up another point. After we secure from sea and anchor detail, grab your boss and stop by my stateroom. We gotta figure out a way to get you off these boats. My new Top Snipe isn't supposed to be riding around in one of those things."

"Aye, aye, Captain. Anything else?"

The captain looked around again, shook his head. "Not at the moment. You gents be safe."

"Will do." Brian ripped off a salute, which the captain returned before turning away.

Coleman's radio crackled.

"Chief, we got permission to run the boat in the skid."

"Rog. Fire her up."

"I'll try." Coleman climbed into the boat.

"Something on your mind, Coleman?"

"Yeah. Why are you on the boat today? A-Gang call in sick or something?"

Brian pulled himself into the boat and found a seat on the inflated rubber sponson. "Found out yesterday that no one in A-Gang can swim."

Coleman smiled and shook his own head. "Seriously?"

"Yep. Not one of them."

Coleman was incredulous. "Un-fucking-believable. Who joins the Navy and can't swim?"

"You know, Coleman, I asked them the same question."

"And?"

"Brooks told me that if he has to swim, something has gone seriously wrong with the ship."

"Well, he ain't wrong." Coleman continued shaking his head in disbelief. "Alright, Chief. Here goes. Hope the boat shop did their job."

Coleman grabbed the ignition switch and moved it upwards to 'Start', his face contorted in a mask that was half-expectancy and half-prayer as the boat's big turbo-charged diesel coughed to rumbling life. Coleman scanned the gages and Brian turned to check the exhaust. The initial puff of opaque black smoke was clearing away and a shimmering haze was beginning to drift up from behind the boat. The two sailors looked at each other, Coleman's eyebrows raised in a question that Brian answered with an approving nod. They let the boat run for twenty minutes, keeping a wary eye on the various temperature and pressure gauges in a manner that, under normal circumstances, would have been chalked up to simply being good engineering practice. But this wasn't a normal circumstance.

Brian had gotten a lengthy history of the boats from the ship's Chief Engineer. During the previous few months, both boats had experienced all sorts of engine trouble. Beginning as nothing more than a series of minor annoyances, the problems had become serious enough that both crafts had required a trip to the naval station's small boat shop for overhaul. In the massive bureaucracy of the United States Navy, the requisitions for overhaul were never actually approved or funded. After no small amount of finger-pointing the requested overhauls were cancelled. Each boat got a quick once over, a fluid change, some software upgrades, and a trip back to the Williams, all of which had occurred within the last forty-eight hours.

No one onboard the ship was confident that the engine problems had been resolved, least of all Brian. He'd been horrified to find out that both boats had sputtered to a halt in the frigid waters of the North Sea two months earlier, belching black smoke like a pair of defunct, fire-breathing sea-monsters.

"Coleman!" Brian had to shout over the rumbling of the diesel engine.

Coleman looked over. Brian shouted again, drawing his hand back and forth over his neck like a knife. "Shut her down!"

The order was acknowledged with a quick thumbs-up by Coleman, who pressed the ignition toggle down to the 'Stop' position. The boat's engine sputtered and stopped, a faint ticking noise and the scent of diesel exhaust the only remaining evidence of the operational test.

"Sounded good, Chief. Thought they didn't have time to fix anything."

Brian nodded in bewildered agreement. He'd leafed through the maintenance records and a stack of correspondence between the ship and the boat shop. What he'd read and what he'd just witnessed didn't mesh. This had been too easy. "It did sound good. Looked good too. Let the Officer of the Deck know?"

"Will do, Chief. When do they put us in the water?"

Brian peeled part of a soaked sleeve back and looked at his watch. "Ship leaves in forty minutes or so. They'll want us in the water early. Figure ten minutes, give or take."

"Good. I'm going to the head. That mess decks coffee'll go right through ya."

"Good idea. Back up here in five. Let our fearless leaders over there know?" Brian pointed at the two officers huddled in the ship's starboard side windbreak.

"Will do. Be right back."

★ ★ ★ ★ ★

"Man the Boat Deck."

The order came, loud, metallic, and crystal clear, over the ship's 1MC announcing system. The result was immediate and chaotic, more than twenty sailors appeared on the boat deck, each one hurrying to strap on safety gear and tuck pant legs into boots and socks. When everyone was gathered, the ship's Bosun Mate Chief, a gruff, round man with a receding hairline and the demeanor of an Abrams tank called everyone together for a safety brief, which ended with his typical admonition.

"Pay attention. Follow directions. Keep your head in the game. Don't do anything stupid."

With that advice, he directed everyone to their respective stations and walked over to the boat crew, popping off a quick salute to the two officers.

"Jesus, dude. Those mechanics can't swim?" He guffawed, slapping Brian on the back with one of his inhumanly large hands.

Brian shrugged. "It's gonna be a long ten months."

"You got that right. Be even longer if that boat dies again."

"Yeah, let's not jinx anything, Jason."

"Me? Jinx shit. Never."

Brian grinned. "Just so long as she runs like she did this morning. A broken engine would be par for the course, though. Cause I've got nothing else going on, right?"

Boatswain's Mate Chief Petty Officer Jason Roberts laughed again before commiserating. "Yeah. What the hell's up with that shit? Engineering loses all those folks, Top transfers, and you pop in a few days before we haul in lines and blow this popsicle stand. You expecting more help or is it just gonna be you and Tim until you both retire?"

"Shit, Jason, I'm betting it's just us."

"Don't give 'em any ideas. You two pull this off, they'll start trying this shit with other ships."

Brian rolled his neck from side to side, trying to get it to pop. "So, do a shitty job?"

Jason winked. "Well..."

Their conversation was interrupted by another 1MC announcement.

"All visitors are requested to depart the ship. USS James E. Williams expects to get underway in approximately twenty minutes."

As the families and friends of the crew began finding their way across the brow and down to the concrete pier, Roberts slapped Brian on the back again, smiling. "Alright, bud. You ready?"

"Let's get this over with."

"That's the spirit."

The older chief walked off, barking at his sailors, ensuring everyone was in his or her proper position. Satisfied, he got on his radio and requested permission to put the boat at the rail. When permission was given, Roberts became an automaton, dispensing clear orders which were followed. The seven-thousand-pound craft, raised several feet by the ship's boat davit, was swung outboard and lowered. The bosun eyeballed the placement, judged it correct, and ordered the boat secured to the rail. His sailors complied, taking strain on the boat's bow and stern lines and cinching it tight against the Williams' grey hull before tying off to a pair of cleats. Roberts inspected again and ordered an adjustment before obtaining permission to load the boat crew. Permission was given and the crew boarded the craft. Coleman got on first, taking his place behind the wheel. Brian, Lieutenant Eckersley, and Ensign Strater followed, each scrambling into position for the next step. At a thumbs up from Coleman, Roberts requested authorization to lower the boat to the water.

The craft's lines were untied and the davit began lowering the boat to the choppy waters of the harbor. Brian kept an eye on the distance between the boat and the surface. At just two feet, he called for Coleman to start the engines. Coleman hit the toggle switch just as the craft's hull made contact with the water. The diesel rumbled to life, jettisoning a cloud of black smoke. As he pulled the quick disconnect from the davit hook, Coleman called out.

"Cast off lines."

At the front of the boat, Ensign Strater unhooked the bowline, an effort duplicated by Brian at the stern. A pair of thumbs up told Coleman the boat was clear of all lines. He reached down to the throttle, bumped it up, and drove away from the ship. Once clear, everyone took their normal places. Brian sat down on the sponson to Coleman's immediate right.

"Stern light up, Chief?"

"Yeah. The lanyard on the cotter pin is missing though. Remind me to have A-Gang fix that today."

The coxswain nodded. "With luck, that'll be the least of our problems."

Brian was still sitting in the same spot an hour later, listening to the rumble of the boat's diesel engine and smelling the exhaust as it swirled around the seven-meter-long craft. Small waves lapped over the bow as the boat idled along beside its mother-ship.

"Clearin' up a bit."

Coleman's voice startled Brian, bringing him back into the moment. He looked around. Ahead and to one side, the pale golden light of a winter sun was fighting to break through the drizzle. To the other side, less than two-hundred meters away, USS James E. Williams glided through the brown-green waters of the harbor. From the mast, a massive battle ensign furled and curled in the winds, the red, white and blue of the flag rolling and whipping like a sea of grain.

"Helluva sight, ain't it, Coleman?"

"What's that?"

"The ship."

Coleman turned his head briefly. "Sure is."

The boat officer chipped in. "Never been outside for a departure, Chief?"

Brian shook his head. "Nope. Never. This isn't half bad."

Coleman pitched in again, shifting the boat's course to stay abreast of the Williams. "Hell, Chief. All we need now is a couple of fishin' poles."

"I'll pass."

"Pass?" Coleman was incredulous.

"Yeah. I don't fish. Not since I was eight or so."

"Damn, Chief. How do you relax?"

"Who said I get to relax?"

Lieutenant Eckersley laughed. "You mean like our darling swimmer there?" He gestured to the front of the boat, where Ensign Strater was leaning against the gun mount. The young officer's body weaved back and forth with the rocking of the boat as his head bounced around.

"Young pup got rocked to sleep," opined the boat officer.

"Wake him up, Sir?"

"Gently, Coleman."

Coleman laughed, shared a sideways glance with Brian who latched on to one of the life lines running down each side of the small craft. When he saw Brian was secure, Coleman goosed the throttles and spun the wheel left, then right, then back to center.

The boat jumped through the water, the added horsepower slinging the tiny craft across the surface. Ensign Strater awoke, scrambling for a hold on anything as a small, icy wave broke over the boat's rubber bow. His panicked voice rose over the sound of the engines as Coleman reduced power.

"What the hell?"

"Sorry, sir," Coleman apologized. "Debris in the water. Didn't want to hit it."

The young officer was standing, clutching the gun mount like his life depended on it. Beyond the young officer, out in front of the boat, Brian could see the waves building through the channel, whipped up by the brisk wind.

"You might want to sit back down, Mr. Strater. Got some waves ahead."

The young officer looked out in front of the boat, then turned to Brian. His eyes went wide.

"Chief."

"Just some waves, sir," Brian started to explain. The young officer was pointing aft now. Everyone turned to look.

Heavy black smoke was pouring out of the rear end of the boat, a thick cloud of exhaust that obscured everything.

"Coleman, cut speed. Mr. Eckersley, get the bridge on the radio."

Coleman's right hand dropped off the wheel, chopping the throttles back to idle while Lieutenant Eckersley hailed the bridge. "Mother, this is Norman."

Brian began unfastening latches on the engine access as a static laden response came immediately.

"Norman, Mother. Go ahead."

"Mother, we're havin' engine trouble out here. Heavy black exhaust.

Chief Thompson's checking the engine now."

"Mother copies engine trouble, Norman. Can you make it to the next turn?"

"Wait one, Mother."

The lieutenant turned to look at Brian, who'd heard the exchange. "Chief?

"Gimme two minutes?"

Coleman yelled. "Chief. Fuel pressure's bouncing around."

The big diesel engine began coughing and sputtering, plume after plume of black smoke issuing from the rear of the craft. Brian turned to speak, to order Coleman to kill the engine, but the boat beat him to the punch. The entire craft shuddered as the engine shut down, shaking on its rubber mounts as it shook off the last few rpms. He moved a gloved hand to his face, wiped off a combination of sweat and icy sea spray. He turned to the boat officer. "Mr. Eckersley, we're gonna need a tow."

5

DEGUERRA

DEGUERRA HAD GIVEN HIS EXECUTIVES two weeks to find viable options for securing the future of TitanX Security, relegating each of the company's most senior personnel to a fortnight of stress-filled days and sleepless nights. The group had worked round the clock, looking at the company's dire financial situation from every possible angle. Quite a bit of blood—Paul had had a run in with an electric stapler —sweat and tears had been spilled to generate the document sitting in front of the TitanX CEO.

Nick hadn't looked at the paperwork yet, choosing to leave the cover sheet in place. He thought it odd that—after a lifetime of making critical, life-and-death decisions in some of the most extreme tactical environments on the planet and pushing strategic policy for this organization—here he was, afraid to look at a sheet of paper. His brain kept reviewing the problem as the boardroom door opened and his three most senior advisors filed in—each followed by at least two aides toting enormous three-ring binders.

Nick had built a private security organization that exclusively served the needs of the United States government. For fifteen years he'd refused to provide services to anyone at odds with his country—even when the opportunity to do so was lucrative. He'd turned down offers from corporations in Israel, Venezuela, and Russia over the years. That kind of loyalty had been rewarded with more business opportunities than Nick knew what to do with. He'd done his best and he'd tried to keep it simple. He provided manpower that freed up the American military to do what the taxpayers expected them to do.

Nick knew that was key. Soldiers weren't cops or security guards. Soldiers belonged out in the weeds. Hunting bad guys.

In the field, Nick had hated giving up shooters to guard some outpost when it meant that he'd had to go into the field short of personnel—because to go out unprepared meant that getting the job done was harder, that there was a greater chance of failure. America had almost always been about superior firepower, about bringing the full might and fury of the world's largest arsenal to bear on those who challenged the safety of her people.

The sheet of paper scared Nick in a way he'd not thought possible. It was the death warrant of the company itself and it represented multiple failures. Nick had failed to safeguard his fortune. That knowledge was bad enough. It made his gut turn. But the realization that he'd failed to take care of his people, the people on whose backs he made his money, grated on Nick's pride. He depended on those people and the people they were responsible for. His financial future depended on them. To a man who'd never ceded the field to a single foe, the sheet of paper in front of him looked like the white flag of surrender. Nick closed his eyes. Unless he did something, this defeat, a single piece of copy paper transformed by the addition of ink from a laser printer, would be followed by more. This company was surrendering. He was surrendering. And the terms of the surrender were incalculable.

Nick felt his blood pressure rising. He took a few deep breaths.

"Nick?" It was Bev. Her concern cut through his thoughts. "Are you alright?"

"I'm fine." Nick shook off his concerns. "Okay, folks. You've had two weeks to make your cases. Let's see what we've got. Bev?"

Bev cleared her throat. "Nick, in front of you, you have the recommendations for the future of TitanX, in order of strongest recommendation to weakest. I would add that the right answer here is likely a hybrid of the options we are presenting."

Paul shifted in his seat and shot Bev a poisonous look that Nick caught.

"Paul? Something to add?"

All eyes turned to TitanX's Chief Operating Officer, a man whose position was less about running the organization than it was about running the actual contractors who worked for the company. Burkhart was, like Nick, a retired Special Forces soldier. What he lacked in university and business-world credentials, he made up for by being one of the finest training officers the United States Army had ever produced. The old adage, "those who can't do, teach", did not apply to Master Sergeant Paul Samuel Burkhart, United States Army, retired. He was a man who'd been there and done that. He'd smelled the smoke, had come home with the t-shirt, and now he taught other people how to wear it.

Nick figured he knew what was coming. "Go ahead, Paul."

"Nick. Have you looked at those recommendations? I mean really looked at 'em?"

"Honestly, no. I have a pretty good idea what you three are going to say."

"Nick. The top recommendation on that list is to entertain foreign contracts. Are we really gonna do that? Don't get me wrong. I understand I'm not in the Army anymore and that's the only way we stay afloat for the next eight years, but you heard Bev two weeks ago. The number of contracts we'd have to win is outrageous."

"What's your point, Paul?" Nick asked, a tinge of anger creeping into his voice. The others around the table looked down at their notes. It was clear to Nick that they'd heard this multiple times in the past two weeks and had tired of it.

"Nick, if we do this. If we go after these foreign contracts, it won't be overnight and it won't ever be enough. We'll lose employees and operators. We'll have to lay folks off until we secure new contracts. Lots of folks."

Turner turned to Paul. "We've been over this, Paul. It's unavoidable. If we don't entertain foreign contracts, we lose everyone. We simply cannot afford to keep everyone and…"

Paul cut him off, his voice raised. "And you didn't want to hear me the last two weeks, Danny. Neither did Bev. But I get my say now. Those are my men and women. My troops. And you want me to just up and tell them to go home because the election didn't go our way?"

"Paul," Nick tried to keep his voice even and calm. "You wouldn't be telling them that. I would."

"Oh! That's so much fucking better!" Paul almost came out of his chair. "Sorry, folks. We didn't see this coming and, well, we have to let you go. The company is going under, you see. No money to pay you with. So sorry about this. Good luck. Tell your starving families we're sorry too!"

"Paul. That's enough." Nick snapped.

"No, Nick it isn't. You hired me to take care of the people and that's what I intend to do. Bev's data says that, with the number of contracts we'd keep after Evans shuts everything down, we'd experience more than eighty-five percent reduction in staffing until we secure new gigs. Eighty-five percent! Do you know how many people that is? Do you have any idea how much time I spent to get all of those people onboard and trained? Do you?"

"Paul, I know how much work you've put into our folks, but it does not change the fact that Evans is going to pull the plug on almost every contract we have and we cannot just keep folks on the payroll indefinitely while we search for other opportunities."

"So, we just fire them? Unceremoniously dump eighty-five percent of our folks because we didn't actually think Evans was going to win the goddamn election? Jesus, Nick. A fuckin' blind man could have seen that coming!"

Turner spoke up again, trying to defend his turf.

"Paul. What were we supposed to have done differently? Legally, we cannot even pursue some of the contracts we're talking about today without the government cancelling our contracts with them. If an audit turned up even a single proposal to an unapproved client, the government could, and would, pull every contract we have now. We'd be in the same boat we're in now."

Bev came to Turner's aid. "Paul, this isn't personal."

"Like hell it isn't. Have either of you two ever been fired?" He shook his head before going on. "Who am I kidding? You two grew up with silver spoons up your ass. Neither of you knows what it's like to be broke as shit."

Nick held a hand up. "But I do, Paul. I do know what it's like." He turned to Bev and Daniel. "Would you two excuse us?"

★ ★ ★ ★ ★

Nick got up, walked to one of the sideboards and began sorting through the bottles there. After selecting an expensive bottle of scotch, he poured two fingers into each of the two tumblers he'd pulled from the waist-high cupboard.

On his way back to his chair, he placed one of the glasses on the table in front of Paul. Flopping down in his own high-backed chair, Nick took a sip. He watched Paul over the rim of the clear glass.

Paul picked up his glass and eyeballed it. "Company going down the damn tubes and we're drinking a two-thousand-dollar bottle of scotch. Are you kidding me?"

"Jesus, Paul, you gotta get a handle on that temper of yours." Nick took a sip. "Besides. The scotch is paid for and open. Can't exactly get a refund."

Paul leaned back in his chair, closed his eyes, and drank.

"I know, Nick. Christ. I'm sorry. I just can't watch people lose everything."

"It won't be everyone and they're not losing everything." Nick pointed out, after another sip. "Hell, Paul. We pay better than anyone else out there. These are big boys and big girls. You've trained them well. They'll land on their feet somewhere."

Paul snorted. "Nick, you know as well as me that that 'somewhere' you're talking about is one of the hundreds of companies that can't do business with the United States government. Aside from huge pay cuts, anyone going that route won't ever get vetted on another federal job. And those that don't go that route are going to end up guarding car dealerships and shopping malls for a third of what we pay them."

Nick had to admit that he did know that, but it also didn't change the facts. TitanX was in trouble. Paul continued. "Look Nick. I know I'm not here because of my business savvy. You hired me to build an army, so to speak. I can't compete with you, Daniel, or Bev when it comes to this side of things. I know that. But dammit, Nick. These are people. They're my people. They have families. You can't just throw them away."

"Then find me a solution, Paul. You say it yourself in your classrooms. Stop bitching and start fixing. Something along those lines. So, get me a solution. All I hear right now is bitching."

Paul blinked at the rebuke—shocked to have his own words thrown in his face. "Nick, you have friends on the hill and even more in the Pentagon. Have you even talked to them? Tried to work something out?"

"Of course I have. Been trying to call in favors for months. Hell, I've been dialing non-stop for the last two weeks, same as you guys." Nick stopped, taking another sip. "A few minutes ago, you were ranting about not seeing this coming. Paul, we all saw it coming. From the point when Evans looked like a lock for the nomination, I've been pinging on every contact I have about our situation. There is, literally, nothing they can do. The new president has too much support for this initiative, both here and abroad."

"So, is this really gonna happen? Just like that? One guy gets elected and we're forced to close our doors or kick four thousand employees to the curb?"

Nick stood, still holding his glass. Paul leaned forward, placing his elbows on the table and holding his head in his hands.

"Paul, the people didn't elect a new group of lawmakers. Not this time. They elected a whole new way of life. Christ, Paul, this country's been at war for almost all of its existence. Sooner or later, the public was gonna wise up. Parents are tired of sending their kids off to war and families are tired of getting their loved ones back in body bags."

"So that's it. We either close down shop or scale back and tell most of our troops to go home?"

"For at least the next four years, yes. Listen, Paul, I know how much you love your folks. I know you put your heart into them. That's why I brought you onboard. But nothing short of World War three is going to change the mind of the president or the public. And with the shift in control of the two houses, he has the political horsepower to make this stick."

"Nick. What the hell am I supposed to tell my people? Can we at least give them a head's up?"

"I don't see how that could hurt. Gives them time to prepare. We can also use some of our contacts to hook folks up with other companies."

"I'm not sure I like that."

"I know, Paul. I know. But it's the best we can do right now."

★ ★ ★ ★ ★

Twenty minutes after Paul left, Nick was still sitting in the boardroom, nursing his second drink of the afternoon while his brain picked through the options—close up shop or jump ship.

Nick had survived downsizing in the Army. He'd watched qualified and capable soldiers sent home for no other reason than that the Army didn't have the budget to keep them. He'd heard plenty of horror stories about the castaways ending up unemployed and destitute. The idea that some of his own employees would end up trying to survive on food stamps and a monthly unemployment check while they hunted for jobs grated on him—but he didn't see a way around it.

Well, not one he was willing to tell his executive staff about. He had one idea. His brain argued with itself for the hundredth time in two weeks. What he was thinking about doing was madness. That he'd even discussed it out loud with one person was sheer-fucking-insanity.

But was it as mad as just sitting here drinking whisky and watching your fortune evaporate and your troops lose their jobs?

Nick forced his brain back to the present. He hadn't been wrong when he'd told Paul that they couldn't afford to keep folks on the payroll in the hope that the world would shift again. That wasn't good business sense and they didn't have the cash to pay folks for sitting around on their asses for four years. Sure, the company pulled in a shitload of money with all of the contracts, but that was the problem. The bottom line was a mirage. Each contract called for a number of contracted security personnel to be paid a certain number of dollars, with added payments for overhead and training and a myriad of other expenses. In the end, there wasn't a lot of wiggle room and, if he was perfectly honest, much of what appeared to make TitanX wealthy would vanish when the contracts were cancelled.

Nick took another pull at his drink. He leaned back in the chair, the cushy leather enveloping his body as his brain kept going over his limited options, searching for another answer. Nick's eyes opened back up after exhausting every other possible idea.

Nick reached forward and pressed a button on the tabletop phone. The voice of his assistant came clearly through the intercom.

"Yes, sir?"

"Chuck. Where's Mike Nixon right now?"

Nick heard fingers tapping on keys—Chuck Warner was one of the old guard, a man who preferred the 'antique' keyboards with large, noisy keys.

"Sir, Mike's in San Diego right now. On leave."

"Get him here. Yesterday."

"Yes, sir."

Nick was waiting when his guest walked into the TitanX boardroom eighteen hours later.

"Mike, how the hell are ya?" Nick crossed the boardroom, clasping Mike's hand in an iron grip that threatened to grind the younger man's knuckles into bone meal.

"Doing fine, sir. And you?"

"No complaints. How's your mother?"

Mike was caught off guard. He should have known better. You didn't get to be CEO of the world's largest private security firm without having a few tricks up your sleeve. Besides, Nixon hadn't really kept his mother's health a secret. Still, getting asked about her situation point-blank by the man who signed his paychecks was a unique experience.

"She has good days and bad days."

"Alzheimer's?" Nick asked.

"Yes, sir." Mike said.

Nick shook his head. "Went through that with my grandfather. Awful to watch. Harder on us. Physically it's still your family, but sometimes..."

Mike finished for his boss. "But sometimes, when they don't recognize you. Yes, sir. That does suck a bit."

"I'll be damned. Didn't think you frogmen ever admitted that anything sucked." Nick grinned.

Mike smiled back and relaxed slightly.

Nick continued. "So, Mike. Bet you're wondering why you're here."

"That question has crossed my mind, sir."

Nick raised an eyebrow. Mike explained. "Sir, twelve hours ago I get recalled to New York. Today I rate your personal assistant as a driver."

Nick grinned at that. "I really shouldn't let Chuck drive people around. He's a bit..."

Mike nodded. "Yes, he is."

"He doesn't get out much." Nick laughed. He turned to the sideboard. "Can I fix you something?"

Mike shook his head. "Just water."

Nick reached down and extracted a bottle of water from the mini-fridge before pouring himself a cup of coffee. He gathered both drinks and headed for Mike. After handing over the bottled water, Nick flopped into his chair at the head of the table, signaling that Mike should take a seat.

"Mike, I've got a job for you. I'm working on a contract that's going to be fairly lucrative."

"How long is the assignment?"

"A few weeks' worth of work. Nothing major. I'm heading over to Scotland soon to work out the details."

Nixon unscrewed the cap from his water. "We don't have it yet?"

"Let's just say it's out for bid and we're the only bidder." Nick paused. "Can't get much easier than that, especially with all of this going on." He waved at a stack of newspapers.

"Sir, I heard about the contract troubles with the new president's policy. My apologies."

Nick took a sip from his cup. "Yeah. That's a bad situation, but we've got some of the best folks in the business working on it. We'll figure it out. Pull in new clients here and there. Attack it bit by bit."

"Will that work?"

"It won't completely even out the losses, but it'll help. I don't know that we'll be able to save everyone, but we're working on it. Anyone we can't save; we'll damn sure try to place them somewhere. Recommendations. Good, solid evaluations." Nick paused and took a drink. "By the way, don't spread that around. Don't need folks panicking. Only way we get through this is to have everyone focused and performing. Present a good, strong product and we'll save some folks a lot of heartache."

"I understand sir. My lips are sealed."

"Let's talk about that. In the service you had some access to code-word stuff, correct?"

"Yes, sir."

"Okay. This contract is to be considered code-word. The executive staff isn't cleared for this."

Mike frowned. "I normally get my marching orders from Mr. Burkhart. Am I to assume…"?

Nick nodded. "That's correct. All communication for this contract will be between your team and myself. No one else."

"Must be some contract."

Nick smiled and took another sip. "Son, you have no idea."

Mike listened quietly as the CEO of TitanX explained the details of the contract. When Nick finished, Mike whistled. "Holy shit, sir."

6

EVANS

"ALRIGHT, FOLKS, HOW'S THIS GONNA WORK?" The President directed his question at the members of his senior staff. Every eye in the room turned to the Chief of Staff, who was pocketing a handkerchief.

"You okay, Leslie?" The President asked.

"I'm fine. Eyes still watering from that swab check." Barnes noted. "There's gotta be a better way to test for this thing."

Evans noticed several staffers reach for their own noses. He grinned.

Cathy Bettencourt, the Secretary of the Treasury, wrinkled her nose up like a small child. "I'm not so sure that some of the testers didn't work at the Agency's black sites. Getting those swabs shoved up your nose every day surely qualifies as an enhanced interrogation technique."

The Director of National Intelligence, Ophelia Adams, leaned around the Secretary of Defense. "Can't confirm or deny that, Cathy."

The president was rubbing his own nose now. "I don't know about that, but having someone shove a wooden stick up my nose everyday has to be giving the protective detail ulcers by now." The president turned to the Secret Service agent standing by the door. "Isn't that right, Jack?"

The agent didn't even crack a smile. "We manage, Mr. President."

The president smiled and looked at DNI Adams. "Ophelia, you think they'd tell me if they didn't like me getting tested?"

"I think they'd tell you anything they didn't like. Their job is to keep threats away."

"Even at the cost of having someone tickle the front lobe of my brain every day?"

"Even that."

The president shook his head. "It's a catch-22, isn't it? They have to swab me to make sure I haven't contracted Covid, but the swabbing itself is dangerous in the Service's eyes. Some crazy bastard could just shove that stick right through my brain." Evans paused, thinking. "You know. We all hate the test. I assume that the public does too. Anything we can do about that?"

"Not really," Barnes admitted. "This is the most accurate testing procedure we have. The National Institute of Health and CDC claim that some less-invasive tests are on the way, but there's no timeline for that yet."

"Find out what we can be doing to help? We're still losing hundreds of people each day and the dozen vaccines under development haven't been testing well. If we can't vaccinate for this yet, we should be able to help make the testing less, um, intrusive."

Barnes made a couple notes. "I'll make some calls. At the very least we can get congress to push some more funding through for research and development."

"Good. What's up next?"

"Planning is already underway for your first G20 Conference." Barnes pointed out. He flipped through his notes. "April. Chennai."

Evans groaned. Economics was not a strong point. It was, at best, a pair of grades on a very old college transcript. Courses he'd passed through brute force. He viewed any economic theory beyond the Keynesian Cross as something akin to witchcraft.

"Mr. President," Cathy explained. "For the month prior to the conference, you'll be getting visits from some of my best people. They'll be briefing you on just about anything you may need to know."

The president nodded his thanks. "Okay, so I don't need to be Adam Smith or John Nash for this. What else?"

"The withdrawal," Barnes noted.

Evans grinned. "How do we kickstart that?"

"Well, Mr. President, we have a couple options. We can let Congress push for the withdrawal of troops or we can direct the Pentagon to do it with an executive order."

"Pros and cons?" The president inquired.

Alice Freytag, a graduate of Arizona State and the Deputy Chief of Staff fielded that question. "Sir, either way gets the job done. There are enough opposition folks left in congress to slow it down a little, but those are mainly folks who either have major defense contractors behind them or constituencies that almost solely rely on defense spending. They can't stop anything and they really are caught between the proverbial rock and a hard place. Hell, sir, there are three new senators from states overwhelmingly in favor of the withdrawal who have constituents that will lose jobs because of it. An executive order, in this case, gives the whole process a giant shove forward and it gives some political cover to some of our allies who may need it in the midterms."

Barnes nodded. "I agree, Mr. President. Starting the process here will let some of the folks on our side of the aisle point elsewhere when their constituents ask questions. It even gives some political cover to some people across the aisle who we might need on our side for other policy initiatives. It's a win-win from both of those standpoints." The Chief of Staff pointed at the president. "Bottom line is simple. This is something you need to be in front of. This is your initiative. This was your candidacy and this is your presidency. The executive order is the way to go, even if it's just a shove in the direction congress is already leaning."

The president leaned forward and picked up a cup of coffee. He'd been in the job for two weeks and was still getting used to the sheer volume of day-to-day tasks that demanded his attention. He was already having trouble sleeping, his mind refusing to shut off as he crawled between the sheets. The coffee helped, at least during the day. It probably wasn't helping the insomnia. He put the cup back down and looked around the room.

"Frank? Do you have any issues with this?" The president asked.

Franklin Tolchanov was the Secretary of Defense. He shook his head. "None, sir. I'd prefer to get moving on this."

Evans nodded and turned to Bettencourt. "What's the economic impact here?"

"That's something we need to dig deeper into. We got some rough numbers during the campaign, but nothing specific. Are we talking about across the board?"

"Yeah." The president said. "I assume OMB and CBO will have estimates laying around somewhere. This isn't exactly a new idea."

Barnes was scribbling notes as Bettencourt answered. "I would imagine that would be the case. I don't know that it will be a significant reduction. The world's a pretty big place and people still think we need to be the world's police."

Barnes finished writing. "I agree. Congress will want a small reduction, but the actual dollar amount will be a small fraction of the defense procurement budget." He looked at the opposite couch, where the communications director and press secretary sat. "Regina, how does this play out at the local level?"

Regina Kelly, the White House Communications Director, was a Penn State graduate and Rhodes Scholar who'd grown up in West Baltimore. The second youngest of eight children in a single-parent home, she'd worked her way up from rock bottom and had the scars to prove it.

"Mr. President, I'd have to check with the Pentagon first, but I'd imagine that procurements and military manning or recruiting would actually change very little. We have about a hundred and seventy thousand troops deployed around the world at any given time. There are about sixty-thousand troops deployed to the region and only about twenty thousand of those troops are deployed in Iraq, Afghanistan or Syria. I would hazard a guess that the biggest savings would come with the reduction of contracted security professionals. It's a fairly large amount of money but it is spread among an extremely small group of companies. Those people will get the message and immediately realize that their livelihood is on the line. That could present a problem. Most of those companies are in democratic bastions. That could be a thorn in our side in the mid-terms in two years. We need a public relations strategy for that."

That made sense, the president thought. He noted the smile on his SECDEF's face and assumed the two had talked already. He turned to his Chief of Staff. "Leslie, best first move?"

Barnes nodded at Tolchanov. "Best option is to have SECDEF and his team in for a meeting. Say two days to put the numbers together?"

Tolchanov nodded. "Two days works. We started pulling old plans and estimates right after the inauguration."

"Do it." The president ordered. "We'll hold off on the executive order for now. I do want someone working on the language for that, but it can wait until after we have firmer budget estimates."

The group nodded as the president went on. "You were all there during the campaign. I don't have to tell you how big this issue is. I don't know that the average voter understands or even cares that ending this war might ultimately cost Joe or Jane Taxpayer his or her job, but I do know that we owe it to the public to consider that possibility and maybe have a plan for that. Any questions?" There were none. "Alright, people. What else?"

DNI Adams cleared her throat. "Mr. President, I know we covered it during the daily brief, but we really should put a working group together to look at the India-Pakistan thing. That could bite us in the ass."

Evans made a note on a pad of paper. "Explain."

"Well, they had that dust-up a few days after the inauguration. Sure, no one was killed, but shots were fired and about fifteen Indian troopers ended up in the hospital. Now we're hearing lots of rumblings out of India. Nothing official. Just bits and pieces of locker room talk. Chest-thumping mostly, but potentially serious chest-thumping."

Barnes looked up. "Like what?"

"Like they're tired of dealing with this particular threat. Like they're ready to draw a line in the sand with respect to Pakistan and the terrorists that base from there. They have a legitimate complaint. They deal with plenty of incidents and cross-border incursions by groups that we can loosely tie to Pakistani leadership. In this case, three of the Pakistanis involved were former ISI officers." Adams thought for a moment. "Leslie, ever see Ghostbusters?"

The Chief of Staff nodded. "Sure."

"Remember the scene when Wenkman is shocking the kid in the lab and the kid gets pissed and starts screaming?"

Barnes nodded.

"Same thing. India gets shocked and shocked and shocked. Eventually they throw their hands up and say they've had it."

Evans leaned back in his chair. "Alright. Ophelia, work with Leslie and get it set up. I don't want this blowing up into something that derails the withdrawal."

Adams nodded as the president wrapped the meeting up. "Anything else, folks?"

★ ★ ★ ★ ★

Franklin Tolchanov was a short, feisty, barrel-chested man with a crew-cut, unchanged since a six-year hitch in the Marine Corps. His gait, also unchanged in the three decades since he'd left military service for the University of Kentucky, was a precise and efficient thirty-inch pace that carried him into the cabinet room of the White House ahead of four of his principal staffers. He strode immediately to Leslie Barnes and grasped the Chief of Staff's outstretched hand.

"Morning, Leslie. How's it going?"

"Great, Frank. Great. How's the family?"

"Great. Ruth's cancer free and our oldest just made me a grandpa."

"Congrats! We were all pulling for Ruth. Glad to hear she's in the clear."

"Yeah, well the docs at GW caught it pretty early. A few months later and things might've been different. She lost a lot of weight, but nothing some good chow can't fix."

"That's good to hear. Well," Leslie gestured to the oval table dominating the room, "should we get to work?"

SECDEF smiled. "Let's do this."

After taking a few minutes to situate everyone, the Chief of Staff kicked off the meeting. "Frank. I really appreciate you getting this together."

SECDEF waved off the comment, pouring a glass of water while he did so.

"It was easy. We always have the budget numbers and plans around. Just a matter of dusting everything off and updating a few spreadsheets." He paused to take a sip of water. "Leslie, is he really gonna make this happen? Pulling out everyone but the embassy folks?"

"That's the plan. Is it a problem?"

"Hell no." Franklin's southern drawl came on strong. "Shit, Leslie. This move'll solve more problems than it presents. It'll end up saving money."

That surprised the Chief of Staff. "How so?"

"Christ, Leslie. Do you know how expensive it is to keep folks and gear over there? Hell. Maintenance costs alone will drop twenty percent with this move. Fuel, munitions, replacement costs. All of it goes way the hell down when you bring folks back stateside. The folks that build the gear will lose out a bit when they're not replacing units that have either been run to shit or blown the hell up, but we can't stay in a war forever just to keep throwing money their direction. Throw in the cost of housing and feeding everyone. We get screwed on that too, by the way. We try to appease the local governments and suppliers by procuring from local resources and they fleece us for it."

"I hadn't thought about that. What's the biggest problem you see?"

SECDEF took another sip and leaned back in the stuffed leather chair. "That's a fifty-fifty question. The intel and national security hounds will tell you that moving the troops out creates a security risk. Maybe a vacuum of power or something like that."

"And you don't agree." It was a statement, rather than a question, but Frank answered anyway.

"No. Not really. Listen. Everyone over there, the government types, I mean, have either asked or told us to leave. We're no more welcome than a plague rat. We're not in power, cause we're not really an occupying army any more. Sure, we have boots on the ground, but not in that kind of capacity. Haven't been in that business since the second world war. The folks in power there say we're not helping matters and the folks who want to be in power use our presence as an excuse to attack the people we're trying to help out." The SECDEF went silent for a few moments before speaking again. "No, Leslie. I believe those folks will throw a parade after we leave. Right before they start shootin' each other again."

Leslie leaned his elbows on the table and rubbed his temples. "We've been there for almost twenty years and things haven't really changed. What are the optics if we pull out?"

"You'd have to ask the intel guys or maybe the historians, but probably not much different than leaving Vietnam. We look whipped, whether it's true or not. There'd probably be some muscle-flexing by the various groups over there. ISIS, Al-Qaeda, Taliban or what have you. On this side of the line, you'll probably have some hand-wringing and pearl-clutching from folks who say that leaving sends the message that the terrorists win and that this move will just encourage the bastards."

"Will it?"

"Leslie, those people will say whatever they want, whenever they want, and either edit or create the videos to support it. To the people who follow them, it doesn't matter if it's really true, it just has to be believable to them. Besides, counter-terrorism is largely an intel operation. Relatively speaking, my budget for the intel side of that part of the world is very small. Hell, man. If we leave, it's a good bet that things calm down a bit. When those people aren't shooting at us or trying to blow up my equipment, they spend their time going after the people they think help us. Again, they don't much care whether that info is true or not. A lot of innocent people have died in the past twenty years for that reason alone."

"You really don't have a problem with this?"

"Hell no. Two reasons. I'm tired of flushing money down the toilet in that region and the DOD has plenty for those troopers to do. Sure, we'll keep a carrier battle group patrolling the Persian Gulf, but boots on the ground? No sir. I'm fine with ending that part of the equation."

"Any big impacts on suppliers or contracts?"

"Not much immediate impact to the supply chain. Procurements will stay the same for now and drop off later as we replace whatever gear we leave behind. Biggest impact will be to private contractors."

"How much are we talking about?"

Tolchanov shrugged. "It's a piece. The private security business is a thirty-billion dollar a year industry. On our end, we spend nearly a billion per year to use private operators in the region. That's just us at DOD and the intel folks. Most of it, about eighty percent, is one firm."

"Really?"

"Yeah. There's an outfit based in New York called TitanX. Owned by a retired Army special forces guy. Nick DeGuerra. Good man. We've been using them for about fifteen years or so. They're gonna get hit hard."

"How hard?"

"It depends on how they handle it. Say it takes a year or so to completely shut everything down. That gives them a year to go looking for other customers. That probably won't stop the bleeding. More than ninety-percent of their business is with the US government."

"Jesus."

"Yeah. If they find other clients, the best they can do is lose about sixty or sixty-five percent of their revenue stream. If they don't, they're out of business."

"How many employees?"

"Somewhere around four thousand."

Barnes made a mental note to reach out to the new representative and senator for the district. Both were democrats and both would be unhappy if the US government rendered four thousand of their constituents unemployed.

"Leslie?"

"Yeah?"

"This has to happen. We've been pissing money away over there for more than forty years. It may be sacrilegious coming from a person in my job, but there are better ways to spend that money. I'm supposed to say spend it on more troops and ships and guns. Hell. For what we've paid in the last two decades, we could've rebuilt the military and paid for every kid in this country to go to college. It's a no brainer."

7

———

THOMPSON

BRIAN BLINKED INTO THE DARKNESS as one hand groped for the alarm clock. It was one o'clock in the morning and his three hours of fitful sleep were not enough. He half rolled, half fell out of the six-foot-long metal cubby that was his rack and stood, rubbing the sleep from his eyes and attempting to stretch away the aches and pains that came with years of sleeping on a three-inch foam mattress.

Fighting off a blurry headache that was a by-product of too much stress and too little sleep, Brian struggled into a faded set of blue coveralls that had been hanging on his locker door. Fresh from the laundry, there was a faint scent of fuel permeating the coveralls that never seemed to go away. There was also a persistent dampness to the fabric, courtesy of the nearly defunct heating elements in the ship's dryers.

He opened his locker and reached inside, retrieving two small gold anchors, a leather name patch, and a cotton, khaki colored belt with a gold buckle. He set the items on his rack and pulled on a thick pair of soft and warm black socks before slipping each foot into his black leather boots. He tied the laces, rocking back and forth with each roll of the ship. Brian squared away his uniform, lacing the belt through the loops on the coveralls, affixing the anchors to the points of his collar, and sticking the name patch on a strip of Velcro above his breast pocket. He reached back into the locker and withdrew a few additional items. A small, dark green notebook went into his back pocket and he dropped some pens in a pocket on his left shoulder. With that, he closed the locker door and left the berthing compartment, already thinking about each item on an absurdly long to-do list.

The ship was quiet at this early hour, the dim red glow of the darkened ship lighting giving the entire vessel an eerie, abandoned feel. Brian walked forward and began climbing up the first ladder. He didn't really mind the darkened version of the ship. He could think, could organize. It was peaceful during the night, none of the chaos that seemingly characterized every waking hour on this ship.

Brian reached the next deck up and began walking the engineering spaces. He roamed the ship, looking and listening as he walked. He heard the humming of four hundred and forty volts of electricity flowing through the switchboards and the swoosh of various fluids moving through the piping systems. He noted the high-pitched whine of the gas turbines that moved the ship and generated power as he took time to talk to each watch stander. Satisfied, he turned his mind to breakfast.

Brian climbed out of main engine room number one, his last stop, and walked forward to the Chiefs' Mess. He entered and surveyed the dim scene. One chief was knocked out on the soft brown microfiber sofa under the television and two more were sitting quietly, eating their breakfasts and trying to wake up before their respective watches. The chief on the sofa twitched slightly and moved a little. Poor bastard, Brian thought.

The sleeping chief had been up for nearly seventy hours straight, chasing down faults in the destroyer's weapons systems that had ended up being engineering problems. During maintenance on some of the ship's electric buses, the automatic transfer of electricity to an alternate power supply hadn't happened. Brian's electricians had begun combing the system and had found additional glitches, all of which needed repair for the ship to keep the Williams' guns working in an emergency.

Brian walked to a row of cabinets where he grabbed a cup of pre-packaged cereal and a glass for orange juice. He filled the glass before taking a seat. He was greeted by a pair of grunts as he devoured his breakfast.

Five minutes later, Brian made his way to Central Control, the ship's nerve center for everything engineering. Chief Tim Guillory was wrapping up his shift as the Engineering Officer of the Watch and looked exhausted.

Guillory was a few years older than Brian. He'd grown up in the Louisiana bayou and hadn't joined the Navy until his twenty-third birthday. He'd told Brian that he'd woken up one day tired of living hand-to-mouth. He'd thrown a few items into a bag, hopped into a car, and visited the nearest recruiting office.

"Tim?"

"Just finishing up," said the older man.

Brian waited for him to finish writing in the logbook, amazed again that the man's heavy bayou accent was almost unnoticeable. Unless he was watching football, Brian thought. Then it comes out full-force. He'd witnessed that twice in his first weekend aboard. First as Tim watched LSU play. The second time during Sunday Night Football. Brian smiled at the memory of Guillory jumping on the Chief's Mess couch while yelling 'Who Dat?' after an overtime win.

Tim signed the log and turned around. "Damn. You're early."

"I can leave," Brian grinned.

"Oh hell no."

"Alright, Tim, whatcha' got?"

"Plant is the same as before. Shifted the generators for water-washes on number two and three. Two ACs online. LPACs are the same. Prairie and masker both on. Same fire pumps online. Just shifted fuel suction about twenty minutes ago."

"No problems?"

"None. Except for the water-washes, it was a fairly quiet watch."

"Works for me. You're relieved."

Guillory announced his relief to all spaces and headed for the door, leaving Brian to watch over the plant. He looked around at the sailors in the space and climbed into a tall, leather captain's chair in the middle of the room.

"Alright, folks, time to shift equipment."

"Top, PACC. Fuel pumps shifted forward and aft." A sailor announced nearly six hours later.

"Pumps shifted aye. Thanks, Cruz."

"No problem, Chief."

Brian leaned over to note the routine shift in the logbook. As he did so, the door to the space opened to admit several additional officers and sailors. Brian looked at his watch. Half-past seven. Time for quarters, a traditional morning meeting throughout the Navy.

"Morning, folks," he said with a not-quite-feigned cheerfulness.

A chorus of greetings, some grumbled, some enthusiastic, emanated from the new arrivals.

Each person in the room was part of the department's leadership. Chief Guillory was there. The ship's Chief Engineer, Lieutenant Owen Walker, stood by along with Chief Warrant Officer Grady Larsson, the ship's Main Propulsion Assistant. The ship's Damage Control Assistant, Lieutenant Junior Grade Leslie Hunter, was also present, as were several brand-new officers. Ensigns Jeffrey Strater, Joanna Keisling, Tom Szepanski, and James Kilgore were, respectively, the division officers for the department's main propulsion, electrical, auxiliary, and repair divisions. Each division officer was accompanied by at least one senior petty officer.

Brian looked around, pulling out his notebook and a pen. "I don't have anything new for you today. Got a few sailors missing eval inputs. We've got about a month before we sign those, so hit those folks up this morning. Need the info by close of business today. Let's go around the room. Who's first?"

Each officer and petty officer took turns outlining work for the day. Brian scribbled notes and asked a few questions about parts and schedules, getting a fresh update on the day-to-day lives of his sailors and their gear. Electrical division was doing routine maintenance and continuing to troubleshoot the bus transfers. Main propulsion and repair divisions were doing a good deal of space preservation, cleaning and painting mostly. Brian turned to face Ensign Szepanski.

"AUXO, whatcha got?"

"Nothing much aside from the RHIB. We need an hour to change filters on the ship's steering hydraulics later. We can do the offline units first and then shift."

"When?"

"Whenever the bridge is good with it. We're flexible."

"I'll let the captain know, Chief," the Chief Engineer said.

"Thanks, sir," Brian turned back to the AUXO. "Now, about the

RHIBs."

The petty officer behind the AUXO, a machinist mate named Donaldson, spoke up.

"Chief, we've looked over the whole fuel system. No idea why there's water in the gas tank or how it got there. We checked everything. Every hose. Every connection. Even the intercooler."

Brian scribbled a note. The boat had been out of commission for two weeks. When it had been craned onboard, they'd pulled a fuel sample that had been short on fuel and long on seawater. The Auxiliary Division sailors, collectively known as A-Gang, had descended on the broken boat and had found nothing. There was no apparent cause for why the fuel tank had water in it. They'd pumped almost twenty gallons of saltwater out of the tank before finally getting a sample that was straight fuel.

"What's the tech manual say?"

Donaldson cocked his head. "Chief, you ever see those things? Like eight volumes. A thousand pages each."

Thompson nodded. It rankled him that they'd not used the tech manuals. Not even opened the damn things. "Tell you what. After I get off watch and grab some chow, I'll head up to the boat deck. AUXO, can you have a couple folks up there with the schematics and manuals?"

"Sure, Chief, but don't you have other stuff to do?"

"Nothing that can't wait until tomorrow. There's a disciplinary review board later, but nothing that concerns me. Some deck guy got his ass beat down in the combat berthing. We've got a lot going on, but we're gonna need that boat soon. We've got three more practice boardings before we hit the Suez and that's assuming we don't get told to do any real-world ops between now and then. Ignoring that, we have upkeep to worry about. We can't do maintenance on the good boat until this one's fixed."

"And he's getting tired of the XO giving him shit about it," the ship's Chief Engineer pointed out.

The Executive Officer, XO, was Lieutenant Commander John Polian. An enlisted machinist's mate before earning a commission, the man's wicked sense of humor now had a new target in the person of Brian. The jibes weren't personal. It was the XO's way of getting his new

Top Snipe to relax a bit. Brian rolled his eyes as the REPO launched his XO impression.

"Gawdahmnit, Chief! How long does it take to fix a little leak? I could've rebuilt an entire boat by now." It reminded Brian of a particularly poor JFK impersonation.

Most of the sailors in the room broke into laughter.

Brian motioned for quiet. "Alright. Alright. REPO, if he ever hears you doing that, all hell's gonna break loose."

"True, but I'm already the most junior officer on the boat. How much worse can it get?" He was grinning ear to ear.

"Oh, I'm sure I can come up with something," a gruff New England accent wafted into the room.

Brian turned to see the XO enter Central Control. "Morning, XO. What can I do for ya?"

"Oh, don't mind me. I'm here to listen to more of Ensign Kilgore's stand-up." He walked over and slung an arm over the Repair Officer's shoulders. Ensign Kilgore, face flushing red, inspected the floor by his boots. "Now, you folks were talking about boats?"

★ ★ ★ ★ ★

An hour later, Guillory reappeared in Central Control to re-assume the role as USS James E. Williams' Engineering Officer of the Watch, or EOOW, a circumstance that Thompson reminded himself needed fixing. The two Engineering Department chiefs were the only qualified EOOWs onboard.

As he headed to the Chief's Mess for a refill on his coffee and some leftovers from breakfast, Brian let his mind wander over the possible problems with the boat. He was so engrossed in thought that he walked right past the entrance to the Mess and squarely into the ship's maintenance coordinator.

"Jesus, Brian, you look like shit."

"Gee. Thanks." Brian grumbled.

Chief Petty Officer Douglas Franklin, known throughout the ship as 3MC, was one of the ship's oldest chiefs. Pushing fifty, with the belly and balding head to show it, the Virginia native was one of those souls who'd come to the Navy late in life. He'd joined at thirty-five and had just passed fifteen years of service. He was a good guy whose job did not endear him to the majority of the crew. Doug Franklin's appearance in your office usually denoted some sort of error in your weekly maintenance reports—documents that almost all sailors loathe.

"Where ya headed?" Doug's slow, southern drawl was deceptive. While it appeared to make him seem a bit slow, Brian knew the southerner to be smart as hell, with a memory to match.

"Mess. Coffee."

"Me too."

The two retraced Brian's earlier path and entered the mess, walking right into a lively discussion about the recent ranking of the ship's second-class petty officers. Both filled a mug with fresh coffee and found ringside seats.

"Your boy fucked up his early promotion recommendation awful fast." The comment came from Kyle Corcoran, the ship's Sonar Chief, and was directed at one of the vessel's Fire Control Chiefs, Steve Whitmer.

"Fuck off, Kyle. How many of your folks got ranked above 'promotable'? Steve pointed out reasonably. STGC Corcoran had three second classes and none of them ranked above promotable, Navy-speak for a C-average.

"Bound to be a lot more if your boys are settin' the bar that damn low," quipped Corcoran. He got a pair of middle fingers in return.

Brian leaned towards the ship's Command Master Chief, a big, burly former Bosun's Mate, and whispered. "Okay. What the hell did I miss?"

Master Chief Logan Carrillo, the ship's senior enlisted sailor, turned and grinned. "Apparently Petty Officer Randolph was late to watch this morning. OPS said something about expecting more from a senior second class and Randolph lost his mind."

Brian smiled. "No shit?"

"No shit," Carrillo said. "Even suggested that OPS may have a somewhat inappropriate relationship with his own mother."

Brian snorted. Carrillo continued. "I'm sure you can imagine how pissed OPS is. He wants Randolph's head on a platter."

"I'll bet."

OPS, the ship's Operations Officer, was a Naval Academy graduate who liked to constantly remind the enlisted sailors that he possessed a college degree and was, therefore, better than them. The lieutenant, a Washington-state native named Lance Caldwell, was a bit of a pain-in-the-ass. The man was intelligent, but his inability to interact with people caused a lot of trouble.

"You know. That's not like Randolph." Brian said. "He's a quiet kid. Does his job well. Never in trouble."

Carrillo nodded. "That's why he's coming in here for a Disciplinary Review Board first. Kid won't tell Steve shit."

Brian nodded again and the two turned to watch Steve and Kyle continue to needle each other. Brian noticed something. He turned to Carrillo, whispering. "Logan?"

"Yeah?"

"What's Jason up to?"

Carrillo turned. Roberts was sitting at the far end of the couch, keeping one eye on the Randolph argument and the other on an object hidden by one of his thick legs. The resident prankster kept glancing down at whatever was hidden by his leg, followed by a quick glance at the two bickering Chiefs and an occasional glance towards the stand-up fridge by the door.

Brian followed the man's gaze toward the fridge. There was an object perched on top of the fridge, something Brian was sure hadn't been there earlier that morning. It was a small, dark rectangle that was…moving? Brian looked closer. The black box had little orange pieces sticking out of one end.

What the hell?

Carrillo elbowed Brian in the ribs, getting his attention. He nodded at Roberts. Brian shifted his gaze. Jason was sitting there, about twenty feet away, with an enormous shit-eating grin on his face and his index finger hovering over whatever was hidden by his leg. Jason winked at Brian and his finger descended.

Brian heard a motor kick on. Before he had time to even wonder what it was, a series of six muted pops came from the box on top of the fridge and six, neon-orange foam darts raced across the room, targeted on Steve and Kyle.

Most of the darts bounced harmlessly off of their targets, but one scored a direct hit—splashing down in Steve's freshly-filled cup of coffee and splattering some of the molten liquid on his hands.

Steve's expletive was lost in an eruption of laughter. The argument between Kyle and Steve dissolved quickly and Brian lifted his coffee towards Jason in mock salute.

Carrillo stood up, gesturing for everyone to quiet down. "Alright folks. I'm sure you all have shit to do. I need Brian, Jason, Doug and Kyle on the board at sixteen hundred. Everyone else can witness, but keep your traps shut. Aside from that, I have coffee with S-2 division at ten." He checked his watch. "Ship wide field day starts in twenty minutes. Unless you're on watch or fixing the RHIB with Brian, I need you out getting the ship clean. Got it?"

He was answered by a chorus of groans and three semi-serious attempts to volunteer to help troubleshoot the RHIB. He ignored all of it. "Now, clean up after yourselves and get out in your spaces. Serious. Don't let me catch you in here during field day."

'Field day' was a traditional, weekly deep cleaning of the ship's interior spaces—a two-hour evolution that usually left the ship smelling like a mix of pine cleaner and fuel. Unlike most naval traditions, this one was universally disliked by every sailor without the title 'Executive Officer' attached to their name.

Brian got up with the rest of the chiefs, refilling his coffee one more time and wiping down his spot at the table. As he headed for the door, he got two more volunteers to help with the boat.

It took two minutes for Brian to get back to his desk in the Engineering Log Room, a space just around the corner from Central Control that was part office space and part storage for technical documentation. Brian fired up his desktop computer, slipping his access card in a slot on the keyboard and typing a PIN when prompted. The computer opened Outlook automatically and updated the inbox. Brian scanned the emails listed as unread.

There.

Brian saw the email with his wife's name attached to it buried between an emailed advisory message and a reminder to submit evaluations for E-5s. He clicked on the email and opened it. Within the first two words, he breathed a sigh of relief.

False alarm. Sorry. You'd think I'd know real labor pains from false ones by now. :) Kids are okay. Already looking forward to summer and it's only February.

How's the ship? The kids liked the pictures you sent of that boarding. The PAO(?) or whoever took them did a good job. I did have to explain to the younger kids what you were doing. When I mentioned the word pirate, they both wanted to know if you knew Jack Sparrow. SMDH.

Well, I have to get off here. Two more weeks until the due date.

After this surrogacy, I think I'm going to call it quits. What do you think?

Love you.
April

Brian typed a quick response and logged off. He picked up the coffee mug and a set of sunglasses and headed out of the Log Room. As he headed for the Boat Deck, his brain began reverting back into its technical mode—thinking about the busted RHIB and trying to picture the mysterious source of the leak.

8

———

THOMPSON

BRIAN HAD VAGUE IDEAS about just how foul he smelled as he fell into one of the empty chairs in the Chief's Mess. Except for standing watch, some admin, and thirty minutes here-and-there for meals or trips to the head, he'd spent almost every hour of daylight for the past two days sitting in the RHIB, helping to tear apart the engine and fuel system while the Mediterranean sun beat down on the boat's fiberglass deck. He'd sweated through every set of coveralls he owned as he and two of the ship's junior engineers worked to find out why the fuel tank was filling with seawater.

The three of them had gone through the system piece-by-piece, marking off each component on a schematic after confirming that particular piece was not the cause of the problem.

An hour before, Brian and the two engineers had been sitting in the boat, tightening the last few fittings back down and ready to go back to the drawing board when one of the sailors, an Electrician's Mate Third Class named Gearhart, had started trying to manipulate one of the deck plates back onto its frame. While trying to secure the plate in place, the young sailor's hand had brushed a clear, plastic line running just below the deck framework. After sticking his head below the level of the deck to see where the line ran, he'd sat back up and asked a simple question. "Hey Chief, what's this line for?"

Brian sat in the relative comfort of the Chief's Mess, the cool, conditioned air flowing over him as he tried to rehydrate. Sweat dripping from one cuff formed a puddle between his feet as he leaned forward in the chair. He'd have time to eat and shower before heading to Central Control for another six-hour watch, during which time there were no scheduled evolutions.

He looked up as the door opened. The CMC walked in and deposited his cover on a hook by the door. He grabbed a coffee mug, filled it and sat down opposite Brian. "Captain said you got the boat fixed. Nice job."

"That sucked."

"I'll bet. What was it?"

"Something that wasn't on the drawing."

"Seriously? What?"

"Ever seen the fuel tank on one of those?"

Carrillo thought for a moment. "Not that I can remember."

"The old boats used to have a vent right on top of the fuel tank. Ours still does. Sort of."

"Meaning?"

"The old vent is still there, but it's been modified. Someone ran a line from the vent, forward under the deck, to the front of the sponson. In our case, it got installed by the boat shop before deployment. It's actually zip-tied to the gun mount."

"And?"

"Normally the installation comes with a little ball-check valve. Air can escape the tank, but water can't get in. The installation of the line was to prevent gas fumes from building up below the decking."

Carrillo's face broke into a broad grin. "No."

"Yep."

"Those idiots installed the check valve upside down, didn't they?"

"Yep. Gearhart found it. Wanna know the really bad part?"

"It's marked. Like 'this way up' or something, isn't it?"

Brian reached into the breast pocket on his coveralls and extracted a small, black tube, which he handed over. Carrillo picked it up and turned it over. On one side, stamped with a little arrow, was the word 'UP'. He shook his head. "So, it would only fail when the boat was actually in the water, right?"

"Yep. We ran it in the skid about an hour before we put her in the water. No problems. Ran smooth as hell. But once she starts taking waves over the front end..." Brian's voice trailed off.

Carrillo had been in the Navy for almost three decades and had developed a moderate loathing for civilian contractors like those in the boat shop. He shook his head and handed the valve back. "How much time did y'all spend on that thing?"

"Since we left? What? Two, almost three weeks. Last few days? Maybe sixteen hours a day."

"Fuckin contractors."

Brian nodded and gulped the last of his water before standing up for a refill. Carrillo cocked his head. "How come you guys didn't see it when you took the boat apart?"

"They rigged part of the line to the underside of the decking. When we pulled the decking up, the line pulled off of the old tank-mounted connection." Brian shrugged. "When we looked at the tank, all we saw was the old set up. The line was laying in the bilge. I added it to the drawing in bright red pen."

"I'm assuming there was no mention of this line in the tech manuals?"

Brian sat back down with a full cup of water. "Funny you mention that. A couple days ago, I asked the same question at quarters."

Carrillo was nodding. "And?"

"And Donaldson gave me this 'Chief, have you seen how thick the manual is' bullshit. I don't think those people have ever opened a manual."

"That's not good. A-Gang has its hands in too much shit for that nonsense."

Brian nodded. "Tell me about it. I don't get it. All jokes about machinist mates not being able to read and needing picture books aside, those damn books really do help."

"You think it's more than just the boats?"

Brian thought about it for a second. "Honestly, yes. Which means I have something else to keep an eye on."

Carrillo nodded. "I've been through that before. Let me know if you need help and get some rest."

"Thanks, but I've got the next watch. I'll get a good six hours after that."

"That reminds me. How're you and Tim gonna get off of that six and six shit? Captain's been asking. You two standing that rotation and trying to do everything. That's a recipe for disaster, Brian. Or burnout. Or both." Carrillo referred to the watch rotation where Brian and Tim were trading off responsibility for the ship's engineering plant every six hours, twenty-four hours a day, seven days a week.

"Get someone qualified. We've got two possible EOOWs. The previous top snipe did a hell of a job prepping them. They just need a little tweaking and a full drill set."

"How long?"

"Maybe a month. Both are really good on each watch station, just gotta get 'em thinking about the whole plant. The whole ship."

"Well, keep at it. Need anything?"

"I gotta clean up before watch. Have someone stick a plate of food in the fridge for me?"

"Got it. No seafood, right?"

"Yeah. I'll take whatever else they've got tonight."

"Done. Go clean up. Get some rest after watch. You really do look like shit."

Brian headed to the door. "Everyone keeps sayin' that."

The ambient noise in the aft Chief's berthing—mostly the flow noise from an air conditioning unit and the sound of four middle-aged men snoring—was shattered by the trilling of the phone. Brian Thompson sat bolt upright in his rack at the noise—or tried to. His forehead smacked the rack light positioned just twelve inches from his face.

"Sonofabitch..."

While Brian held his forehead with one hand and searched for the switch for his rack light with the other, he heard another chief answer the phone. After some mumbling, there was a knock on the side of his metal-framed rack.

"Brian?"

"Yeah?"

"It's Tim in CCS. Said he needs you there."

Brian groaned. "Tell him I'll be there in five."

Brian wriggled sideways out of his rack, his forehead aching, and began to put a uniform on. In three minutes, he was out of the berthing compartment and climbing the ladder towards Central Control.

"What happened to your head?" Tim pointed.

"Rack light. What's up?

"Sorry to bother you, but number one reefer died about ten minutes ago and the aux rover can't get it restarted."

"Crap." Brian looked around. "What time is it?"

"Three."

Brian did some math in his head. Less than thirty minutes of sleep. "Alright. Let the rover know I'm headed to the reefer decks. I'll shift units. He can continue his watch."

"Rog."

It took Brian twenty minutes to pump the refrigerant back into the unit and isolate the downed reefer, after which he called Central and requested permission to start the standby refrigeration unit. After getting the go ahead from Guillory, Brian flipped to the portion of the operational procedure for starting the offline compressor and ran through the procedure step-by-step. He knew the operation of the unit by heart, but on thirty minutes of sleep, he wanted to make sure there were no mistakes.

After another twenty minutes, the stand-by unit was placed online and Brian called Central to let Tim know that he was starting to troubleshoot the broken unit.

"Hey, Chief, what happened to your head?" Brian started at the voice of the Aux Rover.

"Rack light." Brian returned to his work, eyes and fingers running over the troubleshooting guide in the technical manual. "How's it going?"

"'Cept this reefer, watch is pretty quiet."

"Yeah. Night watches are supposed to be quiet." A thought. "Brooks, you still have the logs for number one reefer?"

"No. I left those with Chief Guillory when I picked up a blank sheet for number two. Want me to get 'em?"

"Sure. I wanna see what the unit was doing before it shut down."

"I'll be back in five. Need anything else?"

Brian fished in his breast pocket and pulled out his shipboard debit card. "Yeah. Coke? Get yourself something too."

"Thanks, Chief. Be right back."

Petty Officer Brooks was back in the promised time, bearing operational logs and two ice-cold sodas. He sat down on the space tool locker. "Find anything yet, Chief?"

"Not really." Brian popped the top on the soda, the resulting hiss spraying a little soda on his palm. He wiped his hands on a rag and took a gulp before taking the logs from Brooks. As he drank, his eyes ran through the recorded readings—zeroing in on abnormal discharge pressures here and there.

Brooks watched Brian work. He'd only been in the Navy for eighteen months and the process of translating pressures and temperatures into operational problems was still something he hadn't quite mastered.

Brian muttered. "Well, sonofabitch."

"What?"

Brian held the log sheet up so the junior sailor could see the readings. "Look at the last set of readings."

Brooks looked. One reading was obvious. "Compressor discharge is high."

"And what causes that?"

Brooks thought for a minute. "Easiest answer is a shut valve."

"But?"

Brooks closed his eyes, thinking. "But the unit has been running for a week. Shut valve would have been noticed. Plant woulda shut down already."

"Correct. What else?" Brian could see the gears turning in the young man's head. When he didn't respond, Brian took another tack. "Does the unit have a control valve for the compressor?"

"No."

"Okay. Then what controls discharge pressure?"

The sailor's eyes closed again and then snapped open. "Oh shit. The water reg valve."

"Right. Look. Seawater injection temp has been going up and the discharge pressure rose too. What's that tell you?"

"The reg valve isn't moving?" It was an answer in the form of a question, complete with the kid's voice rising at the end, but it was the correct answer.

"Yep. Water reg valve isn't operating properly."

"So, what do we do?"

Brian looked at his watch. "Well, you continue roving and I'm gonna look at the valve and see if I can find what's wrong."

★ ★ ★ ★ ★

Brian walked into Central Control an hour later, his brow furrowed. Guillory finished reviewing a set of logs, handed them back to one of the engine room operators and looked up.

"Brian. What's up?"

Brian looked around at the rest of the watch standers in the room. "Folks? Can you excuse us for a minute? I'll cover the PACC."

The junior sailors in the room nodded and filed out of the space. When the last left, Brian dogged the door down and sat down in an empty seat. Guillory was watching him. "What gives?"

"Tim, who did the maintenance on the reefer units before I got here?"

Tim sat back, searching his memory. "When I first got here, it was a guy named Baker. He left a year before you got here."

"Transferred?"

"No. Got out. Went back home to go to school. Good kid. Good evals. We tried to get him to stay."

"No problems with him?"

"None. Why?"

"Who took over for him?"

"I think Donaldson's been signing for the maintenance. Why?"

Brian reached into a pocket and extracted a rusted bolt, which he handed to Tim. The gas turbine chief rolled it around in his hand.

"Retaining bolt?"

"Sort of."

"Sort of?"

"You know how a water reg valve works?"

Guillory kept rolling the bolt around in his palm. "Vaguely. Spring loaded valve, right? Tighten the spring and the pressure needed to open the valve goes up."

"Right."

"So, the bolt broke?"

"This isn't the retaining bolt. This was wedged into the valve after the original retaining bolt broke."

Realization dawned on Tim's face. "Jury-rigged repair?"

"Yeah. Instead of replacing the broken parts, someone just wedged the valve in place."

"Were you able to fix it?"

"Didn't even try yet. Started looking over the rest of the unit. Found this." Brian reached back in his pocket and pulled out a pale green circle. The painted object was roughly the size of a quarter and three times as thick. As soon as it hit Tim's hand, it began pulling towards his tungsten wedding ring.

"A magnet?"

"Yep."

"Where?"

"On top of a solenoid valve. Painted to look like part of the valve."

"Magnet keeps the valve open." Tim was thinking aloud.

"Yep." Brian confirmed. "That, some jumpered pressure switches. One jumpered safety. And some other shit."

Tim sat back and rubbed his face. "This is all we need. Jury-rigged repairs and gun-decked maintenance."

Gun-decking, claiming that something was done without actually doing it, was a cardinal sin in the Navy. Next to thievery, gun-decking anything in the Navy was something that both men had grown to hate. It was, after all, a question of trust. If you couldn't trust a sailor, then he or she was of no use to the ship.

"Where's CHENG?"

Tim glanced at the clock on the wall. "Should be in Combat."

"Alright. I'm heading to see him."

Brian got up off the chair, collecting the bolt and magnet from Tim. He'd taken two steps from the door when an alarm went off on the console behind him. He turned to look at it. Tim beat him to it. "Number two reefer just shut down."

"Why?"

"Says high compressor discharge pressure. You don't think..." Tim's voice trailed off.

"I'll find out in a few minutes. Heading down there."

"Alright. Let me know what you find."

An hour later, the captain walked into Combat, settling into his reserved seat and placing a mug of coffee into one of the chair's built-in holders. He looked at Brian and Lieutenant Walker. "Jesus, Chief. When's the last time you slept?"

"Been awhile, sir."

"Well, after we talk, you get some rack time. Got it? I know you and Guillory got shit going on, but you two are on track for a pair of nervous breakdowns."

Brian's face contorted into a grimace, an expression that did not escape the captain's notice.

"Am I to assume that whatever you're gonna tell me precludes the idea that you'll get some sleep soon?"

"You could say that, sir."

"Well, let's have it."

"Sir, we've had both refrigeration units fail in the last three hours. Number one failed early this morning and number two failed while I was troubleshooting number one."

"By failed, you mean fixable soon or down for the count?"

"I'll know more when I start tearing them apart, but for now, they're both down for the count. Worst case."

The captain pointed out the obvious. "We're in the middle of the Med with no way to keep food cold and a hard date to get through the Suez."

"Yes, sir. Assuming I don't find anything crazy, we have the parts for a rebuild of both. It's gonna take around seventy-two hours to get one unit up and running."

"We're gonna lose a lot of food."

"Yes, sir."

"If the rebuild doesn't work or you find something crazy?"

"Then we'd need to pull in somewhere and have the units replaced."

The captain took his cover off and rubbed his head. "CHENG?"

"I think we try to fix them, but we send the report off ship."

Commander Allen raised an eyebrow. "Get the warning off early in case we need help?"

"Yes, sir."

"Chief, how confident are you?"

Brian blinked. "Can I fix it?"

"Yes."

"We have the parts to rebuild just about every individual component on the units. I can't repair a damaged casing, but I suspect that I'm just going to be replacing and repairing lots of little things. A valve here, sensing line there. Switches. Solenoids." He shrugged. "I've got this."

The captain got up. "Chief, get moving. CHENG, I'll be in my stateroom. Get the report up for my signature as soon as possible."

"It'll be there in thirty minutes sir."

The captain nodded. "Thank you, gentlemen."

After the captain left the space, Lieutenant Walker looked at Brian. "You didn't mention the jury-rigging."

"Getting the unit up and running matters first. I'll handle the jury-rigging later."

9
KHAN

LIEUTENANT GENERAL SAEED KHAN was a large man, even by western standards. He stood a hair over six feet and tipped the scales at just over two-hundred and thirty pounds. The general—who'd just celebrated his sixty-first birthday—did not look his age. Even the face, swarthy and dark as it was, was surprisingly free of wrinkles. The lone hint of the career officer's true age were the wisps of grey hair beginning to creep up the man's temples and residing in his thick mustache.

Khan was a man who'd been there and done that. After receiving a degree in chemistry from Quaid-I-Azam University in Islamabad, he'd won an appointment to the Pakistani Military Academy. Since graduating first in his class at PMA, he'd been everywhere and had done a little bit of everything. During the Soviet-Afghan War he'd been a tank commander, driving M-48 tanks given to the Pakistani Army to help bolster the defenses of a nation staring at the Russians on one border and the Indian Army on the other. During the Persian Gulf War, he'd deployed to Saudi Arabia with several Pakistani brigades to help defend the areas around Tabuk. Despite his current position, he'd been involved in nearly every border dispute with India for the last two decades—a situation that had slowly, but steadily escalated in recent years.

Khan shook his head at that. Every year seemed to be filled with such incidents, mostly in the Kashmir region. The previous year, a stand-off between the two nations had resulted in several bloody engagements. Before that, a never-ending series of attacks and counter-attacks had killed hundreds. India usually claimed their strikes were against targets known to be terrorists, usually Jaish-e-Mohammed or some similar group.

Pakistan usually claimed the dead were innocent civilians—a claim that was debatable in the general's mind—before launching retaliatory strikes. On those occasions that the Indian claim proved accurate, a slew of extremist organizations within Pakistan usually added their own brand of retaliation to the mix, further confusing the situation.

And therein lay one of Khan's biggest problems. With recent incidents on the Kashmir front and the resulting counter-attacks and retribution exacted by both the Pakistani government and various extremist groups, his own position had become precarious. The Indian Prime Minister had, very publicly, drawn a line in the sand a week ago. He claimed that Pakistan's inability and unwillingness to deal with the terrorist element within their borders represented a clear danger to the people of India. The man had gone on to present evidence that several of the groups had threatened Indian forces with nuclear weapons. When several reporters had noted that no terrorist organization had access to nuclear weapons, the Indian PM had corrected them with a curt "not yet".

Khan had ample reason to concern himself with this problem. He was the Director General, Strategic Plans Division. Among his many duties, he was in physical possession of every nuclear warhead in Pakistan.

While each branch of the military technically had nuclear weapons at their disposal, Strategic Plans actually held the keys to the armory, as it were. As the head of Strategic Plans, he devoted most of his time to three issues. He was responsible for the planned use of such weapons. This was a minor concern, mostly because war planning had existed for decades and such plans required only the occasional tweak or adjustment. Research and development were another area of responsibility for the aging general, but again, these were minor issues largely because Pakistan was home to some of the world's finest scientific and engineering minds. If he was honest with himself, Khan had to admit to spending most of his waking hours, and more than a few sleepless nights, fretting about the security of his arsenal.

The security of Pakistan's nuclear weapons had long been the subject of debate on the world stage. While men like Khan denounced such criticism as nonsense and attempted to reassure the world that there was no such threat, everyone secretly harbored doubts. The general knew that the Pakistani government—and military, for that matter—was divided. On one hand were men who prioritized their work ahead of everything except family. On the other were those who viewed the performance of their jobs as secondary to their religious responsibilities. These men, a faction of religious zealots, were men who subjugated everything to Allah's will.

Khan stopped himself.

It was not Allah's will that guided such men. Not strictly. It was man's interpretation of Allah's will. Twisted versions of the Prophet's words. Interpretations made by men who thought exactly alike. A distorted echo chamber of voices all screaming for the same thing.

And that, Khan knew, was the world's biggest fear—that one or more of these devices would eventually fall into the possession of a religious fanatic with the will to use it.

In addition to the stresses and worries put on him by his position, Khan had another problem. He'd been at this game, soldiering and policy-making, for almost forty years. He felt he'd given everything to his country—and gotten nothing in return. He was an intelligent and gifted engineer. In another life, he often thought he would have pursued a career designing things. The idea that he could design one of the weapons under his control fascinated him although, as a young man, he had frequently entertained the possibility of designing shuttles to ferry astronauts into space.

But I didn't choose that path. I chose this one. And now I'm stuck. I got this position through trust. Because I haven't been bought. I've stayed honorable. Not corrupt. And where has that gotten me?

As his fellow career officers and the politicians they worked for spent the last four decades enriching themselves—frequently at the public's expense—Khan had never been provided the opportunity to participate. He'd always been left behind, usually under some sort of pretense that such opportunities were not acceptable for the man in charge of safekeeping the nation's nuclear weapons.

Khan understood the reasons he held his posting. He understood the criticisms his program faced with respect to security. He understood everything about his job. But he understood one thing no one else considered. Despite his youthful appearance and seemingly abundant energy, he was old, tired, and—with retirement looming—flat broke. For decades, he'd lived on his meagre government salary and now—when his body and family were both letting him know they'd been through enough—he had nothing to show for the work he'd dedicated his entire adult life to. And that wasn't the worst of it.

Khan knew that his government was weak and would eventually cave to pressure from the outside world. They would acknowledge the security concerns everyone had about Pakistan's arsenal. When that happened, he'd be the scapegoat. Whether that eventuality was the result of political pressure or the consequence of some sort of terrorist incident did not matter. Either way, it would probably cost him his head.

This was why he was sitting in a luxury suite in Edinburgh, Scotland. He'd received a phone call the previous day from an old friend who'd mentioned that a trip to Scotland, a friendly round of golf, and a discussion of items of mutual interest might be in order. Khan didn't have the slightest clue what his old friend wanted. He didn't play golf, but he knew the phrase 'items of mutual interest' meant that his friend had something of great import to discuss. That such discussions could potentially be very lucrative, and the knowledge that this particular friend was an extremely wealthy man factored heavily into his decision to fly to Europe.

He looked around the suite, wondering again what this might be about, knowing only that the man he was waiting for was a serious person who would not have gone to all of this trouble for something trivial. When there was a knock on the door, Khan stood and clicked off the television that he'd not really been watching. He glanced at the wall clock as he heard his guest being escorted through the anteroom.

Punctual as ever.

Nick DeGuerra came into the room like a bull in a china shop, shunning any sort of formal introductions normal among powerful men and grabbed the general in a bear hug. Khan returned the hug just as ferociously. Both had wide, genuine smiles plastered on their faces.

"Nicholas, my friend. It is great to see you."

"The pleasure is mine, Saeed. What's it been? Five years? Six?"

It had been seven years since they'd last met face-to-face. Khan smiled again and waved to the couch. "It's been too long, my friend.

Please, have a seat."

The two men sat. Nick was still smiling. "Been a long time since Saudi. How ya been?"

"Do you watch the news?"

Nick laughed. "Yeah. I do."

"They pretty much get it right. My government is divided. Extremists on both sides."

"Capitalists versus fundamentalists?"

"Secularists versus fundamentalists would be more accurate. Half of the government wants to appease the will of Allah before all things and the other half wants religion completely out of government service."

"Separation of church and state?"

"Something like that."

"Hey. We can't even get that one right. We've been trying for damn near two-hundred and fifty years. Hell. It still says 'In God We Trust' on our currency."

"But your religious fanatics do not blow themselves up in the middle of Washington D.C."

"Touché. But ours don't have to. They can wreck everything through lobbying. More civil. More damaging."

One of the Khan's assistants brought in a tray of bottled water and set it on the coffee table between the men. Khan thanked and dismissed the man, asking the rest of his staff to leave the suite.

"No bourbon, Saeed?"

"Not this time. Sorry."

Nick cracked the top off of a bottle of water and took a long pull. He looked around the room and raised an eyebrow.

Khan smiled. "As paranoid as ever. The room is not bugged. My staff swept it twice."

Nick smiled. "Saeed. I've been seeing some pretty disturbing stuff coming out of Pakistan."

"Such as?"

"The secularists are losing control of the government. It presents a unique threat to the region."

Just like that, Khan thought he knew why Nick was here. "You are speaking of my control over certain weapons."

"Yes."

"I can assure you that my weapons are quite secure."

"I see a lot of things that suggest otherwise."

Khan leaned forward. "Nicholas, I do not know if you are here on behalf of your government or not. I suspect not. I do not imagine you are a supporter of your new president and I do not imagine that Evans would send such a message through you. I can only assume that you are here in some professional manner, especially given the situation your company finds itself in."

"What situation is that?"

Khan said. "We both know how much you stand to lose if President Evans abandons the region. How much of your business is tied to the region? Eighty percent?"

Nick winced. "Closer to ninety."

"And TitanX will not survive without conflict in the region?"

"I wouldn't put it that way. An American presence in the region benefits my bottom line."

Khan smiled at that. In more ways than one. If my intel is correct. "An American presence in the region causes more conflict than it deters. Having Americans in our lands gives the more extreme elements of Islam a target, if you will."

"Our lands?"

"Nicholas, the only reason we met and served together in the first place is because the Saudis wanted to limit the number of westerners in the Holy Land. Why do you think I was at Tabuk?" He paused to take a drink. After clearing his throat, Khan continued. "Why don't you tell me why you're here?"

Nick looked at the floor between his legs and shook his head. "Saeed, I need contracts to make up for what I'll lose when we pack up and leave the Middle East. I know Pakistan won't hire us to guard bases, but I figured..."

"Nicholas, if you know we won't let an American private security firm guard our conventional installations, why would you think we'd bring you in on strategic ones?"

"Actually, I was thinking about a strict training contract. Bring my guys in, examine how your folks do business, provide training and advisory services."

It was Khan's turn to shake his head. "There is absolutely no way I can do that."

"Saeed, look at it this way. The world thinks you have a security problem with your nukes. Hell, half your government thinks you have a problem. I'll bet you have nightmares about the religious fanatics in your government seizing the arsenal and handing it over to one of the dozen or so groups that use your country as a hide out."

Khan blinked. Nick continued. "You know what my folks can do. You've been to the facility and you've personally worked with some of my top people. We can significantly increase the proficiency of your staff and we can use our resources to help you weed out anyone who might pose a threat and recruit and train new troops. Worst case scenario, in the event that your worst nightmare comes true, it might be enough to buy you some time until the cavalry arrives."

Khan frowned at the bottle of water in his hands. "Do you know how many troops I lost last month just because they could not pass the vetting process?" And that, the general didn't say, was far less scary than the alternative—that people with questionable loyalties had not been found out.

"No, but we can help you fix this. We can't change the minds of the folks in your government, but we can help you show the world that you take your security seriously and make anyone willing to try and steal those things seriously consider the consequences."

Khan closed his eyes for a minute, thinking. He'd pitched a very similar plan to his own staff just weeks before. Nearly all of them agreed that just improving the recruiting and training processes was a step in the right direction. The object—the general well knew—was deterrence.

Make yourself a hard target. Make the mugger leave you alone and go after easier prey.

Deterrence would work against the dozens of little fish Nick referred to. Whether it would work against the big game hunters out there who thought that possession of a nuclear device might help them establish themselves—that was another matter entirely. But Pakistan had no internal resources for training to that level. The closest neighbor with those skills was Israel and asking them for help was unthinkable. He opened his eyes. "Are there legal restrictions to your offer?"

"Mainly conflict of interest, but I'm gonna lose most of my US government clients anyway."

"How soon could you get me a proposal?"

"Forty-eight hours work?"

"Get it to me and I will take it before the committee."

"What will they say?"

"They'll say yes." Khan confirmed, thinking that this might just save his own skin.

"Really?"

"As you mentioned. The secularists know we have a security problem and the fundamentalists won't want foreign governments poking around. They'll agree as long as we keep your involvement small and covert."

Nick smiled and extended his hand. "Thanks, Saeed. I needed this."

"Just make sure you send the very best. I cannot have this blow up in my face."

"Done."

Khan watched Nick. Now that business was concluded, he'd expected the American to leave. But Nick made no such move. He just sat there, wringing his hands. "Nicholas? Is there something else?"

DeGuerra looked around. "You sure nobody is listening?"

Khan smiled. "This room is clean. I told you this. My adjutant, Colonel Raza, swept it twice this morning."

Khan watched as his guest seemed to struggle with himself. Finally, the American looked up. "Saeed, you looking to retire soon?"

The question took Khan by surprise. Almost. "Nicholas, I am one of those people who will work until it kills me." The irony of the statement made Khan smile inwardly.

"Because you want to?" Asked Nick.

"Because I have to." Khan answered, watching to see if DeGuerra interpreted his comment correctly. He did.

"That bad?"

Khan nodded. "Being an honest man does not pay well in this world. I have dedicated my entire life to ensuring the security of my country. I am not wealthy and all I have managed to do is make myself... how do you say it...a target of opportunity?"

A moment of silence ensued.

Nick cleared his throat. "Meaning what, Saeed?"

"Meaning I have few options. I can retire now and be blamed for any problems my successor finds. I can wait for the government to acknowledge that the world's concerns about Pakistani nuclear security are probably valid. Or I can wait for someone to steal a nuke." Khan attempted a gallant shrug. "All of those scenarios will have the same detrimental impact to my health."

Nick took a breath and exhaled. "How much would you need to retire?"

Khan cocked his head. "Are you offering me a job?"

"That wouldn't be a retirement now, would it?" DeGuerra smiled.

Khan deflated a bit. "I suppose not. I don't suppose you are generous enough to fund my retirement just because we're friends?"

"Not exactly what I'm asking."

"Then what are you asking, Nicholas?"

"Saeed, your job is to protect Pakistan's nukes, right?"

Khan thought he saw where this was going. "That's right. Why?"

"Do you suppose I could come up with twenty million reasons for you not to do your job?"

Khan blinked and his mind raced. He said nothing. His mind worked on the problem. He evaluated his own position between two factions of government, both of which, ironically, did not believe that he was doing everything he could to safeguard the most valuable strategic assets Pakistan owned. He tried to look at all the angles and process every outcome. He played out the mental chess match as fast as he could. What should have been an easy no for a man who'd never failed to take his duties seriously became a fight between his soul and forty-odd years of suppressed desires. As the thoughts crackled across his mind, Khan slowly realized what his wife and children had been telling him. In his blind adherence to duty, he'd never appreciated how he was being used by his own government. He'd been lectured frequently on his own worth by his wife, but he'd never taken her seriously—always responded with the same lecture on ethics and loyalty.

And where has that gotten me? Nowhere. I've sacrificed my entire life for the security of a nation that is—what? Ungrateful? No, not quite that. Unaware? That was closer. And the people in charge? What am I to them? Expendable?

Khan knew he'd never be rewarded for being successful. But failure, he realized, would mean his death and the death of those who were close to him.

His wife and children had been right all along. Now, sitting here, confronted with Nicholas' proposition, he began to see how his own superiors saw him. He was a dog. A mongrel. A well-trained one that never asked for more than was given to him, but a dog nonetheless. And he was going to be thrown out in the street like a dog. Whether or not he was executed first was the only remaining question.

Khan began to feel something he'd repressed for decades and it surprised him. He felt the twinges of anger well up inside him. He remained silent for nearly three minutes before speaking. "What is it, exactly, you have in mind?"

10

THOMPSON

THE REFRIGERATION MACHINERY room was trashed. The tiny space—a ten by ten room stuffed with all of the gear, gages, and piping necessary to keep the ship's food stores cold or frozen—was awash in an inch of seawater that sloshed back and forth as the ship rocked. Bits of plant life that Brian had cleaned out of the strainers and condensers floated on the surface as the water splashed towards an overwhelmed deck drain in the corner. A collection of tools—wrenches, screwdrivers, and multi-meters—covered every flat surface in the room. One corner of the room was cluttered with a pile of broken components and the soggy, discarded boxes of replacement parts. A single trash bag had been affixed to a door handle and was filled with more than sixty-five hours-worth of soda cans, noodle cups, and candy wrappers. The room stunk. A fetid mixture of oil, sweat, and the scent of decomposing biological life overwhelmed the ability of the space's tiny exhaust fan.

Brian stood in the middle of the space, facing one unit, his back to the other. His filthy coveralls, soaked through with a briny mix of sweat and sea water, hung limp on his frame. Dirty rags and a pair of combination wrenches protruded out of one rear pocket, the other held a green notebook and an unopened soda. His face was drawn and sallow, the eyes rimmed in red from stress and a lack of sleep.

He hadn't slept since the units had died and his body was rebelling. When he wasn't fighting to keep his eyes open, he was busy trying to ward off the double vision that occurred when his eyes were trying to focus on tiny details. Except for six-hour stints as the EOOW, he hadn't left this room except for the occasional trips to the head and vending machines. He'd practically lived down here like some sort of Tolkien-esque creature, struggling against the desire to look after his own well-being and the need to meet a looming deadline.

The ship had transited most of the Mediterranean while Brian had been squirreled away turning wrenches and repairing wiring. It was stressful. If at least one of the units was not repaired and operational in the next seven hours, the captain would be forced to delay the ship's trip through the Suez Canal and divert somewhere to obtain assistance. That detour would also involve sending a message to the USS Laboon to let that crew know that their return trip to Norfolk from the Horn of Africa would, after seven months on station, be delayed by a few more weeks.

Brian ran through the system line-up for the fourth time, using a grease pencil to mark off each step as he checked, re-checked, and triple-checked the position of each valve and switch on the USS James E. Williams' number one reefer. Satisfied that he'd not missed anything, he called Central Control.

"CCS. EOOW."

"Tim. It's Brian. Permission to start number one reefer?" He read off the applicable procedure's acronym.

"Wait one." A brief silence before Tim came back on the line. "Granted. Start number one reefer."

"Start number one, aye. I'll call you back in a few." He hung up after being wished good luck.

Brian turned back to the unit. Over a period of almost three days, he'd almost completely rebuilt both units, checking, testing, and repairing or replacing nearly every component. During the course of the repairs, he'd found no less than fifteen parts on each machine that had, in some way, been "fixed" with a variety of back-alley mechanic repairs that one might see at a disreputable auto dealer. Brian wiped sweat from his brow with a filthy sleeve and told himself to focus.

He reached up and pressed the start button. As the needles on various pressure and temperature gages began to move, he held his breath.

★ ★ ★ ★ ★

An hour later Brian rapped on the door to the captain's stateroom. A gruff voice commanded him to enter. He turned the knob and pushed open the door.

Commander Allen had his back to the door, busy scribbling notes on a report that Brian couldn't make out and didn't have much interest in anyway. When the captain finished, he turned and stood, motioning for Brian to have a seat. "Well? How are my reefers?"

"Number one is online. It's been running for about an hour."

"Out-fucking-standing. And number two?"

"I'll test number two after my next watch. That one took a little longer to repair. Found a few vacuum leaks during testing that needed to be fixed. Number one will hold the load and Senior Chief Loeffler's folks are checking to see if we lost any food."

The captain turned his head, looking at the clock and digital map displays mounted above his desk. "Jesus that was close. Will the repairs hold?"

It wasn't meant to be an offensive question and Brian didn't take it that way. It was just something the captain had to ask.

"Yes, sir. There's a pressure switch that'll need to be replaced soon. We didn't have a new one onboard. Other than that," Brian shrugged.

"Great job, Chief. But now we've got something else to discuss." The captain stood and shut the door. "I've heard some rumors about why you've been down in the reefer decks for three days. I imagine you can guess what they are."

Brian nodded. You didn't lie to the captain, especially about something like this. "What have you heard, sir?"

Commander Allen stretched. "Oh. The word gundeck comes readily to mind."

"Captain, what I've found suggests that is the case..."

Commander Allen raised an eyebrow. "But you want to make sure before you throw MM1 to the wolves."

"Yes sir. I haven't looked at the maintenance records yet. I'll know tomorrow and we can figure out where to go from there."

"Chief, if he did it, he's toast. I know you know that, but I have to say it. I need to know that you understand what parts of your job aren't getting done while you're off fixing someone else's fuck ups. You have the largest department onboard. One third of the crew works for you and you're the one turning wrenches. Not supposed to be that way." Brian started to protest, but the captain held up a hand. "I know. Some jobs have specific training requirements and whatnot. I get it. But you and Guillory can't do it all. It's not possible. You know that as well as I do."

"Yes, sir."

"Listen, Chief. I appreciate the hard work. Saves our ass. But you can't do it all. This was an emergency and I get that. But let other folks get their hands dirty. As long as it doesn't pull us off mission, let folks fall on their face. It's good for them. Understood?"

Brian nodded.

"Good." Commander Allen stood and opened the door, latching it in place to protect against the ship's slow rolls to port and starboard. "Get some rest, Chief. And thanks again."

★ ★ ★ ★ ★

A few hours later, Brian looked up from a set of maintenance reports. He rubbed his knuckles into his eyes, causing flashes of light to bounce around behind the closed lids. It was a pet peeve of his wife's, something she always warned him was bad for him. He chuckled aloud as he recalled his usual retort. He reopened his eyes to see people staring.

"What?"

"You're giggling to yourself, Chief." Said the operator on the PACC, Propulsion and Auxiliary Control Console, a twenty-two-year-old gas turbine electrician named Kate Becker.

"Thought about something my wife said."

"What's that?"

"Rubbing my eyes is bad for me."

"Hell, Chief. What part of this job isn't bad for you?"

"That's what I say."

Becker turned back to the console, scanning the pressures and temperatures displayed there, keying in codes to shift the screen through each page of equipment readouts. When she finished, she turned back to Brian.

"You've been looking at that stuff for three hours. What are you looking for?"

"Just reviewing maintenance records."

"Or seeing if MM1 gun decked the reefers?"

Brian looked up. Becker laughed. "He's a piece of shit, Chief. He brags about his 'redneck fixes' to everyone." She actually used her fingers to form quotation marks during the assertion. "Christ, Chief. Once, me and Cortez were down trying to get the oily water separator to work and saw him trying to patch a seawater leak on the strainers with duct tape."

Brian blinked. "And?"

"He got smacked on the wrist for it. That's all. He was the old A-Gang chief's boy so he never got in trouble. Always talking about hunting and fishing. Hell, Chief. He was never on the watch bill until you got here."

"Seriously?"

"Seriously, Chief. If you ask him if he fucked up the reefers, he'll probably admit it. He'll say they were temporary fixes until he could order parts, but he'll admit it."

"No one's that dumb."

The Electric Plant Operator, Electrician's Mate First Class Vernon Soto, laughed out loud. "You don't know Donaldson that well, do you, Chief? It ain't that he's that dumb. It's that he thinks he's that smart. That dude probably thinks all of those things you found were clever little repairs."

Brian began rubbing his eyes again, thinking. He had a splitting headache that was equal parts lack of sleep and stress. "Okay you two. Thanks for the advice. Keep this to yourselves. I have to get CHENG down here."

"Fair enough." Becker said. "Hey, Chief?"

"Yeah?"

"Your wife have that baby yet?"

Brian gestured to the computer screen on the console. "Haven't heard anything. Had a false alarm a few days ago. She emailed me about an hour ago and said everything was quiet on the home front."

"How much longer?"

Brian had to think about that. He knew the due date, but calculating time from the present meant knowing what day it was, something his brain wasn't able to lock onto at the moment. He looked at the logs, checking the date there. "Shit. Two more days. Something like that."

Petty Officer Becker shook her head. "I'll pass. My sister is pregnant and I can't say that it looks fun."

"Amen to that." Brian noted, placing the maintenance logs in a pile on the deck.

He reached up and pulled the phone off of its rack, dialing the number for Lieutenant Walker's stateroom.

"Is this how you want to handle this?" The USS James E. Williams' Command Master Chief asked.

"Yeah. I talked it over with CHENG. Short of Donaldson admitting that he jury-rigged all of this stuff, I can't prove it. But there is enough evidence that he blazed off maintenance without actually doing it. If he had actually followed the procedures on these five maintenance cards, all of which were procedures he signed for on a weekly basis, he would have found seventy-five percent of the shit I just fixed. Maybe more. I'm pretty tired and calculating all of this is beyond me right now." Brian said.

"And how long does this go back?" Carrillo was flipping through the print outs Brian had handed him.

"At least a year. I only went back through the last four quarters."

Carrillo handed the stack of papers back to Brian. "Alright, get the paperwork done. Let MA1 Gramble know I want a DRB scheduled for tomorrow."

"Will do."

Carrillo shook his head again. "Jesus. Just what we need. Any problem getting rid of him?"

Brian shook his head. "None. Not with shit like this going on."

"You know what this means?"

"Yeah. I have to check everything he's touched."

"Well...you, Tim, CHENG, and AUXO."

"I can use the rest of A-Gang. They're young and inexperienced, but they know when something ain't right."

"Ain't?"

"Shut up. I'm tired."

"Y'all's a good word, too."

"Dickhead."

"That's Master Chief Dickhead to you."

Brian rolled his eyes and downed the last of his coffee.

"Alright, Master Chief Dickhead. I've got some paperwork to do."

11

NIXON

MIKE NIXON TUCKED A FACEMASK into his pocket and left the headquarters building of TitanX. He meandered through the compound to the barracks building and the hotel suite-like room that he was currently using as a residence.

The four-man team he'd put together had been approved by Nick DeGuerra earlier in the week and had spent the past few days taking care of all of the routine administrative work that preceded a contract deployment. They'd been briefed in on the contract to covertly evaluate and train an elite group of Pakistani security guards. Mike, and most of his team, didn't believe for a minute that anything related to Pakistani security really qualified as "elite"—a notion that had been reinforced by a lifetime of military and private-sector experience for each man.

What the Pakistanis they were to evaluate and train were responsible for guarding hadn't come up during any briefings, but it didn't take a genius to make logical guesses and everyone but Mike had constructed incorrect hypotheses. The closest the squad had come to a consensus was that they were to work with Pakistan's equivalent of the United States Secret Service.

They'd been through a thorough medical screening conducted by TitanX's resident physicians. Each man received an array of shots and prophylactic prescriptions to be taken immediately upon arrival in Islamabad and a brief detailing coronavirus protocol in their destination country.

This morning, the team had sat through one last briefing on the current state of training for their new client. After the presentation,

DeGuerra reiterated an instruction that had become routine over the past week. All reports for this assignment were to be addressed only to Nick. No one else. They'd been assured—again—that their presence in Pakistan was going to be a closely held secret, that they were to keep an extremely low profile during this trip.

Mike thought about that as he walked past the small commissary and turned to head towards the barracks. It made sense. He wasn't an expert on Pakistan by any measure, but he had a vague idea what would happen if word got out that Pakistan had hired an outside entity to improve the security of their nuclear weapons program. There were two sides to that particular sword. On one hand, it would demonstrate to the world that Pakistan was making a concerted effort to address the concerns nearly everyone had about their ability to maintain control of their nuclear arsenal. The flip side, which was just as razor-sharp, was that such information would be nothing short of a public admission that the rest of the world had been right—that the security of Pakistan's nuclear weapons was highly suspect.

He could see it now. If Pakistan got outed on this front, it would be akin to admitting on a global stage that their weapons were not secure and Mike was certain an array of terrorist groups would line up like shoppers on Black Friday to snatch one of the live nukes.

As he passed through the front door of the barracks, he waved his identification at the guard by the front desk and tried to calculate the size of the shitstorm that would hit the region if it became known that Americans, especially private security types, were helping to secure an 'unsecure' nuclear program.

Two hours later, Mike stepped back onto the sidewalk outside of the barracks building. There, curbside and loading bags into the back of a Chevy Suburban, was the largest member of his team. He headed that way.

The man looked up; a massive grin displayed through a heavy, black beard.

"Mike."

Mike smiled, stuck out his free hand. "How goes it, Dave?"

Dave Fogarty was, like Mike, a retired SEAL. He was a six-foot six-inch behemoth of a man who tipped the scales at more than two-hundred and seventy pounds. They'd served together in the Navy, but it had been two years since they'd crossed paths.

"Almost packed."

"Good." Mike paused. "How's the family?"

"They're good. Pop retired. How're your folks?"

Mike cringed. They'd not had much time to catch up during the week. "Dad passed away two years back."

Dave looked up. "Sorry, man. Didn't know. He was a good man"

"It's okay. Mom's still mom. Has her days."

"She still make that green bean casserole?" The two men had spent a week on leave at Mike's childhood home when both had been assigned to SEAL Team 4 in Virginia Beach. During the trip, Emma Nixon had baked a casserole from tuna fish, egg noodles, cream of mushroom soup, green beans, cheddar cheese, and water chestnuts. The concoction had been a disaster that both men felt obligated to eat after seeing how proud Mike's mom had been of her creation.

Mike shuddered at the memory. "Christ, no. Even mom eventually realized it was an abomination."

A head peeked around the rear of the suburban. "Someone say casserole?"

Brian grinned. "Good morning, Miguel."

Miguel Jimenez was a former Delta operator who'd grown up on Chicago's south side. He stood a hair over five and a half feet and barely broke one-fifty on the scales. He had the lean build of an endurance runner and, despite his slight frame, retained an ant's propensity for carrying a disproportionate amount of his own body weight.

"Morning, Mike. What's this I hear about casserole?"

Dave turned. "Miguel, you don't really wanna know."

"That bad?"

Dave gestured to Mike. "You wanna tell him?"

Mike shrugged. "Vomit in a dish, Miguel. We about ready?"

Miguel laughed and hefted another bag. "Got a few more bags. You know, this'd go faster if you squids quit holdin' hands and helped out." He stacked it in the SUV.

Dave turned, launching a bag towards Miguel that weighed at least eighty pounds. "You're just jealous. I've got Mike here and you're stuck bunking with a PJ."

A fourth man, tall and lanky with a shock of red hair on his head and a matching, scruffy beard exited the barracks. "That's CCT, dickhead." Andrew Cook had been a member of the United States Air Force for twelve years, a full decade of which had been spent as a Combat Controller, a single-man unit frequently attached to Navy, Marine, and Army special warfare teams to coordinate airborne firepower in support of a variety of missions. "And I seem to remember calling in airstrikes to save your big ass more than once."

"Yeah, yeah." Retorted Fogarty. "Wouldn't have happened if the intel was any good."

Mike nodded. "Hard to argue with that."

Miguel voiced his agreement as well. "Murphy's law doesn't have shit on military intelligence."

A chorus of "amens" were accompanied by laughter as Dave placed the last of the baggage in the truck. "Mount up, clowns. Let's get this show on the road."

★ ★ ★ ★ ★

The TitanX team climbed back into the SUV after stopping off for a lunch of fast-food burgers and fries. As Andrew directed the vehicle back onto the interstate, Miguel reached forward and tapped Mike on the shoulder.

"Mike?"

"Yeah?"

"We really getting paid six figures for training a bunch of guards?"

"That's about the size of it."

Miguel whistled. "That's some serious dough. What's the boss' share?"

Dave leaned forward to catch the answer. Each man had been promised two hundred thousand dollars for this contract. Mike turned. "In addition to our salaries, another four big ones according to Chuck."

Dave blinked. "Four mil?"

Mike nodded.

"What's so special about these people?" Miguel asked.

"What do you mean?"

"Mike, we get sent off to train folks all the time. Mostly our own people. Never been a secret before. What's the big deal? Pakistan's on our side, right? Why are these guys so special? Not that I'm complaining. Easy gig. Big ass paycheck."

Mike turned back to the front of the vehicle. It hadn't been covered in the briefings, but they'd find out in twenty hours anyway.

"It's not the guards who're special. It's what they do. Specifically, it's what they're guarding."

Dave turned. "What. They gonna let us train the presidential guard?" The smile froze on his face when Mike answered.

"It's the SPD."

Andrew spoke first, navigating his way through the light traffic on 87 South. "Fuck. You serious, boss?"

"SPD?" Miguel asked. "What's that?"

"Strategic Plans." Answered Andrew. "Pakistan's footballs."

Miguel's eyes went wide. "Nukes? We're training the security force for their nukes? Jesu Christo."

"Who else knows?" This came from Dave.

"Just us and DeGuerra." Answered Mike. "And Chuck, apparently."

Dave chewed on that for a second. "Secrecy makes sense. If it got out that Pakistan hired us to fix their security, that's basically admitting that their nukes aren't as safe as they would like everyone to believe."

"So why wasn't this part of the briefing with Mr. DeGuerra?" Asked Andrew.

Miguel handled that one. "Because those rooms back at headquarters aren't exactly soundproof. It's an office building, not one of our old team buildings at Bragg."

"So? It ain't like India is spying on TitanX." Andrew opined.

"No, but corporate espionage is a real concern. Especially for us. We're the largest firm in the biz and pulling some James Bond shit and planting a few bugs ain't all that hard." Miguel pointed out. "All you gotta do is find a pissed off janitor or admin weenie."

The four men sat in silence for a moment before Miguel spoke again. "Jesus. The boss is really sweating this shit. Isn't he?"

"He is." Mike thought before continuing. He'd told Nick that his lips were sealed regarding the state of the company. But that wasn't fair. They needed to know. "Gents. Do you understand what the US withdrawal means for the company?"

"I'm sure we lose a little business." Remarked Andrew.

"A little business is an understatement. More than ninety percent." Miguel barked. "What the fuck?"

Dave leaned forward over Miguel's seat. "Mike. TitanX takes in hundreds of millions in contracts. Are you saying they put all the eggs in one basket?"

"It would appear that way." Mike thought for a few seconds. "Listen guys. I'm not a business major. I don't make the calls on stuff like this and I'm definitely not invited to board meetings. I'm just a knuckle-dragger with a degree in history, but Nick was worried when he briefed me. I don't get the impression that the company can survive long without a serious shift in how they do business."

"Or who we do business with?" Asked Dave.

"Something like that." Mike replied. "I got the impression that this little training op is Nick testing the waters. He even said as much when he pitched me on the contract. If we're successful in something like this, maybe he can start expanding enough to keep the company from going under."

"Hate to be the one to break it to you, but that ain't gonna happen." Miguel said.

Mike turned. "Why's that?"

"Cuz he can't ever go public with this contract."

"He's right, Mike." Chipped in Andrew. "The world can't know that an American private security firm helped the Pakistanis get their nuclear shit together."

Mike nodded, turning back towards the front of the truck. "Good point."

"There's one cool thing about this." Miguel was leaning back in his seat again, snacking on the remainder of his fries.

"What's that?"

Miguel's face broke into a wide grin. "We get to use the company jet."

12

DEGUERRA

DEGUERRA WATCHED from his office window as the SUV disappeared down the access road and headed towards the highway. Once the vehicle was out of sight, he turned back to his desk, pressing a button on his telephone as he fell into his chair. Chuck Warner's voice came over the intercom.

"Sir?"

"Chuck, can you see if Secretary Tolchanov will take a quick call?"

"Yes, sir. Wait one."

Nick heard a nearly silent click as he was placed on a temporary hold. After about fifteen seconds, Chuck Warner came back on the line. "SECDEF on line two, sir."

"Thanks, Chuck." Nick picked up the handset and pressed the appropriate key on the phone, affecting a jovial tone as he spoke. "Secretary Tolchanov, thanks for taking my call."

"Christ, Nick. How many times I gotta tell you? The name is still Frank."

"Sorry, Frank. Force of habit."

"Those die hard, don't they? What can I do for you?"

"Well, I'd hoped to talk to you about business for a bit."

"Yeah, I figured you'd be callin' sooner or later. This policy shift is gonna do some damage, isn't it?"

"That depends on what we do. If there's no chance of maintaining these contracts, and no chance to acquire some new ones, we'd have to branch out to more foreign clients."

"Which'll hurt you if we ever need your services in the future.

Conflict of interest and all that?"

"Correct."

The line went silent for a few seconds before SECDEF spoke. "Shit, Nick. I'm sorry. We have some nickel and dime stuff out for proposals. That's the competing contract stuff you've probably already seen. All of the big money contracts are tied up for the next few years and those all have options attached that could extend them for quite a while. As far as the no-compete stuff goes, I've got nothing right now."

Nick sighed. "I figured. It was worth a call. Hell, Frank, I've already called half of Congress."

"Yeah, I know. A few of the appropriations folks have mentioned talking to you. They don't much like knowing that they're gonna lose a few thousand jobs heading into midterms."

"Frank, if I don't find something, we won't make it to the midterms."

"I know, Nick. I know. We even briefed the president on that, but with things relatively stable in the region and the massive support for the withdrawal, it'd be political suicide not to do this. For the first time in decades, a sitting president has overwhelming support for an issue from both sides of the aisle. Hell, I'm supposed to beat the war drums and find ways to spend on defense and I even think it's time to do this."

"I know. We'll come up with something."

"I sure as hell hope so." Frank commiserated. "Your folks have done a helluva job over the years. Nothing stateside can hold you over? Private sector stuff. Guarding Google or Facebook or something?"

"We're working on that. It won't be much. Just a band-aid on a wound that needs a tourniquet. Working to try and save as many jobs as possible. Got feelers out and folks sniffing around for us."

"Frank, I know this puts your firm in the hurt locker, but nothing short of a shooting war can derail this. Hell, the people over there have been asking us to get the hell out of their countries for almost a decade and demanding we leave for the last five years. You heard what the president of Iraq said a couple months back, right?"

Nick wrinkled his brow. He'd watched that one live on television. "You mean that Iraq can't be Iraq while law enforcement troops are wearing American uniforms?"

"Yeah. Hate to say it, but the man has a point."

Nick grimaced. "Yeah. He does. That shenanigans in Kashmir causing any problems with this?"

"Not really. A few minor dust-ups and lots of posturing and bluster."

"Even with India drawing that line in the sand?" Nick queried.

"That's only a problem if one side completely loses their shit. Know what I mean?"

"I do." Nick sighed. "Well, Frank, best of luck."

"Look, Nick. I'll keep an eye open. If I find anything that'll help, a non-compete proposal request or something, I'll give you a call. Best I can do."

"Thanks again, Frank. I appreciate it."

"You're welcome. Can't promise anything."

"I understand."

The call disconnected a moment later and Nick replaced the handset in the cradle. He'd spent every day since the inauguration trying desperately to save his company and, more important, his personal fortune. Nothing was working.

According to the stack of newspapers on his desk—he still preferred the hard copies to the digital versions—the new president was set to sign an executive order mandating the removal of American forces from the Middle East and Afghanistan. The order, which had garnered approval from nearly every major ally—the Saudis understood but weren't thrilled and Israel was privately hovering between disbelief and anger—was set to take immediate effect and was scheduled for completion before the 2022 State of the Union.

TitanX, and Nick's substantial personal wealth, were on death row with the execution date set. Nick had been unable to wrangle a stay from any of his high-profile contacts. What grated on the CEO was that he couldn't even get people to argue his case. In less than a year, he'd lose ninety percent of his business and personal assets and nearly everyone with the power to do anything about was already asking what funeral home to send the flowers to.

Nick picked up the report in front of him. Hundreds of millions would be lost in the next twelve months. Thousands of his employees would be without jobs. All of his plans for the future, along with the blood, sweat, and tears he'd put into building his empire would vanish.

In less than a year, TitanX would diminish—they'd no longer be the primary security firm for overseas government installations. No. This time next year the company's most lucrative contract would be the provision of physical security and training to some defense supply depot in Pennsylvania.

As he ran each scenario to its inevitable conclusion, he found impenetrable brick walls blocking his way. There were no real tactical victories to be had in this war. He only knew of one way to save his company, but to do it—to go ahead with the plan that had formed over the last few weeks—was what? Madness? Treason?

It couldn't be madness. He was a sane person, trying to protect his own interests and those of his people—well, the ones who worked for him at least. And treason? That was something clearly defined in the Constitution as the act of giving aid or comfort to the enemies of the United States. And he wouldn't be doing that? Would he? No. He'd be pushing the government back into the fight—forcing them to keep doing the job they'd started. The United States couldn't just leave the Middle East. And leaving Afghanistan was unthinkable. Aside from killing his company, the move would leave power vacuums. And who'd fill them. Al-Qaeda? ISIS? Someone worse?

Nick's mind chewed on the idea. If he went through with this, American troops would flood into the region and the power vacuum that the pundits feared would never exist. If it never existed, no one could step into it. What his plan really did was to ensure security, not disrupt it. If that was true, then this wasn't about TitanX's bottom line or earnings statement. It was about ensuring national security.

He looked at the numbers Bev listed in the appendices of the first report and counted the hundreds of millions of dollars listed there. He looked at the numbers listed by his personal accountant and calculated the losses there. He weighed the pros and cons of what he was considering and examined the risks for the hundredth time in a week. He told himself it wasn't about money. He told himself it wasn't pride and it wasn't anger at losing his company. Okay, his brain conceded, it wasn't completely about those things. Besides, hadn't he already embarked on this course? He'd just sent Mike Nixon and his guys off to Pakistan.

The first step had been taken. But was it a commitment to execute the rest of his idea? No, he told himself. It wasn't.

Mike and his team would go to Pakistan and train some folks. They'd come back. Nick and his team would continue to keep the firm from going under. The fight would be valiant, but doomed. And Nick would watch it all evaporate like wisps of smoke. His company. His people. His fortune. All of it would just slowly go away like some slow, drawn-out illness for which there was one inevitable end.

My money. My company. My legacy. Gone.

The CEO of TitanX made his decision and reached for the intercom button that would connect him with Chuck Warner. "Chuck, I've got a few calls to make. No disturbances for the next half hour."

"Yes, sir. And your ten-thirty appointment?"

"I should be done by then."

"Very good, sir."

Nick pressed the button again, disconnecting him from his assistant. He reached into the pocket of his suit coat and pulled out a cellular phone that he'd purchased two days earlier. He dialed a number from memory and waited as the phone trilled. It was answered on the third ring.

"Yes?"

Nick struggled to get his emotions under control. "You have authorization to begin stage one and stage one only."

"Yes, sir."

★ ★ ★ ★ ★

Will Patterson sat at his desk and looked at the phone in his hand. Over the last two weeks, he'd helped his boss develop a plan to save TitanX, but he'd not been sure that DeGuerra would pull the trigger on the op. He'd estimated a ten or fifteen-percent chance that he'd even be told to execute one portion of the plan. Now he had authorization to go through with the first step and—even though DeGuerra had withheld approval for the follow-on portions of their plan—it had sounded like the man was considering the probability that each stage would be necessary.

As he leaned back in his chair, Will's brain raced through the past few years, thinking about his time with the company and what his life had been like before he'd been employed here. Nick had given him a second shot at life. This company, his co-workers—they were all the family he had. He had to protect that. Didn't he? If he didn't, what did that make him?

★ ★ ★ ★ ★

Will was one of a handful of TitanX employees that DeGuerra used to fix corporate problems. That made him unique. What made him even more unique was the fact that the thirty-five-year-old Patterson was the only operator-qualified employee of TitanX who wasn't a military veteran.

As a young man, he'd been in and out of various juvenile detention centers throughout Texas—mostly for a few minor robberies and the occasional assault and battery charge. After growing out of the system—both juvenile hall and foster care—he'd graduated to the world of adult crime, spending most of his time helping to mule drugs across the US-Mexico border.

Muling was something he'd shown a knack for. A set of fundamental skills and rules, aided by a little luck, had vaulted Will from the ranks of the merely reliable to the realm of the trustworthy. By age twenty-five, he was pulling in just under ten-thousand dollars a month for maybe fifteen days-worth of actual work. For a kid with a tenth-grade education and no real job prospects, that kind of money was hard to pass up. Life for the young Texan was comfortable, something the young man expected to continue for the indefinite future.

Three days before his twenty-sixth birthday his luck had run out. He'd been arrested by Border Patrol with twenty kilos of uncut heroin after an unmanned aerial vehicle had picked him up walking through the wilds of south Texas. It was an accident. Murphy's law. A few agents had been testing a new camera system and had just happened to fly over the wrong place at the wrong time.

Will had been swept up and escorted to the nearest detention facility where a swarm of prosecutors and law enforcement officers had descended on him within hours. He'd endured hours of threats and pleas and good-cop, bad-cop routines without uttering a single word.

Unwilling to deal—primarily because his overactive imagination could picture the consequences his former employer might consider—he'd stood trial and been convicted. In short order, the prosecutor, judge, and jury had wrapped him up in trafficking charges and left him on the doorstep of his new home—Federal Correctional Institution Three Rivers, a medium-security prison south of San Antonio, Texas.

Prison hadn't proven all that difficult. As a mule, he'd learned to keep his head down and avoid standing out—a tactic that worked doubly well in prison. Muling had rules. So did prison. One simply needed to follow the rules to survive. He got up when he was told to get up. He ate when he was told to eat. He didn't pick fights and he didn't cause trouble. He barely spoke.

Will made parole his first time up, gaining his release after only three years behind bars. As a not-yet thirty-year-old with multiple felonies on his record, he should have been nervous about his prospects upon release. He should have been worried. He wasn't. He had a plan.

Model inmates enjoyed a few privileges during incarceration and Will had taken advantage of each. After earning library access, he'd finished his high school diploma. He'd entertained vague ideas about trying for college, but the realization that every college application asked about his criminal record forced him to examine other options. Over the course of a few weeks, he'd come across the name of a company that seemed to pop up everywhere. Using his limited access to the internet he'd researched TitanX Security. After watching every training video on the corporate website, he'd decided it sounded like something he might want to try—if he was ever given a second chance outside of the Three Rivers prison complex.

He'd come out of his shell to ask some guards if they'd ever heard of TitanX and, as luck would have it, three had been former employees of the security firm who'd left in order to spend more time with their families. They confirmed the excellent pay and benefits and explained the training program. They'd also pointed out that TitanX probably wasn't interested in hiring a convicted felon. Despite the prison time, Will wasn't accustomed to hearing the word no. It rankled him that he might have ruined the next fifty years of his life before the age of thirty.

Ultimately, he decided that the worst-case scenario was rotting in jail for the better part of two decades. Only slightly less awful was the prospect of making parole and being told that his new dream job didn't have a place for an ex-felon—a situation which would involve either a return to his criminal ways or spending the remainder of his natural life waving flags for highway construction crews. With that thought in the back of his head, Will Patterson set out to make himself as hirable as possible, preparing for the possibility of release from prison.

Already possessing an abnormally high tolerance for pain, Will joined the iron pumpers in the prison yard, packing on almost thirty pounds of muscle in the last six months of his incarceration. He started running, usually laps around the yard, but occasionally on the two treadmills designated for inmate use. His body adapted quickly to long distance running and, within months he found he was able to maintain a six-minute pace for miles. At one point, less than a month before his release, he'd actually challenged one guard to a race on the treadmills. One hour. Whoever ran the furthest. The guard, a frequent competitor in state and regional marathons, had accepted after gaining permission from his supervisors, only to lose the challenge when Will cleared nearly eleven miles in sixty minutes.

By the time he'd left the prison, Will had transformed himself physically and mentally. Gone was the immature, poorly-educated drug mule who'd been perp-walked in the front door. He'd set himself up to at least try TitanX. What the hell, he figured. Worst they could do was turn him down. In that case, he was certain that the local Department of Transportation office would be happy to hand him a radio and one of those hand-held stop signs.

Less than a week after his release from FCI Three Rivers, Will Patterson—dressed in an off-the-rack suit and carrying a small duffel bag with the remainder of his clothes and belongings—presented himself to the guard on the access road leading to the TitanX compound. After a few phone calls, he'd been escorted onto the property and into a waiting room where he'd been introduced to the two men who'd decide his fate. The older of the two had handled the introductions.

"Hi. I'm Paul Burkhart and this is Mike. Understand you're here about a job."

Will shook the offered hands. "Yes, sir. I read about you guys on the internet and wanted to give it a shot."

Burkhart sat down. "You know, our application process is online. You didn't have to come here."

Will nodded. "Yes, sir. I just haven't applied for a position in a while and wanted to meet you people in person."

Paul smiled. "Fair enough. Tell us about yourself. Military background?"

"No, sir. Never been in the military. They weren't exactly interested in me." Will saw Paul's eyebrows raise and noted that Mike didn't move a muscle.

Paul stated the obvious. "I can only think of a few reasons the Army would turn someone down and none are good. What's up?"

Will didn't even have to clear his throat. He just leveled his gaze at Paul and explained. "I got in bed with some pretty bad people and got busted muling heroin across the border. Did three years in a federal pen down in Texas. Made parole last month and came here."

Paul looked down at the table. The tone of his voice indicated how he felt about the situation. "Okay. Lemme get this straight. You're a convicted felon, sent up the river for drug trafficking. You made parole and you came here."

"Yes, sir." Will replied. As much as he tried to control it, he was nervous. His pulse raced.

"Why? You have to know who we are and what we do. You have to know we can't hire you. So why make the trip? Why bother?"

"Sir, to this point, I've done nothing useful with my life. Those drugs I carried across the border likely damaged some folks. Sure as hell they caused trouble. I got some makin' up to do in this life and I figured this was a place to start. I can't join the military, but if I can do what you folks do, free up the military guys to go make the world a better place..." Will shrugged. "Hell, sir. That's enough for me."

Paul shared a sideways glance with Mike. It was the first time Mike had moved since the introductions. Paul went on.

"Listen, Mr. Patterson. You have no formal training and you're a convicted felon. Even if you made it through training, how can we use you? Damn near every contract we have requires a background check and that doesn't take into account that, as a felon, you can't carry a firearm. What are we supposed to do with that?"

Will swallowed. What he would say next would probably be his last chance here. "Mr. Burkhart, you said nearly all contracts require background checks. Not all. I am willing to do whatever it takes. I will scrub toilets here to earn a chance to do what you guys do. I don't care what it takes. The lawyer who handled my release mentioned that I can petition to seal or expunge my records in a few years, depending on my behavior. I want to be able to make that happen."

A knock on the door interrupted whatever response Burkhart had ready and all three men turned to see DeGuerra enter the room. Introductions were made and Will repeated his story at DeGuerra's request. Paul explained again that there was simply no way to employ a man convicted of trafficking narcotics before Nick interrupted the discussion and motioned for both Paul and Mike to follow him into the hall.

"Mr. Patterson," Nick said. "If you will excuse us for a few moments."

Will had stood as his interviewers walked out of the room, his heart racing. He'd been supremely confident walking up the access road to the guard shack. Now, he was close to panic. He knew that the three men were just outside the door, discussing his fate. He was certain that he would be sent packing.

The door opened. Only Paul and Mike re-entered the room and resumed their seats. Will continued standing, unwilling to risk collapsing into the chair. Paul broke the silence.

"Mr. Patterson, Mr. DeGuerra reminded me that, among our thousands of employees, we do have one individual who has been in your situation before. He also reminded me that that person has given us years of hard work and faithful service."

Will took a breath, the iron grip on his lungs loosened a little bit as Paul continued.

"Mr. Patterson, here is what I propose. We are willing to hire you as a temporary employee doing exactly what you offered. You'll be part of the janitorial staff."

Will could hardly believe it. It wasn't what he'd wanted, but it was a foot in the door. He reached a hand out, to say thank you. Paul held a hand up.

"Hold on. I said you'd be a part of the janitorial staff and you will be. At night. Part-time. You came in here and pitched going through our training program. That will be your day job. Mr. Nixon here will be your training officer and I will be keeping a close eye on you. Our trainees normally get one do-over here. You don't get that. Fail to do your evening job to our standards and you're out. Fail to meet the training standards and you're gone. Is that clear?"

Will's knees almost gave out. "Hell yes. Crystal clear, sir." His voice wavered and he was trembling.

Mike spoke for the first time. "Why don't you sit down, Mr. Patterson." Will sat as Mike went on. "Listen. This ain't gonna be easy. If you don't have it in you to follow the rules and work your ass off, I'm gonna find out quick."

"Yes, sir. I understand." Will replied.

"I hope so. You'll be in a class with fifteen others, people who've done their time in the service and put in the hard work to get here. You're gonna have to outwork each and every one of them every single day or I will kick you to the curb."

"I understand. I won't disappoint you."

"I hope not. I want you back here at eight in the morning. We have some paperwork to do and the doc is gonna have to see you."

"No problem, sir. I'll be here."

"Good. The guard said you walked up the road. You need a ride back to wherever you're staying?"

Will looked uncomfortable. "Uh. No, sir. I'll be fine."

Paul glanced at Mike and spoke. "Where are you staying, son?"

Will looked at the floor briefly. "Well, sir. I hadn't quite worked that out yet."

Paul turned. "Take care of it, Mike?"

"Got it. I'll get him a room in the barracks for now."

A knock on the door brought Will back to the present.

"Enter."

The door opened and one of the TitanX staff came in. Will gestured to a cheap folding chair on the other side of the cluttered desk. The new arrival, who was technically the manager of this particular camp, fell unceremoniously into the chair. Will greeted him with a smile.

"Alex."

"Mr. Patterson." A nod. "Should I ask what you'll be telling the home office about my lovely facility?"

Will smiled again. This facility was Camp Mercury, a detention facility where the American military could drop off individuals with suspected ties to ISIS, Al-Qaeda, or any of the other insurgent groups running around Iraq for safe-keeping. Located in Umm Qasr, just a few miles from the Kuwaiti border, the facility housed over four hundred detainees.

"You have nothing to worry about on that score. A few training issues to deal with, but I suspect that's probably a paperwork drill rather than an actual procedural problem with your staff. Everybody I interviewed and observed seems to know their job forwards and backwards."

It was Alex's turn to smile. He worked his staff hard and took pride in their performance. "That's nice to hear. Back to New York or off to audit another poor soul?"

"Funny you mention that. I was supposed to audit our facilities near Bagram next, but there's been a change in plans."

"Missing out on the joys of Afghanistan? How will you ever cope?"

Will laughed. "I suppose I'll get over it."

Alex stood to leave. "Well. I need to get back to work. Just stopping by to hear the voice of judgement and see if you need anything else."

"Actually. Part of the new orders do require your assistance."

"How can I help?"

Will reached across the flimsy desk and handed Alex a small index card with eight names and numbers written on it. He had prepared the card the previous week at his CEO's direction, not knowing whether it would be used. Alex examined the names for a few moments before looking up. "What gives?"

"Corporate got a call asking us to transport these individuals to Camp X-Ray."

"Gitmo? What for? Not that I mind. Most of these guys are

nobodies, likely picked up after a neighbor decided to get even for some dumb shit and finger them to the local Army outpost."

"No clue. Maybe they're not nobodies. Someone with some pull wants them in Cuba right quick."

Alex handed the card back. "Fair enough. Need escorts?"

Will nodded. "Yeah. Small detachment. Just make sure to bag 'em and restrain 'em."

"Clean 'em up first? Change of clothes?"

"Probably a good idea. Thanks, Alex."

13

THOMPSON

"REPAIR FIVE, CENTRAL. Send one attack team to the secondary boundary."

The damage control phone talker acknowledged the order and relayed the instructions to the ship's Auxiliaries Officer, Ensign Tom Szepanski. As the Locker Officer for Repair Five, all casualties and damage in the ship's engineering and propulsion plant were his responsibility. There was pride to be had in successfully managing this locker, but right now was not the time. He had a team on scene with less than twenty minutes of air left in their SCBAs, the self-contained breathing apparatus that all naval firefighters wore. He turned.

"Messenger, Tell the locker leader to send the next team."

"Aye, aye sir." The young sailor, almost unrecognizable in a flash hood and battle dress, left the locker and walked around the corner towards the mess decks, which served as the staging area for the repair locker's personnel. After entering the space, he quickly found the Locker Leader and relayed the message.

The chief listened and nodded. "Thanks. Let the Locker Officer know they're on the way." As the young sailor retraced his path back to the locker, the Locker Leader turned and bellowed. "Gearhart!"

A sailor across the space, in full fire-fighting turnout gear and surrounded by a full team of identically dressed sailors, looked up.

"Get your team to the secondary boundary, starboard side access. Check in with the scene lead."

"Aye, aye Chief." Electrician's Mate Third Class Ricky Gearhart turned to his team. "Team two. Follow me."

The team, under Gearhart's direction, snaked their way across the mess decks and out the aft door. They moved through the ship's starboard side passageway, careful to avoid catching any part of their gear on the panels and valves that lined the walls. The team kept walking forward, past the ship's medical office and the repair locker where Ensign Szepanski and another junior sailor, a plotter, were updating the charts used to track all the damage control efforts on the ship.

As the team approached the forward bulkhead, Gearhart checked in with the Scene Leader. The sailor directed Gearhart's team to go 'on air' and each member of the team reached down to their left hip and detached a small black regulator from the equipment belt that was part of the SCBA rig. The regulators were placed onto the front of each sailor's facemask and turned the ninety degrees required to lock the device in place and activate the airflow. Each mask fogged briefly and cleared before a series of thumbs-up told Gearhart his team was ready. He relayed this information to the Scene Leader and was directed to enter the auxiliary space and relieve the hose team.

Brian watched the new attack team approach his position. Each member of the team stepped over and around the firefighting gear strewn across the deck. In his brain, he made mental notes for everything they did, right or wrong. The spacing looked good and they were communicating well, despite the masks and noise. The fourth and sixth sailors in line had each been forced to steady themselves while stepping over an 'empty' fire extinguisher and each had grabbed onto a power cable leading to a 440-volt motor controller. He'd have to point that out during the debrief.

Under Brian's watchful eye, the newly arrived attack team relieved the original group of firefighters in the prescribed manner and began to 'fight the fire'—in this case a set of red and white flags that were being waved by yet another sailor standing in front of Brian. Within two minutes, the egressing team of firefighters were up the ladder and out of view. That they'd turned their backs on the simulated fire was a problem he'd have to remedy.

Thirty seconds, thought Brian.

It took only twenty-five for his radio headset to crackle to life. "Top, Boats. Attack team is out of the space and off air."

Brian reached for the transmit button clipped to the front of his uniform. "Top aye. Break. XO, Top."

Another crackling voice. "Go for XO."

"Sir, all training objectives have been met. Recommend secure from drill."

"Roger that, Chief. I'll let the captain know."

"Thanks, sir." Brian released the push-to-talk button and watched as the new team continued to battle a simulated fuel fire, nodding in approval.

After about sixty seconds, the loudspeakers in the space erupted with the announcement everyone was waiting for.

"This is the XO from CCS. Restore all casualties. Restow all gear. Set material condition modified zebra throughout the ship."

Brian reached out and placed his hand on the shoulder of the sailor in front of him. At his direction, the sailor stopped waving the flags, giving his arms a break for the first time in nearly an hour. He then approached Petty Officer Gearhart and signaled for the team to remove their regulators and exit the space, which they did gladly. Brian smiled at that. He remembered all too well what getting dressed out was like. Known as 'sucking-rubber' by shipboard firefighters, getting into turnout gear and fighting real or imagined fires was a stressful, dehydrating process that everyone knew had to be practiced constantly.

As Brian left the space and headed aft to Central Control, dodging around sailors putting gear away and coiling up hoses, he thought about the very idea of drilling. Much as every sailor purported to hate these drills, they were necessary.

Brian knew that very few ships had ever been sunk because of a single problem. What killed ships was an accumulation of issues, known as cascading casualties. A fire here, flooding there, with a pinch of electrical failure for seasoning. Eventually, if enough problems piled on top of each other, the ship's ability to recover was put in jeopardy. As he made the turn into CCS, he thought about that, wondering how many ships the US Navy had lost because the crew hadn't been fast enough, or good enough. Or maybe just spread too damn thin? That sounds familiar.

The XO was standing in CCS when Brian entered, the microphone for the ship's 1MC announcing system in his hand. He was watching the DCA, the ship's Damage Control Assistant, and waiting patiently. After a few moments, she turned.

"XO, material condition modified zebra is set throughout the ship. Recommend secure from general quarters."

The XO turned to Brian. "Debrief?"

"Have to be later, sir. The chiefs have a DRB on the schedule in twenty minutes." Brian turned to the DCA. "You good with that, ma'am?"

She nodded. "Eighteen hundred? Mess decks?"

The XO put the microphone to his lips. "This is the XO from CCS. Secure from general quarters. Now set the normal underway watch, section two. Damage Control Training Team debrief will be held at eighteen-hundred on the mess decks."

The XO placed the microphone back in its metal holder and shut the cover for the 1MC control panel. He turned back to Brian and the DCA.

"So. How'd we do?"

★ ★ ★ ★ ★

Fifteen minutes later, Brian strode up the port side passage towards the Chief's Mess. Ahead of him, back to the bulkhead, was Machinist's Mate First Class Caleb Donaldson. As Brian approached and turned to enter the Mess, Donaldson spoke.

"This is bullshit."

Brian turned and looked at him. His eyes traced over the uniform briefly, finding all sorts of issues—loose threads here and there, wrinkles, dirt, paint and oil stains, an unbuttoned breast pocket, and a wad of God-only-knew-what stuffed into the left-side cargo pocket on the pants. Brian turned and entered the mess.

Inside, he found most of the board members already in place and the CMC going through the review board's legal paperwork with the ship's Master-at-Arms, Petty Officer Gramble. Carrillo looked up as Brian walked in.

"Not a bad drill."

Brian nodded, reaching over two seated members of the board to retrieve his coffee cup from the pegboard. "They're getting better. A few things to fix. Some safety violations and procedural issues. That last attack team was cutting it close. The team in-space only had a few minutes of air left when they got relieved. Gearhart is pretty good, but he's probably gonna end up in Shaft Alley if the captain kicks Donaldson off the ship."

Carrillo looked surprised by that. "Why?"

Brian examined his cup. "Gearhart knows the AC plant, the sewage system, and the electronics for fuel transfer valves. He's really good and that space has all of it."

Carrillo nodded. Kyle Corcoran entered the mess and selected a spot on the couch. "Hey, Brian."

"Yeah?"

"How come we always use the main and aux spaces for this drill?"

Roberts reached over and punched the sonar chief in the arm. "Because it's a main space fire drill, dumbass."

Carrillo looked up from the documents he was reviewing, an eyebrow raised at Corcoran. "Kyle?"

"Seriously. We never practice any of this shit in shaft alley or three gen. Which brings up another thing. How in the hell do we even get a fire team into shaft alley?"

"Safest way is the port side access by berthing five. Beats trying to climb down vertically into the middle of the space." Brian noted.

"What if the fire is on that side of the space?" Corcoran pressed.

Brian shrugged. "Man's got a point. There's no easy way to access that space and egress is even worse."

Roberts punched the sonar chief again. "He's still a dumbass."

Doug Franklin walked in. "Y'all see the news? There were a couple more bombings in Kashmir and a few firefights last night. India just released a statement claiming that they've gotten more bomb threats about nukes."

That caused heads to turn. Franklin continued. "Apparently India is pissed. They're saying they'll respond in kind from now on. Like that mutually assured destruction shit between us and the Soviets."

Brian shook his head and took a few steps towards the coffee machine and filled his mug. Information Systems Technician Chief Petty Officer Charlotte Ibanez sidled up next to him with a concerned look on her face.

"Fuck, Brian. I wouldn't drink that."

"Why's that?"

"That brew has been cooking down since before breakfast."

Brian looked down at his mug. "I'll take my chances."

Charlotte laughed. "Should I notify Doc now or wait a few?"

"If I keel over, give it a few before you call doc. I need the sleep." Brian grinned and headed over to the couch. Since this was his sailor, he wasn't permitted to be on the board. He found an opening in the demilitarized zone between Kyle and Jason and squeezed in.

"Brian, see your boy outside?" The question came from Franklin.

Brian nodded over the top of the mug. "You mean the uniform?"

"Yeah. Cares about that as much as he cares about maintenance."

"Shit." Brian paused. "Hey, Master Chief."

Carrillo looked up from the paperwork, peering over his glasses at Brian. "Yeah?"

"On the way in here, MM1 expressed his opinion of this situation."

"Which is?"

"That this is all bullshit."

Carrillo rubbed his temples. "This is gonna be delightful." He turned to MA1 Gramble. "You ready?"

"Yes, Master Chief."

Carrillo stood up. "Alright folks. Listen up. Everyone had a chance to read the statements and charges so let's go over the ground rules. Only MM1, MA1, myself, and the board members are allowed to speak while MM1 is in here. The rest of you will restrain yourselves until I open the floor for discussion. Is that understood?"

The group nodded as Carrillo resumed his seat. "MA1, bring him in."

Ten minutes later, after Donaldson had 'reported as ordered' and the administrative procedures had been observed, Carrillo finally opened up the questioning.

"So, MM1. Why are you here?"

"I don't fuckin know."

The CMC took a breath and put his pen down. He looked directly at MM1 Donaldson. "MM1, this is your only warning. You will maintain military discipline. Understood?"

"Aye aye, Master Chief."

"Now. Let's try this again. Why are you here?"

"I don't know. This is some kinda witch hunt."

"Are you saying you didn't do all of these things?" Carrillo gestured to the packet of materials in front of him, which included several photographs of the 'repairs' in question.

"No. I repaired the reefers so they worked. I didn't do anything wrong."

Senior Chief Loeffler, the ship's leading culinary specialist, leaned forward at the board table. "MM1. Are you saying that I would find your repairs listed in a technical manual?"

"No, Senior Chief. But I fixed those things so they worked and used what I had."

"Used what you had?" inquired the Senior Chief. "Explain that."

"I used the parts I had to keep the system running."

"And used parts to conduct repairs that are not part of any technical document, correct?"

"I doubt it, Senior Chief."

Ibanez, seated next to Senior Chief Loeffler, spoke up. "MM1, are the parts you used to conduct these repairs listed as approved parts in those technical manuals?"

MM1 wavered. "Well, no ma'am."

Ibanez nodded. "Okay. So, you're saying that you used parts that aren't approved to conduct repairs that aren't authorized by any technical authority on a piece of critical equipment. Is that accurate?"

"Ma'am," MM1 started.

Ibanez cut him off. "Chief."

"What?"

"I'm a Chief. Stop calling me ma'am."

"Yes, Chief."

"Now. Is what I said accurate?"

"Well, yes. Sort of." Donaldson said.

"Sort of?" Ibanez raised an eyebrow.

"Well, Chief. Not everything's in them books."

Ibanez leaned back, adopting a surprised look on her face. "Please, MM1. Do tell. What's missing?"

Donaldson mistook Ibanez's sarcasm for genuine interest. "Well, the stuff I did worked. That stuff shoulda been put in there." Donaldson smiled.

Ibanez smiled back and softened her voice, something that most of her fellow chiefs recognized as dangerous. Donaldson didn't know her well and he took the change in her demeanor and tone as a sign that he'd proven his point and won the argument.

"MM1. What is your opinion of the repairs made by Chief Thompson?"

"They're really good, Chief. Couldn't have done better myself."

"And do you know where he learned these repairs?"

Donaldson thought for a second. "Experience, probably."

Ibanez reached down to grab something off the deck. When her hands reappeared, they were holding a three-inch thick binder, the cover of which designated it as the technical manual for repairs of a shipboard refrigeration unit.

"Would it surprise you to learn that Chief Thompson followed the procedures in this book?"

"It would, Chief."

"Why's that, MM1?"

"Ain't nobody read that book, Chief."

"I'd be inclined to agree with you. It's a pretty large manual. Except for one thing." She flipped the binder open and made a show of looking through the pages as if she couldn't quite find what she was looking for. Donaldson leaned forward. After a few seconds of silence, she flipped one last page and feigned relief. "Here it is. Wasn't quite sure I'd read that right."

Donaldson was curious now. "Read what, Chief?"

"Oh. I was just thinking that there was probably another reason that Chief Thompson wouldn't have to read this manual to know what it says about fixing refrigerators."

Donaldson's eyebrows went up. "Why's that, Chief?"

She flipped the book around so it was facing him. "Oh, nothing much. It just seems that the person who helped write the manual would have a pretty good grasp on what's in it." Her finger pointed to the page and there—about halfway down a list of twenty sailors, in bold, black letters—was the name MMC(SW/AW) Brian Thompson. Donaldson's face dropped as Chief Ibanez continued.

"MM1, why do you think the author of this manual would leave your little repairs out of the final version?"

Donaldson didn't quite know what to do with that. "I don't know, Chief."

She flipped through more pages of the manual, finally settling on the troubleshooting and diagnosis section.

"Donaldson, can you tell me the difference between the words should and shall?"

"Yes, Chief. Should is a suggestion. Shall is mandatory."

"What does that mean?"

"It means I have to do something that says shall."

"And do you know what this book says about the broken pieces of equipment that you repaired?"

Donaldson was visibly nervous now. His voice shook. "No, Chief."

Ibanez began reading. The formatted language was the same in each case. If X has failed, the technician shall—and so on.

Donaldson listened, still unable to see where the line of reasoning was taking this interview.

"Chief, it doesn't say anywhere that I have to read that manual."

Ibanez smiled up at Donaldson, like a spider with a juicy fly caught in her web. "Funny you should mention that." She turned to her right. "3MC?"

Franklin cleared his throat and picked up the large stack of papers in front of him. He showed them to Donaldson as he spoke.

"MM1. What are these?"

Donaldson's voice shook as he answered. "Maintenance records, Chief."

"Your maintenance records?"

"Yes, Chief."

Chief Franklin flipped through the records. "Almost a full year of records. Do you know what they say?"

"That I did all of my assigned maintenance, Chief."

Franklin looked up. "Well, they say you claimed to have done all of your assigned maintenance. I took the liberty of looking up anything assigned to the reefer units. One-hundred-and-twenty-six checks in the last eleven months. All of which have your signature saying that the checks were completed and that no follow-on action was required." Franklin paused and pointed. "This is your signature? Correct?"

"Yes, Chief."

"So, you can imagine my shock when I find that eighty-two of these checks involve inspections or other maintenance actions which would have been impossible to complete without either noticing the broken components or fixing them?"

"But, Chief, it don't say to..."

Franklin cut him off. "Au contraire, shipmate. In each case, there is an instruction printed on the maintenance requirement card to follow the procedures outlined in the technical manual right there." He indicated the manual laying open on the table.

Donaldson went silent.

Carrillo asked a few questions, which Donaldson refused to answer. After asking Donaldson if he had anything to add and getting a curt "no", he directed MA1 to escort MM1 out of the space. As the door shut, the CMC looked over his glasses again at Brian. "Anything to add?"

"Nope."

Jason asked. "Can he be fixed?"

Brian shook his head. "Not here. I spent more than one hundred hours fixing that man's fuck-ups. That's one hundred hours where I wasn't seeing to the needs of the other one hundred and four sailors in my department. Send him home."

Carrillo scribbled down a few notes before looking up.

"Alright folks. Thanks for your time. Recommending we skip the XO on this one and go straight to the captain. Suez transit tomorrow, so mast will be delayed a couple days. Questions?"

Everyone shook their heads. Carrillo stood.

"Alright. Walk the ship, talk to your folks. Everyone rest up. Gonna be a long transit. Brian, come with me?"

"Sure thing." Brian heaved himself up off the couch and followed Carrillo out the door. Because it was chow time and the passage by the mess decks was one-way traffic, it took four minutes for the pair to walk the long way around the galley and enter Carrillo's office by the serving line. When they got the door shut, Carrillo sat and waved Brain to the tiny bench that served as a seat.

"Wouldn't be doing my job if I didn't ask. You understand what sending Donaldson home does, right?"

"Do I know that I'll be the only AC&R tech onboard? Yeah. I know that." Brian answered.

"But do you understand what that means? You're a department chief. You aren't supposed to be doing maintenance. Sure as shit ain't supposed to be turning wrenches."

"I know that. What exactly can I do? Can't have him doing that shit." Brian pointed out.

"Agree. It's an elegant trap. You can do it and shouldn't be. He can do it and shouldn't. You're in a tight spot and you have a lot on your plate. We haven't even transited the Suez yet and the captain wants to know how we'll make sure you don't burn out."

"Getting some new engineering chiefs would help."

"I know that. We keep bringing it up with DESRON and the commodore. Nothing yet. Hell, I've emailed the detailers myself. Problem is..."

Brian cut him off. "Problem is we got stuck in an admin loophole. We still carry most of those old chiefs on the books. Right?"

Carrillo nodded. "Yep. Except for the legit transfers and those billets got gapped by BUPERS because we were supposed to go into drydock. I don't know if that will change any time soon."

Brian raised his hands. "Look, Logan. I'm not asking you for miracles. Just keep the press on. And yeah, I know ditching MM1 will hurt over the next few weeks, but I also know I won't be spending the rest of deployment wondering what goofy shit he's done to a piece of gear or waiting anxiously for another nasty surprise."

"You sure?"

"Positive. Anything else?"

Carrillo smiled. "Yeah. One thing."

Brian was suspicious. "What?"

The master chief opened his notebook and shuffled through some papers. After a few seconds, he selected one and handed it to Brian. "This came in right before DRB. I think you may want to find an open phone line and call home."

Brian looked down at the sheet of paper. It was a message from the American Red Cross, sent by his oldest son. The message was simple and to the point.

April Thompson gave birth to surrogate baby and both are healthy recovering. Notification to service member. Service member's presence is not requested or required.

Brian looked up, an exhausted smile on his face. Carrillo smiled back.

"That's a hell of a thing. Carrying a baby for someone else." Carrillo held out a hand. "Congrats. Tell her we're all proud of her."

Brian shook the offered hand and stood. "Thanks. I gotta call home."

14

EVANS

DESPITE A REQUEST by the White House Press Secretary to hold all questions until the end of the announcement, the President knew that the Rose Garden would explode when he read the next line on the teleprompter. He could see the reporters scooting forward on their seats. They knew what was coming, mostly because it was obvious and because they'd been provided advance copies of the announcement, attached to an official press release, upon their arrival at today's briefing.

In just his second month in office, it amazed the new chief executive that the members of the press corps would "report as ordered" just like a group of well-disciplined sailors, even in the late-February freeze and frost of the former malarial swamp that was Washington DC. The President, with a shiver that had little to do with the icy winds, wondered briefly if the scrum to follow was anything like being on the trading floor of the New York Stock Exchange. He breathed in. He glanced around one last time, cataloguing the media outlets. New York Times. CNN. Fox. MSNBC. Washington Post. NPR. Even C-SPAN was here.

"I have just signed Executive Order 14002 directing the immediate withdrawal of all United States military forces from the Middle East and Afghanistan."

The press pool exploded. Voices shouting questions and yelling for clarification drowned out the clicking of cameras, the flashes of which Evans was surprised to see against the bright, crisp midday sun. The president, who raised both hands and was trying to wave the reporters back to their seats, couldn't hear anything beyond the repeated "Mr.

President!" He decided that the remainder of his prepared statement wasn't going to happen without answering a few questions first. The president selected a reporter from MSNBC.

"Ms. Gregory?"

"Mr. President, how does this order affect stability in the region? Couldn't the withdrawal of our forces create a power vacuum? What kind of message does this send?"

Evans smiled. The question was, relatively speaking, a softball. He took a swing. "As you know, most of the governments in the region have been asking us to leave for some time. The biggest message that we are sending by maintaining a large footprint in the region is that we do not trust the citizens of those countries to manage their own affairs. That message alone invites conflict."

A reporter from NBC raised her hand and yelled a question. "Mr. President. Is this a smart move, given the rising tension and recent incidents between India and Pakistan?"

Evans took a breath. "Ms. Anderson, we are monitoring that situation carefully and working with both sides to reduce tensions in the area. We don't believe that our military presence on the ground influences that dispute one way or the other."

The president pointed at another journalist from the Los Angeles Times, whose name he could not recall.

"Mr. President, you said 'most governments'. Are you referring to Israel? What is their opinion of this move? How does this affect the relationship between Israel and Palestine?"

"Israel has publicly come out in favor of our withdrawal, citing an uptick in extremist activity on both sides of that conflict during our presence."

The LA Times reporter scribbled and pressed.

"And what do the Palestinians think of this move? Could this be seen as an abandonment of our efforts to keep the peace and find a resolution to the question of Palestinian sovereignty?"

Evans smiled again. "Let me be clear. The removal of US forces in the region is not an abandonment of the region. We are not leaving everyone there to their own devices. This shift in policy is simply a removal of our troops from the area with the acknowledgement that the countries involved can, and should, be responsible for their own security. My predecessors have worked to make this happen. The countries involved have worked very hard to make this happen. It's time." The president placed his hands on the sides of the podium, an unconscious affectation he'd adopted over the last few years.

"For more than two decades, the United States has adopted policies in that part of the world that are more stick than carrot. We have been quick on the trigger and slow on dialogue. We are not washing our hands of the issues. We are shifting to policies that involve heavy doses of diplomacy and discussion. The commitment of American troops, the decision to place our young men and women in harm's way, should always be the last resort and should never be a long-term solution."

A reporter from Fox stood, arm raised, pencil in hand. The president gestured for him to ask the next question.

"Mr. President, it sounds like you're saying that we prematurely committed troops to Afghanistan and Iraq. After the 9/11 attacks, do you believe that an immediate and forceful military response was unjustified?"

Evans resisted glancing towards his Chief of Staff, knowing that Leslie Barnes was standing off to the side with an "I told you so" twinkle in his eye. "I believe that we have been too quick to default to military intervention in the past. I do understand that, in the aftermath of the tragic incidents on the morning of September 11th, the public cry for vengeance was loud and clear. I also understand that decisions made in anger rarely solve the issue at hand. That is why we are adopting this shift in how we do business in the region."

The Fox reporter smelled blood in the water and moved in.

"So, Mr. President. You're saying that FDR was wrong in declaring war on Japan less than twenty-four hours after the attack on Pearl Harbor because he was acting out of anger."

The president smiled. "No. The decision FDR made was necessary. In that instance, we were the victims of a bloody attack signaling a breakdown in diplomatic efforts after years of talks. I do not consider that to be an irrational decision made in anger. In the case of the 9/11 attacks, there was no diplomacy beforehand and the attacks were committed by individuals who were not representatives of a military or state organization. I believe a military intervention against the Taliban and Al-Qaeda was warranted, but not immediately and not with the information we had in hand on September 12th."

The president leaned forward; the smile gone. "Since 2001, more than sixty thousand men and women have been killed or wounded as a part of the War on Terror. The reasons for those troop deployments have been studied countless times. By Congress. By universities. By individuals." Evans pointed at the reporters. "Some of you have authored books on the subject. Two of you had those books top the best-sellers list. In nearly every study, regardless of agency, the same conclusions pop up. We were unprepared. We moved too fast into a situation we didn't know enough about. We will not make that mistake on my watch. We are bringing our troops home. We are not down-sizing. Those troops will rest up and train. When they're done training, they'll train some more."

The NPR reporter in the back shouted.

"Train for what, Mr. President?"

The smile returned. "Steve. We live in a real world with real problems. This executive order doesn't change that. There are individuals, agencies, and nations who would do us harm. While our primary focus will be on creating dialogue and the use of diplomacy, I don't want anyone to get the wrong idea about my willingness to use the military if I have exhausted all lesser means or cannot reasonably employ such measures. In the case at hand, we have to give these people a chance to govern themselves. Just as our founding fathers would not have welcomed the idea of British troops remaining on American soil after the revolution, neither will we subject other sovereign nations to govern under the supervision of American soldiers. We will continue to provide assistance, when requested, in other forms. It is in everyone's interests that these nations are self-sustaining and the United States stands by to assist in the development of infrastructure."

Twenty minutes later, Evans walked into the Oval Office. Barnes, clad in a rumpled navy suit, was waiting for him. The president looked at his Chief of Staff, grimaced, and pulled a twenty-dollar bill from his pocket. He handed the bill to his smiling advisor.

"Lucky bet, Leslie."

"Sucker's bet, Mr. President. No way in hell was Fox gonna let you off on that one."

"Could've been worse. I don't know that he's used to hearing a democrat agree with the position he took in his book."

Barnes grinned. "Bet that conclusion was really popular around Fox News. Republicans like warfare, traditionally-speaking. It's good for the economy."

"Sure, Leslie. We declare war, ramp up government spending, provide lots of jobs building planes and tanks and ships and bombs. Unemployment goes down. National debt goes up. And lots of young kids come home in caskets and wheelchairs. But the DOW loves it, so what's the harm, right?"

The Chief of Staff flopped down into one of the chairs. "Look at you. You understand economics after all. I'll cancel those pre-Chennai briefings for you so we can get some real work done."

"Let's hold off on canceling those. That little remark represents ninety percent of my ability to understand the economy of this country, let alone those of the other nineteen members of the conference."

The president slipped out of his jacket and loosened his tie. He slumped back into the custom chair behind the Resolute Desk, sunlight pouring in through the thick, bullet-proof window behind the desk—oddly green and distorted by the sheer thickness of the glass. He had a pounding headache that, he assumed, resulted from reading a never-ending pile of briefs and point papers.

"Not a bad day. Good idea to ask the majority leader and speaker to address the crowd next."

"Hell, Mr. President. They practically begged to. This is a huge deal. It really is. We're finally taking the training wheels off."

"Think they'll be alright?"

"Hell yes. Like SECDEF said, except Israel, they've all been telling us to leave for years. Sure, there's probably gonna be a little backsliding at first, especially in Iraq and Syria, but it's time to kick the birds out of the nest and see if they can fly."

"And we're always there with a safety net?"

That had been one of the unspoken agreements over the last few weeks. The United States would maintain normal diplomatic relations with each government with financial incentives. The idea had come from one of the Speaker's junior staffers and was the equivalent of a neighborhood watch program. Everyone talks and problem solves together. Everyone helps keep each other in line. Do that, and the United States leads the way in putting together economic aid packages for anyone who can consistently play nice with everyone else. And show measurable efforts to deter and eliminate terrorism.

"Those aid packages are gonna be expensive, Leslie."

"They are, but it won't be as expensive as keeping troops deployed there. And I'd rather hand them piles of cash than another generation of kids. If you think about it, we actually save a bit in the end. We're already shipping them money. We're just removing the military cost from the equation and offering a slightly bigger carrot. It might be optimistic, but making it more lucrative to fight against terrorists and dictators than it is to just look the other way or participate might actually be the key. Hell, Daniel, it might even be possible to begin changing the public image those folks have of us."

"From heavily armed assholes to Santa Claus?"

"That's the idea. Right now, we generate our own enemies. We're not seen as favorable to begin with. Every time our troops engage someone over there, we make the image worse. We need to work on changing that. That's a complicated problem that you'd need ten or fifteen terms in office to solve. It's a mix of religion and culture that most people over here don't get. It's the global equivalent of telling your rebellious teenagers how to live their lives. All you end up doing is pushing them farther away. And we've been doing that for decades over there. We're acknowledging that it's time to change tactics."

"That's fair." The president yawned as the intercom buzzed.

"Mr. President, FLOTUS and the kids are here."

Before the president could acknowledge the announcement, the door to the Oval Office opened and his kids burst into the room, with Alicia trailing behind. He got up and walked around the desk, catching a giggling Daniel Junior and picking him up.

"And what have you been up to today?" Evans smiled at his son.

"Daddy, they have ice cream."

"They do?"

The child, with some of the aforementioned treat drying on his t-shirt, nodded emphatically. "Giant buckets. Chocolate. Vanilla. Stachio."

"Pistachio?"

"That's what I said. Stachio. And banana."

"And you brought me some?"

The child leaned closer to his dad, hand covering his mouth with a sticky hand, whispering. "No, but I know where it is."

The president whispered back. "Should we go get some more?"

Daniel Junior nodded wildly as his father put him down. He turned to see his daughter Elizabeth taking up station on the chair behind the massive antique desk. "What about you? You coming for more ice cream?"

She nodded and jumped back out of the chair, racing around the desk to her father's side. Evans looked at his wife.

"Shall we?"

Alicia nodded. "Sure, but you're staying up with them all night."

"Deal." The president turned to his Chief of Staff. "You joining us, Leslie?"

Barnes laughed and patted his stomach. "I think I'll pass, Mr. President. Besides, I've got a few more meetings today."

"Anything I need to be concerned about."

"Not at all. Routine stuff. Go on. I know how to find you."

The president turned to his son. "Alright, young man. Lead the way."

15

NIXON

"THESE GUYS SUCK," said Miguel, expressing his qualified opinion of the Pakistani SPD's physical security staff. "Aside from changing mags and pulling the trigger, they don't know shit. I'd be surprised if half of them can do anything other than punch holes in the sky with a loaded weapon. And that's the easy stuff. They can't think tactically. They're sloppy. They're undisciplined. And their admin is for shit."

The rest of the team nodded in agreement as they sat around a picnic table at the SPD Headquarters and Garrison compound in Rawalpindi. They'd been in-country for a week, observing the security detail perform their normal, day-to-day duties and conducting a variety of special drills and evolutions. What they'd witnessed had been written up in an assessment, complete with recommendations and training plans, which they'd been scheduled to present to their host over two hours ago. Dave leaned over the table.

"How's the general gonna take this, Mike?"

Mike looked up and shrugged. "He's only really got two options. Believe us or don't."

Dave pressed. "Those were his internal training reports though." He was referring to the status reports the general had provided to TitanX. "If you read those, you'd think these guys were ready for anything. I wouldn't hire these guys to run security at fucking Walmart. They're that bad."

Mike nodded as Andrew chimed in. "Now we know why the rest of the world worries about their ability to keep the nukes safe."

Miguel grinned. "Yeah. Forget terrorists. Half the gangs I grew up around could figure out a way to steal one of these things and there ain't shit this guard force could do about it."

Mike smiled. "Well, let's maybe be more diplomatic than that when we get in there."

Miguel sipped his water and looked at his watch. "What gives? We've been waiting two hours."

Mike took a long pull on his water. "The general is defending our presence here. Apparently, some of his associates are having second thoughts about letting us assist."

Dave almost barked, spitting water across the table. "They're gonna be even less thrilled with our report. How in the hell does this work, Mike? We know they're shitty guards. They have to know it. But if we say it that blatantly, they might get pissed and send us home."

"Again. They can believe us or not. If they send us home, that's on them. Nick says he's already given Khan an overview of our assessment. They talked for a couple hours yesterday. Tryin' to smooth the waters a bit."

"Bet that went well," replied Andrew. "It's a bit insane, isn't it?"

Miguel turned. "What's that?"

"How governments will lie to themselves, make policy decisions based on those lies, and then vehemently defend the policies."

"They all do it," noted Miguel. "Hell, we do it and most of America accepts policy as an article of faith."

"Doesn't make it any less insane," Dave announced. "Hell, I'll bet that concept alone lengthened the Cold War by at least a decade."

"On whose side?" Andrew asked.

Dave shrugged. "Does it matter?"

Miguel raised his bottle of water in mock salute. "Good point."

Mike cut off the discussion, nodding towards the headquarters building. One of Khan's staffers was walking down the steps and heading their way. "Look alive, gents."

The staffer approached the table where the four Americans were standing and introduced himself as Colonel Pervez Raza. After Mike introduced his team and handshakes were exchanged, the colonel invited them to follow him.

"General Khan apologizes for the delay. As you know, some of the ministers, while recognizing the need for assistance, are uncomfortable with the idea of American involvement."

Mike spoke for the group. "No need to apologize and we understand the concern. If the situation was reversed, I think you'd find more than a few members of our Congress who'd be extremely angry with the arrangement."

"Besides, sir. We aren't Americans." Miguel interrupted. His comment caused the colonel to stop in his tracks. A confused look crawled across the man's face.

"What do you mean?" Asked Raza.

"We aren't here as American representatives. We are private contractors who just happen to come from the United States." Miguel smiled.

Raza rolled his eyes and headed off, grumbling. "Yes. That's so much better."

Andrew punched Miguel in the shoulder. "Smooth, Miguel."

"What?" Miguel asked, smiling.

The group, led by Colonel Raza, entered the building and passed through security with nothing more than a perfunctory wave from the three guards at the main desk. The four Americans shared a look. Raza led the Americans through the building and into the office of the Director-General of the Strategic Plans Division. The office, a minimalist affair for one of the highest-ranking officers in the Pakistani military, consisted of little more than a large writing desk and a conference table. A stand against one wall supported a bank of televisions, one of which—the Americans noted—was tuned to a CNN. As they entered, General Khan stood and waved them each to seats around the relatively small conference table.

"Gentlemen, I apologize for the delay. As Colonel Raza no doubt informed you, there are still individuals who are uncomfortable with the arrangement I have made with your company."

"General, thank you for seeing us." Mike replied. "We appreciate the trouble you are going through to host us."

Khan smiled painfully and waved to a sheaf of papers that Raza had just placed in front of him. "Mr. Nixon, I've read your preliminary findings. Your report varies significantly from the monthly reports I receive from my staff. We are not politicians here. Let us deal with each other as soldiers. I need frank assessments, regardless of how you think I may react."

"Fair enough, sir." Mike answered. "There are a series of significant issues with the security staff, all of which stem from their initial training and all of which present your enemies with an opening. Your nuclear arsenal is extremely vulnerable."

"How vulnerable?" Khan was flipping through his report as Mike delivered his assessment.

"General, you have anywhere from thirty to forty guards on duty at each of the storage sites at any given time. My team here could steal a nuclear weapon from any one of them with little more than a week's planning. With a month to plan, we could accomplish the same feat and your detail would never know." Mike watched for his host's reactions. He noted that Raza didn't even blink. The general's reaction was more congruent with his expectations.

Khan's head snapped up; an eyebrow raised. "With only four men? And what weapons?"

"Maybe a sidearm each. Nothing major."

"Impossible," the general contested. "I know that we have security concerns, but what you say is impossible."

Miguel spoke up for the first time. "General, it isn't that hard. If you've read the reports, then you know that one of the concerns we have regarding the current guard force is discipline."

"Your point, Mr. Jimenez?"

"You operated out of Tabuk during the first Gulf War, correct, sir?"

"That's correct," the general confirmed.

"And your troops got into a few skirmishes that went overwhelmingly your way. Correct?"

The general saw where this was going. He'd authored a book on his victories, a book this man had clearly read. "And you think that the same level of overconfidence exists in my staff that existed in the Iraqi Army? That it causes discipline issues?"

Mike interrupted. "General. I know it seems far-fetched, but have you looked at the appendices to the report?"

"I have not," the general admitted.

Mike flipped in his copy to Appendix B. "General, if you'll turn to page B-1." The general did so as Mike elaborated. "This appendix describes, in detail, how my team could accomplish what we have just claimed."

The general scanned the pages and turned to Raza. "Have you read this?"

The colonel nodded grimly. "I have, sir."

"And?"

"It is possible."

"I see." Khan went back to his copy. He had to admit that the plan was clever. Simple, but clever. He looked up to see Mike watching him. "What do you propose, Mr. Nixon?"

Mike cleared his throat. "Sir, as you can see, we've outlined a plan in which we could steal a nuke without firing a shot. Let us do it."

"Absurd." The general almost shouted before closing his eyes. "You will have to excuse me. It has been a somewhat stressful day. What you ask, Mr. Nixon, is impossible."

"I understand," said Mike. "This is a sensitive topic for any nation, but especially yours. You've been under the microscope on this issue for a while now. But without a red cell test you'll never really know. Without hard information, Pakistan will have to live under a cloud of suspicion and scrutiny." Mike was talking about the practice of having a team from one's own side brainstorm and conduct penetration attacks to simulate what the bad guys would do.

Khan nodded and turned to Raza. "Your opinion?"

Raza stood. "General, given certain precautions and restricting access to the results of such an experiment, I believe such an exercise would be invaluable. If these gentlemen can do what they say, what's to stop a much larger force from doing the same thing?"

Khan turned back to Mike. "Mr. Nixon, you said a month and you could steal one of my nukes without my country ever knowing it was missing?"

"Yes, sir."

"You have two weeks." Khan gestured to Raza. "The colonel will make arrangements for the dummy site."

★ ★ ★ ★ ★

Forty minutes later, Mike Nixon was standing on the balcony to his room, an encrypted satellite phone to his ear. DeGuerra picked up on the second ring.

"Mike?"

"Sir."

"How'd the brief go?"

"About what you'd expect. They weren't exactly thrilled with our assessment, but they seem to understand that it's probably more accurate than their own reports."

"And your proposal in Appendix B?"

"They went for it. The general's staffer, a Colonel Raza, is making the arrangements. Completely blind test. Except for the Colonel, everyone guarding the dummy facility will assume that they are guarding real nukes."

"Mike, you really think you can pull this off?"

"Sir, did you read the rest of the report?"

"I did."

"Then you know this isn't that difficult. It's a simple red cell drill."

"Alright. Be careful." Nick conceded. "Good luck, gentlemen."

"Thank you, sir." Mike disconnected the call and walked back inside his room where Dave, Miguel, and Andrew were waiting.

"So, what did the boss say?" Asked Dave.

"Gentlemen, we have an op to plan." Mike grinned.

Miguel stretched lazily and started to speak. He was cut off by a buzzing on the desk in the room. Mike turned his head to look and realized the buzzing was a text on his personal cell.

"Shit," Dave said. "How'd you get a signal here?"

Mike shrugged and picked up his phone. It wasn't hard to guess who was texting him. He unlocked his phone and selected the proper icon. He looked at the little red number. Twenty-seven unread messages. Two of the messages were from Julie, his mother's live-in nurse. Both messages from her were variations of the same thing. Mom's having a bad day. She's okay, just upset. Call her if you can. The remaining twenty-five were from his mom, half of them different versions of the same subject. Michael, I can't find your dad. Is he with you? Michael, I went to your room and you weren't there—an interesting twist since Michael didn't have a room at his mother's southern California home. As he scrolled through the messages, his heart sank. The remaining messages were erratic. One was a cell phone picture taken of a photograph of Mike at his BUD/S graduation. Mike knew the photo sat on the mantle above the fireplace. The text message that accompanied the picture was wrenching.

Michael? Who is this in the picture?

Mike sat heavily in the small chair by the desk. His team, who'd been haranguing Miguel about his lack of diplomatic skills, went quiet.

"Boss, you okay?" Andrew asked.

Dave looked at Mike, shifting his eyes from the cell phone to Mike's face. He turned to Miguel and Andrew. "Guys, give us a minute?"

"No problem. We'll be next door." Miguel announced as both men got up and left the room.

Dave watched the door close and turned back to Mike. "Your mom?"

Mike handed the phone over, screen unlocked and text messages visible. "Yeah."

Dave took the phone and scrolled through the messages. "Sorry, man. Look, if there's somewhere you need to be, we'll understand. We got this if you need to bolt."

Mike leaned back and looked at the popcorn ceiling. "No. This job is just a few more weeks. She'll be okay until then. I'll just call when I can."

"You sure, boss?"

Mike nodded. "Yeah."

Dave eyed him. "You're worried she won't remember you at all soon?"

"Something like that. At least she still knows my name. For now."

"True." Dave agreed. "Seriously Mike. We got this if you need to head home. You ain't got shit to prove to us. You know that."

"I know." Mike stood and accepted the phone back. He looked at it briefly before pocketing it. "I'll be okay. I'm gonna go find a landline to use and make a call. Then we have work to do."

Dave stood. "Alright. I'll get those two started. We'll be here when you get back."

Mike headed to the door. He stopped before exiting. "Thanks, Dave."

"No problem. Hey man. I spent more time at your house those first few years than at my own. Like having a second family, ya know? Say hi to her for me?"

"Think she'll remember you?" Mike asked.

"Does it matter?"

Mike smiled. "Probably not. Thanks again, Dave."

★ ★ ★ ★ ★

Less than a mile away, Colonel Raza sat at a cheap metal desk—ironically a surplus one manufactured three decades earlier in the United States—and stared at the wall. He blinked and wondered about his new set of orders.

Raza had read the brief the Americans had given Khan. Probably before the old bastard had read it himself. That wasn't fair, Raza knew. He had only two jobs and both were straightforward. Khan wore several hats and, unfortunately, one of them meant dealing with politicians and frequently bending to the will of that class of people.

Raza shook off the train of thought and blinked again, thinking over the Americans' proposal. It was straightforward and simple, but more than that, it was possible. With those four men, and the plan they'd submitted, it was probable that they would succeed. Likely even.

But that was not the reason Raza found himself sitting in this tiny little office and blinking at the wall. There was another, more disturbing reason for that. Khan had ordered a twist to this test—a minor wrinkle he claimed was necessary. If the Americans tested the deepest levels of Pakistan's nuclear security, Khan wanted to assess everything. Raza understood the logic of the small change in plans, even though he was convinced it was madness. What was it the Americans liked to say? Go big or go home? Well, Khan was going big. The crazy old bastard had ordered one of the dummy devices to be replaced with an actual warhead. Even as Raza sat at his desk selecting soldiers for transfer to the dummy site, he knew there was a group of armed guards readying one real weapon for transfer. Khan was inserting live nukes into the test and had tasked Raza with ensuring that his orders were carried out. That bothered the colonel for several reasons, mainly because of the pure recklessness of the idea.

Raza was not, had never been, devoutly religious, but he whispered a silent prayer that this would not blow up in their collective faces. When he'd finished chuckling at the irony of his thought, he turned his attention elsewhere. From a drawer, he withdrew a small, portable tape player with an earpiece. From a pocket inside his uniform jacket, Raza withdrew a small cassette. The colonel pressed play, listening carefully to a recording of the conversation between Khan and DeGuerra in Edinburgh. Raza made a few mental notes, rewinding here and there to ensure he'd not missed anything. Raza got up and paced through his office, thinking as he walked back and forth in the overheated room. On the tape, Khan hadn't put up much of a fight against DeGuerra's proposal.

That was curious, wasn't it.

Maybe the folks in the ministry weren't all that opposed to the Americans? That made sense, didn't it. Khan didn't have that power. Someone had to okay the contract and the idea behind it. If that was true, Khan's lukewarm protestations on the tape were simply pro forma, as were the ministers' current gripes. Raza rolled that around in his brain briefly before nodding. That made sense.

As he paced, the tape played out fully and stopped. Raza ejected the tape and flipped it to the other side. He had no reason to do so, it was simply an instinct remembered from a distant childhood. Raza closed the player and pressed play. The scratchy voices of DeGuerra and Khan came through again, discussing retirement. The colonel looked curiously at the player in his hand. He pressed stop and resumed pacing.

What was this?

Raza searched his memory and couldn't remember hearing anything about a retirement conversation. He pressed play and listened.

It took less than thirty seconds for his blood to freeze.

16

THOMPSON

BRIAN NOTED THAT EVERYTHING INSIDE the skin of the ship was clean, antiseptic—something he knew and had accepted over the past seventeen years of service but which seemed especially poignant on this deployment. Everything here was ordered and structured and as it should be—a condition determined by a set of standards and regulations to which sailors like Brian were inseparably married. Grey paint. White paint. Neatly stenciled acronyms on all the pipes and color-coded handwheels on every valve. Everything labeled in such a way that even the most obsessive-compulsive organizers on the Home and Garden network would have been hard-pressed to object to.

Engine rooms notwithstanding, the air on the ship was conditioned and clean.

It's comfortable here. Seventy degrees. Maybe seventy-two. Kept that way by massive air conditioning units humming away down in the bowels of the ship.

Brian continued waxing poetic as he transited the passageways and hatches between him and the boat deck. He reached the airlock leading outside and opened the first door, stepping past the frame, into the void beyond. His hands closed the door, dogging it down tight. He didn't even think about the movement. Over the past seventeen years, the action had become purely automatic. Muscle memory. You opened the hatch, stepped through, and shut it—checking to make sure you didn't slam the hundred-pound piece of steel on someone's hand in the process.

Brian stood in the airlock, flexing his jaw, trying to relieve the pressure in his ears before turning. He opened the second door and stepped past that frame into a strange new world—his senses reported in as he closed the door behind him, muscle memory again taking over a task that his brain had little time for.

The heat was the first thing he noticed. Inside it was nice and cool. Even the engineering spaces on this ship weren't uncomfortable. Out here a searing blast furnace pumped fire into his lungs and scorched his windpipe. In mere seconds since the transition from air-conditioned comfort, sweat was already forming all over his body, soaking his uniform while every biological cooling mechanism worked at maximum capacity.

The sunlight was the second thing he noticed. Inside, the sixty hertz buzzing of fluorescent lighting never assaulted his eyeballs like this. Sure, you got the occasional headache from the constant, near-invisible pulsing of the tube-shaped lights, but no one acknowledged the lights' existence until one went out. The sun could not be cast aside so easily. The light blazed down on the ship and everything on it, threatening to blind anyone with the temerity to venture outside without eye protection. Even with sunglasses, Brian's pupils contracted to pinpricks as his eyes tried in vain to protect themselves. He could feel the searing heat blistering his retinas, torching nerve endings he'd once read about in a high school biology class.

As Brian ventured further aft, heading midships for the open section between the fore and aft stacks, the smell struck him. It was a curious miasma that was equal parts fresh and putrid—changing at the whimsy of the winds. When the slight breeze whipped in from starboard, the clean smell of the ocean greeted him—the occasional spray of saltwater and unsoiled air blew across his face. But as the wind shifted, coming from land, it carried the smell of raw sewage and garbage, with a hint of burnt rubber and just a touch of smoke as garnish.

Brian had never deployed to this area of the world before but, in his first few minutes outside, he determined that the shifting winds were maddening. His nose couldn't adjust quick enough and his stomach rebelled. Get used to it, he told himself. You've got at least six months of this shit. He made the turn, crossing over to the starboard side of the ship where the rest of the boarding team was waiting.

Past the dozen bobbing heads, Brian got his first glimpse of Somalia. The sunlight, still blazing, danced on sapphire-encrusted water, stretching off to a horizon devoid of anything Brian could recognize as civilized. There, just a couple miles away, was the Somali coastline—a brown strip distinguishable from this distance. Brian could make out wrecked structures, vehicles, and—barely—people. From his vantage point, Brian could see nothing even remotely inviting and he reprimanded himself for the thought. Brian knew there were nearly three million people living in Mogadishu, most of whom occupied themselves only with the chore of surviving. Those people— who should have been able to count on some sort of functioning government to help them out—worked themselves to death just to live long enough to see another sunrise.

Technically, they were not the reason the Williams was floating offshore. The reason for that, and part of the reason so many struggled in this East African nation, was the corrupt minority who spent most days squeezing every last drop of wealth out of those around them.

Smoke rose into the sky, carried on the shifting breeze towards the ship. A few wrecked hulls dotted the coastline, remnants of ships which had made unscheduled stops here. Brian looked at it all, even though the scene to port was more comforting. He took it all in as a tiny little voice in his head greeted him.

Welcome to Mogadishu.

He approached the rest of the boarding team, fastening the chin strap on his tactical helmet. He went over his gear once again, making sure the extra strap material was tucked away or taped firmly in place. He ran his hands across his body armor, ensuring the pouches were firmly shut before checking to see that his M-9 Beretta was securely locked in its thigh holster and that his M-4 rifle was secured by the plastic clip on his left side. Satisfied, he gave the boarding team leader a thumbs-up and moved to the lifelines to put his eyes on the boat.

Roberts joined him there, patting him on the back as he spoke. "Been on station less than twenty hours and we've already got a boarding to do. Crazy shit."

Brian nodded, examining the boat. "Helluva way to start out, eh? Who did the boat walk through?"

"Coleman and Brooks. Gearhart helped out a bit too. No problems." Brian nodded again. "Jesus it's hot here."

"With all that shit on? I'll bet. Stinks too." Jason gestured at the column of smoke drifting from the city. "Who're you guys after?"

"No one. Not really. Small cargo ship. Compliant boarding. Hell, I think the ship's master requested it."

"Well, you be careful out there. You break something and Tim's pretty much screwed." Both men laughed.

"I'm not boarding today. Just along for the boat ride and to work on my tan."

"You need it. You're starting to look like Beetlejuice." Jason's radio crackled to life and he answered it before turning back to Brian. "It's time."

The Boarding Officer, a Lieutenant Junior Grade named Lee—but who went by the callsign Bruce for boarding evolutions—had received the same radio call as Roberts and designated the Boarding Team Lead to escort the rest of the team to the ship's flight deck. Brian walked up as the remainder of the team headed further aft.

"Ready, sir?"

"Yeah. We load the boat in five mikes."

Brian nodded. "How'd you get stuck with 'Bruce' as a call sign?"

The lieutenant grinned. "Captain found a picture of me from a judo tournament when I was eight. Last name Lee." He shrugged. "Almost unavoidable."

"You still do judo?"

Lee shook his head. "Nah. Got my ass kicked a lot. Took up chess. Lots safer."

"Chess masters don't do hip throws?"

Lee grinned again. "Apparently not."

Brian allowed a smirk to eek its way onto his face. "Academy grad?"

A shake of the head. "Virginia Tech. Math major."

"Math major?" Brian's head cocked to the side.

Lee shrugged. "What can I say? I'm a walking stereotype."

"I'm assuming 'Bruce' doesn't bother you?"

Another shake of the head. "Better than getting stuck with 'Bug'. How'd that happen?"

Brian smiled. "Two of the guys walked into the gym when I was doing squats during the Suez transit."

"I heard about that. Jones claims you had four hundred pounds on the bar."

"Sounds about right."

Bruce turned. "What are you, like a buck fifty, soaking wet?"

"More on a good day."

"Christ, Chief." Lee shook his head.

Four hours later, the small boat was back in the skid on the starboard side of the USS James E. Williams. A crew of two machinist mates and two deck seamen were conducting post-use maintenance on the boat while the boarding team had gathered on the mess decks for the debrief. Any member of the crew walking past the closed doors of the crew's mess might have mistaken the goings-on there for a party instead of the serious debrief that was supposed to be occurring. Inside the mess decks, Commander Derrick Allen was waving for silence with one hand and pointing at a laptop screen with the other.

"Are you serious?"

The question was directed at one of the team members, a Fire Controlman Third Class named White who was always the first team member up the wire-rope ladder and on deck of a target ship.

"Well, sir. Yes. I got to the top of the ladder, determined the area was clear, got over the rail and saw him there, face down on the deck with his hands behind his head and his ankles crossed."

"And you zip tied him and moved him across the deck?" The captain asked.

FC3 White smiled. "Yes, sir."

The captain turned to Lieutenant Lee. "And did we find out what the young man was doing there?"

Lieutenant Lee grinned. "Well, sir. It seemed that he was unaware that the ship's master requested our visit. Apparently, the young man isn't exactly the most popular person back home, gets bullied a bit. Well, he saved up a few paychecks and managed to purchase a handgun during one of their recent stops. Just the handgun. Didn't have enough left over for clips or bullets."

The captain rubbed his eyes. "Poor kid thought we were there for him?"

"That seems to be the case, sir." Lee said.

"And his own captain didn't tell him otherwise?"

The Boarding Officer shook his head. "No, sir. Just left him there, scared to death."

The CO sighed. "What an asshole. Did we confiscate the gun?"

Lee shook his head. "No sir. It was legally purchased and unloaded."

One of the team, a Bosun's Mate named Christensen, called out from the back of the group. "Only because he was too broke to buy the ammo, sir."

The room erupted in laughter again and it took a couple of minutes for the captain to quiet things down again. "Alright folks. Alright. Good boarding. Lessons learned?" He looked around at the team.

Lee stood. "Well, sir. While it's funny, the situation with the young man could have been dangerous. When FC3 encountered him, she had no way of knowing why he was there. Her moving him cleared the area for the rest of the team to board, but it also left the area unsecured for a minute. If we move him, we don't have control of the entry point. If we don't, we're just hoping he isn't wired up with explosives. We'll have to figure out a way around something like that."

The captain nodded. "Good point. Anything else?"

"Just gotta replace the ladder. Saw two spots on my way up where the wire rope is either kinked or damaged. A couple of bright, shiny nicks. I'll put the supply request in today and BM3 Christensen is going to swap the damaged ladder with one of the spares."

The captain rose from his seat, shutting his notebook and tucking a pen in his breast pocket. Everyone else got to their feet as Lieutenant Lee called "Attention on deck!"

The CO walked out of the room. "Carry on."

★ ★ ★ ★ ★

Brian walked into the Chief's Mess thirty minutes later, heading to the row of stainless-steel cupboards lining the inboard bulkhead. Carrillo and several others were sitting around drinking coffee and taking much needed breaks from a busy first day on station. Carrillo lifted the remote and silenced the television. "Brian. Wanted to ask about Kyle's comment."

Brian selected a cup of Ramen and turned around. "Which one?"

"The thing about a fire in shaft alley. Do we have a process for fighting that kind of fire?"

Brian began pouring hot water into the cup of noodles. "Not really."

Carrillo turned back to the television. "You aren't concerned?"

Brian sat down to wait for his dinner. "It's not that." He paused, thinking. "I mean, what can we really do? There's only one good way in and one way out."

"So why don't we practice it?"

Brian had to rack his brain for a few moments, searching for the answer. "Probably because there isn't a requirement or drill package for it." He picked up a fork and poked at the boiling noodles.

"I mentioned it to the captain. He wants to run the next few drills down there."

"Okay." Brian scooped a forkful of noodles into his mouth.

"You don't sound convinced."

Brian swallowed his bite and put the fork down. "What do you want me to say?"

Carrillo shrugged. "You usually have an opinion."

"Logan, I'm tired as hell and I have watch coming up. You told me to do something and I'll do it. End of story."

Carrillo turned around. "I didn't tell you to do it. I said it needed done."

"And I'm the one that writes the drill packages."

"You don't need to be. Have someone else do it. Like DCA."

"DCA? Really?" Brian said. "The person getting drilled writes the drill package? That's how we do things?"

The room went silent when Carrillo muted the television again. "Something you wanna say?"

Brian glared at him. "Nope. I'm fine. Just one more thing to do."

The CMC stared at Brian for a few moments. There was an edge to his voice that Brian missed. "Brian. You okay?"

"I'm fine. Just got a lot going on."

A snort of laughter escaped from some of the chiefs. Carrillo shot them a look before turning back to Brian. "Brian, 'a lot going on' is one hell of an understatement. You got what, a couple weeks' notice before showing up to this shit show. Your wife just gave birth. Kids. Donaldson. Boarding team. Damage control teams keep doing the same stupid shit. Most of engineering is on your shoulders. Half the gear in your department is wrecked. The rest is breaking left and right. You're pale as shit and you look like you've lost at least ten pounds since you've been here. And you clearly aren't sleeping."

Brian just sat there. *Then get me some damn help.* Carrillo went on as if he could read Brian's thoughts. "Listen, we're trying to get more chiefs out here for you. You know that. But at this rate, you're going to burn out long before anyone gets here to help you."

Brian felt the anger rising in him, felt his face flush. He snarled. "And my option is to what? Just let things be? I don't turn wrenches because I fucking want to, I do it because we need those systems and, in most cases, we need them quickly. What should I do? Just leave shit broken until I get help?"

Carrillo pointed. "That's not what I'm saying and you damn well know it. Not everything is a right now issue. And you can't do it all yourself. No one can."

"It is when we send off a message telling the rest of the Navy it is." Brian shot back. "Sure, if we were part of a battle group, this wouldn't be that big of a deal. There'd be another ship around to back us up for a few days while we got our shit together. But that ain't the case. We're out here alone. If I just let shit go, we'll be getting pulled off station for repairs every two weeks for the next six months."

Carrillo sat there, a calm expression on his face. Brian realized he'd been yelling. He looked down at the table.

"Brian, what happens when you burn out or your body shuts down because you've stressed it out? Who fixes shit then? You aren't wrong. We need the gear working to stay on station. And that can't happen if the person who fixes the gear kills himself through stress and neglect. Again. You can't do it all yourself and you can't do it all today."

Brian kept looking at the table. He knew Carrillo was right. In a few weeks, he'd gone from a state of relative relaxation to a near-permanent state of stress and anxiety. He wasn't sleeping. What sleep he did get wasn't beneficial. He felt that an impenetrable cloud of doom and gloom existed around him, always waiting for some new casualty to befall him. He had turned into some manic Eeyore, always predicting and expecting the worse.

Brian realized that everyone was staring at him. He snapped. "What?"

Carrillo raised his hands. "Brian. What's going on? Why do you think you need to do it all?"

Brian sat there, fuming. Carrillo continued, his finger pointing at Brian. "Dude. You can't fucking do it all. No one can. I don't know what this is. I don't get this superman routine you have going on, but it ain't working."

Brian's brain raced. He stood. "Then get me some fucking help!"

Carrillo came off his seat. He towered over Brian. "Listen dammit! Your department is going down the tubes while you're down turning wrenches and shit. Whatever this is, it needs to stop. You need to figure it out. You need to trust people to do their fucking jobs so you can do yours. If you can't do that, if you can't explain this drive to me, then get the hell off my ship!"

The two men stood, their faces inches apart, breathing heavily.

17

NIXON

"BOSS, IS THIS SUPPOSED TO BE THIS EASY?" Miguel whispered, his Bluetooth-enabled earpiece picking up the sound and broadcasting it to each of his teammates on the four-way conference call.

Mike's eyes scanned the area while he answered. "That's kind of the point here, Miguel. Our boot camp recruits are less relaxed than these guys."

Miguel watched the Pakistani soldiers around him. "I was never relaxed in boot. The drill instructors made damn sure of that. Sergeant Weatherly was a scary son of a bitch. Not like the eight-week long tea party the Air Force put on."

"Fuck you, Miguel." Andy Cook's voice broke in.

Miguel smiled. "Love you too, buddy."

Dave Fogarty came on the net. "He's got a point though. Got eyes on ten guys. Rifles slung, cigarettes out. We're simulating a delivery of a nuke and no one seems to give a shit."

Mike looked around. "The world ain't worried about ISIS or Al-Qaeda assaulting one of these places and taking a nuke by force. Well, not only worried about that. They're also concerned that these guys will just lose one through pure negligence."

Mike's team was conducting a red cell drill. They were playing the part of a bad actor and had been authorized to attempt to infiltrate this dummy storage site after claiming that they could—with minimal planning and nothing more than sidearms—steal a nuke without anyone knowing the weapon was gone.

They were halfway to their objective. Eleven dummy warheads waited behind a massive blast door twenty feet from the truck that Miguel was driving—each one an exact replica of an actual nuclear weapon, minus the physics package required to wreak havoc and destruction. As far as the Pakistani guards knew, the warheads were real. General Khan had, apparently, kept his part of the bargain—going along with the ruse that this was an actual storage site and ensuring his people believed as much. Mike and his team marveled at the logistics involved in that little bit of trickery. In just one week, Khan had identified and set up a site for this exercise and had made the necessary arrangements to ensure that anyone wearing a Pakistani uniform believed the site was real.

★ ★ ★ ★ ★

During the final briefing before the red cell exercise, Mike had asked about the process, incredulous at the speed with which a such a monumental task had been accomplished—sure that a similar move in the United States would take years while politicians, the military, a variety of environmental protection organizations, and about ten thousand lawyers argued over the project. Khan had smiled, genuinely pleased with himself. He'd explained that he had, the very day he'd authorized this test, visited one of Pakistan's active storage sites under the pretense of conducting a facilities inspection. After an hour, he'd declared the site's buildings and bunkers unusable, making a great show of chastising and firing the compound's commander and replacing him on the spot. Within an hour of the performance, he'd ordered the immediate relocation of the entire operation to a more up-to-date facility.

When Mike had asked about the former commander's fate, Khan had shrugged it off. "Mr. Nixon, the facility was poorly maintained. He was responsible. These are nuclear weapons. What would you do in light of such failure?"

Remembering the look on the general's face and the nonchalance with which the man's imprisonment had been communicated made Mike second-guess his initial impression of Khan.

That there should have been twelve weapons instead of eleven at the new facility hadn't been mentioned by a single member of the security detail. Mike's plan counted on that. Over the previous three days, he'd confirmed the shipment of the twelfth device independently. That had been done easily. He'd identified a likely target and had offered to reimburse the man in exchange for a little information and copies of the proper paperwork. After some minor haggling, Mike had walked off with a complete set of transfer orders for a nuclear weapon—with Khan's signature in the proper places—for the bargain price of seven hundred dollars.

From there, it had taken Miguel, Dave and Andy two days to build their own replica device. Khan had watched the entire operation quietly, commenting once that he could not tell the difference in external appearances between the original and the American-created fake. Mike and his team had accepted the compliment with smiles, but had demurred when Khan had asked for the name of the individual who'd supplied the fake transfer orders.

★ ★ ★ ★ ★

The newly installed commander on the post—a captain—had given the false paperwork a cursory glance before continuing the inspection himself.

Miguel whispered. "What do you suppose he's looking for?"

Mike grinned. "A bomb."

Miguel smiled back. "Shouldn't be that hard to find. Think he'll notice two?"

Mike turned in his seat, making a show of watching the soldiers smoking nearby. "Hell, I don't even think he noticed that there were two devices on the paperwork."

Mike looked behind him at the crate holding a pair of weapons. One was the twelfth warhead that the Americans were purportedly escorting to the site. The other was the American replica which bore the same serial numbers and markings as one of the original eleven devices in the bunker.

The scenario Mike had briefed to Khan and Raza had been absurdly simple and it relied heavily on the complacency of the Pakistani guard force. If you were ordered to do something, by someone you trusted, that thing was done. It was expected to happen. You didn't question it. The guards' faith in the integrity of their chain of command was, as Mike suspected, so complete that the guard detail either failed to notice the two non-Pakistani males in the lead truck or just assumed that the obvious outsiders belonged there.

This was as simple as it got. Play off of trust. Waltz into the facility because they let you in. Drop off the "real" dummy device and swap the replica for one of the originals. Drive off into the sunset and then gift wrap the stolen "nuke" and leave it on Khan's desk. Simple. Easy. Mike grinned at the ridiculousness of it all.

Mike watched as the captain of the guard finally boarded the truck, stepping over and around the Pakistani guards to verify the serial number of the shock-proof crate in the bed of the truck.

"About time, mano. Jesus." Miguel griped. "You notice he didn't have them open the crate?"

Mike nodded in agreement. "These guys don't question anything."

Andrew's voice popped up on the call for the first time.

"Well, they don't exactly have the same military justice system we do. Questioning orders here likely gets you a lengthy prison term. Or worse."

"Bet this was what the Soviet army was like," Dave opined.

"That's a rog. How are you boys doing out there?" Miguel asked.

Dave and Andrew were on separate roofs of neighboring buildings, purportedly to keep an eye on the "big picture" side of the delivery.

"Three's good," Dave responded. "All quiet."

"Four's good. Convoy diverted to the vehicle park once you guys made it in the front door."

Mike's head turned. He and Miguel looked at each other.

"Seriously? All of them?"

Andrew came back on the line. "That's affirm. Ain't nothing between the front door and the guard shack but two dudes on foot patrol."

Miguel started to smile, but stopped when Dave spoke again.

"Hey gents. Shouldn't the outer security door to the bunker have shut after you were admitted?"

Mike turned to look behind them but couldn't see past the array of lamps set up to illuminate the immediate area. He spoke as his brain tried to recall every detail from the procedural manual Khan had given them. "Three. You saying the doors are still open?"

"That's affirm six. I can see the floodlights and one tail light from my pos."

Miguel grumbled. "Idiots."

As Mike was making a note, the captain of the guard climbed down from the back of the truck and walked to the driver's side door, rapping on the thick metal with his knuckles. Miguel opened the door and exchanged a few words that Mike couldn't make out.

Miguel turned. "He says they need to inspect the cab. We have to get out."

Mike nodded and whispered into the earpiece. "Three, Four. You catch that?"

Dave and Andrew acknowledged before Mike went on. "Gents. A few more minutes for inspection, then thirty minutes to offload and make the switch. We'll be out of here in forty mikes."

Mike opened his door, stepping down and away from the vehicle—following the directions of the sergeant on his side of the truck and making additional notes as he did so. On the opposite side of the massive truck, Miguel did the same.

The captain of the guard climbed up into the truck and behind the wheel—making a show of inspecting the cab. Mike turned to watch the other seven guards—noting that all but one of them appeared confident in their performance. Only one young man, who Mike pegged for no more than nineteen years old, stood guard by the open door that Mike could now see—his rifle held at low-ready, eyes looking out and away from the events behind him. Good for him, thought Mike.

Mike had turned to the nearest guard to ask who the young man was when he heard the truck's engine rev. His head snapped up to see the truck lurch backwards into the group of smokers.

While Mike was still processing the truck's movement, Dave's voice screamed into his ear.

"Incoming! Get the fuck down!"

Mike dropped to the deck as an explosion rocked the bunker's entrance. The blast knocked out the lights and sent a spray of deadly fragments slicing through the air, tearing apart the guards that the truck hadn't run over. Mike kept his head down, fighting the urge to look up as another explosion rocked the bunker. Over his earpiece he heard Andrew yelling.

"RPGs!"

Mike pulled himself up after the second blast and moved in a crouch to put the truck's slow-moving bulk between himself and the bunker's entrance. He flinched when klaxons erupted throughout the facility. The truck was halfway through a three-point turn with four guards just beginning to clamber out of the back of the moving vehicle. They moved, rifles up, toward the entrance to the bunker as Mike continued moving. More explosions rocked the front of the bunker and Mike could hear the distinct rattle of AK-47s.

"Team, Six. Check in." Mike yelled.

"Dave's up. Moving. Unknown number of hostiles moving through the gate."

"Miguel's up." Mike turned to see Miguel crouched behind a wall, his sidearm out and pointed downrange.

Mike moved to Miguel's side, drawing his own pistol. "Four. Check in."

Silence.

As Mike and Miguel watched the truck amble through the bunker entrance, Dave's voice came back on the call.

"Six. Got eyes on Four. Andrew's down."

"Rog. Four's down," Mike repeated. "Where the fuck is the truck going?"

Dave answered. "No idea, but the Opfor just wiped out the four guards chasing it out of the bunker and shifted fire away from the truck."

Mike's brain raced as the battle raged outside. From his limited vantage point, he could see fire raking the buildings to either side of the transport. "Dave. Can you get to Andrew?"

"Affirm. The rifle fire has shifted. I can get there."

"Do it. Get him and meet us at the back of this bunker in five mikes."

Miguel voiced the only dissent. "What about the truck?"

"Just a truck. Not our problem. Gents, we cannot get caught here. Our presence will not help the SPD. Word gets out and all hell's gonna break loose for the Pakistani government."

Miguel nodded in the dark. "Roger that."

Dave's voice confirmed as well. "Roger. See you in five."

Mike turned to Miguel. "Move."

Miguel grabbed Mike's shoulder and squeezed, a signal that it was time to leapfrog backwards toward the emergency exit. As Miguel rose to begin the first jump a group of men entered the bunker, pouring fire into the bodies of men torn apart by the first two blasts. Both Americans froze, dropping as low as they could but keeping their feet under them.

"Fuck. What do you wanna do, boss?" Miguel whispered.

Mike looked around. "Think they can see down this far?"

"Hell. I can barely see you."

Mike kept his eyes on the gunmen. "We move to the emergency exit. Stay low. Watch your step."

"Roger that."

Mike eased away from the wall to start the exfil. In the pitch black he didn't see the piece of broken pipe laying on the floor. His toe bumped the shattered steel tube and sent it clattering away towards Miguel.

All four gunmen swung their rifles towards the noise and squeezed off rounds. Mike screamed, "Move!"

Neither American worried about engaging the gunmen. They raced over debris toward the door they knew to be in the back, left corner of the bunker. Bullets raked the area, pinging and snapping off piles of concrete and metal debris as the former SEAL tried to reach in his shirt for the key card that would open the security door. He stumbled, tripping over a pile of rubble as a cloud of bullets transited the space his upper body had just vacated. Miguel was nearly to the door when Mike regained his feet and sped off.

With the key card out, Mike crashed into the door, feeling for the card slot as a hail of gunfire raked the area around him. Miguel, tucked behind a half-wall of concrete, was returning fire with his pistol.

Mike's hands continued searching the darkness as bits of concrete pelted his face and arms—amazed he hadn't been hit yet.

There.

He inserted the card and saw the tiny green light flash. He crouched as he pulled the door open and reached back for Miguel. "Move!"

Miguel continued firing downrange as Mike pulled him by his collar towards the door and the tunnel beyond. Miguel's pistol locked open on an empty mag. Still moving backwards, his thumb found the magazine release as his left hand drew a fresh mag from his web gear. He had the mag halfway inserted when his eyes saw a flash at the far end of the bunker. He turned and shoved Mike into the tunnel.

"RPG!"

Forty yards away the bulbous end of the RPG leapt off the launcher and raced toward the door. In the excitement of the moment, the gunman shot high and the rocket-propelled grenade hit two feet above the security door's mantle, expending much of its energy on the reinforced concrete of the bunker itself.

The blast flung Mike and Miguel into the tunnel and down a set of rough concrete stairs, slamming each man's head into the hard surface. They landed, blind, deaf, and unconscious, in a heap at the bottom of a short flight of concrete steps. A second explosive round rocked the area they'd just vacated, wrenching the massive security door in its own frame and sealing that end of the passage.

Mike's eyes opened reluctantly as his brain played catch-up. He was face-up in a tangle of arms, legs, and debris with his head propped on something soft. At his feet he could see a blurry set of steps, down which water flowed like a waterfall—which explained why his entire back felt wet.

He blinked once. Twice. Then a third time, trying to clear his vision. Without moving his head, he could now see the top of the stairs. The heavy security door was bent, forced in against its own frame. He could see shafts of light pouring through cracks in the frame, one of which illuminated a broken sprinkler pipe from which water continued to flow.

The air was heavy with the smell of cordite and smoke and Mike remembered why he was laying at the bottom of a set of stairs. He struggled to sit up, using one arm to prop himself up while the other tried to remove whatever it was that was laying across his chest. Mike looked down, his head throbbing as he did so. His hand rested on a boot.

Mike turned to check on Miguel and was relieved to see the other man blinking.

"Miguel?"

Miguel groaned. "Fuck."

"You hit?"

Miguel pushed himself up onto all fours and rocked back onto his heels. He ran his hands over various parts of his body, checking for injuries. "I'm good. Fucking hell of a headache though." Miguel turned to look behind him, his gaze falling on the wrecked door ten feet above them. "That how we came in?"

Mike nodded, trying to stand. "Yeah."

"Dave and Andrew?" Miguel was pulling himself up.

Mike reached to touch his ear. The earpiece was gone. He stuck a hand in his pocket and pulled out his phone. The screen was shattered, with whole chunks of glass missing. Mike pushed the power button on the side of the phone and held it in place. Nothing.

"Phone's shot. Yours?"

Miguel was looking at his own phone and shaking his head. "Nothing. What the hell was that all about?"

"No clue." Mike steadied himself against the wall. "Let's get the hell out of here."

"Take it slow, mano. My legs are wrecked."

Mike took a step and wobbled. "Mine too. Use the wall."

The two men proceeded down the passage, sloshing their way through puddles of sprinkler water, struggling to control the movement of each leg.

Miguel broke the silence. "Captain of the guard knew. Didn't he?"

Mike nodded in the dark, picturing the scene when they'd have to tell the General that one of his own was in on the attack. "Yeah. Khan's gonna be pissed at that. Wonder how many others?"

Miguel didn't say anything for a few minutes, focusing on his plodding and painful footsteps. Then, "Hey Mike. Doesn't this seem odd? All of that to steal a truck?"

Mike shrugged as well as he could under the circumstances. "Maybe they thought the bombs were real."

"No way they're that dense."

"It's possible. Figure they heard about the new facility, ask their guy about it and he tells them. As far as the captain or any of the guards knew, those things were real."

Mike and Miguel reached an intersection. Mike thought back to the blueprints he'd checked out while planning this fiasco. The left tunnel headed back to the main bunker and offices. He pointed to the right. "That way."

Miguel limped off. "Shit. Terrorists willing to knock off a nuke site?"

"Terrorists who did knock off a nuke site," Mike corrected. "Well, sort of."

They reached the end of the passageway, finding another security door. Mike pulled the key card out of his pocket, wondering how it had survived the blast and praying that it wasn't damaged after laying in the water under him. He swiped it.

A red light blinked and a buzzer sounded. Mike swiped the card again. Nothing. He tried wiping the card on the cleanest and driest part of his clothing before swiping it a third time. Red light. Buzz.

"Now what? Back to the bunker?"

Mike was about to speak when the door beeped, clicked, and was ripped open.

Floodlights poured into the alcove where Mike and Miguel stood. Neither man saw the rifle butts that knocked them unconscious for the second time that evening.

WILL WAS EXHAUSTED. He'd been in the air for the better part of five days and was looking forward to a few hours of sleep.

As ordered, Alex O'Neil had run through the bureaucracy of transferring eight of Camp Mercury's detainees to Will's care for delivery to Camp X-Ray in Guantanamo Bay, Cuba. Four of those men were still aboard the TitanX corporate jet as it made its final approach to a fixed base operator fifty miles northeast of San Diego.

Will smiled, thinking about how easy it had been to make four human beings vanish. He'd signed for the eight detainees, half of whom were guilty of nothing more than being in the wrong place at the wrong time when the US Army rolled into town. Will, four guards, and eight prisoners had left for Basra before hopping their way across southern Europe and the Atlantic Ocean to Cuba.

The Camp X-Ray operations officer, a major in the United States Army with flag-level aspirations, had been shocked to arrive on the tarmac and find eight detainees ready for turnover. He'd been told to expect four men and he'd come equipped with the paperwork to do just that. More bureaucrat than soldier, the operations officer had no intention of sticking his neck out on this issue.

Will knew that Camp X-Ray was controversial and he'd not been surprised when the young major had described, in detail, the big, rolling pile of shit that would land squarely on him should he be found to have detainees that he did not have the proper paperwork for. For Will's benefit, the major had even outlined a scene where several angry senators would crawl up his ass while apologizing profusely to the detainees.

In view of the guards, Will and the young major had gone over the fouled-up paper-work—with each man making several exasperated phone calls. In the end, Camp X-ray only took the four prisoners they'd arranged for and Will had agreed to return the unwanted men to their point of origin.

Will, four guards, and four detainees had made the long trip back to Umm Qasr. Once there, Will had released the guards from their responsibilities—a circumstance that each man happily accepted after almost forty-eight hours in the air.

As the guards rode off the flight line, Will had walked back onto the plane and had hidden each of the remaining detainees, bound and gagged, in smuggler's holds built into the jet's interior. By the time the ground crew had arrived to perform maintenance and refuel the craft, Will was sitting in one of the plane's comfortable chairs, going over some paperwork and reports for the home office in Schroon Falls.

That had been twenty-seven hours and three stops ago. Technically the craft had enough range to make the twenty-one-hour flight with only one stop, but the TitanX pilots were a conservative bunch and Will was in no great hurry. He had plenty of time.

The plane landed smoothly despite a gusty crosswind, the mild squeak and bump of the main gear followed by the touchdown of the nose gear announced another safe landing. Will smiled to himself.

He was going over the next few steps of Nick's operation in his head as the aircraft taxied to a hangar. Customs would board in the hangar and perform a cursory inspection. Will had arranged the flight to arrive at the airport's busiest time as a hedge against a more intensive search of the craft. He wasn't concerned that they'd find his human cargo. The holds were too well disguised for that. They'd been engineered by careful men with plenty of experience creating and installing such compartments for individuals and organizations on both sides of the law. Will was just trying to stack the deck in his favor.

The plane entered the hangar and the stairs were dropped so a harried-looking man in a sweat-soaked button-up and tie could board the plane. He greeted everyone and held a hand out.

"Good afternoon. Passport please."

Will handed over his passport.

"Welcome home, Mr. Patterson." The man was pale as death and was sweating profusely. That worked in Will's favor, but there was one risk. The last thing he needed was this guy passing out on the plane.

"Thanks. Are you okay? Can I get you some water or something? You don't look so good."

The official waved it off. "I'm okay. It's just hot out there and we're a little busy."

Will commiserated. "I heard. We had to hold pattern for other planes to land."

"My apologies, sir." The official turned his head side to side, glancing around the plane.

"No apology necessary. It's just good to be home. Inspecting our camps and facilities in the Middle East is a bit hairy."

"I saw the stamps in your passport."

"Bet that raises eyebrows," Will joked. "We run or provide security for most of the US' facilities over there." Will figured being overtly obvious about his recent travels was a better play than acting, being coy, or trying to pull off the 'I'm sorry, can't talk about that' routine.

"Ah." The man replied. "Not often I see some of these stamps. It does raise a few alarms."

"Need to see my paperwork for the trip? Notes and stuff?" Will offered, trying to appear overly eager.

"No need. I've got three more planes after this one." The customs officer stamped the passport before handing it back. "Again, sir. Welcome home."

Will took the passport. "Thanks. Sure you don't need water?"

The man shook his head and turned to the door. "I'm fine. Thank you anyway."

Will watched the official leave before popping his head into the cockpit.

"Hey. Smooth flight, guys. Thanks."

"Not a problem. Need anything?" The pilot asked.

Will shook his head and made a show of checking his watch. "No. I'm gonna hang out in the cabin for a bit and wait for rush hour to end." Will glanced out of the windscreen. "Besides, it doesn't look like my rental is here yet."

The co-pilot looked up. "Need me to call someone about that?"

Will declined. "Nah. Thanks for the offer. I've got enough to keep me busy until it gets here. You guys enjoy your time off."

"Will do, sir."

Three hours later Will walked down the steps, wheeling the last of four massive bags to the black SUV sitting next to the plane. He placed the bag in the back, climbed behind the wheel, and headed for the airport's exit road. As he drove past the security checkpoint he yelled over his shoulder.

"We're clear."

Will's announcement was followed by the sounds of zippers being undone and grumbling. As he drove down the road, a man climbed into the front passenger seat. Will glanced at him. "You guys okay?"

The man just stared—Will could feel the eyes on him, burning into the side of his head. He could smell the guy too, but there was nothing to be done about that. Not yet anyway.

"Is there a problem?" Will didn't bother looking over.

The man in the passenger seat spoke, his voice heavily accented. "Is there a problem? We've been manacled for almost a week. We've spent the last day stuffed into cargo-holds on your jet with little food, little water, and no way to relieve ourselves and you ask if there is a problem?"

Will ignored the sarcasm. The man was justifiably angry. Will supposed he'd be angry too. "Listen. It was the only way to get you here deniably. You can be angry all you want, but I got you here." Will glanced at the man. He looked pissed.

"Where are we?"

Will gestured out of the windows. "Look around. Where do you think you are?"

The man turned, looking out of the tinted windows at the passing road signs. It took a few seconds before Will saw his eyes go wide. He turned to the back of the vehicle and spoke to his companions. Will continued driving and listened as the group conducted an energetic conversation in Arabic. The man finally turned back to Will.

"You brought us to America. Why?"

Will turned. "There's time for that later. The green bag in the back has food and water. I suggest you eat."

"But why have you…"

Will cut him off again. "Listen. We've got a two-hour drive. We can't exactly stop and get you gentlemen food and drinks. I suggest eating and hydrating. Explanations come later."

The man in the third row found the green bag, opened it, and passed snacks and bottled water forward. The man in the passenger seat collected two bottles. He opened his and took a long pull before handing the extra bottle to Will.

"Mr. Patterson. You cannot expect us to wait patiently for an explanation after telling us that you have smuggled us into America."

Will drove with his knee as he popped the top off the plastic bottle and took a drink. "How'd you guys end up in our custody?"

The man in the passenger seat smiled grimly. "We were collected by your soldiers, your naval commandos."

Will nodded. "What for?"

"For nothing. We did nothing. Just another example of…"

Will cut him off. "Cut the shit. I've seen your files. You got picked up during a raid on a bomb factory. All four of you."

"If you know this, why did you ask?"

Will ignored the question. "The men who picked you up—the naval commandos, as you call them—what do you know about them?"

The man shrugged, stuffing cheese and peanut butter crackers into his mouth. "What do you mean?"

"What I mean is this." Will jerked a thumb over his shoulder. "Two hours down that road is Coronado, California."

The man looked out the back of the SUV and back at Will. "So?"

"Coronado is home to the training center for those men who put your ass in that prison camp in Iraq."

The man in the passenger seat shrugged again—a gesture that was starting to grate on Will's nerves. "So?"

Will looked at the man. "Wouldn't you like to get even?"

The man cocked his head. "You say this is a training center for your naval commandos. We got picked up by a small handful of such men. Why would we take on an entire facility?"

Will smiled. "First, they're called SEALs. Second, they aren't armed here. Just a bunch of trainees running around the beaches."

The man nodded. "And what, exactly, would you have us do?"

"You guys are bomb-makers, right?"

"Possibly." The man replied, finishing one package of crackers and opening another.

Will smiled at the man again and got a grin in return. The man took a long pull while one of his companions peppered him with what Will assumed were questions in rapid-fire Arabic.

"What does he want?" Will asked.

"He wants to know why you are helping us."

Will kept his eyes on the road, thinking about how TitanX was going under and that this company was the only family he had left.

His blood boiled at the thought that the only people who he cared about, the people who'd given him a second shot at life, would be crushed by the uncaring politicians in Washington DC. Men busy driving a policy change to appease millions of voters who didn't live in reality, who didn't see or understand that the world was filled with dangers. "I have my reasons."

Will navigated the dark twists and turns of Proctor Valley Road. It had been a long, stressful drive from the fixed base operator to this point. Southern California traffic was notoriously bad and, on this night, had been even worse than normal. Major accidents on both major north-south interstates had pushed local traffic onto the back roads, turning what should have been a two-hour drive into a four-hour debacle.

To make matters worse, Will's passengers had never stopped questioning him. Despite his best efforts to either dodge topics outright or placate the men until they reached their destination, they'd not let up. Will couldn't blame them. If he'd been bound and gagged in a cargo hold for twenty-four hours, he'd have questions too.

Will found the turn-off, a dirt access road framed by a pair of concrete posts with a heavy chain slung between them. Will and two of his passengers manhandled the chain out of the way before driving the vehicle a few yards down the dirt road. Once inside the property, the passengers had put the chain back while Will used his feet to obscure the tire tracks at the access road's entrance. Satisfied that everything looked undisturbed, Will and his passengers climbed back into the truck and slowly drove up the dusty road.

The SUV came to a rest between a run-down, two-story farmhouse that would not have looked out of place in the rural Midwest and a large pole-barn that seemed in much better shape than the home.

Will turned to his guests. "Gentlemen. There are rooms in that house for each of you, plus clothing, showers, food, and drinks. Clean up. Change clothes. Eat. Get something to drink. I ask that you meet me in the kitchen in thirty minutes."

One man in back eyeballed the house, speaking in Arabic as he did so. The man in the front passenger seat responded and turned to Will.

"Are we prisoners here?"

Will pointed at the man's wrists. "If you were prisoners, I wouldn't have taken the cuffs off. No, gentlemen. You are free to go."

"Free?"

Will shrugged. "Sure. You may go in that house, clean up, eat, and leave. You do not have to listen to what I have to say."

"And if we just leave, you will not call the police?"

"No. I wouldn't have to. The only direction you can really go in and survive is towards San Diego. North and East of here is nothing but barren desert. Sure, there's the random town here and there, but you'd never make it that far."

The man in the passenger seat glared at Will. "And why is that?"

"Four men, with your physical appearance, this close to the Mexico border." Will shrugged again. "Hey. Feel free to take your chances, but I'll tell you. Folks this close to the border are kinda antsy, what with all the cartel violence down south. Chances are good that someone sees you and calls border patrol. And that's if you're lucky."

"If we're lucky?"

Will shrugged. "It's America, man. People here love their guns. What can I say? Folks out here see four raggedy-looking gents like you, figure you for illegals who jumped the border. Hell. They'll probably just shoot you and drag you out into the desert for coyote food."

The man thought for a second. "Or we just tell the truth about how we got here.”

"If they give you the chance, sure. You could. I wouldn't advise that."

"And why not?"

"Two reasons. First, no one would ever believe you. My organization is the largest private security firm in the world and has hundreds of millions of dollars in government contracts. You are four Islamic State operators who escaped from a prison camp. We can drown your claims pretty quickly."

"And the other reason?"

"I swapped the information in your files with the information from the files of the four men back in Guantanamo Bay."

"So?"

"So, right now, your official files say that we have no evidence you've ever committed a crime and that you should be released from US custody as soon as is practicable. A simple phone call from me explaining that in my state of exhaustion I messed up the ID procedures puts you four gentlemen right back in prison."

"We've been in prison before."

"Not for the reasons I'll add to the files." Will smiled. "Gentlemen, come in the house. Get yourselves cleaned up. Get some real food in you. Listen to my proposal. If you decide it's not worth your time, so be it. I won't stop you from leaving as long as you leave me and my organization out of it when you get caught."

After a short conversation among themselves, curiosity and full bladders won the day. All four guests stepped out of the vehicle and into the house.

★ ★ ★ ★ ★

Will and his four guests sat around the table, freshly washed and fed. One passenger reached for the pot of coffee sitting in the middle of the table and refilled his cup as Will spoke.

"Gentlemen, if you could strike at the SEAL training facility, would you do it?"

The front passenger from the long drive, a man named Farid, translated for his companions. The three men nodded as Farid answered. "Before we agree, you need to explain why you are doing this." He leaned forward. "Why should we do this for you? Why help you? Your organization runs the prison we were held in."

Will nodded. "That is true. We run that prison. It is also true that my organization is not happy with our own government."

"How so?"

"Despite what I told you before, my organization has been threatened by the government of the United States. The new president has decided to cut ties with us, a decision that will hurt thousands of my colleagues and their families."

Farid took a sip of coffee. "Mr. Patterson, have you seen what your government has done to my country? Have you seen the millions that your people have helped to hurt?"

Will nodded. "I have. Which is why I understand where you're coming from. You worked to help protect your people. To keep them safe and..."

Farid cut Will off mid-sentence. "To keep them safe from people like you. Mr. Patterson, you cannot expect us to see your situation and ours in the same light, especially when your people are the cause of our problems."

Will put his mug down on the table and looked at his guest. "I was a criminal, a prisoner like you. I was arrested for trafficking drugs into the United States and spent three years in a federal prison." Farid blinked. Will continued. "When I was released from prison, no one would give me a second chance. I had no home. No job. No money. Not even everyone at my company wanted to give me a shot. There was one guy there who fought for me, who wanted to give me a chance at building an honorable life for myself. That man will lose everything if the government closes us down."

Farid said. "I can understand and appreciate your loyalty to your people Mr. Patterson, but that still does not obligate me to help you. If we do this, wouldn't it make matters worse for my people?"

Will shook his head. "Actually, what I have in mind would drive the very people you have a problem with right into your arms."

"And how would you do this?"

"An attack on a military installation here, especially this one, shows that the Islamic State can strike at the heart of the US military. The military would have to respond by sending troops to your backyard, where you can get at them easily."

Farid lied. "But we are not Islamic State. We are..."

Will interrupted him. "First, you are Islamic State. You know it and so do I. Second, it doesn't matter. Americans won't care whether you are Islamic State or the Iraqi Boy Scouts. They'll see what you do. The FBI will figure out who you are. And those two things combined will piss people off. Enough that they'll rethink pulling out of the Middle East."

"Mr. Patterson, the whole point of a jihad is to push people like you and your kind from our lands. Why would we do something to invite more such people?"

Will grinned. "Funny. You have folks like Bin Laden, Zarqawi, Baghdadi running around saying that your duty is to strike at infidels wherever you can. It's a lot easier to do that when the infidels are in your backyard."

Farid rolled his eyes. "Two of those men are dead."

"So's the third."

Farid shrugged. "Possibly. Baghdadi has been declared dead before. Ask your CIA."

"That doesn't change anything." Will pointed out.

"It doesn't?"

"Those men were martyrs to your cause. From what I understand, that's some sacred shit. You'd have to be a pretty cold bastard to ignore that."

"I don't see how this helps your organization. The response you're talking about wouldn't save your company."

Will nodded. "Farid. Saving the company is someone else's job. This operation is strictly personal."

Farid nodded. Will knew the man across from him had joined ISIS after a wayward American drone strike had killed his wife and infant son. "Mr. Patterson, that is something I understand. Not necessarily a sound strategy, but I can understand. If we were to accept this mission, how would we strike at the training camp in Coronado?"

Will explained, describing his idea and outlining an inventory of the materials stored in the barn forty yards away. When he finished, Farid smiled at him.

"Anything else, Mr. Patterson?"

Will reached into a pocket and pulled out a piece of paper. He handed it to Farid. "That is a transcript of an interview."

Farid scanned the paper. Finished, he looked up. "And?"

"In there you admit to having contacts in Norfolk."

Farid folded the paper and set it in front of Will. "I have many contacts, Mr. Patterson."

Will leaned forward and tapped the paper. "But this one works in the shipyards. For the Navy. Who is he?"

Farid thought for a moment. "What do you need with him?"

"Does it matter?"

Farid shook his head. "His name is Calvin. Calvin Robinson."

"Who is he, Farid?"

"Former Navy. He's an engineer who we trained to make bombs. IEDs. We recruited him in college."

Will grinned. "How do I contact him?"

An hour later, Will ended his call to Norfolk and dialed an international number. The phone rang once before it was answered by a man thousands of miles away.

"Yes."

Will smiled into the night. "Your work order is approved."

"When is work to begin?"

"Immediately."

The line clicked off.

19

JOUDA

IBRAHIM JOUDA STARED at the phone in his hand. His brain worked to process the information he had. He was being directed to attack and destroy the American prison camp at Umm Qasr. That wasn't surprising. He and his team had considered that target before. What was shocking him was how the operation had come into being.

Almost a month ago, he'd met an American who'd promised that this opportunity would come to fruition. The same man had provided an entire backpack full of intelligence on the target—maps, blueprints, watch schedules, armaments—with three conditions. Ibrahim's team was to free every prisoner at the site. They were to burn the entire facility to the ground. They were to leave none of the staff alive.

The same American—a man who called himself Jason—had just, over the phone, given his operation a green light.

Ibrahim sat on the steps of his home in Basra and thought. Could this be a trap? He'd considered that possibility before taking the proposed operation to his leadership. Technically, as the operational commander for Islamic State forces in the region, he hadn't needed to do that, but trust did not come easily to Ibrahim—especially not when the person providing you the intelligence was an American employee of the company responsible for the target's very existence.

The council had voted unanimously for the proposed operation, providing almost one-hundred additional men and an array of operational planners for the strike, the latter being largely unnecessary. There was only one viable way to attack this target and it did not take a military genius to plan that operation.

Despite the council's eager support of the proposal, Ibrahim still had reservations. He had not yet been able to discern the American's motivation to help his organization. He'd pressed the American at every opportunity and had, once, been given only the vaguest of answers.

The man, Jason, had claimed to be unsatisfied with his government's actions. Ibrahim had pushed for more, trying to discover some deeper answer. His efforts proved futile. The American never broached the subject and ignored any comment or question Ibrahim had posed on the matter.

In the end, Ibrahim had decided that it wasn't necessary to understand the man's motivations. It wasn't unheard of for Americans to be dissatisfied with their own government and westerners joining the cause wasn't without precedent. The American was angry. And, as Ibrahim well knew, anger at the western world was a most useful tool.

If successful, his organization would claim responsibility for the attack. They'd praise Allah while the media specialists would work their magic and launch another recruiting campaign using video made during the assault. He knew that the propaganda value alone was worth taking on the operation, but that didn't answer his question. Why was the American helping us? Ibrahim decided that he'd probably never find out.

Ibrahim had little need for religion, at least not the kind preached to the young zealots. He'd grown out of his youthful fanaticism a long time ago. There was a God and He had a plan for Ibrahim, a calling to use his knowledge and skills to help the followers of Islam. It was that simple. He didn't need—had little desire to hear—the angry calls for vengeance and retribution. It was enough for him to keep the corrupting influences of the western world at bay. He saw little need—or legitimacy—in strategies that involved pursuing his enemies beyond his own borders. Publicly, he'd recite the mantras about how this was Allah's will. But that was performance art. What he believed now, after nearly two decades of fighting—first with Al Qaeda and now with the Islamic State—was that the formation of a caliphate was necessary. Not because God wanted one, but because his people needed their own land. A place to be secure, a place where his culture could be left alone—unaffected by, and protected from, outside influences.

To Ibrahim, the concept of jihad had morphed from some vaguely misunderstood religious duty to a mission of necessity. His people were persecuted and corrupted everywhere they went. They needed their own place, somewhere they could call home and be free of the mindless distractions and threats posed by the outside world.

"That doesn't answer your question about the American," Ibrahim muttered quietly. "And now you sound like an Israeli." He chuckled at himself as the door opened behind him.

"Telling yourself jokes again, Ibrahim?" A hand came down on his shoulder. Ibrahim looked to his right to see his friend plop down on the steps beside him.

"No, Kasim. Just thinking."

"Good."

Ibrahim cocked his head at Kasim. "Good?"

Kasim's arm dropped across Ibrahim's shoulders. "Yes. Good. Thinking is good." He poked Ibrahim in the chest. "You thinking is very good. You not telling yourself jokes is something to praise Allah for."

Ibrahim narrowed his eyes. "Why?"

Kasim grinned, his white teeth contrasting with a heavy black beard. "Because, my friend, you are not funny."

Ibrahim turned. "My children think I'm funny."

Kasim was beaming. "They'll learn better." Kasim glanced at the phone in Ibrahim's hand. "What does your American say?"

"He says the operation should go forward."

"Good."

Ibrahim removed the battery from the phone and looked at Kasim. "Is it? Is it good? Why is this man helping us?"

"Does it matter?"

"What do you mean?"

"Ibrahim, the council thinks it is worth the risk. If the information is accurate, as it appears to be based on reports from our own people, the operation will be a success."

"And if the information is wrong?"

Kasim shrugged. "Then, inshallah, we will all be martyrs and the media people will have different videos to release. Either way, we win."

"I don't like not knowing what this man is up to."

"Me either, Ibrahim. But you have no control over that. You do have control of almost two hundred of the faithful, all willing and ready to execute the plan we've spent two weeks developing. It'd be a shame to tell everyone to go home."

Ibrahim nodded. "You're right, as usual. Are the men ready?"

Kasim smiled warmly. "Of course. We can be on the road in two hours."

Ibrahim nodded, his mind drifting elsewhere again. He stared at the powerless phone in his hands. "Get them moving. Everyone to their starting positions."

Kasim nodded, clapped him on the shoulder again. "It will be fine, Ibrahim. You'll see."

★ ★ ★ ★ ★

Alex O'Neil leaned forward on his desk and looked at his watch, a venerable old Casio G-Shock. He rubbed his eyes with his knuckles, a habit that felt therapeutic but had to be bad on the corneas. It was late and he was tired. He'd spent the better part of his day inspecting the massive detention camp. His staff, which he thought undersized for the needs placed on them, had implemented every corrective action recommended by Patterson's report and today's tour had verified that every aspect of the guard staff's performance was up to the high standards demanded by corporate headquarters.

A knock on the door didn't stop him from rubbing the exhaustion out of his eyes.

"Yeah?"

The door opened and a head poked through the gap. "Alex? You busy?"

Alex shook his head and waved his operations officer into a seat. The man, a forty-year-old former Army cop named Lee Weaver, looked as exhausted as Alex felt. "What's up, Lee?"

"Remember the foul-up a couple days ago with the eight detainees?" Weaver had a bit of southern drawl that almost two decades of military service and private security deployments hadn't quite erased.

Alex nodded. "Yeah. Will looked like shit after being in the air that long."

"That he did." Lee confirmed. "Poor bastard spent what? Three days straight in a plane?"

"Closer to five if you count the trip back to California."

"Five days in a fuckin' plane? The hell with that. Longest I ever spent on a plane was the hop here, and that was broken up over two days."

"World's a big damn place," Alex noted. "Was there something you had for me?"

Lee blinked and looked down at a notebook he'd carried into the office. "Yeah. Sorry. The detainee count came up four short today and I can't find the four guys Will brought back. Today was the first day I should've had them back on my count, what with processing and all. But I can't find 'em." Lee handed over the transfer documents for the men.

Alex sat up in his chair and accepted the paperwork. He wasn't alarmed. It wasn't unusual for the detainees to play games during the counts. In a place where the prisoners had no contact with the outside world and little in the way of love or respect for their captors, harassing the guards and making life difficult for them was the sport of choice. Alex explained that to his operations officer, forgetting that the man in front of him already knew it.

"Alex, I'm sure you're right, I just haven't had the chance to do a proper search and the evening reports are due to you in a half-hour."

"I appreciate the heads up. Go ahead with the search and let me know what you find. I'm gonna rack out when I'm done here." Alex stood to shake Lee's hand, folding the papers and tucking them into a pocket. He'd file them later.

"Will do." Lee stood to leave the room, eyeing his boss. "You okay?"

"I'm good. Been a long day. May have to strangle the idiot who writes my schedule."

Lee's forehead wrinkled in confusion. He started to respond, but was interrupted when the radio on Alex's desk crackled to life.

"Mercury Six, Mercury Two-Two. We're taking sustained harassing fire from the rocks north of our position."

Lee turned to the radio. Mercury Two-Two was one of the external patrols wandering the area immediately outside of the fence line. Aside from serving as a visible, physical deterrent, the mounted, sixteen-man patrol served as a tripwire, triggering the occasional attack before the opposition was ready to launch.

Receiving harassing fire was an occupational hazard for the staff at the camp—even more so, both men knew, for the roving patrols. For as long as either man could remember, local insurgents had gathered to take weekly pot-shots at the men guarding the camp, a hazard that had resulted in casualties over the years.

The report of harassing fire wouldn't normally get more than cursory attention from two of the camp's top employees—the individual team leads and watch commanders were all more than capable. It just wasn't often that the incoming fire was reported as 'sustained'.

As Alex and Lee listened in, the watch commander—Mercury Six—got on the net and directed the response.

★ ★ ★ ★ ★

Ibrahim crouched low among the rocks above Camp Mercury's east side, viewing the camp through a powerful set of binoculars taken from the remains of an American convoy his men had ambushed the previous year. He was less concerned about this operation than he'd been four hours earlier. The American's information had been accurate. The camp's security force guarded the open areas to the west and south of the camp, leaving the hills and cliffs to the north and east to do the heavy lifting in those sectors.

In the notes he'd received, the American had pointed out that, while the camp staff knew there were paths and routes through the hills, they didn't believe that a large enough force could move through the area to pose any great threat to the camp itself. Instead, the notes went on, the security detachment relied on motion sensors set throughout the rocks to provide any early warning.

The American had appended his notes with maps on which every motion detector was identified. Red circles on the map indicated the maximum effective radius of each detector. Using the map, Ibrahim and twenty of his men had spent the last two hours creeping through the rocky outcroppings, either dodging each sensor like a group of master thieves or disabling them. Ibrahim had worried about doing that, certain that severing the power to the sensors would set off an alarm. The American had assured him that this was not the case.

Once in position, Ibrahim had directed his group to their positions. He'd broken his team into groups of four—two heavy machine guns and a two-man mortar team per section—each of which had a specific sector of the base to target. When his teams were in position, weapons at the ready, he'd contacted Kasim with permission to initiate the attack.

Ibrahim covered his watch with a hand and pressed a button to light the face. Four minutes had elapsed since the first shots had been fired. Ibrahim could hear gunfire from one of Kasim's teams in the distance. He counted off the seconds silently as he raised a pair of binoculars to his eyes.

According to the intelligence reports, the patrol under fire would be talking to the command post and would be directed to push out, away from the camp to drive the threat away. Ibrahim couldn't see Kasim's team, but he could see the patrol under fire. Another four-vehicle patrol was idling near the camp's main entrance, just waiting for...

"There." Ibrahim whispered to himself. Through his glasses, he could see the secondary patrol break into two elements and advance, moving away from the camp.

As the patrol moved off, a third four-vehicle patrol took up the original force's position. Ibrahim checked his watch again. Six minutes in. The advancing patrol would be engaging Kasim's men now and when they did...

Through the cool night air, the sound of gunfire intensified. What had been the sporadic sound of a few AK-47s was replaced by the sound of heavy machine gun fire as Kasim's original shooters had been joined by twenty others, each of whom operated old, but reliable, DShK 12.7mm guns.

As Kasim's DShK emplacements shredded the mobile patrol, Ibrahim turned to the crew nearest him and waved.

Wumpf.

The first mortar round headed down range and was followed immediately by the sounds of additional rounds from the other three teams—each of which had a list of targets, complete with the adjustments each of the 82mm mortars would require to shift fires.

★ ★ ★ ★ ★

What the hell?

Moments before, just after he'd heard the surge in gunfire and the screams from Mercury Two-Two, he'd heard several muffled thumps—barely audible against the background noise.

"Mortars incoming!" A voice on the radio had screamed as the telltale whistling of the shells became audible. Alex and Lee dove to the deck as the first round hit less than fifty yards from Alex's office.

Alex hugged the ground as the overpressure wave from the first blast blew the glass from his window across the room. He pushed his face into the gritty floor as hard as he could as several more explosions rocked the camp.

A brief lull in the shelling allowed Alex to look up. On the other side of his overturned desk, he could see Lee crumpled on the floor and unmoving. Alex crept around the desk, staying low.

Lee was unconscious—a massive bruise was forming on the right side of the man's face. Alex shook his head. His ears were ringing and he had a pounding headache. Outside, the thumps and whistles of mortar fire had been replaced by the crackling of automatic weapons fire and the constant snapping and smacking noises of bullets slamming into the structures nearby. It briefly crossed Alex's mind that the fire wasn't coming from the same place it was earlier—that it sounded closer and higher than before. He pushed the thought aside as he raised himself into a crouch and hefted Lee's limp form from the dirty floor.

★ ★ ★ ★ ★

Ibrahim's mortar teams were shifting fire as the machine-gun sections raked the prison camp's staff structures with thousands of rounds—each man with carefully selected, overlapping fields of fire that avoided the portions of the compound housing inmates.

Off in the distance, Kasim's teams had destroyed the first sixteen-man roving patrol and were engaging the second, third, and fourth roving patrols.

From his position, high in the rocky outcroppings, Ibrahim could see the camp's staff scrambling. Everyone he saw was scurrying around—trying to avoid the withering fire from Ibrahim's position. Very few of the defenders were working to engage their tormentors.

Ibrahim looked down the line to his right and got the signal that the mortars were prepared for the next volley. He nodded at the figure in the dark and—within seconds—was rewarded with the renewed sounds of 82mm high-explosive ordnance being sent downrange.

★ ★ ★ ★ ★

Alex was halfway out the door, with Lee slung over one shoulder, when the second volley of mortars began falling in the camp. Hanging on tight to the body of his still unconscious operations chief, Alex sprinted to cover, heading for a reinforced concrete alcove just fifteen yards from his half-destroyed office.

Mortars rained down on the camp, sending showers of dirt, bits of concrete, and shards of lumber and shrapnel slicing through the air. Bullets peppered the area, raking the ground at Alex's feet as he half-ran, half-stumbled to relative safety.

Alex was ten feet from the alcove when a mortar round hit the structure. The explosion blew him backwards, slamming him into a pile of rocks that he'd just passed in his dash for safety. He felt a flash of pain in his back when he made contact with the rocks, knowing instantly he'd broken something.

Alex's world spun as he laid at the base of the rocks. With his head lolling to one side, he could see the guard towers along the main fence line burning in the distance. The only sound his brain could process was the deep ringing in both ears.

Alex tried to get up, but realized that his legs weren't working. As the shells and bullets razed the camp, showering him with more dirt and debris, he tried to turn his head to look around. A stabbing pain gripped his neck and shot down his left side and his neck begrudgingly made a ratcheting turn, shattered bones cutting into nerves and muscle as his head rotated.

Off in the distance, he could see a fire raging in the camp—the flames licking up the sides of buildings that were all but destroyed.

An object on the ground between Alex and the nearest fire caught his attention—something he couldn't quite make out. He commanded his eyes to blink rapidly, trying to generate tears to wash out caked up dirt.

The object looked long and cylindrical, starting close by and reaching off into the distance. As Alex's vision cleared, he became aware that it was someone's arm. He blinked. A watch. On the wrist. Lee's watch. Alex's one working arm reached out to haul his injured employee behind the rocks.

The arm moved easily as Alex pulled. Too easily.

Alex had just enough time to realize that it was Lee's arm—and only the arm—before one last mortar landed directly on top of the rocky outcropping where his half-paralyzed body lay.

Ibrahim's team had released the four hundred inmates of Camp Mercury after ensuring that every guard was dead. The orders had been clear on that. Leave no one alive.

The orders had been clear on one other point. Burn the entire facility to the ground. Nothing was to survive. Not a single document at the camp, hard-copy or electronic, was to be recoverable.

Ibrahim looked on as the one hundred and eighty-nine remaining members of his force moved through the camp one last time, burning and destroying everything except the food and weapons they would be leaving with.

Satisfied that his orders were being executed properly, he turned and pulled a small cell phone and battery out of the thigh pocket of his pants. He placed the battery in the phone and held the power button until the phone began its booting process. When the small screen on the phone indicated that the device was ready for use, he dialed a number from memory. After three rings, a familiar voice answered.

"Yes?"

"Mercury."

The phone clicked off.

Ibrahim smiled.

20

WATKINS

RAY HAD WOKEN UP—after too little sleep—with a low-grade migraine and a stiff neck. Despite the aching skull and soreness, the sixty-three-year-old businessman and former soldier had rolled out of bed at an ungodly hour to begin a breakfast and exercise routine prescribed by his doctor and ruthlessly enforced by his wife and oldest daughter.

After choking down a protein shake—a strawberry flavor that he joked was more straw than berry—he'd stretched and gone through a series of body-weight exercises similar to those he'd done for twenty years in the Army. When he'd completed that part of his routine—something his father had always called 'setting up'—he'd walked into the garage and jumped on the treadmill.

That is where his morning routine had ceased to be routine. Ray had struggled through the first two miles of his morning run and was just congratulating himself on not quitting when the shoelace on his left foot had let go.

The shoe had loosened within a few paces despite Ray's best efforts to alter his stride and keep the shoe in place. Instead of stopping the treadmill and fixing the shoe, Ray had attempted to pull the shoe back into place in mid-stride. For a few awkward paces, the fix worked. By performing an absurd-looking, one-legged, high-knee maneuver, Ray had actually slapped the shoe back in place. When he tried to use the same awkward stride to yank what was left of the laces tight, the wheels fell off.

In mid-stride, with his left knee almost waist-high and the treadmill set to maintain an eight-minute mile pace, he'd misjudged his grab at the dangling shoestring, tangling one of his fingers in the mess of laces crisscrossing the top of the sneaker. Sensing danger, he'd immediately attempted to jerk his hand clear of the flat, orange laces.

In his desperate attempt to remove his entangled fingers, he'd pulled the shoe off his left foot, stopping the appendage in mid-stride. His brain, sensing the impending disaster, flung the shoeless foot out too far and too wide. The stride, already off balance, placed half of his foot on the carbon-fiber side of the treadmill while the other half touched down on the spinning tread.

Ray had wobbled momentarily before tripping and falling onto the moving track. His torso made the briefest of contact before his whole, one-hundred-and-seventy-pound frame was launched into a pile of cardboard boxes.

His wife heard the crash and had run into the garage to see her husband lying upside down amid the detritus of another household goods move, fingers still entwined in the bright orange laces of his left shoe. To Ray, that had been bad enough. What made it unbearable was the way she'd broken down in hysterical laughter after verifying that he was no worse for wear.

The subsequent two hours hadn't been any better.

Ray's driver had shown up with his morning ration of intelligence reports and coffee twenty minutes later than normal after a pair of wrecks had forced him into a lengthy detour. Ray was halfway through a follow-up report describing an attack on a Pakistani military site when he'd reached down and grabbed the paper cup of coffee and raised it to his lips. While the length of the drive had ensured that the coffee had cooled from nuclear to merely scalding, it did nothing to ensure that the lid stayed securely in place. Ray had tipped the cup to his lips and was rewarded with a lap full of scorching hot, drip-brewed coffee.

That was why Raymond Watkins, National Security Advisor to the President of the United States, now stood in his corner office in the west wing of the White House in his boxers and t-shirt. As he struggled into the spare suit he'd stashed at the office, he glanced at the wall clock. He was late for a briefing with the president and he still hadn't finished reading his morning material. That the reports were now as coffee stained as the shirt, coat, and pants piled on the floor was—for the moment—forgotten.

Ray got himself together after a brief struggle. He checked his tie in a mirror and used one hand to verify that he had, mercifully, remembered to zip his fly while the other hand punched the intercom. "Tell the president I'm on my way."

"Yes, sir." The line clicked off.

Ray grabbed an armful of stained briefing folders and raced out the door.

The president put the report down and eyed his advisors warily. His Secretary of Defense smiled back.

"Based on this, you're saying that the withdrawal will begin when?" The president pointed to the document in front of him.

SECDEF put his coffee cup, a wide-bottomed affair with a presidential seal on one side, down. "As early as next month is possible, but not necessary. We should stick to the original plan. These places are in good shape, relatively speaking, but ghosting them a few weeks early might cause problems with each country's internal timetable."

The president looked up. "Ghosting?"

Tolchanov smiled. "Sorry sir. A phrase my kids use. Apparently, it's a term for a break up where nothing is said. One of the people just vanishes. No 'Dear John' or anything. Just radio silence."

Evans grinned. "There are a few people I wish I could have ghosted over the years."

SECDEF nodded. "Old girlfriends?"

"Admirals." The president stretched. "Of course, going radio silent on Fleet Forces Command with a thirty-billion-dollar ship and ninety-odd cruise missiles probably isn't a great career move."

The Chief of Staff looked up from his own copy of the withdrawal briefing. "Didn't one of our submarine commanders do something like that once?"

Evans nodded. "Back in the late nineties. One of our boomers was reported to have left its patrol area without informing anyone."

Barnes looked up. "Seriously?"

"That was the report. USS Florida, I think. Squadron commander issued the usual statement about being unable to confirm or deny the report."

"Jesus."

The president shrugged. "It happens. I left my patrol area hundreds of times."

"Without telling anyone?" Tolchanov said.

"Well, no. But I wasn't carrying part of the strategic nuclear arsenal."

"Doesn't that make it worse?" Barnes asked.

"Not really. Boomers aren't supposed to be a visible deterrent. The idea behind carrier battle groups is that they project power clearly. Like the big-ass bouncer at a bar. You know he's there and you try to behave. These boats are meant to be invisible. Like the monsters under the bed."

"But leaving the patrol zone?"

"Most likely came across a stray submarine and moved out of the area to avoid detection."

Barnes shook his head. Tolchanov grinned. "Leslie. Just think of it as hide and seek with nuclear weapons."

Barnes rolled his eyes. "Do me a favor, guys?"

The president and SECDEF looked up at the rumpled man.

"Leave that comparison out of any press briefings?"

Regina Kelly added her voice to the conversation for the first time. "I second that request, gentlemen." She turned to the Secretary of the Treasury, a sixty-five-year-old graduate of American University. "Cathy, are these figures right?"

Cathy Bettencourt nodded. "Been over them a few times. CBO and OMB both agree on these estimates. Looks like we actually end up saving quite a bit of money. Everyone involved noted that the maintenance and replacement costs for previously deployed units will drop significantly once they're back stateside. Even with the proposed increases in training time."

"Leslie, is this something we want to point out during a briefing or are we letting the press discover this on their own?" Evans said.

"As much as I'd love to wave the flag about this cost savings, this isn't the time. This is about troops coming home and trusting these places to govern themselves. That's the message." Barnes paused. "Maybe we can arrange a convenient leak or two in a few weeks, but for now, let's not go there."

The door had opened halfway through the Chief of Staff's opinion, admitting a frazzled National Security Advisor. Ray arranged his papers and turned to the president. "My apologies Mr. President."

Evans waved it off. "I heard you've had quite the morning, Ray."

"You could say that. Fell off the treadmill. Dumped liquid magma on myself in the car."

Alice Freytag laughed. "Video or it didn't happen."

"I'll refer you to my wife for the first incident and my driver for the rest." Ray smiled. "On second thought, just talk to the driver. My wife is probably still laughing her ass off."

Evans leaned forward. "How, exactly, do you fall off of a treadmill? I've seen it on video, but never in person."

"It's complicated." Ray demurred. "Where are we?"

"Dodging my question, Ray?" The president asked with barely concealed glee.

The National Security Advisor stiffened. "Not at all sir. It's just a matter of national security and not all of the characters in this room have a need to know."

The president looked around. "They are a pretty shady bunch."

"Who among us hasn't pitched an operation to sabotage Mr. Watkins' sneakers to the Chinese or random terrorist groups?" Kelly said.

Ray's head snapped up. "How in the hell do you know about my shoes?"

"I haven't." Freytag ignored Ray. "Although there was a guy at a bar a couple weeks ago. Kept asking the odd question about Ray's shoes. How thick were the laces? How many eyelets? That kind of thing. Maybe I should have turned him in?" She shrugged.

"What did I do to deserve this?" Ray asked.

The staff broke into laughter for a few seconds before the president waved his hand. "Alright folks. I think that's enough fun at Ray's expense this morning. Ray, we were just discussing the withdrawal plans and schedule. Any new concerns?"

"No sir. Israel is making some noise, but Jack," Ray nodded to the Secretary of State, "is handling that. India is still pissed about the most recent incidents, but they're not trying to lay this at our feet. They're sticking to the script and blaming Pakistan for all of their troubles."

"And threatening retaliation. Don't forget that. The Indian PM has gone the 'eye for an eye' route on each of his last three press statements regarding Pakistan." SECSTATE leaned forward from his position on the couch. "Ray's correct on Israel. They are voicing the expected concerns. We're abandoning them, leaving them at the altar. That kind of thing. I've had several conversations with Prime Minister Baratz about this. He'll continue to voice his concerns in public, mostly because that's what his constituency expects. In private, he'll make sure the leadership there knows we still support him."

Evans nodded. "Do we need to make public statements on the issue?"

"No, sir." SECSTATE shook his head. "We're good."

"A bitching sailor is a happy sailor?" Evans said.

A nod. "Something like that Mr. President."

The president turned back to Ray. "DNI Adams says the area is fairly quiet lately, except for Kashmir that is. Thoughts?"

Ray leaned back. "I agree with her. We don't hear much out of the region that sounds threatening. It is always a possibility that bad folks over there have gone radio-silent ahead of some attack, but I don't think that's the case. This feels different."

"Like everyone took a step back after our announcement to take a breath and think?" SECSTATE asked. "I got the same impression talking to everyone during the transition and after the inauguration. There's almost a sense of relief that we're leaving."

"Except for Israel, the dust-up in Pakistan, and the ongoing issues in Kashmir?" asked the president.

Ray nodded. "And that dust-up in Pakistan appears to be a one off. ISIS claimed responsibility and put a predictable spin on the op. Claimed it was a real bomb. Inflated casualty counts."

"Why attack a training facility?" Barnes asked.

Ray turned. "Simplest answer is that the facility was an easy target. Not much in the way of security and they can get away with claiming to have walked off with a real bomb."

Barnes looked up from his notes. "How's that?"

SECSTATE fielded that question. "They'll build their own bomb using the training case and then film themselves placing it somewhere. When the attack goes off, their propaganda machine will play up last week's attack and theft and make a big deal out of killing infidels or apostates with their own weapon."

"You know," Evans said. "This isn't gonna help Pakistan convince the world that their nuclear arsenal is secure. Sure, it was a training site. This time. The public perception is going to be that a nation that can't protect a training site doesn't have the capability to adequately protect a real one. What if these people go after one of those next?"

"I agree, sir. DNI Adams probably has some data on the subject." Ray looked around. "Where is Ophelia?"

"She had to step out about ten minutes before you got here. She'll be back soon." Said Barnes. He looked at his watch. "Mr. President, you have an appointment in five minutes."

The president looked over his shoulder to the antique clock on his desk. "Fair enough. Alright folks. We'll pick this up tomorrow. Cathy?"

"Yes, Mr. President?"

"Get with Leslie and schedule a time for me to go over the CBO and OMB numbers again."

"Yes, sir."

★ ★ ★ ★ ★

Ray made the short walk back to his office, stopping to ask his executive assistant about the day's remaining schedule.

"Sir, you're free until ten. That's a meeting with DNI Adams. It's a working lunch."

"Good. I'll have time to finish reading all of this." Ray shook the stained, mostly dry, folders in his hand.

"Yes, sir."

The staffer was eyeing him. Ray let out an exasperated breath. "I'm fine, James. Seriously. Just a few bruises."

"Yes, sir."

There was an edge to the man's voice that Ray mistook for nerves. "What?"

"Nothing, sir. It's nothing." James Martin turned back to his computer.

Ray shook his head and crossed to his door. He shoved the door open, took two steps, and stopped dead.

"James!"

The executive assistant walked in with a barely concealed look of mirth on his face. Watkins glared at him. "Mr. Martin. What, exactly, do I pay you for?"

The man was still grinning. "Run the shop for you."

"Very funny. I suppose since you're running the shop, you can explain all of this." Ray gestured wildly.

Inside his office, on nearly every horizontal, antique surface, were eighty pairs of running shoes—each with the laces done up in overly fantastic bows.

Martin could barely contain his laughter. Ray rolled his eyes and moved towards the desk—tossing the three pairs of shoes sitting there on a couch. "Alright, Mr. Martin. Very funny."

"I'll get the owners to collect their shoes, sir."

"I should have them taken to the incinerator." Ray grumbled to himself. Louder, he asked, "Whose idea was this?"

"Sorry, sir. I'm not at liberty to say."

"Thought so. Get her on the phone and collect the shoes for their owners."

"Yes, sir." Martin headed out to the anteroom. In twenty seconds, his voice came over the intercom. "DNI Adams on line two, sir."

Watkins picked up the handset and pressed the appropriate button. "Morning, Ophelia."

"Good morning, Ray."

"Very funny."

"Thought you'd like it."

"What'd you do, raid the White House gym?"

"And the one at OEOB." She meant the Old Executive Office Building. "How are you feeling?"

"I'll live. Tiffany put you up to this?"

"Let's just say she inspired my..." The DNI stopped talking. Ray could hear murmuring on the other end of the line. When her voice came back, the playful tone was gone. "Ray? Can you meet me at the Situation Room in five minutes?"

"Sure, what's up?"

"We're getting word of an attack in Iraq. A prison camp near Umm Qasr. All inmates freed, all staff KIA. That's all I have. See you in five."

★ ★ ★ ★ ★

Everyone in the Situation Room stood as the president entered and took his seat at the head of a heavy, oaken table piled high with papers, tablets, and phones. Evans glanced around the room at the series of electronic displays and flat screen televisions that covered more than sixty percent of the wood-paneled surfaces in the room.

"Alright people. What have you got?"

SECDEF nodded to a two-star standing at the opposite end of the table. The general, whose name the president didn't know yet, cleared his throat.

"Mr. President. At approximately 2140 local time, an insurgent force attacked and destroyed a detention facility near Umm Qasr, Iraq. At the time, Camp Mercury housed some four-hundred detainees, all of which were released by the attacking force. Every member of the camp's staff was KIA and…"

"General," Evans interrupted, "how many soldiers are we talking about?"

"Mr. President. There were only two active military personnel on site. The other sixty-five staffers were private contractors—employees of TitanX Security. We spoke with the Operations Director at TitanX," the general looked down at his notes, "a Mr. Paul Burkhart. He believes that several of his employees were guardsmen or reservists. He's working to get that information to us as we speak."

"ISIS?" Asked Ray.

The general nodded. "They have claimed responsibility, sir. They released a video montage of the attack about thirty minutes ago."

"Mr. President, that means that this will hit the major news networks in short order," Barnes said.

"How does that affect the withdrawal?"

"It'll cause some concern," the Chief of Staff opined. "But, it's just one incident and this facility has been attacked before, if my memory serves me."

Tolchanov nodded. "That's right. They get harassing fire on a weekly basis and the facility has been assaulted three times in the last two years. Usually just a couple dozen guys with small arms. This video shows mortars and heavy machine guns firing down into the camp."

Evans chewed on the eraser end of a pencil. "Okay. It's still early. Leslie, I need you and Regina working on a statement. Frank, you and the general have notifications to make. Leslie, I'll need call sheets for the families of everyone we lost today and a phone conversation set up with the owner of TitanX. Am I forgetting anything?"

Barnes shook his head. "No. The statement will be standard stuff. Our thoughts are with the families. This doesn't affect getting our troops back and we fully support the local, democratically-elected representatives of the people as they deal with the perpetrators. Something along those lines."

The general raised his hand awkwardly, an action he'd not performed in a long time. "Mr. President?"

"Yes, General?"

"About the notifications..."

The president held a hand up. "The military and the leadership at TitanX will make the notifications. I won't be calling anyone until I've gotten confirmation that they have been notified by their leadership first. Fair?"

"Thank you, Mr. President."

Evans looked at his watch. "Alright. Leslie, twenty minutes on the statement?"

"Faster, if I can manage it."

"Twenty minutes is fine. It'll take that long for Steve to do the make-up." Evans stood. "Alright folks. Back here in two hours, unless something else breaks loose. Let's get to work."

21

RODRIGUEZ

SEAMAN TIMOTHY RODRIGUEZ'S ARMS GAVE OUT, dropping him face-first into the moist sands of Coronado. As he struggled to push his soaking-wet and sand-encrusted body back up into a push-up position, a pair of boots entered his field of vision. A low, gritty voice spoke.

"Rodriguez, why are you putting up with this shit? Come on, dude. You can't even push your body up off the sand."

Rodriguez grunted and squirmed, concentrating as hard as he could on straightening both arms. Neither was complying. He almost got his left side up and had just extended a wobbly right arm when he lost control of his left arm. There was a moment where he thought he had this push-up under control despite the fire raging in each of his shoulders and a violent shaking that racked his body. Rodriguez felt the sand giving way beneath his hands right before both arms collapsed.

The boots to his left shifted as the instructor squatted down, the voice barely a whisper.

"Seriously, Rodriguez. You're holding your entire boat crew up. Why are you still here?"

Rodriguez's mind processed the question as he tried to force his arms to do what his brain demanded. The soft voice of the instructor pleaded with him. "Got an idea for you. Ring the bell and I'll get you out of here."

Rodriguez turned his head slightly, looking at the instructor as the deal got sweetened.

"Seriously, Rod. I can get you a good meal, a hot shower, and a nice, soft bed. C'mon man, think about it. Pizza. An ice-cold coke. Hell, man. Maybe even a heated blanket. When's the last time you were warm?"

When was the last time? Rodriguez couldn't count the days. He wasn't even sure what day it was.

Hell Week, a rite of passage for every US Navy SEAL, had started with breakout Sunday evening—a maddeningly disorienting event that started with the instructors breaching the classroom where class 505 was gathered watching Old Yeller. What had been a quiet evening evaporated in a few moments of gunfire, yelling, and high-pitched whistling. Since that moment—when every molecule of Rodriguez's being had been jolted from a quiet peace to a constant state of manic motion—time had become almost irrelevant. All that mattered was getting through the next sixty seconds. For Rodriguez, that was becoming as difficult for him as it had been for so many before him. The BUD/S—Basic Underwater Demolitions/SEAL—class had started Sunday evening with eighty-six students, each believing then that they had what it took. Now—after days of punishment and sleeplessness—only thirty-three remained.

Rodriguez pushed the thoughts out of his head and focused on the task immediately in front of him—completing the prescribed punishment of twenty-five push-ups. In the BUD/S world—where failure was defined as anything not resulting in a win—his boat crew had failed to perform. They'd finished last, or second-to-last, in every single race today and were subject to whatever consequences the instructors deemed appropriate.

After the first race, they'd done twenty-five push-ups after turning themselves into sugar cookies—a process that included diving in the surf before rolling around in the sand to ensure that every part of their person was covered in the coarse-grit sand. After the second race, they'd done sit ups—sitting in two, four-man rows while balancing their small, rubber craft on their hands. After the third race, they'd been sent into a make-shift pool of ice water in the back of a monstrous truck named Old Blue before being directed to complete twenty-five additional push-ups.

The rest of Rodriguez's crew had completed this most recent

course of twenty-five push-ups and were now resting, waiting for their struggling teammate. Rodriguez's arms had given out after twenty-four repetitions and his struggle had attracted the attention of the nearest instructor, a man now offering him some pretty irresistible options.

"C'mon Rod. You really don't have to put up with four more days of this. You really don't."

Rodriguez adjusted, got his arms back under him before his brain flashed a warning. Four more days? Haven't we been out here for four days? What day is it?

The instructor saw the hesitation and confusion on Rodriguez's sand-covered face and smiled behind a pitch-black pair of Oakleys. "You thought we were almost done, didn't you?" He made a show of checking his watch. "Hell, Rod. It's only Monday. We got all day today. And Tuesday. And Wednesday." The soft, reasonable voice trailed off.

Rodriguez's brain was firing erratically now. Monday? That leaves five days. It can't be Monday? Can it? Doesn't matter. Do the push-up. Both arms. Up. He shoved, growling and grunting. He made it halfway up before collapsing again. The voice returned.

"That was so close, Rod. Almost got it. Those arms gotta be burning by now. What about the shoulders? When I finished Hell Week, I always remembered how my shoulders felt." The instructor got down beside Rodriguez and cranked out a few push-ups. "Yeah, good times."

Rodriguez tried to block out the thoughts. It couldn't be Monday. It had to be Wednesday. Didn't it? A bed. A shower. Sounds nice. Fuck that. A push up. Just one push up. But a shower does sound nice. Rodriguez shook his head. Just one damn push up and you can stay. He did mention pizza, didn't he? From where? Rod! One push up and you can finish this shit.

Under the watchful gaze of his instructor, Rodriguez shoved against the sand, heaving his body up. Three inches. Six inches. His arms shook. The fire in his shoulders raged. His teeth ground into each other.

"Back straight, Rodriguez. Get your ass outta the air."

Rodriguez dug his fingers into the sand, struggled to bring his hips down and straighten his back.

"Back straight, Rod."

Rodriguez tried lowering his hips. As soon as they passed the level of his shoulders, the weight became too much and his arms gave out again. He collapsed into the sand while his brain screamed at him. No! Push, goddammit! Push!

The instructor spoke softly. "Rodriguez. Look up."

Rodriguez picked up his head, looked at the instructor—a twelve-year veteran known to students and staff as Ripley. The man, a Chief Petty Officer named Gary Janicek, was pointing at two filthy trainees climbing into the back of a white pick-up truck.

"See those guys? Know where they're heading?"

Rodriguez looked at the sailors. Like him, they wore dirty, wet, sand-encrusted fatigues and orange life jackets. From this distance, he couldn't see their faces, although they moved normally. Ripley's voice came back as the truck drove off.

"They're off to a life of comfort. Warm food. Sleep. A long-ass shower. Ain't that what you want?"

Rodriguez shook his head.

"You don't want a hot shower and a warm bed? I can make that happen. All you gotta do is ring the bell. C'mon, dude. We both know you don't want this life. Save yourself the pain. Six more days of this shit says you don't have it. Quit now. Ring the bell."

Six days? How the fuck was that even...

Rodriguez's brain began talking again, reasoning. There can't be six days left. There can't be more than two. He's fucking with you, Rod. Just to see if you'll quit. It's a game, but it's his game. If you want to play, you just gotta do one...fucking...push-up. Just one.

Rodriguez ignored the pleading instructor. He closed his eyes and took one breath. Then another. Then a third. As he exhaled, he shoved with all his might—feeling like the weight of the world lay across his shoulders. His entire upper body burned. His arms shook. Each shoulder felt like someone was ripping away the muscle. Rodriguez strained, fighting to pull his elbows in and lock them in place. He felt the right one lock straight and his body swayed left. He shifted his left hand in the sand, pushing it wider to compensate. A growl escaped through his clenched jaws as he straightened his left arm. His eyes locked on the shaking appendage, willing it straight as he shoved one last time.

The arm locked in place and Rodriguez held the position. He breathed raggedly as his whole body convulsed. As loud as he could, he yelled.

"Twenty-five."

Rodriguez looked up at his instructor.

Ripley nodded and turned away. "Boat crew three. You have this race off. Get water."

Rodriguez collapsed back into the sand.

Ripley strolled over to a group of instructors, one of which tossed him a bottle of water. As he unscrewed the top and took a long drink, another instructor—SO1 Harrison Fremont—walked up to the group.

"Well gents, couple more races and off to," he pulled a schedule out of a pocket, "log PT. Jesus. We trying to make the whole class quit?"

"Nah." One of the other instructors said. "Just Rip's boy."

There was a general murmur of agreement and the nodding of heads as Rip looked over at Boat Crew Three.

"Face it, Rip. Your boy ain't gonna make it. How close did he come to quitting during those push-ups?"

"He'll be fine." Rip shook his head. "He might have thought about it, but he did the push-up."

"This time." SO1 Fremont pointed out. "What happens next time?"

Rip finished the water. "Guess we'll find out."

"Are you sure he's part of your family?" another instructor asked. "I mean, he seems a hell of a lot smarter than you, but..."

Rip ignored the remark and watched his nephew help get boat three ready for the next race. "I'll be right back."

He headed off to talk to his sister's oldest child.

Farid Saadoun climbed into the passenger side of a small box truck painted to look like a United States Postal Service delivery vehicle and looked out the window.

"Anything else, Mr. Patterson?"

Will shook his head. "Just remember what we talked about. Those drums in the back are wired up twice. There's a switch on the floorboards that'll trigger the devices. Just watch where you put your feet. Deadman switch is the little black button in the glove box. That one is wired to a pressure sensor in your seat. Don't use it unless you have to."

"Mr. Patterson, have you considered the possibility that we will just disappear without doing anything?"

"The thought has crossed my mind. Have you considered the possibility that I wired a remote detonator into the device? Martyrdom is less cool when you don't take the enemy with you."

Fuck you. Farid glared at the American. "Understood, Mr. Patterson."

Will inclined his head. "Good luck, gentlemen."

Farid nodded and rolled up the window. Will watched as both trucks rolled down the access road with their cargo of fake packages and real explosives.

BUD/S Class 505 was back on the grinder in the main compound. Earlier in the day they'd finished the boat races and log PT before hefting the boats onto their heads and shuffling to chow and the pool. The class was in bad shape. They'd lost three guys after lunch—men who simply could not bring themselves to leave the chow hall for the next event. At the pool—during medical checks—they'd lost three more. One had clearly torn a muscle in his calf—the knot on the back of his knee had been the size of a softball. While the instructors were trying to figure out how he'd even been walking, two more students were diagnosed with advanced staph infections.

A quick meeting of the instructors had resulted in a change of schedule. The pace was reigned in slightly and the instructors were even more alert for medical issues than they'd been over the previous few days.

Rip looked on as the students were led through a much-needed stretching routine that was peppered with a reduced load of push-ups, flutter kicks, and dead hang competitions. SO1 Fremont sidled up next to him.

"Man, whatever you said to your boy lit a fire in his ass."

Rip nodded. "Told him he was disappointing his pops."

Rodriguez's father—Rip's brother-in-law—had passed after a long battle with lung cancer while Rodriguez was still in Indoc. Faced with the choice to attend the funeral and drop to the next class or stay with 505, Rodriguez had stayed. As much as they knew it had to hurt, the instructors had offered the young sailor no quarter. They couldn't. It just wasn't how things were done.

Fremont whistled. "Harsh, dude. Harsh."

"Maybe. He chose to stay and that kid has spent the last four weeks feeling sorry for himself. You don't skip your dad's funeral and then not have something to show for it."

"Well, it's working. Look at him." Fremont pointed. The students were doing dead hang competitions while being sprayed with hoses. Rodriguez had just won four events in a row.

Rip looked at his nephew. "About damn time."

Farid was trying to calm himself. He breathed as the vehicles drove, stopping and starting in heavy traffic, down the Silver Strand. He rolled his neck as they turned right onto Tarawa Road and merged into the line of vehicles waiting to enter the base. Farid checked his mirror to ensure that the second truck was immediately behind them. It was.

Both trucks crept forward. They were within seconds of their objective and it seemed—to Farid at least—like the process for each vehicle to present identification to the guards and gain access to the post was interminable.

Before they'd left, Patterson had assured them that the paperwork he'd given them would withstand the topical scrutiny of the most knowledgeable gate guard.

"And what if they suspect us anyway," Farid had asked.

"Then you stomp on the gas, take the first left, and race to your objective. Response time for an emergency at one of the gates is ten times what you need."

"And four men with our appearance won't raise alarms?"

Patterson had shrugged at that. He'd told them that they'd probably be mistaken for Mexicans without even apologizing for the inherent racism in the observation. Farid could've punched the man.

As his vehicle inched towards the guard, he reached forward and pulled the clipboard off the dashboard.

"Good morning, gentlemen." The guard was dressed in woodland camouflage and wore black web gear with the word 'Police' emblazoned in large, blocky, yellow letters across the front. "You guys are early today."

After making sure his foot was clear of the switch on the floor, Farid leaned over and handed the clipboard out of the window. In barely accented English, he replied.

"Sorry. I start vacation as soon as we're done."

The guard accepted the clipboard and made a show of flipping through the pages there. He leaned back and looked at the second truck. "Two trucks today?"

"Yes, sir. More packages than usual."

"Looks good." The guard turned and beat on the door to the guard shack behind him. After a second and third guard came out of the shack, he turned back to the truck. "I'll have you gentlemen pull over there by those cones and these gentlemen will give both vehicles a once over before you head in."

Farid pulse quickened. "Is there a problem, sir?"

The guard handed the clipboard back. "No. Just standard to inspect delivery vehicles."

"Oh. Okay." Farid accepted his clipboard. His mind was racing.

"Farid?" The driver was looking at him.

"Let them inspect. If they try to open the back doors, we leave."

"Patterson did not mention this."

"I know."

"Is it a trap?"

Farid looked around as the vehicle rolled to a stop in front of two orange road cones. "No. Other than these two guards and the one at the gate, I see no one else."

One of the two new guards approached the driver's side door. "Gentlemen. I need you to step out of the vehicle and follow me while my associate inspects your truck."

Farid's driver pretended to unbuckle his seatbelt, his eyes pleading for instructions.

In Arabic, Farid whispered. "Go!"

The guard, a Petty Officer Third Class named Jacobs, backed ten feet away from the vehicle, waiting for the driver and passenger to step out and join him. The revving sound of the engine got his attention. As he watched, the postal truck moved forward rapidly. Jacobs reached for the radio on his left shoulder. Both vehicles were thirty feet from him and accelerating towards the pop-up barricade just inside the gate.

"Barricade." Jacobs yelled.

Inside the guard shack, a fourth member of the security team slammed his hand down on a two-inch wide red button designed to raise the thick, steel barrier within seconds.

In the security command post four blocks from the gate, the watch commander heard the call and got on his radio. He ordered all mobile patrols to the vicinity of the main gate. A scanner in the BUD/S instructor office broadcasted the call to two instructors working on administrative chores. One of these, an SO2 who figured he'd let the senior instructor know there was an issue, headed for the door leading to the grinder.

★ ★ ★ ★ ★

Farid knew the steel barriers were there. If the one-foot-thick steel posts raised before they got past them, the mission was over. Sort of. Farid was not going to take any chances. He popped open the glove box and pressed the button inside, activating the dead-man switch. He watched anxiously as the yellow line marking the barrier's location swept under the front of his vehicle.

"Left. Now!"

★ ★ ★ ★ ★

Jacobs watched as the barricade popped up, clipping the second postal truck as it raced away. The rear of the second vehicle jumped into the air with the force of the impact—the steel posts striking just aft of the rear axle and shearing the bumper off.

Jacobs saw both trucks turn. "Both vehicles cleared the barricade. Heading south on Trident Way!"

The sound of squealing tires caused Rip's head to pop up. He'd been signing off on the recent drops while the Hell Week class did another set of flutter kicks. He stood, wondering what idiot was drag racing around the base. Had to be staff, he decided. Students didn't drive here. He was halfway across the grinder when one of his junior instructors burst out of the office door.

"Rip. Security alert. Car ran the gate."

Rip's brain moved into high gear. Tires squealing near enough to hear and a report of a vehicle running the gate propelled him to action. He could only assume the vehicle was coming to this spot. This grinder was famous. You could find it on Google Maps and it wasn't a closely held secret when Hell Week was going on. He began shouting.

"Vehicle inbound! Get the hell off the grinder!"

Fremont dropped his hose as other instructors looked around. "Where to?"

"Through the building, to the Indoc grinder. Through the next buildings 'til you hit the beach. Move!"

The instructors began moving. Two had to corral Boat Crew Four as the delirious students attempted to head off toward their inflatable crafts. Rip searched the grinder, grabbing students and pushing them in the right direction. Rip didn't see his nephew anywhere. He shoved a few more students in the right direction, yelling for them to move faster as he turned around and scanned the blacktop. He spotted his nephew by the pull up bars.

Rip ran that way, waving his arms. "Rod! Get your ass moving, boy!"

Farid held on as the truck swayed, dangerously close to tipping as it took the left turn at speed. He had two targets on this road. The first was the building on his immediate left, the headquarters of the training facility. Keeping his ass firmly pressed into the seat, he turned to look out the rear windows. He watched the second vehicle turn as his own vehicle raced on. They had three blocks to build up speed and he could see the target.

"Faster!"

The engine strained as the vehicle raced towards the gate. Farid judged the distance and whispered a prayer before unbuckling his seat belt.

Two guards stood at the security barrier on the northwest corner of the BUD/S Instructor Offices/Grinder compound watching the white truck race towards them. The senior one, a Petty Officer Second Class slated for BUD/S class 506 raised a Mossberg M500 shotgun to his shoulder, aiming at the base of the grill.

Petty Officer Grierson depressed the trigger and the gun roared, sending a slug into the radiator. Steam sprayed from the engine as he racked another round into the breach and aimed just above the hood on the driver's side. He depressed the trigger again and saw the windshield spider web as the vehicle swerved. Grierson grabbed his fellow guard and raced to his left.

★ ★ ★ ★ ★

Farid watched in fascination as the world tipped sideways. The second shot from the guard had killed his driver—whose dead body had leaned onto the wheel at the last second. The truck had veered left before traveling over the curb and through the guard post. As the vehicle continued, it struck a heavy, commercial-use generator stowed behind the shack. Already unstable from the passage over the curb, the impact with the generator box tipped the vehicle on its right side.

The vehicle skidded ten feet before Farid's bodyweight shifted and released the pressure sensitive trigger installed there and sent an electrical signal eight feet to the blasting caps embedded in fifty pounds of ANFO.

22

EVANS

THE PRESIDENT FINISHED SHAKING HANDS with the front office staff of the Washington Nationals as the defending World Series champions filed out of the Oval Office for a photo op on the South Lawn. As the door closed, Evans turned and lifted the custom jersey he'd just been gifted.

"I don't have to wear this, do I?"

"For the cameras?" Barnes cocked his head. "Yeah. You do."

"That sucks."

"Why's that?"

Evans worked the buttons on the front of the jersey. "The Cubbie faithful are gonna think I've ditched them."

"The Cubs?"

Evans slipped the jersey on. "Growing up in Indiana limits your exposure a bit, especially in the eighties. The occasional Cards or Reds game made it on air, but Chicago was always broadcast. Every game. Easy to get hooked."

"Really?"

"Yep. During the summer, I'd get up, do chores, watch Bozo the Clown before lunch and the Cubs after lunch. Channel nine was a hell of a babysitter."

"No night games?"

Evans buttoned his jersey. "Wrigley didn't have lights 'til eighty-eight."

Both men headed for the door. "Ever play ball, Leslie?"

Barnes shook his head. "Nope. Too uncoordinated. You?"

"Can't hit a moving ball."

"Let's hope you can catch one."

"Yeah. Drop one or fumble a grounder and the press'll have a field day."

Barnes opened the door. "I can only imagine the headlines."

"Mr. President?"

Evans and Barnes turned to see Regina Kelly behind them.

"Regina, aren't you supposed to be out there with the Nats?"

"Yes, Mr. President. There's a change in plans."

"No one told me," Barnes said. He pulled his phone from a pocket.

"Sorry, Leslie. This just came up." Kelly apologized. "Mr. President, you're needed in the Situation Room."

Evans looked at his watch. He had forty-five minutes until the next scheduled update. "Something break loose on the Camp Mercury attack?"

Kelly shook her head. "CNN and other media outlets are reporting an explosion in San Diego."

★ ★ ★ ★ ★

It took two minutes for Evans to make his way to the situation room. He was struggling to remove the jersey.

"Well? What do we know?"

An Army officer pointed to the bank of television screens—each of which was tuned to a different news channel. "Mr. President. Preliminary reports indicate two explosions in Coronado, California. Details are still sketchy."

Evans eyed the screens—most of which were broadcasting the same shaking images. Piles of debris and rubble marked spots where buildings had once stood. Small fires dotted the wreckage. Teams of first responders darted around. Evans noted the presence of what appeared to be military personnel digging into the detritus. Before he could ask about the military, the camera angle changed.

The overhead shot—a helicopter, the president decided—showed the remains of a building sitting near a crater. The building, what was left of it, surrounded a partially obscured section of pavement dotted by what appeared to be dozens of bright, yellow footprints.

"Shit" Evans said. He turned to SECDEF. "BUD/S?"

Tolchanov nodded. "Yes, Mr. President. Preliminary reports say that at least two vehicles, purportedly belonging to the United States Postal Service, ran the gates and detonated vehicle-borne IEDs on the complex."

"Casualties?"

"Unknown at this time, Mr. President," SECDEF said. "It'll be a while before we know, but CNN is reporting that a Hell Week class was on the grinder during the attack."

"What are we doing about this?"

Tolchanov turned away from the screens. "I've ordered all military and government installations to Force Protection Condition Delta. Essential personnel only. Gates are closed and security staffing is being doubled."

"Okay. I know it's a bit early for this, but I'll ask anyway. Who did it, why, and what are my options?"

"We don't know yet." Said the National Security Advisor. "No one has claimed responsibility. If it was a nation-state, we have military strike options available. Something measured and strong. If it's a terrorist group," Ray trailed off.

"If it's a terrorist group, my options are limited because of who they are and how they work?" Evans stated the obvious.

"That's about the size of it, sir. Short of this being some domestic group trying to prove a point about the military-industrial complex or an eco-group angry about the SEALs detonating C4 out at San Clemente, the likely culprits are the same people we've been at war with since 2001. You know the difficulties involved in retaliation there."

Evans felt his face flush as he watched the screens and listened to the back and forth from his national security council. He leaned forward to ask a question when Tolchanov pointed at one screen.

"Major! Turn up CNN."

An Air Force major used a remote to unmute the appropriate television—the anchor's voice became audible halfway through the statement. She sounded calmer than the president felt.

"...received by fax just moments ago. The message indicates that the Islamic State is responsible for today's attack on the Navy base in

Coronado, California. The statement, issued to several media outlets, claims victory over the United States and her allies and goes on to cite America's withdrawal as a clear surrender to…"

The fax machine in the corner of the room buzzed as the Secretary of Defense directed the major to mute the television.

Evans glanced at each person seated around the table. "Thoughts? Opinions?"

"The claims are basic chest-thumping Mr. President," Tolchanov said. "Nothing more."

"I agree, Mr. President," Ray said. "We knew they'd claim victory when we announced the full withdrawal. The rhetoric was inevitable. Frankly, it took a lot longer than I thought it might. The actual attack is the bigger issue. If what they're saying is true, they've just proven that they can reach out and hit us at home. Again."

"Any chance this is someone else? Domestic terror?" Evans asked.

Ray shook his head. "Possible, but unlikely. These groups, Al-Qaeda and ISIS and whatnot, tend to be pretty honest when they claim credit for something. That said, everyone but ISIS tends to be a bit more, um, discerning."

"Discerning?"

Ray shrugged. "Best word for it, Mr. President. The Islamic State guys have always been more chaotic than the rest of the groups. As crazy as it sounds, some of these organizations actually have strategic visions outlined. They tend to only authorize and claim operations that align with their objectives. There are outliers, but mostly it needs to be their guy doing something approved by their leadership. ISIS is different. They'll take credit for anything if they have even the slimmest connection."

"And the target?" Evans asked.

SECDEF leaned forward. "It's a military base. Makes sense as a target for both groups. SEALS have been a pain in the ass for them for twenty years. Could be either. My money is on ISIS."

"Why?" Evans asked.

A shrug. "Gut feeling. If it was just the grinder and the SEALS, I'd say Al-Qaeda. But targeting the HQ building with the civilians working there? That feels excessive. And excessive violence for shits and giggles is damn near a trademark for ISIS."

"Violence for violence's sake?" Barnes asked. "For what purpose?"

"They're terrorists, Leslie." SECDEF said. "The purpose of terrorism is to terrorize. When they started off, they'd pick fights and blow-up things for the hell of it. Zarqawi used to get a kick out of starting firefights with two opposing sides. His folks would take a few potshots at whoever was available and wait for the cavalry to show up. Then they'd fire on the newcomers and melt away to watch the show. Hell, when Bin Laden was alive, he publicly criticized the Islamic State and their prolific tendency towards violence. He even tried reining them in once or twice."

"Gents," Evans intervened. "If this was ISIS. What do we do?"

"We go after 'em," Ray said.

Tolchanov nodded. "We set the agency and the FBI loose."

"Gotta know who the 'them' is before we do that," Barnes pointed out. He turned to ask the Director of National Intelligence a question and didn't see her. "Where's Ophelia?"

Tolchanov answered. "She's on a call with the directors of the FBI and CIA. She'll be here shortly."

On cue, the door opened to admit DNI Adams. "Mr. President, my apologies." She took her seat at the table. "I just got off of the phone with Directors Albright and Waller."

"Not a problem Ophelia. What's Albright have?"

"CIA doesn't have anything more than what the news is reporting. They're shaking some trees, but nothing's come of it yet."

"And Waller," asked Barnes.

"FBI is already on scene and Director Waller is sending more agents to aid in the investigation. Information is sketchy. Local guy says two blasts. Best guess is ANFO—same stuff McVeigh used in Oklahoma City. They'll confirm or contradict that as they collect and analyze evidence. Sorry, Mr. President. It's just too early to have concrete details."

"Have you seen the claim of responsibility?"

"I have."

"And?"

"CIA and FBI both say it sounds genuine. It has the same language and rhetoric as past claims. The syntax and cadence seem to be consistent with the claims we've received after other incidents."

"I'm gonna have to go on television in a few. Is that something I can say?"

Leslie Barnes shook his head. "Not exactly. Let the reporters bring it up. If they do, you can explain that you have seen the claim and that the resources of the United States government are looking into it. Something like that."

"Can you work on that with Regina?"

Barnes held up his phone. "She's already on it."

Daniel Evans nodded. He was about to stand and order hourly updates when the young major with the remote stepped forward and un-muted the television.

"Excuse me Mr. President. You may want to see this."

Will was watching the news coverage while the TitanX corporate jet was being readied for departure. During a commercial break, he decided to take advantage of the complimentary coffee service. He'd had a busy and sleepless two days and his body was screaming for rest, but he figured he'd compromise with caffeine for now.

Will collected his cup, slipped it into one of the sleeves provided to avoid burning his fingers, and returned to the couch. A breaking news banner flashed across the screen and he lifted the remote and raised the volume several notches.

"CNN has received emails from four individuals claiming to have carried out the attacks at the Coronado Naval Base today. Each email declared the American withdrawal from the Middle East as a victory and contained a video message from the sender. CNN is working to verify the authenticity of these videos and has forwarded the emails to the Federal Bureau of Investigation."

"Sonofabitch!" The profanity drew a disapproving glance from the woman tending to the complimentary food and drink spread. Will apologized for his language and fished a cell phone out of his pocket.

He was scrolling through his contacts when he stopped himself.

Instinct told him action was needed. But what action? What could he do? Will's mind raced as an attendant entered the lounge to inform him that his flight was ready. He told himself to be patient and put the phone back in his pocket. He finished his coffee and collected his bags before heading for the door.

In twenty minutes, the private jet was aloft and climbing through cloud cover. Will flipped on the in-cabin television and found a station covering the attacks. He had to wait fifteen minutes to finally see the videos.

★ ★ ★ ★ ★

Evans looked around and decided that being president was a surreal experience. Less than an hour ago, he'd been sitting in the situation room discussing a terrorist attack on American soil. Not just any soil, either. The BUD/S grinder. One of the American military's hallowed places.

In his career with the Navy, Evans had worked with the SEALs, had listened to the tales—each man describing his experiences on that tiny piece of real estate. They spoke of that small section of blacktop in a way that reminded him how it had felt standing on the beach at Normandy during a family vacation.

Now he sat behind his desk, going over some of the never-ending administrative paperwork that came with his job. Fifteen feet away, Daniel Jr. was fast asleep on one of the Oval Office couches—the remnants of a grilled cheese sandwich dotting the visible side of a cheek. Elizabeth was perched in one of the ornate chairs, curled into a ball and watching one of her cartoons on the ever-present tablet.

A gentle knock on the door caused Daniel Jr. to stir. It did not, Evans noted, distract Elizabeth from the intrigues of her cartoon cats.

"Mr. President?"

Evans looked up to see Leslie Barnes enter his office. The president noted that Barnes was entering from the door leading to the secretary's anteroom as opposed to using the one that connected the Oval to the Chief of Staff's office.

"Leslie. What's up?"

"You know those four videos CNN reported? Before airing the videos, CNN forwarded the emails containing the videos to the FBI."

"ISIS?"

"Yes, sir. Early analysis says the videos were shot in the vehicles used in the attack by a prepaid cell phone purchased about an hour from Coronado."

"That was pretty quick."

"The videos had timestamps, as did the emails." Barnes read off of his notes. "Besides. These guys weren't exactly covert about it."

"Anything else?" The president asked.

"There is a portion of the emails that CNN is not making public. The versions they forwarded to the anchors and producers are truncated."

"Okay. Why?"

The Chief of Staff handed over a single sheet of paper. Under the salutation was the same paragraph CNN and every other major news network had been broadcasting and dissecting for the last thirty minutes. Below that was a second paragraph.

"As the Americans prepare to depart our lands, the faithful will fly the Black Banners of Khorasan and pursue those who have ravaged our people and our nation to their very own doorsteps. Our brethren around the world have a new ally working from the very heart of the west, people who may not believe as we do but who are willing to support our cause. We thank them, unbelievers that they are, for their support and announce our new campaign. If we can no longer engage the cowards of the west on our soil, we will do so on theirs."

Evans looked up. "Leslie, this says..."

"I know. These four guys say they have a new ally and they insinuate that that person or persons is here, in the United States."

"Any chance this is just bluster? They do a lot of that. I mean, over there, they tend to back it up. But they're always saying that an attack here is imminent."

"Maybe so. In this case, I don't think it's bullshit. FBI thinks these guys really were ISIS. Not stringers. The real deal. The bureau also thinks the claim about help from inside is probably true."

"How?"

"You're not gonna like the answer."

"Try me."

"The names the men gave in the video match the names of four men we had in custody in Iraq."

"Had?" The president cringed. "Please don't tell me we pulled the catch-and-release mistake with these guys."

Barnes shook his head. "Worse. These four guys were all listed as detainees at Camp Mercury."

23

NIXON

MIKE TRIED TO FOCUS on his surroundings while his brain catalogued a lengthy array of aches and pains. His head felt like someone was using a jackhammer to pry his skull open and his first conscious action was to take a few deep breaths to lessen the pain. His extremities and torso were sore and battered in a way that he'd not felt since his final years as a SEAL. As his eyes traced the grid of the tile ceiling, he commanded his fingers and toes to wiggle and was relieved when each responded.

He was laying on a narrow bed and could feel pressure on both shoulders when he tried to shift his position.

"Good. You're awake." A faceless voice spoke.

Mike tried to sit up, but was foiled by restraints he'd failed to notice. Two straps held his upper body in place with another pair on each side to keep his arms still. Mike's pulse raced and he struggling against the restraints.

"Sir. Please. You're in a hospital. The restraints are in place to keep you from ripping the IVs out of your arms."

The voice was quiet and soothing. Mike stopped struggling. He closed his eyes and let his mind search his body for the aches that had to be there. He felt one insertion on the back of his left hand—could feel the tape pulling at the skin there. His mind searched more and located a small, stabbing pain in the crook of his right elbow. He decided he might be in a hospital. He opened his eyes and tried to focus on the person who had to be near the foot of his bed. The blurred outline of a man in a white lab coat began to take shape.

"Where am I?" Mike half croaked.

"A private hospital in Islamabad. The military found you unconscious after an accident and brought you here on orders from General Khan. You know him?"

Mike blinked. The man—doctor—had come into focus. He was short, with dark skin and jet, black hair streaked liberally with grey. He held a clipboard, flipping through various pages and scribbling notes as he talked. Mike noted that the man's lightly accented English was perfect and that seemed strange.

Mike croaked again. "ISIS?"

There was no answer. Mike took a breath and tried to clear his throat. "Who did this?"

A shrug. "An accident, sir. These things happen."

Mike coughed. "Water?"

"Of course." The doctor turned and murmured something Mike couldn't make out. An orderly appeared at his side, holding a large cup with a straw floating around in it. Mike caught the straw on the third try and gulped.

"Slowly, sir." The doctor admonished, watching over a pair of wire-rimmed glasses.

Mike worked the water around in his mouth before swallowing. "Sorry. Hey. Can we get the straps off?"

"Yes. I think so. There is little chance that you'll tear anything out while conscious." The doctor spoke again and the Velcro restraints were removed.

Mike smiled as the last one came off. He was still groggy and the headache was still there, but he could move. That was something.

"How long have I been here?"

"You've been unconscious for a few days. Do you remember your accident?"

Mike's brain worked on that. It was the third time the doctor had referred to an accident. "Not really."

"The general said your truck overturned. Americans should be more careful driving here. My countrymen do not share your affinity for orderly driving."

Mike grunted. "I'll remember that. How'd you know..."

"How did I know that you were an American?" The doctor smiled. "General Khan told me. He left instructions to care for you and your partner as I would my own family and to notify him when you were awake."

"Partner?" The doctor's English was excellent and Mike noted that he'd not used the plural.

"Yes. A small man. Very muscular. He regained consciousness yesterday and is a very amusing fellow."

Miguel, thought Mike. "There were two other Americans in the accident."

The doctor shook his head. "I know only of the two of you that the general's men brought here."

Mike leaned his head back on the pillow. He remembered the report that Andy had been down and knew that could mean anything. He commanded himself to think, but the pounding in his head derailed even the simplest train of thought.

Mike heard the door behind the doctor open and raised his head in time to see Khan enter the room. The general whispered a few questions, collected the answers, and asked for privacy. The doctor nodded, directing his staff to leave before following them into the hall. Khan approached the bed.

"Mr. Nixon. How are you feeling?"

"Where is the rest of my team?"

The general looked around, grabbed a chair and fell into it. He looked like shit. He slouched and there were bags under the red-rimmed eyes.

"General?"

"Jimenez is in the room across the hall."

"Cook and Fogarty?"

"The younger one, Cook?"

Mike nodded.

"Mr. Cook was killed by the mortars fired on my training site. We found his body with several shrapnel wounds. The larger man—Mr. Fogarty—was killed by rifle fire. We found his body under that of Mr. Cook."

Mike swallowed hard. Dave had died trying to carry Andrew's body out of the fray. Khan shook his head and examined his hands.

"I am sorry, Mr. Nixon."

"Who was it?"

Khan looked up. "Who do you think?"

Mike closed his eyes, tried to organize his thoughts. "Right before the attack, the captain of the guard stole the truck with the dummy bomb."

"Yes. I know. ISI raided his home two days ago. I'm sure you can imagine what they found. As it stands, every individual under my command is being interrogated and investigated to ascertain the, um, status of their loyalties." Khan's voice was hollow, distant.

Mike did not want to consider the treatment the Pakistani intelligence service would give every employee of SPD. He looked at the general. The general looked especially pale.

"General?"

"Yes?"

"Do I need to get the doctor back in here?"

"Excuse me?"

"You look like hell." Mike paused. "Pardon me, sir."

The general leaned forward and rubbed his eyeballs. "It is nothing. As you can imagine, my superiors are not pleased with me at the moment, but that is not your problem." Khan stood. "The doctor tells me that you are well. Besides the stitches in your forehead and a mild concussion, you are otherwise healthy and should be ready for travel soon. I will be making arrangements to get you and your team back to New York this evening if I can. It is important that I get you and your team out of Pakistan quickly and quietly. It's not a proper send off, but you understand the delicacy of the situation. Yes?"

Mike nodded. "Sir, what happened at the back of the bunker? We made it there during the attack. The door was stuck. Someone opened it from the outside. Next thing I know, I woke up here." Mike gestured to the room.

"That is my fault. When the alarm sounded, the rapid response team deployed as per regulations. I did not have time to warn them about your team. When they accessed the rear door of the bunker and found themselves face to face with two foreigners, I am afraid that they assumed you were involved in the attack."

Mike touched the bandage on his head. The spot was tender. "I suppose I'm lucky they only butt-stroked us and didn't just open fire."

Khan forced a wan smile. "For that, I am also thankful. Now, if you will excuse me, Mr. Nixon, I have some arrangements to make. After I get you and your team out of my country, I need to talk to those in my government who are very publicly calling for my head."

"Thank you, General. Is my gear here? I need to call my boss and let him know what's happened."

"My adjutant is working to collect your belongings and those of your team. We will get them to you as soon as possible."

"Colonel Raza?"

"Yes. As you can imagine, he is also very busy."

"Calls for his head too?" Mike inquired.

"Of course, but nothing will come of those. What was it one of your presidents said? The buck stops here? Roosevelt?"

"Truman."

"I like this man. It's a good saying."

Mike shrugged as best as his sore body allowed. "It is. But history isn't really kind to him."

Khan stopped at the door. "Why?"

"Truman ordered the bombing of Japan."

"It was necessary, I think."

"Maybe so, sir. But going down in history as the only man to use nuclear weapons? I'll pass on that."

Khan stepped away from the door. "You do not believe Truman was justified?"

Mike shrugged. "General, I'm just a shooter. I don't pretend to know anything about politics. Any nation wants to step on a battlefield and settle disputes in a gentlemanly manner, that's fine. Those bombs killed hundreds of thousands of innocent people."

"It stopped the Japanese," pointed out Khan.

Mike pushed himself more upright. Every part of his body seemed to ache. "Sir, that may be true. Like I said. I'm just a lowly grunt. I don't make policy. But every single time I went out with my team, we were admonished to avoid civilian casualties."

"Times were different then, Mr. Nixon. Do you agree that such weapons are a last resort?"

"I do."

"What if Truman's use was a last resort? Most of Japan's military leadership had no intention of surrendering."

Mike conceded the point. "That may be true, but there were a lot of unknowns in that equation. People guessed what the Japanese would do and how many lives it might cost. I don't have the balls to make a call like that."

Khan shook his head. "Not a politician, Mr. Nixon?"

Mike smiled. "I studied my fair share of history in college."

"Mr. Nixon, I do really have to go, but I want to ask a question."

"Okay."

"If Canada and Mexico were unfriendly to your country and constantly posed a threat to your national security, what would you do? Assume one, or both, had better infrastructure and a decided military advantage. What then?"

Mike thought for a second. "I assume you're talking about India?"

"They pose a threat to us." Khan confirmed. "And they are a nuclear power."

"We went through this with the Soviets for a few decades." Mike noted.

"Not the same, Mr. Nixon. In your Cold War with the Soviet Union, America did not share a contested border with the Russians."

"That's true. In our case, we had a lot of help from friends."

"Yes. America used most of western Europe and portions of Africa, Asia, and the Middle East as a buffer. You had a picket line and some powerful friends. But what happens to a country without such friends?"

The question was a reasonable one, Mike decided. It was almost holy writ that a shooting war between India and Pakistan would end with each nation flipping nukes at each other. "You have friends, General."

Khan turned back to the door and placed his hand on the knob. "Yes, we do. But our most powerful friend is moving out of the neighborhood."

★ ★ ★ ★ ★

It took just over four hours for Khan to make the arrangements to smuggle the two living and two fallen Americans out of Pakistan. His superiors were not happy with him. They'd not wanted the Americans in the country in the first place—certainly not to poke holes in the security surrounding their nuclear weapons program. The attack on the training site was seen as a direct result of the general's misguided intentions. That it had only been a training site helped his case, although more than one minister had pointed out that the successful attack on this training site proved that the actual weapons storage sites were not as secure as the Pakistani government had led the world to believe. Those same ministers also pointed out that the fact that the attackers had only gotten away with a truck and a fake bomb was the only reason the good general hadn't already been hanged or shot.

Khan had escorted the Americans to a remote runway at Nur Khan, a Pakistani Air Force base in Rawalpindi capable of maintaining and operating the government's fleet of Gulfstreams.

Khan, Nixon, and Jimenez looked on as the bodies of Andrew Cook and Dave Fogarty were stowed aboard the aircraft with the rest of the TitanX crew's belongings. When the loading was complete, the general turned.

"Mr. Nixon. Mr. Jimenez. Please pass my condolences to Mr. DeGuerra and the families of Mr. Fogarty and Mr. Cook. While it may not seem like it, your work here has served a purpose."

Miguel nodded.

"How is the council handling this?" Asked Mike.

"They are taking the threat seriously. Publicly, they will continue to proclaim their faith in the security around our weapons. Privately, they are furious. They realize that the arsenal is at risk."

"About damn time," Miguel growled.

The general nodded solemnly. "It shouldn't take a tragedy to gather support and change policy, but that is the world we live in. Now, you men have a plane to catch and I have a government full of headstrong people to deal with."

Handshakes were offered and accepted and Khan watched the two Americans board the aircraft. He turned away as the flight crew closed the main cabin door and walked to his car. After folding himself into the soft leather of the backseat, he pulled a phone from his pocket and dialed a number. It was picked up after two rings.

"Have you found Colonel Raza yet?"

24

THOMPSON

BRIAN FORCED HIMSELF OUT OF THE SEAT and paced around Central Control. All around him were LCD screens showing the status of the ship's complex power and propulsion plant. He should have been worrying about many things. The list of problems he had was growing, fast.

On the ship, two of the ship's air conditioning plants were showing high bearing temps and a myriad of other indications that the machinery wasn't functioning properly. The faulty pressure switch on the rebuilt refrigeration plant had failed and was causing the unit to trip offline prematurely. A vibration sensor reading on one of the main propulsion gas turbine engines was high enough—even at an ordered speed of just five knots—to constantly broadcast a warning alarm. Four spaces were showing active alarms on bilge flooding sensors, even though only one of those spaces had any measurable amount of standing water sloshing around under the deck plates. Ironically, none of the flooding sensors in shaft alley were active. They should have been, considering that the worsening leaks on the propulsion shaft seals were pouring buckets of water into the bilge.

At home, his wife was trying to go through the normal process of recovery from a pregnancy and subsequent birth—only this time it wasn't routine. She was struggling with the recovery this time and he wasn't there to help. He also wasn't there for the kids, all of whom were struggling to adapt to new surroundings, new schools, new teachers, and new friends.

Brian should have been thinking about these things, but he wasn't.

The only thing on his mind was the seemingly gargantuan task lying directly in front of him—keeping his eyes open for the remaining two hours of his current watch.

He'd been awake—again—for longer than he cared to remember. A poorly-executed main space fire drill, three boardings, and emergent repairs on two critical pieces of equipment had conspired to deprive him of sleep.

He leaned on the captain's chair that occupied the middle of the room and tried to focus on the red numbers displayed on the propulsion console. He moved his eyes at random, forcing himself to scan the gages and think about each number. That worked briefly, giving his mind something to process. Eventually, his eyes settled on one readout and the numbers went blurry.

"Captain in CCS!" A voice snapped Brian back from dreamland. He turned to see Commander Allen stepping through the aft door into Central.

"Sir," Brian greeted the captain before announcing the commanding officer's location to the bridge and combat.

"Folks, how's the watch going?" The captain glanced around at the sailors in the space, each of which was busy monitoring their equipment. He was answered with a chorus of murmuring.

"Lively as a tomb in here, Chief." Commander Allen noted. He looked at Brian. "Jesus, Chief. When's the last time you slept?"

"Been a while, captain."

"Yeah? Well, you look like hell. Does Guillory look as bad as you?"

Worse, thought Brian. Much worse. Guillory hadn't slept in almost four days after having assisted in repairs to two of the Williams' gas turbine generators. "He and I are running neck and neck, sir."

The captain turned to the sailor at the propulsion console. "Cruz?"

"Sir?"

"If I told you to get Chief Guillory up here, what number would you call?"

Cruz's eyes drifted to Brian, who nodded. "He's in the Chief's Mess, sir."

The captain glared at Brian. The anger in his voice was barely veiled. "I have two engineering chiefs left on the ship and neither one is taking care of himself? Do I have that right?"

The question was rhetorical. Brian didn't answer. The captain scowled for a minute and then turned and left the space. Brian picked up one of the microphones mounted above his console and depressed the button.

"All stations, CCS. Commanding Officer has departed CCS."

Cruz turned. "Sorry, Chief. Want me to call the mess and warn Chief Guillory?"

Brian shook his head. "Nah. The captain won't go get him. He's looking for CHENG right now. Guarantee it."

On cue, the ship's 1MC announcing system crackled to life.

"Chief Engineer, your presence is requested in the captain's cabin."

Cruz stared at the speaker. "Oh shit. He's pissed. What are you gonna do?"

"Nothing."

"Really." Cruz blinked.

"What's he gonna do? Fire me? Send me home?"

Cruz laughed and turned back to his console. "Good point."

It took fifteen minutes for the Chief Engineer to show up in central. After climbing into the captain's chair, he looked at Brian. "Christ, Chief. Captain's right. You look like shit."

"I've looked way worse."

"Maybe, but he's pretty pissed. We got a long time left on station here and you and Guillory are trying to work yourselves to death."

"You need him down here for this?"

Lieutenant Walker nodded.

Brian made the call and Guillory stumbled into CCS two minutes later bearing a large mug of fresh coffee.

CHENG pointed at the mug. "Is that how you two are doing this? Staying hopped up on caffeine all day?

"Well," Guillory replied. "Caffeine, a never-ending supply of broken gear, and the occasional hit of coke or speed."

The room erupted in laughter.

"Very funny. Listen gents. Captain is mad as hell. We're already short-handed and, for some reason, we aren't getting more bodies from BUPERS. You two are it and you're both working yourselves into oblivion."

Brian turned from the log book. He tried to sound angry, but that effort was too exhausting. "What do you want me to say? We hit a bad stretch. Gear's breaking because the ship hasn't had a decent refit in more than a decade. It's not like we're doing work that a fireman could be doing. We're stuck working these jobs because the regs require specific job training for them."

Lieutenant Walker snapped. "This ship is always having a bad stretch. It's been on a bad stretch for almost twenty goddamn years. What do you two think? That if you stay up and watch everything, nothing else will go wrong?" CHENG paused and took a deep breath. "Look. No one is saying that you're doing the wrong things. The captain realizes that you aren't down in the weeds for shits and giggles. He knows that you two have to be the ones doing or supervising some of those repairs. He gets it. He also has to think of the big picture."

"So do we." Guillory interjected. "We're fine."

It was the wrong thing to say. CHENG turned to Guillory and then glanced at the clock on the starboard bulkhead. "List the immediate actions for a loss of steering."

Guillory blinked for a second and stared at his feet, mumbling. CHENG waited fifteen seconds.

"Chief?"

"Give me a second?"

"I gave you fifteen."

The space grew silent. Lieutenant Walker pointed at both men. "Guys. If you're so damn tired that you have to think that hard to realize that you have no immediate actions here for a loss of steering and wouldn't know until the bridge calls it over the 1MC, then what good will you be when something more complex happens?"

Brian stood and stretched. "I get it. We need to sleep. We'll sleep."

"You got that right, Chief." The lieutenant hopped out of the large chair. "I can't believe I have to say this, but the captain is ordering you two, in fucking writing, to sleep. Admin is typing it up right now. For both of you, your next three off-watch periods are to be spent resting or eating. You are not allowed at your desks or in the spaces when you are not physically on watch."

Brian blinked. "Ordered sleep?"

The propulsion console operator turned around and raised his hand. "CHENG?"

"Don't even fucking think about it Cruz. Now is not the time."

The hand went down. "Yes, sir."

CHENG turned back to his two chiefs.

"Captain will be down here in a few minutes to tell you himself. He's already told Carrillo to keep you two out of the mess during your off time."

Brian was about to object when the speakers crackled to life.

"Central, Main One."

Brian picked up the handheld microphone. "Go for Central."

"Uh, Chief, can you come down here? There's a smell that I can't quite place. Like something burning."

That got everyone's attention. Brian could feel adrenaline dump into his system and welcomed the wide-awake feeling.

"On the way." Brian grabbed his radio off the charger and slipped it into one of the deep pockets of his dirty coveralls. He looked at the CHENG as he clipped the mic to his collar. "Sir? You mind hanging out here for a second?"

"I've got CCS," Lieutenant Walker confirmed.

Brian left CCS and headed forward through the ship. He cut across mid-ships, moving through the chow line to get to the port side passageway that led to the entrance to Main Engine Room Number One. A quick jaunt inboard and down a ladder put him outside the space airlock. Brian pulled a pair of earplugs from his pocket and inserted them in his ears before rotating the locking lever on the door and entering the space.

The heat hit him first. It always did. It was always warm down here. With everything in the space running while the ship trolled the waters of the Somali coast, temperatures in the engine room could—and did—routinely measure in triple digits.

The smell hit him next and it took a few seconds for Brian's sleep-deprived brain to analyze it. Burning oil, his mind reported as his feet carried him around the space. He lifted the mic on his collar and depressed the button.

"All spaces, EOOW. EOOW is touring Main One."

Brian found the Main One Operator on the upper level and tapped him on the shoulder. The sailor turned. "Chief, the smell is stronger on the mid-level."

The two men headed down a nearby ladder. Brian stood, looking around. He sniffed the air. The smell was pungent and irritating. His brain worked on the problem. Shit, he thought. He lifted the mic again.

"PACC, EOOW. Any odd readings on the GTMs or reduction gears?"

A moment of silence ensued before Cruz responded. "Negative, Chief. Readings on GTMs are good. Same for the gears."

"Nothing on the lube oil system looks odd?"

"Nope. Everything looks good. Temps and pressures all within specs."

Brian stood for a few seconds, his brain trying to list every piece of equipment that used a lubricating oil system.

CRACK

The sound reverberated around the space, followed by a thrashing, grinding noise and the high-pitched whine of an electric motor pulling too many amps. Even in the noisy environment of the propulsion plant, the sound was enough to cause Brian to cover his ears. The operator next to him yelled.

"What the fuck was that?"

Brian was scanning the space. A part of his brain classified the noise as a broken shaft on a pump. It sounded like nails on a chalkboard and the ripping apart of thousands of metal cans.

"Shit." Brian pointed. "The RO."

The two sailors worked their way across the space. At a distance of ten feet, Brian was certain. The noise was coming from the high-pressure pump portion of the ship's reverse osmosis water production system. He could see the unit jumping on its mounts as the motor continued to drive the shattered crankshaft. He yelled to the operator as he ran around the unit to the motor controller.

"Kill the breaker!"

The operator headed to the corner to secure power to the damaged gear as Brian pressed the large button that stopped the electric motor. After several additional rotations, the pump shuddered to a halt.

The operator walked back over. "Power is secured, Chief."

Brian nodded and leaned over the pump. A piece of plexiglass over the top allowed him a glimpse into the unit's crankcase. Where there should have been three connecting rods, he saw only debris. He leaned forward a little further, craning his neck to look at the crank end of the unit. A single object was lying on the pump foundation. He reached down and picked it up. It was a brass plug. Three-quarters of an inch across with one solid end, a fitted, rubber O-ring, and one end cut with threads. Brian reached down to where he knew the oil plug was supposed to be and felt around. In seconds he found an opening. He withdrew his hand and looked at it. His fingers were covered in a dark, glittering liquid.

Brian handed the object to the Main One Operator and watched the sailor examine it.

"Well shit. That sucks."

Brian nodded.

Brian and two mechanics disassembled the pump. Brian examined each piece. He found deep grooves in two of the piston sleeves and scoring on all three lobes of the crankshaft. One of the bearings was shot. The wearing rings were gone, ground into miniscule slivers that gave the burnt oil a shimmering look. It was bad, he thought, but not a total loss. Hope died when Brian used his flashlight to examine the casing itself. He saw a four-inch crack just below one of the bearings and his heart sank.

Brian had already figured out what had happened. The pump had had its oil changed earlier in the day. That, he suspected, had gone smoothly until the oil plug had been installed hand tight. The maintenance card called for twenty pounds of torque to secure the plug properly. Without that, the plug had vibrated loose over the course of several hours. It had fallen free. The oil had drained while the pump continued to run. Heat. Metal to metal contact. The result wasn't hard to predict.

Brian watched as the two mechanics worked to free the last piston from its cylinder. They'd been working on it for more than twenty minutes. It wasn't moving.

Brian picked up a camera and held a flashlight out for one engineer to hold.

"Leave it."

Brian snapped pictures of the damage.

"You sure, Chief?"

"Yeah. It ain't coming out. Besides. With that crack..." His voice trailed off.

"What happens now?"

Brian was still snapping pictures, directing one sailor to aim the flashlight. "Well, unless one of you has a pump casing stashed away somewhere, we probably have to fly a repair team and a new pump out."

Brian scrolled through the photos on the camera and stood. He felt his knees and back cracking and popping.

"Chief, what do we do with this stuff?" The sailor gestured to the broken gear.

"Wrap it in rags and box it up. Leave it on the workbench. Don't toss anything until we're sure no one else needs to look at it."

The captain was sitting in an armchair in his cabin, scrolling through the photos on the camera.

"Can't fix it?"

"No, sir." Brian answered. "Not with the parts we have onboard. The casing is cracked. The sleeve surfaces are completely destroyed. That third piston won't come out. We have replacement internals in the supply system, but not a casing."

The captain handed the camera to the XO. Polian scrolled through the photos and whistled. "Damn."

The captain leaned back and took a deep breath. "Alright. I contacted Fleet Forces and the commodore to give them a heads up. I owe them an update shortly and they're expecting the casualty report. Recommendations?"

Lieutenant Walker responded. "They'll have to send the parts and a fly away team for the install."

"Fly away team?" The captain turned to Brian. "You can't do the install if I get the parts here?"

"I can." Brian responded.

"But?"

"But it's clear you want me running my department and not turning wrenches. This is a lengthy repair. The internal parts are easy. Plug and play basically. But the alignment process is a pain in the ass and no one in the department except for Chief Guillory and myself have done it."

The XO looked up from the camera. "This is a critical repair, Chief."

"All due respect, sir. They're all critical repairs."

The XO shrugged and the captain nodded. "Chief has a point. Either a fly away team does this or he and Guillory are stuck down there. Let's get the job and report written. Request outside activity assistance. I want this off-ship in a half-hour. Questions?"

Heads shook and the captain dismissed the group.

★ ★ ★ ★ ★

The casualty report made it off-ship in twenty-two minutes and began its electronic journey to a large list of recipients. Within an hour, it had been read by Rear Admiral-select Gomez and Lieutenant Commander Havner, the latter having had the good sense to keep his 'I told you so' comments to himself. The Commander, Destroyer Squadron Two-Six swore as he picked up the phone. His aide fired up a secure laptop and emailed a list of contacts for parts and assistance.

The email made its way to a short, squat man who served as the port engineer for USS James E. Williams. He wasn't surprised. He'd been arguing for a dry-docking repair period for years for this ship, pointing out the degrading material condition of the ship and her equipment. That this hadn't been caused by either of those conditions didn't matter to him. The port engineer read the message twice before a new email dropped into his inbox. He clicked on the item and read through the message. It said that the mid-voyage repairs were being moved forward and asked him to identify high-priority repair work that could be conducted within the proposed seven-day window.

The man grunted and turned to look at a whiteboard in his cubicle. It took two minutes to locate the right information and he noted that the schedule shift was only four calendar days. He smiled and began typing. It took thirty minutes because he only used two fingers and a thumb to type. He read the email twice, made an adjustment, copied in a distribution list, and clicked send.

An email argument ensued over the next two hours with more than fifty people using the 'reply all' function to advocate for and against various repair suggestions. One man in the email chain took a screenshot of the updated schedule and texted the image file to a recent acquaintance at TitanX Security.

Commander Allen was in his stateroom when the message traffic came through. After signing for it, he read the missive that directed him to proceed to Seychelles for mid-voyage repairs. The message contained a list of the work scheduled for completion during the port call. He noted a few items that would please the Chief Engineer and his Top Snipe.

Calvin Robinson was on his lunch break when his phone rang. He swallowed a bite of his deli sandwich and picked up the phone.

"Hello?"

"Calvin?"

"Hey, boss."

"Calvin. The stern tube inflatable seals, is that something you can install yourself?"

Calvin paused. "Well, yeah. Why?"

"The Williams broke something and they're pulling in for repairs. The Navy is trying to stuff as many repairs into the period as possible. We can't fix the shaft seals themselves until drydock, but we can upgrade the emergency seals in case something else goes wrong. Those damn things are leaking buckets according to the ship's Top Snipe."

"Oh. Okay. When?"

"That's why I'm calling. Go pack your shit. You've got a plane to catch."

"Fair enough boss."

"Get moving kid." The phone clicked off.

Calvin went back to his sandwich, his mind racing.

25

NIXON

THE CLIMB OUT FOR THE PAF GULFSTREAM was smooth—only the slightest bump jostled the exhausted passengers. Miguel and Mike sat on opposite sides of the plush cabin in seats that would convert into comfortable beds as soon as the aircraft reached cruising altitude. In the built-in cupholder of each seat was a small bottle of whiskey—something that both operators found curious given the flight's point of origin.

A speaker on the cabin's forward bulkhead announced that the plane had reached cruising altitude. The standard language about being free to roam around the cabin was followed by the equally-standard request to keep seat belts buckled while seated.

"Does every flight school in the world teach that?" Miguel struggled with the buckle.

"I suppose." Mike looked over at Miguel. The smaller man had stitches across his forehead and both arms sported fresh, white bandages. Miguel got the buckle unlatched and stood. He looked at Mike. "You alright boss?"

"Yeah. Thought my days of losing folks were over."

Miguel took a deep breath and put a hand on Mike's shoulder. "Me too, man. Me too. Have you called the boss yet?"

"Not yet. Khan asked me to wait until we got out of Pakistan."

"You get the feeling he doesn't trust his own ministry?"

"I get the feeling he doesn't trust a lot of people in his own country."

"On that, you are both correct." The voice caused both men to jump. Mike's head snapped around. Miguel was already facing aft. "What the fuck?"

Mike, unable to unfasten his buckle, craned his neck to look around the seat. A man wearing the filthy coverall uniform of the PAF grounds crew was stepping out of the in-cabin restroom.

"Colonel Raza?" Mike said.

The Pakistani adjutant stepped forward, closing the door to the cabin's lavatory. "You gentlemen think General Khan does not trust anyone in the Pakistani government? I will tell you. That is true. More importantly, many in the government do not trust him."

Miguel moved aft towards the Colonel. Raza backed away. "I'm unarmed."

"Who gives a shit? You gonna do anything stupid?"

"Other than stowing myself away on your flight?"

"Yeah."

"No." Raza stated.

"Good." Miguel nodded. "Now move. You're blocking the head."

Miguel used the restroom, washed his hands, and returned to his seat. Mike and Colonel Raza had adjusted the seating so that three of the seats now faced inboard. There was no talking as Miguel resumed his seat without bothering to re-latch his safety belt.

"So, what did I miss?"

"Nothing yet," said Mike. He turned to Raza. "Senior military officials don't stow away on airplanes trying to sneak folks out of the country. What are you doing here?"

"Same as you. Running for my life."

Mike looked at Miguel and back at Raza. "I think we missed something."

Raza leaned forward. "You have missed a lot of things."

"Colonel," Miguel said. "I'm just a lowly grunt. I've had a bad couple of days and I've lost two buddies. This cryptic shit is beginning to irritate the hell out of me. How about you tell us why you're here before I tie you up and throw you out the door over there?"

Raza said nothing. He reached up and unzipped the top of his coveralls. As soon as his hand reached inside the grease-stained uniform, Miguel launched himself out of his chair.

Miguel planted his left forearm across the colonel's neck while his right hand clamped down on the man's wrist. "Sir, you better be scratching a fuckin' itch in there or I will throw you off this plane."

Raza's eyes widened. "My apologies. I have a package for you."

"Mike? You wanna relieve the colonel of his 'package'?" Miguel asked.

Mike leaned in and frisked the colonel. He pushed Raza's hand away, reached into the unzipped uniform and withdrew a crumpled brown envelope.

"You got anything else on you we should know about, Colonel?" Miguel growled.

"No. Just that."

Miguel backed off, letting go of the Raza's arm and removing his forearm from the man's neck.

"Do you always react so forcefully?" Raza rubbed his neck.

"Colonel," Mike started.

Raza interrupted. "Gentlemen, I'm not a colonel."

Mike stopped fingering the package and looked at Miguel. "ISI?"

Raza shook his head. "No. Not exactly."

"What the hell does that mean?" Mike asked.

"It's complicated," Raza said. His eyes fell on the unopened bottles of whiskey. "May I have a drink?"

Miguel handed a bottle over. "Know what else is complicated?"

Raza unscrewed the top of the bottle and took a long pull.

"What's that?"

"Learning how to fly without wings."

Mike was tired of the back and forth. "Mr. Raza. We were flown to your nation as private contractors to provide a professional opinion and recommendations to improve the security around your nuclear arsenal. Instead, we got blown up and lost two men during a training exercise. I think it's time you told us who you are and why you're on this plane. Why did you say you were running for your life? Why did you say we were?"

"Mr. Nixon, how about we start with why you are on the plane?"

"We're going home." Miguel pointed out.

"In that case," the colonel noted reasonably. "So am I."

"Excuse me?" Mike said.

"I am going home. With you." Raza smiled. "And I'm bringing

home that gift that you hold in your hand, Mr. Nixon." Raza took another drink before handing the bottle back to Miguel. "The general provided the alcohol? Cheap bastard."

Miguel took the bottle and nodded. He was staring at the man in front of him. In mid-sentence, he'd heard the accented English of an educated, senior Pakistani military officer disappear.

Mike noted it too. He fished. "Thought you folks didn't drink."

Raza took the bait. "Fundamental Islam forbids it. Catholicism, on the other hand..." His voice trailed off. "How are the Sox looking this year?"

"You wanna explain why you sound like you're from Beantown, Mr. Raza?" Miguel asked.

"Probably because I'm from Beantown, Mr. Jimenez. Grew up a few blocks from Fenway. Went to Boston U."

Mike's brain was racing. "Okay. Stow the family history for now. What's in the package?"

"Open it."

Mike tore open the envelope. Inside was a small device he'd not seen since childhood. "A tape player?"

Raza beckoned for the whiskey again and took another drink. He cringed and coughed. "This stuff is terrible." He handed the bottle back and pointed at the package. "Play it."

Mike did as requested. A pair of scratchy voices could be heard. The player ran for ten minutes before Mike pressed the stop button.

"I am assuming you recognize one of the voices?" Raza asked.

"Fuck, Mike. That was Mr. DeGuerra."

"It certainly sounds like him." Mike looked to Raza. "How'd you get this?"

"How do you think?"

"Khan lied to DeGuerra about bugging the room?" Mike was confused. He was looking at the floor, trying to think despite a lingering headache. "That doesn't make a whole lot of sense unless..." Mike's head snapped up. "You bugged the room?"

Raza nodded. "Flip to side B."

Mike found the eject button and pressed it, fumbling to extract and flip the cassette. "I'm still lost. Why record that conversation? It's just two guys doing business.”

Raza smiled. “Think about what you just heard. A business conversation. Right? Did you hear anything from Khan but reluctance? The CEO of an American private security firm hard sells the general on a contract to review and improve the security around Pakistan’s nukes.”

“Yeah. So?” Miguel asked.

“Mr. Jimenez. Khan can play this tape and claim that his trust was betrayed by an old friend who just happened to run one of the world’s most proficient private security training facilities. TitanX’s reputation will give credence to his story. He’ll get a slap on the wrist.”

Mike stopped fiddling with the cassette. He was trying to think while Miguel questioned Raza.

“Why would the head of Pakistani SPD get anything other than a slap on the wrist for this? It was a training site. Sure, he lost guys and that sucks, but what did ISIS steal? A truck? A dummy bomb? Big fuckin’ deal.”

Raza smiled at Miguel. Mike saw it and felt his skin go cold.

“It wasn’t a dummy bomb.” Mike whispered. The words came out so quiet they were almost covered by the cabin noise.

“What?” Miguel asked.

“It wasn’t a dummy bomb.” Mike turned to look at Raza. “Was it?”

Raza shook his head. “No.”

After a moment, Mike raised the cassette player. “Mr. Raza, what’s on side B?”

Raza’s voice was steady. “Proof.”

They’d listened to side B of the cassette four times and Mike was no closer to making sense of things. He was glaring at the player in his hands as though it would spontaneously play some recorded message that clarified things.

“Okay.” Miguel said for the fifth time in as many breaths. “Colonel… Mr. Raza. Who, exactly, are you?”

“The last name is actually Raza. First name is Peter.” He shrugged. “What can I say? Parents really jumped off the cliff with Catholicism.

As to who I work for...”

"I'm pretty sure we can guess who you work for." Mike pointed out. "What the hell are...were...you doing in Pakistan?"

"When I finished college back in May 2001, the Agency was just getting into the counter-terror game. I mean, they'd done it in the past, but on a small scale. FBI was up and running on the intel and law enforcement sides, but the agency was still trolling the waters. They'd spent nearly a decade figuring out what to do with themselves after the Soviets threw in the towel.”

"Even after the African Embassy and Cole attacks?" Miguel asked.

"Yeah. Remember, back then, all of the old guard had spent the majority of their careers doing one thing. Focusing almost entirely on terror was new to them.”

"One trick pony?" Mike announced.

"Something like that. Anyway, back then, the Agency had maybe a couple handfuls of native Arabic speakers and another handful of area experts. I didn't know that when I applied. I initially asked to join the science and tech arm. My application went into the system and someone decided that a kid who was first-generation American with parents fresh off the boat...”

"The boat?" Miguel asked.

"Okay, the plane. Anyway, CIA liked the background and they liked the idea of having someone inside the Pak Army, especially the nuclear side. Dad had been a well-known businessman in the country and his name still garnered a few favors. I went to the Farm about two months before 9/11 and, after telling my dad I wanted to serve in the Pakistani Army, he made some phone calls. I was practically escorted off the plane to my first classes at PMA.”

"And your position in SPD?" Mike inquired.

"My undergrad was in mechanical engineering. Ending up in SPD was almost inevitable." Raza pointed out.

"I still don't believe any of this. I mean, Nick? Really?" Miguel was shaking his head.

Raza took a deep breath. "Khan's involvement is simple. He isn't trusted by the ministry and the feeling is mutual. He's broke as hell and his head has been on the chopping block for some time. He's old.

He's stressed the fuck out. He's in deep shit. The ministry would gladly blame him for failing to secure nukes and hang his ass to buy time with the rest of the world. He's a desperate man. DeGuerra's involvement is more complicated. Without ongoing conflict, he's doomed. It's greed. Same as Khan, but orders of magnitude bigger."

Miguel took a drink and looked at Raza. "What do you mean?"

Mike thought through the answer aloud. "Remember what I said on the way here? About the company losing shitloads of money? Nick stands to lose big. Way more than the twenty million we just heard about."

Miguel protested. "But Mike, to think Nick helped steal a fuckin' live nuke? C'mon."

"Mr. Jimenez." Raza said.

"Miguel."

"Okay, Miguel. Let me ask you a question. What do you know about Nicholas DeGuerra?"

Miguel shrugged. "Same shit everyone knows. Ex-Army special forces turned businessman."

"Is he rich?"

"Seems so."

"Are you?"

Miguel laughed. "Hell no."

"What's your net worth?"

"I dunno. Got a military pension and some investments."

"Good for you. When you made those investments, did you get any advice?"

"Sure."

"What was it?"

"Don't put all your eggs in one basket. Spread it around a bit."

"Diversification?"

"Yeah. Why?"

Peter Raza reached into a pocket. Mike and Miguel flinched.

"Easy gents. Just getting some notes." Raza withdrew a folded sheet of notepaper from his pocket and handed it to Mike. "That is a list of every corporation that Nicholas DeGuerra has significant interest in. As you can see, he has a substantial financial interest in what

Eisenhower called the 'military-industrial complex'. Mr. DeGuerra has an estimated net worth just shy of one billion dollars, a large portion of which is tied up as capital in America's next generation of warfighting tech contracts and proposals. Not talking rifles and night vision. Talking drones, ships, submarines, tanks. Big-ticket, high-dollar items or, more specifically, the tech developed for those items by a series of small, powerful start-ups."

Mike and Miguel flipped through the sheets. Miguel whistled. "That's a lot of dough."

"Shit, Miguel. He's right. This isn't really cash. Look at this stuff. Nick been throwing money into every portion of the defense industry. Tanks, missiles, jets, guns, bombs. If peace is breaking out…"

"But why steal the nuke? Even if he sets the damn thing off in the Middle East and we blame ISIS for it, he's still gonna lose." Miguel argued.

"He's got a point, Pete. The voters kinda told Congress and the new president that they don't want another war like this. Hell, ISIS could detonate the damn thing in Omaha and it wouldn't help Nick." Mike pointed out. "A massive build-up wouldn't work for this kind of war. It's kind of hard to fight an insurgency with a billion-dollar submarine."

"That's very true." Peter conceded. "Unless ISIS isn't going to be blamed."

Mike looked confused. "I don't follow. Why have ISIS steal the nuke in the first place?"

"Convenience? Khan couldn't really just sign one out and throw it in the trunk."

"Okay." Mike replied. "He hired someone to steal the thing and what? He's gonna set it off and blame Pakistan?"

Raza shook his head. "Us."

"Us? Like the United States? You've been in country too fuckin' long. How's he gonna do that?" Miguel asked.

"Simple. Where are Mr. Cook and Mr. Fogarty?"

Miguel bolted out of his chair. "Fuck you, man."

Mike grabbed Miguel mid-lunge. It took every ounce of strength he had left in his aching body to restrain the smaller man. In a quiet, measured voice, he spoke.

"Miguel. Sit down." Miguel complied, glaring at the Pakistani-American in front of him.

Mike turned. "What the hell, man?"

"Look guys. This is gonna be hard for you to hear, but Mr. Cook and Mr. Fogarty aren't on this plane."

"What do you mean?" Mike asked, trying to keep his voice reasonable. "I saw the bodies loaded onto the plane."

"Did either of you identify the bodies?"

Mike and Miguel looked at each other. "There wasn't time. Khan wanted…"

Raza raised an eyebrow. "Wanted you out of town quickly and quietly? So he could deal with the ministers?"

Miguel protested again. "Bullshit."

Mike's mind was racing. "Even if that's true, a coroner would be able to tell, right?"

"Sure. But only if you got back home and ordered one." Raza paused. "Andrew Cook and Dave Fogarty did die in the attack at the training site. I am sorry, gentlemen. Their bodies are being held by Khan at one of the bunkers the general would use in case of nuclear war."

Miguel twitched. "Motherfucker."

"Why?" Asked Mike.

"He and DeGuerra intend to use it to start a war that will jumpstart American military production in a way that will make DeGuerra one of the richest men on the planet."

Mike began to say something, but Miguel held a hand up. "Hold on. Why'd Khan let us go?"

Raza grinned. "You're on a private plane that has no record of departure in Pakistan. Everyone who knows you're on this plane is absolutely loyal to the General. Every step of the journey back to New York has been planned by Khan and DeGuerra. Khan needs you on the run to sell his narrative."

"Which is?" Mike asked.

"Despite instructions to the contrary, Khan has documented your entire trip and will use it to place the two of you, Dave, and Andrew at the scene when the device was stolen. He will use Dave and Andrew to tie the United States to the detonation. Your 'escape' right now will be delayed when we land due to technical malfunctions. You'll be hidden away in a safe house until the aircraft can be fixed. After the detonation, you'll be killed trying to 'escape' back to the United States."

"I still don't get how that starts a war." Mike reasoned.

"I'll admit that part has me stumped," Raza admitted. "One of the scenarios that scares the shit out of people is the possibility of Pakistan and India flipping nukes at each other. Admittedly, American involvement on behalf of Pakistan in a shooting war would help DeGuerra, but only if the war is sustained. A nuclear war wouldn't keep going for long."

"Agreed," noted Mike. "And hanging my team out there as the perps would almost stop the war cold. I don't see how this works."

Miguel had stopped participating in the conversation. He was fuming. He'd left his guys behind. He couldn't tell if it was his professional or personal pride that was more injured. His eyes traced back and forth over his surroundings, not focusing on anything, until...

"Motherfucker!" Raza flinched as Miguel bolted out of his seat and grabbed a newspaper folded into a rack on the cabin's bulkhead and flipped it open. He repeated himself.

"What?" Mike shouted.

"I know how they're gonna do it."

26

THOMPSON

THE USS JAMES E. WILLIAMS had been tied to the pier in Seychelles for three hours before the first group of contractors and repair technicians appeared on the ship's quarterdeck. Brian had gotten a phone call and he'd dispatched a young petty officer to collect the group and escort them to CCS. While he waited, Brian opened the computer program designed to track work and secured systems. The program had just loaded when workers arrived.

Tim Guillory stuck his head in the room as Brian began authorizing work and pairing off each contractor with the sailor who'd run the tags and secure the systems.

"Brian. Need help?"

Brian's fingers raced across the keyboard, authorizing work and printing danger tags. "Not here. Walk the plant and the pier for me?"

"Rog. Coffee?"

Brian grinned at the screen in front of him. "Do I ever turn down coffee?"

"Sounds good. Be back in a bit."

Brian signed off on the current set of tags and handed them to a sailor with a verbal order to isolate the equipment. He looked around.

"Next?"

A contractor walked over with a portfolio. "Me, I guess."

"Fair enough. What's the job?"

"I'm replacing the inflatable seals for the stern tubes."

Brian smiled. "Read up on those. Sounds better than what we've got now."

The contractor grinned. "They are. More reliable. Fewer problems with dry rot and stuff."

"And the old design was what? Sixty years old?"

A laugh. "Closer to ninety, Chief."

Brian opened the job on the computer and checked the system isolations against a paper drawing. Something looked wrong. He went through the drawing again and looked around Central for a few seconds before finding who he was looking for.

"Cortez?"

The sailor looked up from a set of logs. "Chief?"

"Need you to fix a tag for me."

Cortez walked over and Brian pointed at the screen. "Add this one here to the tags."

Cortez nodded and headed for the door. "Easy. Back in five."

Brian looked at the contractor. "Sorry. Once he's done, we'll get you signed in on the job and get you to work."

The contractor smiled. "No problem. Did my fair share of those things."

"Yeah?"

"Sure. Back in the day when we did all of this by hand."

Brian smiled and leaned back in the chair. "Ah. The good old days."

"Someone say something about the good old days?" Tim was back, bearing two mugs of steaming coffee. He handed one to Brian.

"We were just reminiscing about writing tags by hand."

Tim winced. "What wasn't to love about that? Hundreds of sailors with crappy handwriting bringing you tags they'd spent two hours writing and not being able to read anything."

The contractor laughed. "You don't sound convinced."

Tim took a sip from his mug and headed for the door. "Those days sucked, my friend." He started to walk out but turned back. "Brian?"

"Yeah."

"Saw Bob in the mess. Said the last part you need for the reefers is supposed to be on the flight deck. Pressure switch, I think."

"Thanks. Tell him I owe him."

"Already did. He said two beers, minimum."

"Done."

The contractor waited for Tim to disappear. "Reefers?"

"Yeah. We lost both on the way across the pond." Brian took a sip.

"I heard about that. You did the repairs?"

"Had some help from a few folks."

"Rebuilding both units underway? That's some serious shit, Chief."

Brian was spared answering by the arrival of Petty Officer Cortez. "Tags fixed, Chief."

Brian turned to the screen, verified the fix, and authorized the tags. He turned to the contractor. "You signing as the Repair Activity representative?

A nod. "Sure."

Brian's hands curled over the keyboard. "Name?"

The man handed over an ID card. "Calvin Robinson."

The PAF Gulfstream carrying Mike Nixon, Miguel Jimenez, and Pete Raza touched down at a fixed base operator in Tbilisi, Georgia little more than an hour after the pilot had notified the passengers that there was a mechanical problem with the aircraft. The announcement had given them little time to act.

As the Gulfstream finished its roll out and made the turn towards the line of hangars, Raza led the TitanX operators aft. He'd opened the lavatory door and, with minimal effort, moved the room's forward bulkhead to one side, revealing a small compartment with a built-in ladder.

"This plane was built for smuggling people, or for escape." Raza pointed out.

"Where's it go?" Mike asked.

"Through the cargo hold to a resealable external door."

"We just dropping to the tarmac in Georgia from a plane doing twenty miles per hour?" Miguel asked.

Raza smiled. "No. We're dropping during a turn. Only ten miles per hour. Still in Georgia." He shrugged. "Sorry. Not much choice there."

Mike climbed into the space. "Let's get this over with."

Each of the three men wiggled into the space and down the small ladder. Raza went last, shutting the door to the head and sliding the false bulkhead back into place. They squeezed through the tight passage and into the cargo hold. Once in the hold, Raza handed each man a pair of ground crew coveralls similar to those he wore. As Mike worked his way into the ill-fitting uniform, Miguel zipped his up and examined himself.

"Shit, Mike. I look like a kid who stole his dad's clothes."

Mike looked over. Both sets of coveralls were the same size. Mike's fit well. Miguel's did not. In another situation, the image of Miguel standing with excess length pooled around his wrists and ankles would have been hilarious. "Relax Miguel. It's better than strolling across the tarmac in civies."

Miguel grumbled and began rolling his sleeves as Raza waved them to the escape hatch.

Mike squatted by the hatch and found the locking latches. He reached to undo them before Raza stopped him. Mike saw him shake his head and point. Mike followed the outstretched finger and saw the problem.

Raza yelled over the noise in the hold. "Tamper switches. Open that and the pilots will know."

Mike nodded. Raza held up one finger and dug through one of the zippered pockets on his coveralls. When he withdrew his hand, Mike saw several small pieces of electrical wire. It took a few seconds of work for Mike to realize that Raza was short circuiting the switches. After forty seconds, Raza looked up and gave both men a thumbs up. Mike and Miguel twisted the spring-loaded latches and lifted the hinged panel out of the way.

Wind whipped through the hold as Mike, Miguel, and Raza watched the tarmac roll by. Raza barked instructions, struggling to be heard over the turbofan engines.

"When you hit the pavement, stay low, move to the grass. We'll stay prone in the grass until the plane approaches the hangars." Raza got a pair of thumbs up as the three men felt the plane slow and lean into a turn.

"Miguel. Now!" Raza yelled.

Miguel lowered himself feet first through the hole, using his upper body to drop himself down until his arms were extended. He looked down at the rolling tarmac and, after deciding it was no worse than a parachute landing, let go. He hit feet first, bending his knees and pitching himself into a roll to absorb most of the shock. After two full rolls, he laid out flat on the pavement, glanced at the plane, oriented himself, and began a low crawl towards the grass on his right.

Mike watched Miguel hit the pavement and start rolling before lowering himself through the hatch. When his arms were extended, he let go, dropping himself to the pavement and rolling to absorb the impact just as Miguel had done.

Raza was the last one out of the PAF Gulfstream. When Nixon had dropped free of the hatch, he positioned himself in the hatch and grabbed it by the pair of handles welded there. Praying that the hatch would reseal as designed, he lowered himself down. When he felt the hatch hit the frame, he opened his hands and let go.

27

—————

EVANS

THE PRESIDENT WALKED into the situation room, hoping he didn't look as bad as he felt. He hadn't slept in more than a day, a situation that always reminded him of his days serving in the United States Navy. Evans vaguely remembered reading a passage in a Wouk novel where the main character acknowledged that his lasting memory of the Navy was the inability to sleep more than an hour without being shaken out of his bunk. The thought made him smile. A rarity during the past thirty hours.

Everyone stood as he took a seat at the head of the table where a pile of reports and a fresh cup of coffee awaited him. Evans whispered a silent prayer of thanks for the cup and ignored the briefing documents for the moment.

"Who do I have to thank for this?" Evans held the cup aloft as if it was some holy relic which, given the situation, it was.

Everyone laughed. Evans took a sip and looked at the individuals seated or standing around the table. "You folks look worse than me."

An assortment of coffee cups appeared from behind stacks of binders as Watkins grinned. "Most of us are on our third or fourth cup."

Evans took another sip. His gaze settled on the cup apparently belonging to DNI Adams. "That's an interesting mug, Ophelia."

A cup sporting the tell-tale ears of the world's most famous cartoon mouse was sitting in front of America's most senior spook. Adams smiled. "What can I say? I like Disney."

Evans set his cup to the side. "Okay folks, where are we?"

DNI Adams cleared her throat. "FBI has been busy. Easy stuff first.

Their lab determined that the explosion in Coronado was caused by an ANFO mixture. They're trying to track down suppliers, but that's going to be a dead end."

"And why is that?" Evans could guess the answer.

Adams glanced back at her notes. "The bombs weren't all that large. Nothing like the federal building and miniscule when compared to that accident in Lebanon last year."

Evans nodded, thinking back to the truckloads of fertilizer shipped to the family farm each year. "Got it. The amounts would be relatively small and no one would really document something like that. That's reasonable."

Adams nodded. "A few hundred pounds of fertilizer and sixty gallons of gas doesn't really set alarm bells off for anyone."

Evans moved on. "Okay. I'll assume that they'll run that to ground as best they can. Tell me about the videos."

"It appears that the initial assessment was correct. The videos are legitimate, and the Islamic State is already praising the actions of these four men." Adams pointed to one of the wall-mounted screens.

Twelve pictures, four rows of three, appeared on the screens as the DNI went on. "What you see here is three pictures of each of the four men claiming involvement. The left-most in each row is from the cell phone videos and the center shots are from our own files on each man. All of these individuals were known bomb-makers in Iraq and each was formerly a guest at Camp Mercury."

"That's the TitanX facility that just got overrun?" Evans asked to refresh his memory.

"Correct, Mr. President."

He looked at the screen. "What are the right-hand side pictures?"

Adams looked up. "Traffic cameras."

Evans raised his eyebrows behind the mug of coffee. He swallowed and set the cup back down. "Traffic cams?"

Adams looked at her notes. "It would appear that whoever set this up either forgot to go over the rules of the road with these guys or the drivers were just plain impatient."

"Meaning?"

"These guys picked up twelve traffic citations starting in downtown

San Diego and ending about one mile from the base in Coronado. Four speed-trap cameras, front shot and rear shots. Eight other violations. Running stop lights and illegal turns. FBI has them mapped backwards to one of the I-15 exits."

Evans shook his head. "Okay. We seem to have a grasp on who they were. Next question is how?"

"FBI and CIA are working on those questions. Right now, we don't know. We do know that the last known location for all four was Camp Mercury." Adams said.

Evans interrupted. "But that facility was destroyed, what? Hours before this happened?"

"Give or take, yes."

"That's not enough time to get from Iraq to southern California. Even if everything was staged and ready for them and taking time zones into account. Right?"

Adams thought for a moment She looked at a display on the opposite wall that showed time zones and what portions of the world were in daylight. "It's possible, but just barely. Maybe an hour or two leeway depending on the plane. Have to consider headwinds or tail winds, too."

Evans shook his head. "That's too close. You don't plan something like this and only leave an hour's worth of lag in the schedule. They had to be here earlier."

Adams nodded. "I'd have to agree with that."

"Okay." Evans rubbed his eyes. "That means they weren't at Camp Mercury when it was attacked. If that's true, how'd they escape?"

"That's one of the things the FBI is working on. Some agents from the New York Field Office are heading up to TitanX's corporate headquarters at Schroon Falls to sit down with the execs and figure out what happened. They'll be able to pull detainee records and daily head counts."

Evans nodded. "Fair enough. Keep me updated."

"Yes, sir."

Evans rolled his neck, trying to relax the muscles there. "What's next?"

"Latest casualty count is in. Thirty-four killed in the Coronado attacks and eighteen wounded."

The president nodded. "Status of the wounded?"

"Scrapes and bruises. Most of those people were far enough from the blast that they just got knocked over or hit with bits of debris."

"Most?"

"One of the wounded is in critical condition. He's a BUD/S student who was close enough to the blast that he was thrown about twenty feet into a wall. He is in a coma and on a respirator. Flailed chest, two broken legs, skull fracture, and shattered wrist. Internal bleeding. He's not in great shape."

"Notify his family yet?"

Adams turned. "His family was on scene when this happened."

"How's that?"

"This kid is a legacy. His uncle is one of his instructors."

★ ★ ★ ★ ★

Ripley sat on a cheap chair, forearms planted on his knees, holding a cheap Styrofoam cup of the worst coffee he'd ever tasted. Hospital coffee was notoriously bad. He knew that from personal experience. He didn't give a shit about the flavor at the moment. His thoughts were firmly focused on a room at Balboa Naval Medical Center that was less than one hundred yards from the waiting room where he sat, alone and brooding.

He drained the cup and tried to organize his thoughts. He'd lost men in the field before. That was a hazard that every man who'd ever worn a trident accepted as part of the job.

But those men had the chance to fight back. They'd died with a rifle in their hands. Rod was doing fucking pull ups. And now he's here, wrecked and hooked up like some damn science project to an array of machinery that keeps him breathing and checks his vital signs and then displays the scores like some twisted sporting event. And all because four cowardly dipshits wanted to make some political statement.

With not much else to do between updates from the doctors, Ripley watched the news. He'd seen the cell phone videos of the culprits. He'd felt the rage build while he'd listened to the statements the men had made just before they'd run the gates. The professional part of Gary knew this was how this war went. Terrorists tried to do their thing and men and women like Gary tried to stop them—or find them after the deed had been done. Either to drag their asses off somewhere for a friendly chat or stomp the hell out of the few who fought it out.

And his nephew had wanted to be part of it. Wanted to be part of that line of defense between good people and the parts of the world that thrived on chaos and violence. Ripley had tried to talk the young man out of his choice. He'd encouraged Rod to select another path. Submarines. Nuke school. Anything else. He would've had more success yelling at a wall. Rod had stood firm in his decision.

And now the kid was in a coma with so much of his body broken that it was a miracle he'd lived this long. And Ripley was waiting. For the next update. For his sister—Rod's mom—to arrive from Minneapolis. He thought back to the phone call he'd made after Rod had been airlifted to Balboa. His sister had been through a lot in her life. She'd just lost her husband to cancer. Her only son was in the ICU.

And she did the consoling. Not me. That's my sis. One tough bitch.

He smiled, remembering the time she'd knocked him out cold. He liked to ignore that she was a talented fighter who'd come up one win short of making the Olympic team. She'd clocked him with two lightning quick jabs, a right hook, and a devastating uppercut that had put him on his back for four minutes. His sister was tougher than he was. He had the scars to prove it. Maybe the kid was too.

Ripley crushed the foam cup, remnants of hot coffee stinging his fingers and bringing him back into the moment. He leaned back, his head against the wall, and waited.

28

THOMPSON

BRIAN LEANED AGAINST THE HANGAR DOOR, looking aft past the end of the flight deck. The night air was clear, warm, and humid. Against the crying of gulls and swishing noise of ocean swells gently lapping at the ship's hull, the sounds of needle-guns and deck crawlers rattled the night. Brian tried his best to ignore the racket. He sat there, the non-skid surface of the deck digging into his tailbone while he looked at the lights of Seychelles.

Brian had been swamped. He and Guillory had alternated shifts in Central Control, signing for completed work and authorizing new work as contractors worked around the clock to finish everything needed to get the ship back to Somalia on time.

He took a sip of the soda he was holding, one of dozens that day. Despite the caffeine, he felt his eyes getting heavy.

"Top, Central."

Brian reached up and depressed the button on his radio mike. "Go for Top."

"Any chance you can stop by CCS for a few?"

Brian nodded to no one in particular and pressed the button again. "On my way." He lifted himself off the deck and plodded back inside the ship. In two minutes, he found himself collapsing into one of the empty chairs in Central Control.

"What's up?"

"Nothing." Tim acknowledged. "Just needed a head break. Bladder can't hold any more coffee."

Brian smiled. "I got it. Anything going on?"

"Haven't seen anyone for forty minutes. Be right back." Tim walked out of the space.

Brian leaned back in his chair—letting the seventy-degree air flow around him. The beeps and buzzing of the panels grated on his nerves. As his eyelids drooped, he heard footsteps in the passage and turned to see Tim walk back in the door.

"Thanks man. My bladder thanks you too."

Brian grinned. "Getting old sucks."

A nod. "Yeah, it does. Why don't you rack out for a couple hours? I've got this. I got a nap before I came down."

"And if you need another head break?" Brian asked.

Tim looked around. "I'm sure there's a bottle around here somewhere."

Brian crinkled his face up. "Dude."

"Seriously. Get some sleep. You get any paler, I'll be able to see your internal organs."

Brian nodded and pushed himself out of the chair. He stretched and yawned. Before he headed to the door, he turned.

"Tim. That guy still down in shaft alley?"

"Who? Calvin?"

"Yeah."

"I assume so. The old seals came off okay, but he mentioned having issues with the new ones." Tim looked at the log. "He hasn't signed out yet today."

"Christ. Okay. I'm gonna stop down there and check on him before I hit my rack."

"Rog. Be careful."

Brian walked out of the room, calling over his shoulder. "Yes, mom."

He decided to take the long way to shaft alley, down by the oil lab. The short way was faster, a ladder just around the corner from CCS that dropped right into the space, but Brian didn't think that sleep deprivation and forty-foot vertical climbs were good bedfellows. He made it to the port side of the ship, yawned, turned a corner, and walked smack into the chest of the captain. They both stumbled.

"Sorry, sir."

The captain was eyeballing him. Brian was certain the man was trying to guess how much sleep he'd had.

"Chief. You look like shit. Again."

Brian smiled. "Thanks sir. I feel like shit." The words escaped his mouth before he knew what he'd said.

Commander Derrick Allen crossed his arms and glared. Brian decided that his commanding officer didn't look amused. "Sir. I'm heading to shaft alley to check on a contractor and then hitting the rack. Seriously."

Commander Allen rolled one arm towards himself, glancing at his watch. "And when's your next shift?"

"Supposed to be in one hour. Chief Guillory is covering for an extra hour. He got some sleep earlier."

"Fine." Commander Allen's face changed. "How's the family?"

Brian's shoulders slumped. He'd gotten an email earlier, mostly a long list of ways that his wife said this postpartum period differed significantly from the others she'd gone through. She wasn't recovering as fast. She felt weaker. Postpartum depression had become an issue and she was borderline anemic. The list went on. It was important stuff. Brian knew that. But there wasn't much to be done from his end other than a kind word, a supportive email, and the occasional phone call home.

"She's fine. This one was harder on her."

"Need anything?"

"About six months' worth of sleep and a ride home." Brian deadpanned.

"Smart ass." The captain smirked. "Check on the contractor and hit your rack, Chief."

"Aye aye, sir."

It took Brian three minutes to climb his way down the long route into shaft alley and maneuver past the giant air conditioning plant to the area where Calvin Robinson was installing the second of two inflatable shaft seals.

"Calvin? How's it going?"

Calvin flinched, dropping a screwdriver that clattered against two pipes before spinning to a halt on the deck plating at his feet. That it hadn't veered off into the puddle of rotting sea water in the bilge was nothing short of miraculous.

"Sorry."

Calvin waved the apology off. "Nah. It's okay. I get caught up in what I'm doing."

"How's the install?"

"About done. Finally."

Brian looked at the new seal. It looked like the old units, but there were several noticeable differences.

Such as...

"What's this?" Brian pointed at a box that appeared to be wired to the new seal. Roughly the size of an old recipe card box, there were four pieces of electrical conduit attached to it. One went to the seal. One went to a digital read out that wasn't illuminated at the moment. Brian traced the path of the third line with his eyes back to a nearby power panel. The fourth line simply sprouted out of the top of the box in an array of wires that were all capped, wrapped with electrical tape, and bagged.

"That's the new gage package." Calvin retrieved the screwdriver.

"Thought this was an analog system."

"It was, but the latest change upgraded some of the features. Replaced the old pressure gages with sensors and this digital readout." Calvin dug through his bag of gear and handed over a dirty, grease-stained folder. "Here. Third or fourth tab back."

Brian flipped through the folder, found the appropriate section and read. "Revision four? Shit. I have rev two."

Calvin used the screwdriver to finish installing a screw on the box's cover plate. "No problem, Chief. I can copy this one for you before I leave and email the electronic version when I get home."

Brian kept reading. "Sounds good." He looked from the diagram to the box on the wall and back. "That last set of wires?" He pointed.

Calvin looked up. "Those? They aren't in the package yet. That'll be the next rev, I think. Those are gonna be the hook up for your alarms in Central. Goes through the interface unit and reads on your consoles and everything. The software update isn't ready, so the change wasn't included. Except for a note about capping and bagging for safety."

Brian nodded, still reading when his radio crackled to life.

"Top, Central." Tim's voice.

Brian keyed his mike as Calvin continued with his job. "Go for Top."

"Captain just called. Told me to tell you to get your ass in your rack. His words."

Brian rolled his eyes and keyed the mike. "Yes, mom."

The captain's voice came over the radio. "I heard that, Chief. You got five minutes."

"Yes, sir."

Brian handed Calvin the folder. The contractor had an eyebrow raised almost to his hairline. Brian grinned. "I have a habit of ignoring sleep. And food. And anything even remotely relaxing."

Calvin grinned. "I was the same way. Ran myself ragged."

"Trade jobs?"

Calvin smiled again. "Hell no. Did my time. I like what I do now. Pays better. Get to sleep at home most of the time."

Brian patted him on the shoulder and laughed. "Well, I'd better get my ass outta here. Chief in central will sign off on the work when you're done."

"Sounds good." Calvin turned to finish his work as Brian disappeared the way he'd come. It took him five minutes to set up the last of the wiring for the explosive charges and two more to run a test on the circuit. Satisfied, he attached the leads and collected his gear. Calvin was off the ship and back at his hotel before he withdrew a cell phone and dialed a memorized number.

"Hello?"

"It's Calvin. Your work order is complete."

29

DEGUERRA

NICK ENTERED the executive conference room at the TitanX headquarters in Schroon Falls looking no worse for wear. He'd been busy. After setting Will Patterson loose, Nick had gone back to work, ostensibly doing the work a harried businessman was expected to be seen doing.

He'd spent much of his time in the air, flying here and there to meet with investors, CEOs, the occasional world leader, and whatever elected officials he'd been able to corner for more than five minutes. The ruse was believable, he thought. Some of the meetings had resulted in new contracts. People sympathetic to his predicament—because it could happen to them too—had thrown him a bone or two. It was nothing that would make much difference to TitanX's near-certain fate, but it made for a good show. Just in case things went sideways.

He'd known he'd have to answer for the Camp Mercury debacle. It was inevitable, Nick thought, but not serious. The FBI had shown up a few minutes earlier and Nick was completely calm. The identities of the two men waiting in the room told Nick a great deal. If either man seated in the boardroom had carried the title of Special Agent-in-Charge or Assistant Special Agent-in-Charge, Nick would have assumed that either he or Will had overlooked something. But neither man carried such a title. The FBI had sent rookies. And that made Nick feel relatively safe.

Nick looked at the agents and wondered just how young they were. They looked like high schoolers. "Gentlemen, how can I help you?"

The shorter of the two men spoke. He had a southern drawl that

Nick struggled to place. "Mr. DeGuerra. Thank you for your time. We have a few routine questions. We'll try to make it quick."

"You boys want a drink?" He waved to the sideboard.

Both men shook their heads. The short one spoke for both. "We're okay, sir."

Nick grabbed a bottle and a tumbler and took his seat. "Suit yourselves."

The taller agent had a voice that was lower and devoid of any patois. "Mr. DeGuerra, as you are no doubt aware, the four men involved in the Coronado attacks had previously been incarcerated at a facility operated by TitanX."

"Mercury." Nick nodded, pouring two fingers of scotch. "I've spent most of my free time on the phone with families and next of kin. Shitty deal. Good folks. All of them."

The shorter one cut in. "Mr. DeGuerra, the Bureau offers its condolences to you and your staff. That's a lot of people to lose. It has to be difficult."

Nick paused, the glass halfway to his lips. "Gentlemen, what do you know about my company?"

The shorter one rattled off statistics. Date of founding. Number of employees. Nick cut him off gently. "I don't mean that stuff. I mean how we do business. We train the hell out of our people and send them to some pretty shitty places. Dangerous places. And you know what?"

The short one bit. "What's that?"

"They go. Despite knowing what could happen, they go. Because they're family. We treat everyone that way. This isn't just four thousand people with the same tax ID number on their W-2's. It's four thousand brothers and sisters, mothers and fathers, grandparents, friends, aunts, and uncles. We take care of our people. While they're here and, God forbid, when something happens."

The shorter one smiled. "We understand, sir. We really do. We just have to..."

Nick raised a hand. "Ah. It's okay. I'm sorry. I get preachy when I think about my people. And with this mess."

The taller one leaned forward. "It's fine, sir. Really. We aren't exactly popular people to have to talk to."

Nick took a drink. "I'll bet." He put the nearly-empty glass down. "Okay gents. Fire away."

The short one picked up a pen. "Sir, any idea how those men got out of your facility?"

Nick shook his head. "We're looking into that ourselves. It's a bit difficult. Looks like everything at the camp was destroyed and the stuff we have archived here isn't much of a help. One day they were listed as present and the next day they're on the news. My Operations Officer is giving himself an ulcer trying to piece together what happened."

The taller one looked at his notes. "Is that a Mr. Paul Burkhart?"

Nick nodded. "That's him."

"We spoke to him earlier. He looked pretty rattled."

Nick leaned back. "Wouldn't you be? That man is one of the finest training officers the Army ever created. I hire him, bring him in. He spent years building this team. He developed the training and operations manuals for everything we do here. And this happens." Nick pointed at the two agents. "That'll rattle anyone."

The taller one nodded. "Well, he was helpful. We spent about two hours with him. He walked us through the procedures for the camp."

Nick smiled. "All of them?"

The shorter one grinned. "Yeah. Everything from intake to burial. Everything."

"That's Paul for ya. He's proud of what he's built and this screw up is killing him."

The shorter one flipped through a leather folio and extracted several papers. "Well, we were able to help Mr. Burkhart piece together part of the mystery. These papers were found in the remains at Mercury." The agent pointed at a photograph. "This man, a Mr. Alex O'Neil, was killed by a mortar. I'll spare you the details, but a portion of his body was found and these documents were in one of the pockets."

Nick accepted the papers and examined them. They were copies of documents that were stained and filthy, but legible. The first page showed a hand-written list of eight names and numbers. The rest of the photographs showed transfer documents, one page each for each of the eight detainees. Nick felt his blood run cold.

The shorter agent was talking again. "Mr. DeGuerra. These show that the four suspects from Coronado were transferred from Mercury to Guantanamo Bay with four other individuals. The other four detainees are physically present in Cuba, but the Operations Officer and a few of the guards from Camp X-Ray remember rejecting the four men we're interested in."

Nick leaned forward, trying to look calmer than he felt. "If X-Ray rejected the transfer, my men would have taken these four back to Mercury. That's standard procedure. Happens occasionally."

The shorter agent nodded. "That's what Mr. Burkhart said. There's some more, sir. Something you ought to know."

Nick raised an eyebrow, feeling as if an icy cannonball had just dropped into his stomach. He poured another drink to keep his hands busy. "What's that?"

The taller agent pulled out more sheets of paper and handed them over. Nick looked. Flight manifests and a picture.

"Mr. DeGuerra. Do you know where we can find this man?"

Nick looked at the photo of Patterson and his mind raced. "Will? No. Why?"

The shorter one sat up straight in his seat. "Sir, Mr. Patterson was identified as the TitanX staffer that attempted to deliver the detainees to X-Ray."

"Ah." Nick swore to himself. "You want to know what happened?"

A pair of head shakes. "Mr. DeGuerra, Will Patterson left Iraq with eight detainees and landed in Cuba. He dropped four men off there—the wrong ones according to DNA, we suspect someone switched records—and returned to Iraq with the four from the Coronado attacks. After that, the plane and the men on it, including Mr. Patterson, simply disappeared."

"And you think that Mr. Patterson had something to do with it?" Nick thought about that. He could guess what the next words out of the agents' mouths would be.

"We'd like to find him and talk to him. Did you know that Mr. Patterson was a convicted felon, sir?"

Nick smiled inwardly, relaxing for the first time in nearly ten minutes. This was unexpected, but not unwelcome. He could use this. Worst case scenario, he could gift-wrap Will Patterson as the mastermind here. Posthumously, of course.

30

KHAN

KHAN STOOD ON A CATWALK overlooking a run-down warehouse in Kohat, Pakistan. As his eyes scanned the piles of broken pallets and empty metal shelves, he tried to slow his breathing. He was agitated. Things weren't progressing smoothly. A series of minor annoyances had dogged him for the past day and he'd been trying to convince himself that the missteps were insignificant. That rhetoric had stopped when the two Americans had vanished from his personal plane. The flight crew had found the tamper switches for the smuggling hatch bypassed. Khan's gut told him that something was badly wrong. The Americans had no reason to run. They could not have known about the hatch. Unless they'd had help. And a warning.

Raza, he thought. He had known about the escape hatch and was still missing. But he couldn't have known about DeGuerra's plan.

Then why did he run?

Khan couldn't answer that question and that was troubling.

Below him, several of his men—overseen by the American calling himself 'Jason' and a weapons engineer sympathetic to extremist causes—were preparing the stolen nuke for use. They'd been here since the day after the heist at the Nur Khan dummy site, with only Khan venturing out—usually a quick trip back to Islamabad to deliver progress reports and keep his government informed about the actions he was taking in the aftermath of the attack. He had to appear to do his job.

Khan worried about that. The device was destined for Chennai and that troubled his conscience. He'd struggled with that part of Nick's plan. He feared what would happen to Pakistan. It bothered him that innocent people would suffer when India retaliated.

And they will retaliate.

"You could quit." He mumbled to himself. "Take the device back. Pick up a few radicals from the street. Put them in front of a firing squad." Khan smiled. It would never work. Not with the Americans on the loose and Raza helping them. If that's what was happening.

And what about Nicholas? He's using you, Saeed.

Khan closed his eyes. It was true. He'd used his resources to discover that Nicholas DeGuerra had funded over forty small, innovative businesses. He had been poised to make a killing in the expansive and all-encompassing world of defense technology. Nick had bet most of his personal fortune, and much of his corporation's financial resources on the success of those businesses.

But it had all gone sideways. And Nicholas was angry. And you're stuck in the middle of it.

Khan should have felt sorry for his friend, but he didn't. He had his own problems and stresses and worries. Most of which would be resolved in two days. Just as soon as the crate sitting sixty feet below him landed on the deck of the M/V Dorian. And someone located Raza and the two Americans. He pounded his fist on a railing.

Khan's cellphone vibrated. He answered it. "Hello."

It was Nick. "Where do we stand?"

Khan leaned on the railing. "Delivery is on schedule. Two days. No more."

"Good." There was a lengthy pause before Nick's voice came back on the line. "Since this order is going so well, I wonder if I might place another?"

Khan blinked. "A second order would be difficult for us right now. We have limited stock and my staff is stretched thin."

"Actually, what I'd really need is a modification to this order."

"Sir, this is a non-returnable item," Khan began.

Nick cut him off. "No. I'm sorry. I was unclear. I still want the delivery. I'd like to request a specific technician, if I may. You have someone named Jason there with you. I've worked with him before. I'd like for him to accompany the other two techs we agreed on."

Khan stood still for a few seconds. He looked at the American on the warehouse floor. "I can do that. I would have to adjust the work schedules of my other employees, but your request is not unreasonable."

"Good. And the fee for the change? I know he's a skilled technician."

"Five should cover it."

"I'll take care of that as soon as possible."

"Anything else?" Khan said. He decided that now was not the time to mention the missing TitanX operators.

"Nothing. Thank you."

The phone went dead and Khan resumed leaning on the railing. He'd just increased the value of his retirement portfolio by twenty-five percent. While he wondered why the man heading to a forklift below him was now part of the delivery, the matter was not overly alarming. Nicholas had a problem and he would provide a solution. For another five million dollars.

A smile flashed across Khan's face as he wondered how much his own yacht might cost.

★ ★ ★ ★ ★

Mike rubbed his left elbow while he waited for the coffee to brew. He'd smacked it on the tarmac during the drop from the PAF Gulfstream. That had hurt, but not overly so. They'd had to get the hell off that plane and away from the airport. The second part should have been simple. Just stand up and walk out. With the coveralls, they'd have looked like mechanics heading home after a long day.

The exfil hadn't worked out that way. They'd dropped from the plane onto the grounds of a private airfield in the middle of a half-assed security drill and Mike had left a great deal of himself on the rough concrete runway and taxiway as he, Miguel, and Raza had low-crawled for nearly a mile to avoid the dozens of rent-a-cops wandering around.

"How's the arm?" Raza entered the small, dimly lit kitchen with Miguel right behind him. Both men filled coffee mugs. Miguel placed a full mug in front of Mike before he plopped down in a cheap metal folding chair. Raza searched the cabinets for cream and sugar.

Mike flexed his arm a couple times. "Nothing broken. Left a half-pound of flesh on that tarmac."

Miguel took a sip of coffee and flashed a smile. "They don't teach low crawl to you squids?"

Mike was spared answering when Raza took a seat and leaned on the table. "You gents get some rest?"

Miguel nodded. "Couple hours."

"Good. Gonna be a long day."

Miguel waved his mug at the walls. "How'd you know about this place? I don't imagine the Agency just issues lists of safehouses in some sort of travel guide."

"Before I tucked myself into the hold of that plane, I got a message off to my boss."

Miguel knitted his brows. "Good guess?"

Raza shook his head. "Nope. Just got a travel guide list of places along the planned flight path."

"That makes sense." Miguel was nodding. "And the rest was improvising?"

"Pretty much. Haven't stolen a car since the Farm."

"And the lady we met last night is ditching the car?"

Raza drank before answering. "Keesler? Yeah. She's good people. Went through the Farm together. She'll help us as much as she can."

Mike yawned. "So, what's next?"

Raza took a drink and turned. "Miguel. You said you knew how this was going to play out before we left the plane. Care to explain?"

"Sure. Got a paper?"

Raza stood and left the room. He was back in thirty seconds with a stack of newspapers. Miguel sorted through them until he found one in English, which he flipped through before flattening it on the small table's center. Miguel pointed at a small headline on the paper's right margin.

"This is how gents."

Mike and Raza leaned forward. Mike read the headline.

"The G20? I don't get it."

Miguel flipped the paper around and his eyes traced the article. "Okay. Bear with me. Back on the flight, we kept going around in circles. Nick wants to make a killing and this withdrawal is fucking with his world. That's easy to figure, right? He spends money on companies that make toys for us knuckle-dragging goons to use in a war and without a good conflict or two somewhere, his investments are for shit. Supply and demand gone bad. Like if the whole world suddenly stopped wanting McDonald's."

A pair of nods.

"But we couldn't figure out how it would work."

Another pair of nods.

Miguel leaned back forward. "Guys. It's simpler than that. We know Khan's broke. He's just a guy who finally discovered he's expendable and wants a payday. Pakistan's involvement doesn't matter. They're kindling for the fire."

Mike rubbed his temples. "The world has always assumed that a full-on fight between Pakistan and India would go nuclear, right?"

Raza nodded.

Mike tried to follow the thought. "That makes for a short war and short wars don't make money." He turned to Raza. "Any chance India stays conventional?"

Raza shook his head. "If they know it's a Pakistani weapon or that terrorists from Pakistan set it off? No way. Unless..." Raza stopped talking and looked at Miguel. "No."

Miguel smiled darkly. "Nick isn't trying to start a war between Pakistan and India. He trying to start one with India and us."

"With Pakistan in the middle?" Asked Raza. "How?"

"Read the article." Miguel directed.

Raza read. He looked up. "It just says that President Evans will be attending the G20 virtually because of a positive test for coronavirus in the White House. What am I missing?"

"Same thing we are. Two American bodies." Mike answered. An idea had formed.

"What?"

"You said it yourself, Pete." Mike said. "Khan has Andrew and Dave. If this was about India and Pakistan, what would he need them for?"

Raza shook his head. "Set off a nuke in India. Show off the dead American contractors as evidence that it was some sort of bipartisan covert op? I don't know."

Mike considered that for a few seconds. "This is all guesswork and, honestly, the why and how doesn't really matter right now. We know who and what. That's something we need to move on."

31

EVANS

EVANS SAT SLUMPED behind the Resolute Desk. He rubbed his eyes and contemplated the infirmities of aging. Going days without sleep as a young officer hadn't been fun, but neither had it been as debilitating as it was now. There was something about this job that seemed to trip the body's circuit breakers. It just drew on your reserves more. That realization forced the president to acknowledge another fact.

He hadn't been ready for this. That the notion wasn't as crazy as it sounded should have surprised the president. Despite the preaching and pronouncements made on a campaign trail, no one ever walked into their first term ready to be POTUS. It just wasn't possible to prepare for this job and everything that came with it. There wasn't an internship or training course for this. But here he was, sitting behind one of the most recognizable desks in the world's most recognizable office. And all he could think about was how fast the honeymoon phase of his presidency had come to a screeching halt. That, and a nap.

"So, what do we know?" Evans looked at his Chief of Staff.

"Four positive tests so far. Only Ray and his personal assistant are symptomatic. Ray and his guy are both quarantining at home. But most of the senior staff has been exposed, yourself included. We'll continue to test everyone and those who turn up positive will work from home." Barnes looked more frumpy than usual, but that was to be expected. He'd had less sleep.

"You look like hell, Leslie." POTUS noted.

"I'll survive." Barnes leaned back on the couch. "I'm concerned about Chennai."

"Can't be helped, Leslie." Evans yawned. "I can't exactly show up in person after my staff tests positive for this thing."

"I know. I know. It's just bad optics. You have to bow out of your first G20 because of this. Just looks bad."

"It looks responsible, Leslie. Hell, half of the election was about handling this pandemic. I can't just ignore what I said to go shake a few hands. And we aren't bowing out. We're just not there in person."

"That's the problem. You'll be on the phone for the real work." Barnes pointed at the pile of papers on his lap. "That's where this kind of stuff gets done. The public discussions are pro forma crap. Play-acting for the cameras."

"We'll get the work done, Leslie. It'll be different, but we'll get it done." The work in question was a series of discussions and proposals for trade agreements—or updates to trade agreements—that still required further haggling and negotiation. Everyone from farmers to software programmers had a stake in those negotiations and expected their president to stand eye-to-eye with his counterparts and get the best deal possible. That the conversations would be held over a satellite-based communications system instead of face-to-face was something the Chief of Staff was worried about.

"I know, Daniel. I know. Call me old fashioned, but I like to sit across the table from the folks I negotiate with. Read body language. Stuff like that.

A sleepy shrug. "We'll make the most of it. What's next?"

Barnes crossed a few things off of one sheet of paper and shuffled to the next. "Got a new update on the Coronado investigation in a little bit. You'll get more detail at the meeting, but the basic gist is simple. FBI is still looking for this Patterson fellow. Apparently, he went AWOL from TitanX and took one of their planes. A couple of agents went to talk to the CEO yesterday and he's some kind of pissed at the possibility that one of his own people had a hand in this mess."

Evans didn't bother looking at the sheet on his own blotter. "How long until that?"

Barnes glanced at his watch. "Twenty-five minutes. Sit Room."

Evans nodded. "I'm gonna give Alicia and the kids a call. See how they're doing."

Barnes collected his papers. "How'd they take this?"

"What? Quarantining at Camp David? It's frustrating for Alicia, but they're making the most of it. Kids love it. Cabins and nature and campfires and all that. They're treating it like a vacation. One of the Marine officers took them on a hike yesterday."

"Gotta be awkward." Barnes noted on his way to the door.

The president waved the remark off. "Nah. Not much different than when I was at sea. Well for Alicia anyway. Kids weren't born yet." Evans said. "Besides. What other option was there?"

Barnes smiled tiredly and looked at the couch. "You didn't feel like crashing in here."

Evans shook his head. "Pass. Too much like falling asleep in the wardroom."

"Well, Mr. President. Enjoy your call. Tell 'em I said hi."

"Will do. See you in twenty."

The Pakistani military caravan—seven trucks in all—navigated their way around a pair of wrecked vehicles. The accident—a collision and fire that destroyed both cars—had taken up both of the highway's narrow lanes and had held up the convoy for more than an hour. Khan had briefly considered ordering his vehicles to back track and either go off road or find another, more usable road before an examination of the map and a few quick calculations had put that idea to rest. The last known serviceable road was more than sixty kilometers behind them and off-roading would limit their speed to maybe twenty kilometers per hour. Either option would result in a delay of at least two hours, possibly four. That was, Khan decided, unacceptable.

He wanted to reach his destination. He wanted to be rid of this cargo. He wanted to be rid of the Americans. Mostly, he wanted to return home, collect his wife, and disappear with his newfound wealth. As Khan watched the carcasses of burnt vehicles slip past, he went over the last few steps of the operation in his mind and estimated the time left before he could vanish.

★ ★ ★ ★ ★

Brian bent over the logbook, a cheap, black ballpoint gliding over the page—making the same entry he'd just reported to the bridge—he'd just started the ship's gas turbine main engines. As he finished the entry, the conning officer's voice repeated back the announcement.

"Started one alpha, one bravo, two alpha, two bravo GTMs. Bridge, aye."

Brian sat down to await the next order while the sailors around him monitored each piece of equipment.

"Chief, how's it looking?" Lieutenant Walker entered the room and found an open chair.

"So far so good. Almost everything that got worked on in port has been tested and the readings look good." Brian stretched and yawned. It was early, but he'd gotten some decent sleep for the first time in more than a week. That, plus two cups of coffee and a breakfast of eggs, toast, bacon, and orange juice had done wonders for his outlook on life.

"Everything but the RO?" CHENG asked.

"Yeah. We can't check on that until we're at least twelve miles out. Pump'll work fine inside that, but you run the risk of clogging up everything else. Suck up all the silt and mud."

"Paperwork on those looked good."

Brian took a sip of coffee. "It did. I'd have felt better witnessing the measurements during the install, but they didn't bother notifying anyone."

"Captain has already expressed his displeasure with the repair team lead."

"I'll bet." Brian had been the one to notify the captain that the repair team had ignored the quality assurance checkpoint. The commanding officer of USS James E. Williams hadn't taken it well. "Not much he could do though. We were already up against a hard deadline to get back out, right?"

"Yep. Apparently, there have been two attempted hijackings since we've been off station. Fleet Forces is kind of pissed."

"When aren't they pissed off?" Brian picked up one of the mikes in front of him and ordered one of his operators to make a few adjustments to a piece of gear. The order was acknowledged and Brian watched the readouts change ever so slightly as an unseen sailor dialed in the temperatures and pressures. He turned to say something to the Chief Engineer but was cut off by the Officer of the Deck's voice.

"Central, Bridge. Place one alpha, one bravo, two alpha, two bravo GTMs online."

Brian repeated the order back to the bridge before picking up a second mike.

"All spaces, Central. Stand clear of all shafts and modules while placing one alpha, one bravo, two alpha, two bravo GTMs online."

With the warning given, Brian counted to fifteen in his head. He turned to the petty officer at the propulsion console and gave the order to place the engines online. He watched the sailor depress the buttons marked 'online' in pairs—alphas first, then bravos. Everyone watched the readings as the gas turbine engines engaged. Satisfied, Brian reported completion of the task to the bridge and turned to the Chief Engineer.

"Well, here we go."

★ ★ ★ ★ ★

POTUS was just halfway through a Reuben sandwich and a rather dramatic play-by-play account of his family's morning trek through the trails of Camp David when the door opened and several people entered the Oval Office.

Evans looked up at the intrusion and examined the individuals arrayed on the other side of the desk. Leslie Barnes and the SECDEF were surrounded by a large contingent of Secret Service Agents. Everyone looked agitated and that made Evans curious. He kept scanning the room as he listened to his daughter and noticed a man in attendance that nearly made his heart stop. The president stared at the United States Army warrant officer with a briefcase strapped to his wrist and told his family he'd call back later.

Evans hung up the phone and took a deep breath before. "Gentlemen?"

Tolchanov stepped forward. "Mr. President. Sorry to interrupt your call. We need you to come with us."

Evans stood and collected a few papers. He jerked his chin at the man with the briefcase. His heart was racing. "Why's he here?"

SECDEF stood firm. "Sir. We might have a problem. Warrant Officer Jefferson here is a precaution."

Evans threw the files he'd gathered into a folio and cocked an eyebrow. The man had the briefcase from which a president could authorize the release of nuclear weapons. "He's a hell of a precaution." Evans tried to keep his voice calm and measured. "Leslie?"

Tolchanov and Barnes glanced at each other. Evans caught the look and set his paperwork down. "Gentlemen? What's going on?"

Tolchanov stepped closer to the Resolute Desk and spoke, his voice steady. "Mr. President. We may have an Empty Quiver."

32

EVANS

EVANS SAT IN THE SITUATION ROOM as patiently as possible, watching as his senior staff and an array of military officers and intelligence types busily prepared for the moment at hand. His forearms were planted squarely on the table, a single, capped pen held in both hands—mostly to give them something to do. Fidgeting probably wasn't a good look on a president, especially after being hurried to this room for the possibility of an Empty Quiver scenario. The president almost shuddered as his Director of National Intelligence swept into the room, accompanied by several of her own senior staffers.

"Mr. President. Apologies for being late." Ophelia situated herself.

"What do we know?" Evans thought the question sounded like bad television.

Adams stood and cleared her throat. "Sir, last night we received a report claiming that this man," she pointed to one screen, "arranged for the theft and sale of one of Pakistan's nuclear warheads."

Evans had seen the face before, but couldn't place it. "And who is this?"

"General Saeed Khan. He is currently the Director-General of Pakistan's Strategic Plans Division."

Evans nodded his understanding. "And who bought the nuke?"

Adams pointed at the screen again and clicked a button on her remote. "The warhead was allegedly purchased by this man. Nicholas DeGuerra. Retired US Army major. Rangers. Delta."

"The guy who owns TitanX?" Evans asked.

"Yes, sir."

Evans put the pen down and rubbed his temples. He could feel the headache coming. "Didn't the FBI just talk to that guy about a connection to the Coronado attacks?"

"Yes, Mr. President."

"Okay. First thing. What's the threat? I'm assuming this isn't attached to a missile or we'd be meeting on NEACP." Pronounced 'Knee-Cap', NEACP was the National Emergency Airborne Command Post, a Boeing E-4B jet upgraded to serve as an airborne and mobile command post in the event of a potential nuclear strike.

Adams nodded. "The information we have indicates that the sale was for a warhead only."

Evans noted that the DNI's voice was as steady as ever. He was sure his was shaking. He cleared his throat. "Okay, and where did this report come from? Can we verify this through other channels?

"Answering your first question will take a few minutes. If you don't mind."

Evans waved her on.

"The information comes from this man." Adams changed the image on the screen. "He is Colonel Pervez Raza. He has spent most of the last two decades serving as General Khan's senior aide or chief of staff. During the last few weeks, as the gears began to turn on the military withdrawal, Colonel Raza claims that Nick DeGuerra began reaching out to set up contracts to help offset his projected losses. One of those contracts was a deal to provide four of his top operators to General Khan to analyze and fix the issues with their nuclear weapons security." Adams stopped to take a sip of water. "As you can imagine, Khan's bosses weren't exactly thrilled at the idea, but they've been under tremendous scrutiny for years. The world does not trust Pakistan to secure their arsenal. DeGuerra and Khan knew that and, to prove the point, Khan set up the TitanX operators with a red cell exercise to steal a dummy nuke. According to the report, Khan, in exchange for twenty million dollars, inserted a real weapon into the exercise and then arranged for some of the more radical members of his party to stage an attack and steal the weapon."

The president raised a hand. "Hold on. We're talking about that attack just before the Coronado incident?"

The DNI nodded. "Correct, sir."

"How accurate is this information?" The Secretary of Defense spoke for the first time.

"Colonel Pervez Raza is an American and there's a tape of the agreement." Adams answered.

The DNI passed Evans a folder. He flipped it open as Adams began briefing its contents. "Pervez Raza is actually Peter Raza. He's from Boston, Massachusetts. He was recruited by the CIA out of school and sent to Pakistan after his father, who immigrated here in his forties, used some old favors to secure Peter a place at the Pakistani Military Academy. We'd been getting good information out of him until about a year ago. Pakistani ISI sniffed around him a few times and he was ordered to lay low for a bit."

Evans flipped through a few more pages and stopped. "Who are these two?"

"These are two of the TitanX employees who made the trip to Pakistan to evaluate and train the security detail. Michael Nixon is a retired SEAL and Miguel Jimenez is retired DELTA. They survived the attack at the exercise site and Khan put them on one of the PAF's gulfstreams to get them out of dodge."

Evans eyed the pictures. "What do they have to do with this?"

"Raza stowed away on their plane with taped conversations of DeGuerra and Khan meeting in Edinburgh to discuss this operation. When the plane made an unscheduled stop in Tbilisi, Raza helped them escape Pakistani custody and got them to a local safehouse."

"Escape the plane?" SECDEF asked. "What for?"

Adams shrugged. "Raza's best guess is that Khan letting Nixon and Jimenez head home was a bit of trickery. They were to be held 'safely' somewhere while the plane was under repair."

The president interrupted. "Ophelia, I think I missed a few things. What's Raza claiming?"

"Raza's estimate is that Khan and DeGuerra planned on using the TitanX operators as scapegoats. There were originally four members of the team. The other two, both also former special forces, died in the attack at the Pakistani training site. Khan and DeGuerra planned to detonate the nuke and tie the Americans and Pakistan to the event. Raza believes that the end goal is to get India to blame TitanX, the

United States, and Pakistan. They'll have the bodies of two Americans in custody, and two suspects on the run. The likely scenario is that Nixon and Jimenez were to be killed trying to 'escape.'"

SECDEF leaned on the table. "And what is all of this supposed to accomplish?"

"Raza, Nixon, and Jimenez think the purpose is to start a war."

"How?" Tolchanov wrinkled his brow. "Who with?"

The president took a breath. "That's what I can't figure. How's this work? They can't honestly think I'd nuke someone."

Adams took another sip of water. "Consensus is that Khan is attempting to get the weapon to Karachi. From there, he can load it on a ship and get it close to a major port. He doesn't have to clear customs that way and doesn't risk it showing up on a screening. The yield on their tactical nukes is still big enough to carve out anything within a half mile of the port."

"Okay," said Evans. "But what port?"

"Chennai." Adams said.

Barnes leaned back in his chair and whistled. "Shit, Daniel. Nineteen world leaders are supposed to be there for the next week. These assholes detonate a nuke there, India will respond. They'll have to. Given the recent dust-ups in Kashmir and that ultimatum they broadcast a few weeks ago, they've got no other options."

"And with me pulling out at the last minute? Jesus. That looks like I knew about this. Especially with the bodies of American contractors framed for the theft." Evans leaned forward and rubbed a spot just above his left eyebrow. "Do we believe that India will go nuclear if this happens? They're not stupid and they're not insane."

"Sir," SECDEF began. "It's not a matter of making a stupid or rash decision. Not for them. They will see this exactly as they have indicated for the past few months. They'll see radical terrorism coming from Pakistan to detonate a nuke on Indian soil while the United States is leaving out the back door—and they'll take that as an act of passive support. And that's without a couple of American contractors tied to the event. With that. Hell, sir. They'll probably convince themselves that we had a hand in this."

"I can't see that," Evans contended. "I've met the Indian Prime

Minister. He's not that foolish."

"He doesn't have to be, Daniel," Barnes noted. "India has been bitching about our support of Pakistan and our overarching reluctance to hammer them on terrorism and nuclear safety protocols for more than a decade. They've been screaming it at the world. A stolen Pakistani nuke going off in Chennai, during the G20, with American contractors involved is all of their worst nightmares come true. It'll be one big 'I told you so' moment and they will go to war over this. With Pakistan and us."

"I can buy that," Evans agreed. "But going nuke? I can see them flipping a nuke at Pakistan—possibly. But us? That seems highly irrational. They have a good grasp on the size of our arsenal. They have to."

"Unless they understand that there is no way in hell you're willing to turn India into a smoking ruin over this. If they believe that, this is possible." SECDEF pointed out. "Plus, there is your stance on our continued presence in the region. You either have to keep your word to the American people and stay out of this fight—at which point India will attempt to wipe Pakistan off the face of the earth—or you have to commit troops."

"And we can't just stand by while India destroys Pakistan, can we?" Evans asked. He was starting to see it now. "How much money and aid have we given to Pakistan over the years? How much time have we spent working with them and trying to help them along? And if India knows we're in the fight, it stays conventional. We can't just turn our back and sneak out while India kicks in the front door and sets fire to the place? Can we?"

"No, sir," SECDEF said. "I don't believe we can. There's another reason, apart from the ally and humanity angle. Pakistan has nukes—one of which has already been stolen. If India bum rushes them and all hell breaks loose, it's a fair bet more of those damn things go missing. It's also safe to assume that DeGuerra knows that and is betting that we'll deep six the withdrawal in order to help Pakistan safeguard those nukes. I believe the intent here is to set off the nuke to foment a conventional conflict."

Evans nodded. "Okay. If we can't stop Khan and DeGuerra,

we'll get drawn into another war. That doesn't help DeGuerra save his company. They're still implicated and we'll have no choice but to unleash the Department of Justice on them. Maybe they can both disappear, Khan with his twenty million and DeGuerra with whatever he's got left. Maybe we find them. Maybe we don't. This doesn't save anything. Right?"

Adams shook her head. "I disagree. It doesn't matter now because of Raza and the information he got to us. Without that, the only real complication for DeGuerra is having Patterson on the loose. That's an easy fix. Take those portions of the puzzle away and we'd know little more than what's on the news." DNI Adams pulled another folder from her pile and slid it down the table. "Besides, sir, it's possible that this was never about saving TitanX. Raza pulled some data and I had my folks pulling more for the last hour or so. Nicholas DeGuerra has invested quite a bit of his net worth in the next generation of war fighting tech. Rough estimate is just shy of ninety percent of his holdings over the past six years. All of it in small businesses that have found a niche to exploit. He was betting big on sustained conflict in the region. All of those investments stood to blow up, except..."

Evans looked up from the folder. "Except I got elected." He gestured at the documents in front of him. "If I hadn't won the election and ordered the withdrawal, these contracts would end up paying off big for DeGuerra, right? On the order of tens of billions?"

Adams nodded. "Correct, sir."

"So, this is all about money? Use the rhetoric coming out of India and our alliance with Pakistan to kick off a war that we can't ignore so that this son of a bitch can generate a profit?"

"Except for the tapes and a few witnesses, this is all largely circumstantial. But yes, Mr. President. That appears to be the case." DNI Adams agreed.

The president stood. "Okay. You've sold me. How do we stop this?"

33

NIXON

MIKE NIXON JUMPED when the hand shook him awake. It took a few seconds after his eyes snapped open to recognize Miguel's face in the dark.

"What?"

"Come on, Mike. Pete got a response."

Mike closed his eyes. "Alright. I'll be down in five."

Miguel left the room and Mike stared at the poorly plastered ceiling for a few moments more before swinging his feet out of the bed and hauling himself upright. He was too tired and sore to speculate on the response and, instead, spent three minutes focusing on getting his boots tied and clomping his way to the small bathroom in the hall. When he made it to the small kitchen, he found a fresh cup of coffee waiting.

"Morning," Raza greeted him with a sheaf of papers. "I assume you both have clearances, not that it matters much right now."

Mike and Miguel both nodded and began going through the papers while Raza summarized. "White House has been busy while you boys have been napping. They're raising holy hell trying to find the Khan and the nuke."

"So, they believed us?" Miguel asked.

"Funny enough, yeah." Raza admitted. "As crazy as this all sounds, they did. Someone must've done one hell of a good job briefing this shit."

Mike looked up from the papers. "So, what's next for us? Back home?"

"You'd think so, but no." Raza shook his head. "We're catching the first of a few flights in about an hour."

"To where?" Miguel asked.

Raza smiled. "First Karachi. Then to one of the Navy's destroyers."

"Why there?" Miguel asked.

"No idea." Raza admitted. "Gets us somewhere Khan can't find us?"

"And makes it look like the US government was involved in this mess." Mike pointed out. "Anything else?"

"Yeah. Looks like the FBI is supposed to be heading out to pick up your boss and everyone is scrambling to find some guy named Patterson."

Miguel looked up. "Will?"

"Yeah," Raza nodded. "Know him?"

Mike took a gulp of coffee. "Yeah. He's DeGuerra's little bulldog. Handles odd jobs for Nick. Bit of an asshole. Huge chip on his shoulder. But he's a solid dude."

"Operator?" Raza asked.

Miguel laughed. "Hell no. Can't get a clearance. Did some prison time before Nick hired him."

"He can handle himself though," Mike pointed out. "He's been through the same Indoc course the rest of the TitanX folks go through. What does everyone want with him?"

Raza topped his coffee off. "Apparently he was responsible for transporting four guys from one of the TitanX detention facilities in Iraq to Coronado where they detonated two truck bombs at the BUD/S compound."

Mike's head snapped around. "What?"

Raza turned to Mike. "You didn't know?"

Mike shook his head.

"A few days back, four Islamic State terrorists exploded two ANFO bombs at BUD/S. One at the headquarters and one at the grinder."

Mike just sat there, blinking. Miguel growled. "What the hell for?"

A shrug. "No idea. I don't have much else on that. There were some videos sent by the attackers to the news, but I haven't seen them. If Patterson is DeGuerra's gopher, his involvement makes it seem connected, but that's just speculation. Best guess? Create chaos. Scare people. Make it easier on the president to renege on his promise to get the hell out of the region."

"Casualties?" Mike almost croaked out the word.

Raza finished his cup of coffee. "I don't know. I didn't get any other details."

Mike stood. "You got a phone in this place? A secure one?"

Raza looked at his watch. "Yeah. But you're gonna have to hurry. We got a plane to catch."

Mike sat next to a backpack of newly purchased essentials—a change of clothes, toothbrush, toothpaste and some other toiletries—and waited as the phone rang. Raza stood by, glancing at his watch. The CIA field officer was agitated and Mike knew why. They needed to be on the road and Mike had tried this call four times already. As he glanced at Raza, he whispered a silent prayer that someone would answer. Mike reached to disconnect the call when the ringing was interrupted by a familiar voice.

"Who the hell is this?"

"Rip?"

Gary Janicek's voice sounded hollow. "Nixon?"

"It's me, Rip. Just heard. Everyone whole?"

Seconds ticked by before Janicek's voice came back on the line. "No. We lost a lot of people. Instructors. Students. Civilian staff."

"I'm sorry, man."

Another pause. "Nix. Where are you that you just heard?"

Mike smiled. The man doesn't miss a thing. "Overseas. Might need some help with something. You up for it?"

The hollow voice changed slightly. "Something? What thing?" Janicek asked.

"A hunting expedition."

"Anything to do with what happened here?"

"Possibly. Not quite sure yet. Can you pull some strings and get free?" That was asking a lot. Rip was still on active duty, but Mike was thinking Peter might pull strings and get the man temporary orders.

The silence was longer this time. When Janicek's voice came on the line, it was different again—like he was struggling with something big. "Nix, you remember Rod?"

"Yeah. Your sister's kid. How is he?"

"Those fuckers got Rod, Nix."

Mike blinked at the phone. "What?"

"He joined up and came to BUD/S. Was in Hell Week when this shit went down. He's here at Balboa. He's pretty fucked up."

"Jesus." Mike looked from the phone to Raza, who tapped a finger on his watch. "I'm sorry, Rip. Listen man. I gotta get moving. I'll call back when I can."

"Nix? You gonna find these assholes?"

"Possibly."

Silence.

"Lay down the hate on those fuckers, Nix."

Two unmarked cars pulled up to the first guard shack at the TitanX Headquarters in Schroon Falls. The driver stepped out of the lead vehicle and flashed a set of FBI credentials at one of the two waiting security officers. She spoke to both guards before returning to her car to wait, knowing that additional vehicles were now sitting on every gate, access road, or walking path leading to or from the compound.

Khan sat in the passenger seat of the truck and looked at his watch. One more hour to drive and he'd offload the device and the Americans. After that, he'd be free to vanish according to plan. But nothing was going according to plan. They'd been held up by the traffic accident and had suffered two vehicle problems of their own—both of which had nearly sent him into apoplectic rages.

Less than thirty minutes after clearing the two-car pile-up, the vehicle carrying the device had come to a shuddering halt in the middle of the highway with steam pouring out of the engine compartment. It had taken several minutes for one of the drivers to discover a hole in the truck's radiator and the evidence of shoddy attempts at repair. That had cost the convoy nearly an hour as several men gathered together to haul the device out of the bed of the truck and load it onto another vehicle.

A snapped a ball joint on the front left wheel of the lead vehicle had caused another delay. The truck's young driver had blocked both lanes when he'd panic stopped the massive truck. It had taken another hour—and the strength of every able-bodied man in the convoy—to clear the road.

Dealing with poorly maintained vehicles had stressed Khan to his limits—the general was self-aware enough to admit that. He'd refrained from yelling at the men. They weren't mechanics and they weren't responsible for the failures. They also weren't the biggest reason Khan's blood was boiling.

The biggest thorn in Khan's side right now was Nicholas DeGuerra. His old friend had seemingly forgotten the adage about things that can go wrong and had been calling every thirty minutes to check on their progress. Khan looked at his watch again and noted that the next call would be in seconds. He leaned his head back against the seat and closed his eyes. At least the impatient fool was using different phones with different numbers for each call.

The phone in Khan's pocket buzzed. He'd turned off the audible ring because the only tone available grated on his nerves. Khan answered the call.

"The damn boat is waiting for the shipment." Nick's voice blared through the small speaker, not bothering to wait for any greeting.

"We will make the delivery as promised. The order will be on time."

"The order is already late!"

Khan waited, took a breath. He counted to five. "The delivery to your final destination has a window of several days once shipped. Yes, the vessel awaits this portion of your order, but there is no impact to the schedule you've requested."

There was a pause on the line. Khan hoped Nicholas was taking a moment to get a grip on himself. No such luck. When DeGuerra's voice came back on the line he sounded as agitated as ever.

"Listen. I paid for a service and I have a very tight schedule. For the money this order is costing me, I expect my demands to be met. What part of that don't you get?"

Khan cocked his head to the side when Nick mentioned the

schedule again. "Sir, you have been a client of mine for a long time and I value your patronage. I cannot help wondering if the agreed upon schedule has changed."

The line went silent for a few moments before Nick's agitated voice came back. "Yes, the schedule has changed. This delivery needs to be expedited."

Khan looked curiously at his phone. He thought the problem through and came to one possible conclusion. He went pale at the thought. When he spoke, he found it difficult to keep his voice from trembling. "Sir, is the project you are working on compromised?"

"Fuck yes, it is!" Nick screamed through the phone. "One of my guards texted me a few minutes ago to tell me that the FBI is camped out in front of my gate."

"For the Patterson fool?"

"For me, damnit."

"And how do you know this?"

"Because they only asked if I was on the property."

Khan sat upright. "I will expedite the delivery. Give me one more hour."

"Hurry the hell up."

34

THOMPSON

BRIAN SAT IN THE CAPTAIN'S CHAIR in Central Control eyeing every gage and dial. The ship was only a few hours out of Seychelles and he was in a foul mood.

As soon as the ship had been twelve miles clear of land, Brian had given the order to start the newly installed RO pump—a process that had gone well until the operator had depressed the 'start' button. Everything after that had been a near carbon-copy repeat of the pump's previous failure. An overamping motor had failed to stop when one of the pump's three pistons had seized on start-up. The massive motor had pushed right through and ground the pump's internals to a hot, glittery, oily mess. Again.

Brian had been pissed at the report, but he hadn't had time to go check out the unit himself. His inclination to do so had been preempted by a pair of orders that left him wondering what in the hell was going on and watching the rest of his gear with a stress-filled foreboding.

The bridge had dialed up a flank bell and turned the USS James E. Williams northeast. Brian could see on a display in the corner of the room that the ship was pointed somewhere other than Somalia and he knew that the ship hadn't done more than ten minutes at a flank bell in the few months he'd been onboard. Those two things told Brian something was up, just not what it was. The mystery was further deepened when the ship's 1MC announcing system had ordered all department heads to the wardroom.

"Top?" It was Petty Officer Cruz. "Getting awfully close to losing two Alpha. One Bravo is climbing now, too."

Brian leaned forward in the chair to examine the readout. One engine was running hot, dangerously close to the point where it would perform a programmed shut-down as a precaution against other, more distressing scenarios. The other wasn't far behind.

"Top, aye." Brian picked up the phone and punched in the number for the bridge.

"Bridge. Junior Officer of the Deck."

"Jason, Brian. What gives?"

"No idea, man. None."

"Any idea how long we're doing this?"

"None. Orders are to haul ass on this heading, tell people to get the hell out of our way, and don't run into anything."

"Great," Brian grumped. "Well, if anyone gives a shit, this Speed Racer shit is gonna cost us an engine soon. Or worse."

"Problem?"

"I've got one engine almost redlined and another climbing."

"What's the best available speed on two engines and three engines?" Jason asked. Brian told him, checking a wall chart to verify the numbers. Over the phone, he could hear Jason scribbling the information down on one of the plexiglass boards on the bridge. "Okay, Brian. I'll let the Officer of the Deck know and get back to you if I hear anything."

"Thanks." Brian hung the phone back on its rack and resumed watching the digital gages on the panel in front of him.

The president strode into the Oval Office after meetings in which he had appointed new ambassadors to South Africa and Germany—the previous appointees had both retired due to ongoing health issues. He saw his Director of National Intelligence and Chief of Staff waiting on the couch. Both stood as he entered the room. Evans headed straight for his desk and waved his guests back to their seats. "Ophelia, where do we stand?"

"Frank will be up in a minute. The tapes from Raza left Tbilisi about an hour ago, but the chief of station there typed up a transcript and got it to us after loading Raza and the TitanX guys on a plane."

"And the transcript?" Evans collapsed into the custom chair behind his desk.

Barnes pointed. "There's a copy on the desk there, but the bottom line is pretty simple. We've allegedly got Nicholas DeGuerra on tape, purchasing a Pakistani nuclear weapon for twenty million dollars."

The president cast a baleful look at his two advisors as the side door to the Oval Office anteroom opened to admit the Secretary of Defense. "Allegedly?"

DNI Adams shifted the notes in her hand while answering. "These are just transcripts. We'll analyze the tapes when they get here. Confirm the voices. Make sure that what we have here is what is on the tapes. I don't expect the facts to change."

"We're looking for Khan. What are we doing about DeGuerra?" Barnes asked for the president, who was busy rubbing his temples again.

"The FBI is currently sitting outside the compound at Schroon Falls, waiting for a judge to sign off on the warrant. DeGuerra is on the premises. Once we have the tapes, we'll turn them over to the attorney general's office and they can run things from there." Adams replied.

Tolchanov got himself situated. "Sorry I'm late Mr. President. Getting a few last-minute updates."

Evans waved off the apology. "Go ahead, Frank."

"We just got the Williams turned around. They were leaving Seychelles after some repairs and are heading towards the Palk Strait at best possible speed."

Evans looked up. "My geography is a bit fuzzy. Where is the Palk Strait and how far is that from Seychelles?"

SECDEF looked at his notes. "Palk Strait is between India and Sri Lanka. We figure that's our best shot to intercept this thing. Based on what this Raza guy has told us, we checked on shipping between Karachi and Chennai. Only three vessels set to travel that route in the next week. Motor vessels Dorian, Gustavo, and Invicta are scheduled to sail today, two days from now, and three days from now, respectively. Seychelles is roughly three thousand kilometers and change from Chennai. At flank speed, the Williams can be on station to attempt intercept in around sixty hours."

The president was scribbling down bits of data. "You said Dorian sails first?"

Tolchanov nodded. "Yes, sir."

"And how long until she hits the strait?"

"Her top speed is around seventeen knots. She can be at the strait fifty-six hours after she sets sail."

Barnes looked up from the pad of paper he was using. "That's cutting it close. Can't the Indian Navy intercept?"

SECDEF shook his head. "All they have local are some smaller vessels, mostly small coast guard cutter types. Nothing bigger than a two-hundred-footer and nothing with a boarding team. Most of their big guns are off to the south. They'll turn those hulls around as soon as we tell them what's going on."

"And Williams is the closest we have?" The President asked.

SECDEF shook his head again. "Technically, no. Three destroyers in the Persian Gulf are closer, but that means a transit through the Straits of Hormuz and that will slow them down. Williams has a straight shot and she doesn't have to slow down unless something breaks. We are ordering two of the Persian Gulf destroyers to head to the Palk Strait just in case the Williams does falter."

Evans nodded. "And I'm assuming our last option is an air strike?"

"Yes, sir," Tolchanov confirmed. "We want this thing intact and that means a boarding team. If that's unsuccessful, the Williams can put her on the bottom. Last resort is an airstrike or cruise missiles from elsewhere. If we have to use two super hornets off of Stennis in the Gulf, we can. There are overflight concerns with doing that. Iran is still gonna see them and want to know what they're up to."

The president nodded. "I suppose the commander of the Williams wants to know his or her rules of engagement?"

"It's a Commander Allen, and yes sir, he'll need your guidance."

"Allen?" The president's head snapped up. "Derrick Allen?"

Barnes, Tolchanov, and Adams all looked at each other. Barnes spoke. "Know him?"

"Christ, yes. He was the Damage Control Assistant on my last command."

SECDEF stood. "I'll work on getting a direct line to the Williams for you Mr. President."

Evans nodded. "Thanks."

★ ★ ★ ★ ★

Khan stood next to Will Patterson, both tracking the crate as a crane lifted it through the air and swung it over the forward cargo deck of the M/V Dorian. Throughout his years of military service, the general had seen cranes operate before and the process never ceased to amaze him.

"Funny how precise one of those things can be, huh?" Patterson said.

Khan turned and smiled at the man. He'd been thinking the same thing. "It is." He waved a hand at the trucks. "One last task. Shall we?" Khan began to walk back to where the rest of the vehicles, and his men, were waiting.

Patterson's hand grabbed the general's shoulder and Khan turned. He looked at the hand and then at the face behind it.

"Do you trust these men?"

Khan cocked his head. It seemed an odd question for a man whose own employer had paid five million dollars to set him up. He smiled warmly, as a grandfather might. "I trust these men with my life. They will do as they are told."

The American nodded and followed Khan towards the waiting men and vehicles. The men tasked to ride the ship with their cargo had all swapped uniforms for civilian attire—mostly western-style jeans, t-shirts, and boots. Each, Khan saw, carried a backpack with what few belongings they would need for what was left of their lives. In each face, Khan could see a curious mix of resolve and fear. He supposed that was natural.

Two of the men stepped forward and Khan waved the rest of the group off. The general turned to Patterson. "These men will execute your tasks."

Patterson looked at the two volunteers in front of him. "Who are they?"

Khan looked from the men to Patterson. "Does it matter?"

Patterson glared at Khan for a moment before unslinging his backpack. He opened the top and withdrew four objects—two cellular phones and two items that closely resembled phones. He instructed the two men in front of him as Khan translated.

"These are the remotes for the device. One for each of you in case one breaks or something happens. The ship must be as close to the port as possible before you activate the timer." Patterson demonstrated how to unlock the safety cover and activate the weapon. The older of the two volunteers looked on while the younger began a conversation with Khan.

"What's he asking?" Patterson asked.

"He is assuming that someone will try to stop them and wants to know what to do."

Patterson directed his answer at the man who asked the question while Khan translated again. "The Indian Navy can't do anything. Their coastal defenses are smaller ships which the Dorian's master will drive through, if necessary. Their larger ships are too far away to intercept."

The man spoke again. Khan turned. "And the Americans?"

Patterson looked at Khan. "Smart kid."

"No. There are always Americans around. It's a fact of life."

Patterson nodded and held up the cell phones. Khan translated again. "These phones have one number programmed into them. There is only one American ship close enough to attempt an intercept. It will attempt a boarding first. If that happens, you call the number programmed in these phones."

Khan asked the next question. "And what happens?" He hadn't been told about this part and had assumed these men would simply try to fend off any attempt at boarding using the weapons the ship's master had stashed in their cabins.

"You watch the ship explode."

35

EVANS

THE INTERCOM IN THE OVAL OFFICE chirped to the group waiting around the president's desk. "USS James E. Williams on the line, sir."

Evans depressed one of the flashing buttons on the phone. "Derrick?"

"Mr. President."

"How's your ship holding up?" Evans asked, knowing the answer he'd get before he finished the question. Despite knowing each other and having served together for two years, there was protocol to be observed. The man driving a ship halfway around the world could not, and would not, air any grievances or problems. Not on this call.

"We're good sir. Crew's rested and the ship is holding up."

Evans nodded. "Derrick. You've heard what's happened and you know where you're headed. I suppose you need to know what I want done."

"The message wasn't clear on that, Mr. President." Evans could hear the familiar background noises of a ship at sea over the phone and briefly considered how surreal it must be to announce such routine things as chow times while chasing down a cargo ship with a nuclear weapon onboard.

Evans cleared his throat. "Commander Allen, we believe that the weapon is onboard one of three ships. The Dorian, the Gustavo, and the Invicta are all sailing from Karachi to Chennai. Dorian has already set sail. You are to intercept each of those ships before they reach the Palk Strait and conduct a boarding. Search for, locate, and secure the device. You are authorized to transfer the weapon to the Williams and have a prize crew take possession of the vessel. Questions?"

"I assume this is a non-compliant boarding, Mr. President." It was more of a question than a statement. Evans looked around. SECDEF nodded at him.

"That is correct, Commander. Your boarding teams are to expect active resistance. Anyone on that ship is to be considered hostile and the use of deadly force is authorized."

"And if the boarding is not successful, Mr. President?"

"In that event, you are authorized to fire on the vessel. Put her on the bottom, Commander."

The silence that accompanied those words was deafening.

"Commander Allen?"

"Yes, Mr. President?"

"Godspeed, sir."

"Thank you, Mr. President."

Daniel Evans punched the button to end the conversation and slumped back into his chair. "Okay folks, let's get SECSTATE in here and figure out what to tell India."

Mike Nixon, Miguel Jimenez, and Pete Raza stepped onto the light grey MH-60 Seahawk and fastened their seatbelts for the four-hour flight to the USS James E. Williams. Around them, the flight crew performed the hundred tasks necessary for a quick turnaround. It took less than fifteen minutes for the ground crew at Karachi to fill up the helo's fuel tanks and give the aircraft a good once over. The three passengers sat patiently as the crew chief climbed aboard and took his place. Mike Nixon watched the sailor don a headset and speak into it as the Seahawk's rotors sped up and the craft clawed its way into the sky.

Khan was just sitting down at a cheap plastic table when the phone in his pocket buzzed. Will Patterson heard the vibration and looked up. "DeGuerra?"

Khan nodded and stood, pulling the phone from his pocket as he left the room. "Hello."

"Are you at the safe house?" Nick's agitated voice asked. Khan wondered how long a man could live in such a state.

"We are." Khan confirmed. They'd been here for hours, just as Nick had demanded. "Why are we here, Nicholas?"

Here, precisely defined on a map, was Bhuj—a small city in northwestern India. Within minutes of the departure of M/V Dorian, DeGuerra had called Khan and demanded that he take Patterson and the bodies of the two other Americans to this safe house. Khan had no idea how or when DeGuerra had set this place up and he sensed that the home's existence had also been a revelation to Patterson.

The accommodations weren't luxurious, but they weren't abysmal. There was sufficient room for everyone—Khan, his two remaining aides, Patterson, and the bodies of the two Americans. Even being in India didn't bother the general much, although he wasn't thrilled to be in the same country where a Pakistani nuke was going to be set off.

"You're there because those men need to be caught trying to escape India."

Khan spoke in a measured voice. "And you think I need to be here for that? What purpose does that serve?"

"It's your nuke, Saeed."

"Was, Nicholas. Was. It is no more. I should be halfway to the Caribbean by now. Besides, you need the Indians to find and kill them. Not me."

The line was quiet for a few moments and Khan could hear DeGuerra breathing. When Nick spoke again, Khan was surprised to hear how much calmer the voice sounded.

"Saeed. I know this isn't how you planned this, but I need you to stay put until this thing goes off. Once this is done, you wrap up the loose ends there and disappear. I get my war and you get another five million."

Another five million? Khan paused, thinking. He made a decision. "Nicholas. Is the FBI still outside your compound?"

"Yes. Of course."

"And they are undoubtedly there for you?"

The anger returned to DeGuerra's voice. "Yes."

Khan smiled. "Ten."

"What?"

"I'll stay put for an additional ten million."

The answer practically blew out Khan's eardrum. "You'll stay put for fucking free, Saeed."

"Or what? My friend, you are surrounded by the FBI. You can't actually keep me here. What can you do? Call up your president, apologize, and tell him where I am?"

"You son of a…"

"Nicholas. No need for that. Ten million more and I execute the plan you have suggested. Without that, I vanish the second I hang up this phone and maybe tip off Mr. Patterson about your plans for him as well."

The phone went quiet for long enough that Khan checked to see if the call was still connected. After nearly a minute, DeGuerra's voice came back on the line. "Fine. Ten."

Khan checked his watch. The M/V Dorian would be nearly to India's southernmost point, passing a city called Nagercoil on its way through the narrow strait between India and Sri Lanka. Purportedly capable of up to seventeen knots, the voyage tracker on the internet indicated a sustained speed of only thirteen for the aging cargo hauler. Khan calculated the ship's remaining travel time to Chennai and smiled to himself. An additional ten million for another day of sitting around and eating was, he decided, a worthwhile investment.

The USS James E. Williams had to slow down to retrieve the Seahawk. Brian was thankful for the pause. It was a minor speed adjustment that lasted less than fifteen minutes, but it helped. All four engines needed the breather. Three of the gas turbines driving the ship through the Indian Ocean were within two or three degrees of shutdown and one engine had developed an odd vibration that was registering at warning levels on the displays in Central.

Brian watched the screen above his head, the feed coming from the flight deck. On the screen, the ship's small complement of aviation mechanics worked quickly to fold in the helo's rotors and collapsible tail section to prepare the chopper for stowage in the port hangar.

The phone next to Brian rang.

"Central. EOOW."

"Chief, Captain here."

Brian sat up. "Yes, sir. What can I do for you?"

"Five more minutes to stow the helo and get back up to speed. Plant okay?"

"It'll be fine, sir. We'll get the same warnings a few minutes after you dial up a flank bell, but she'll hold. Not much we can do anyway."

"Rog. I'll be down there in about ten minutes. Find CHENG and Chief Guillory. Have them down there when I get there."

"Aye, aye, sir. Anything else?"

"Not right now. Tell your folks they're doing a helluva job."

"Yes, sir." The phone clicked off and Brian just stared at the handset.

Evans entered the Situation Room. He'd lost count of how often he'd been down here in the last week and supposed that was some indication for how his presidency was progressing. He'd made three calls since giving Commander Allen his marching orders and only one of them had been amiable. Between calls to the Indian Prime Minister, who'd stopped just shy of screaming, he'd snuck in a call to his wife and kids.

"Where are they?"

A lieutenant colonel in the green service uniform of a United States Marine, answered. "Mr. President, the Dorian is just passing Nagercoil, India." The marine used the laser pointer on a remote to show the position on a projected map. "USS James E. Williams is here." The pointer shifted slightly southwest.

Evans examined the map and thought for a moment. "Night boarding. Time to intercept?"

"Approximately two hours, Mr. President."

Evans turned to SECDEF. "Frank, how long 'til the two destroyers from the Gulf are on station?"

"Tomorrow afternoon. They had to do a quick refuel before they left the Gulf."

"So, we can block the Palk Strait for the Gustavo and the Invicta?"

"Yes, sir. India and Sri Lanka are both onboard. I talked to both defense ministers today. Neither is happy."

"How'd you sell it to Sri Lanka?"

"National security. Easy to explain with the G20 happening a few hours north."

"That's not really a lie."

"And it doesn't take a huge leap of imagination for them to figure out the reason. Probably won't guess nuke, but they'll conclude we're looking for some sort of weapon."

"Let's just hope this thing isn't on the Dorian. I'll feel better with more ships in the area. This is cutting it too close."

DNI Adams entered the room and took her usual place. "Mr. President, just got word from Justice. Sealed indictment against Nicholas DeGuerra. FBI is getting the warrant and heading onto the compound to pick him up."

"Do we expect any issues there?" POTUS asked.

"Hard to say. You wouldn't think so. Yes, the man basically has a small military force there, but I don't think they'll get into a shootout with law enforcement. Ninety-nine-point-nine percent of the TitanX folks are just normal people, going about their jobs and trying to pay the bills."

"With no idea their boss is trying to start a damn war. Will he resist?" Evans asked.

"FBI is deploying a couple of hostage rescue teams to assist in the arrest, so, let's hope not."

36

THOMPSON

BRIAN HEARD THE WATERTIGHT DOOR to Central open behind him and ignored it. His main engines were coming back up to speed and he was monitoring the temperatures and vibrations generated by the ship's four, massive General Electric LM2500 gas turbines. Each engine was running hot again, flirting with the programmed over-temp shutdown setting. Two of the engines now had slight tremors, nothing that could ever be seen with the naked eye, but vibrations felt by an array of sensors installed by the manufacturer. As the temperatures and pressures leveled out, Brian nodded and turned.

Besides the normal complement of engineers, Central Control was now packed with the addition of the captain, the executive officer, the CHENG, Lieutenant Lee, Chief Guillory, Master Chief Carrillo, and three men Thompson had never seen before.

Commander Allen looked at Brian. "Chief, you comfortable asking these two to leave the space for a few minutes?" He pointed to the two console operators.

Brian didn't have to give permission. The captain could order central cleared. But he hadn't. He looked to the Chief Engineer and Tim Guillory. Both nodded. Brian turned to the electric plant and propulsion plant console operators. "Becker, Cruz. Can you step outside? CHENG and Chief here will cover your watch stations."

Both sailors conducted a short turnover and exited the room before Brian spoke again. "Okay, Captain. The room is yours."

"Chief, in a few minutes, we're going to set battle stations and get the boarding team ready. We're chasing down a merchant vessel with a cargo that the White House has ordered us to seize. Possibly."

"Possibly?"

The captain shrugged. "The cargo we're looking for is on one of three ships. This is the first one we need to track down."

Brian looked at the people around him and then ran his eyes over the engine readouts again. "Something special about this one, sir?"

"I'll let this gentleman answer your questions, but I came down here to let you know that you won't be on the boarding team for this."

Brian's head turned. "I'm the only small boat engineer onboard."

Commander Allen held his hand up. "I know that and I'm ignoring the regs for these boardings. You'll understand in a few minutes." Brian interrupted but the captain cut him off. "Mr. Raza, if you please."

Raza extended a hand. Brian shook it. "Chief, my name is Pete Raza. One of the three vessels we will be boarding is transporting a stolen nuclear weapon."

Brian's eyes went wide. "What the fuck?"

"Let him finish, Brian." Carrillo said.

"There's a stolen nuke on one of these ships. It is expected that the ship with the warhead won't exactly agree to a compliant boarding. We understand that you and Chief Guillory are the only two chiefs in this department. When the captain mentioned this, I suggested replacing you on the team with these gentlemen." Raza motioned to the two men with him.

"Who are you guys?"

The taller of the two answered. "I'm Mike and this is Miguel. Private contractors working for Mr. Raza."

Brian turned to Commander Allen and Lieutenant Lee. "One boat?"

"Plus both helos." The captain nodded. "On the chance the shit hits the fan, I can't have half of my engineering department chiefs riding around on a boat. We've talked about this. You need to be here, in Central. Not out there playing cops and robbers."

Brian shrugged. "Understood, sir. I'll keep my ass here. I get to stay in radio contact with the coxswain just in case?"

Commander Allen nodded. "Sure. Why the hell not."

The captain started to say something else, but the ship's 1MC announcing system blared to life and requested that he contact the bridge.

As Commander Allen moved to one of the wall-mounted telephones, the two new boarding team members turned to Brian. "Don't like this?" Miguel asked.

Brian continued scanning gages. "Those boats have had some problems. We've worked most of them out, but they make me nervous. I don't like sending people out like that."

"Anything we should worry about?" Mike asked.

Brian shook his head. "Nah. I'm just overly cautious. I'm assuming you both used to be military?"

Mike nodded. "I was Navy. He was Army."

Brian turned. "SEAL and a Ranger?"

"Something like that." Mike allowed.

Brian went back to scanning as the captain hung up. "Is this shit for real?"

The two men shared a look before Mike answered. "It is."

"Who stole the nuke?"

Mike didn't even blink. "Our old boss."

Gonging erupted throughout USS James E. Williams, accompanied by a calm voice on the 1MC.

"General Quarters. General Quarters. All hands man your battle stations."

Meals, sleep, and routine work were forgotten as three hundred sailors darted up and down ladders and through passageways, donning firefighting gear and flash hoods while they buttoned down every access, hatch, and scuttle on the ship. Reports flowed into Central from the outlying repair lockers, giving minute-by-minute updates on the status of the ship. It took just over four minutes for every sailor to reach their assigned battle station and to get the ship ready, a condition which Lieutenant junior grade Leslie Hunter, the ship's Damage Control Assistant, announced to the entire crew after Brian transferred control of the 1MC system to her.

★ ★ ★ ★ ★

"Mr. President?"

Evans looked up from his seat at the head of the table. It was SECDEF. "The Williams is on station. They have visual on the Dorian and just went to battle stations. They'll be hailing the ship in the next few minutes."

POTUS nodded. "Thanks."

Evans knew what was next. Commander Allen would try to contact the Dorian's bridge crew and convince the cargo ship to halt. At that point, the Dorian's master had three options. They could halt—in which case it was unlikely that the Dorian was the ship the Navy was looking for. They could ignore the Williams—which would make them look guilty. Last, they could try to run. That would probably mean this was the correct ship. There was a fourth option, thought the president. But that was something he didn't want to consider at the moment. Evans turned to the DNI. "How long on the New York part of this?"

"Another hour to get the pieces in place. The headquarters is fairly large and they don't want to miss him."

"Any chance he already skipped?" Leslie Barnes asked.

"It's possible. The security guards at the front gate are still behaving like he's there. No traffic in or out so far. It's possible he just climbed a fence and walked out, but there isn't a whole lot we can do about that."

"Fair enough. Keep me updated."

"Yes, sir."

"Mr. President?" It was SECDEF. "Williams just hailed the Dorian."

★ ★ ★ ★ ★

Gregor Varayev had been running cargo ships for nearly thirty years, with the occasional lucrative foray into the transport and delivery of goods that could not be listed on any manifests. Over three decades, the portly captain had become a pipeline for hire for individuals and organizations interested in moving arms, humans, narcotics, and an assortment of other illicit cargo. Varayev had done a lot of interesting things in his thirty years at sea, but trying to outrun the United States Navy destroyer four nautical miles behind him was a wholly new and frightening experience.

Varayev spat on the deck and slapped the volume knob on the radio console, silencing the persistent American voice. Growling, he snatched up a phone and dialed the number to one of the guest cabins.

"Americans, Asif. Get your men ready."

The phone clicked off and Varayev replaced the handset, trading it for a set of binoculars he strung around his neck. Heading for the door to a small, port side bridge wing, Varayev ordered the ship to full speed.

The nearly seventy-year-old Chechen sailor didn't know what was in that crate on the foredeck, only that it came with heavily armed men and a seven-figure price tag for safe delivery. As he raised his binoculars to his eyes and peered aft into the darkness, he felt his ship surge forward. Knowing that the destroyer behind him had at least ten knots on him, he prayed that the men below decks knew what they were about.

At four different entrances to the Schroon Falls headquarters of TitanX, FBI Hostage Rescue Team armored vehicles raced up the access roads—in each case let through by the company's own security staff after the senior agent at each gate flashed a badge and a copy of the warrant calling for the arrest of Nicholas DeGuerra. One vehicle carried Paul Burkhart.

Paul had been returning to the facility when he'd been stopped by the agents at the main gate. A brief discussion between Paul and the on-scene commander had nearly escalated into a physical confrontation. The imminent fist fight had been avoided only when the commander had briefed Burkhart in on the reasons for the raid. As the assault team readied themselves, Paul had worked through the material. He'd experienced every possible emotion. Disbelief had turned to anger. Anger had turned to rage. Rage had led Paul to demand inclusion on the team. The on-scene commander had been reluctant until Paul pointed out that no one else knew the campus like he did.

Outfitted in a bullet-proof vest and a navy-blue FBI windbreaker, Burkhart bounced along in the back of the vehicle, wishing someone had issued him a weapon.

DeGuerra saw the first vehicle on security footage fed to his office wirelessly and froze for almost ten full seconds. After recovering from the momentary shock, he raced from his office, grabbing a phone, a set of master key cards, and his personal weapon—a venerable, old Colt 1911. He hit the service elevator at full speed, swiping a card across the reader and slipping between the doors just as the first matte black truck discharged its team at the building's main entrance.

Asif Bukari beat on the door across from his cabin, yelling for his men to deploy before racing aft to the first of two ladders that would take him to the main deck of the Dorian. As he mounted the ladder, he heard the footsteps of men racing to catch up. It took two minutes for Bukari and the rest of his team to reach the cargo hauler's fantail. They could just make out the shadowy, low-slung silhouette of a destroyer in the black distance, white crests of foam rolling at its bow. Asif barked orders.

"You two, spread out and stay here." He pointed at two others, one of which had the backup phone and detonator. "You two, fore deck. Stay between midships and the crate."

"And if we can't?"

"If they get past the four of us and you can't stop them, detonate the device. Remember. It takes thirty seconds." Asif patted the man on the arm. "Go. Now."

The two men departed at a run and Asif pointed at the last man. "Come with me. Midships at the boarding point."

Mike Nixon sat on the small boat's rubber sponson, kitted out in borrowed gear, M4 rifle at the ready. He watched as the Williams increased speed again, the height of the white, foaming wake gleamed against and behind the hull of the ship as she raced forward in the darkness. A curt 'hold on' from the coxswain behind him reminded him to grab one of the lifelines as the rigid hull inflatable boat leapt forward alongside its mother ship. The driver kept the destroyer between the target and his small craft. Over his radio earpiece, Nixon heard the chatter between the boarding officer and the Williams' commander.

"Showtime, boss." Miguel yelled.

37

DEGUERRA

NICK DEGUERRA SLIPPED THROUGH THE DOORS of the service elevator and into the maintenance tunnel complex. He was halfway down the main passage in the tunnel when the doors slid shut. Ahead of him, fluorescent lighting buzzed and illuminated one of the branch hubs—a six-way connection of halls that led off to other portions of the TitanX compound. The tunnels under the facility normally served two purposes—they were an efficient way for the maintenance crew to get to and from the offices, ranges, barracks, and classrooms that dotted the facility and they became an alternate pathway for headquarters personnel to move about in the frequent snowstorms that plagued upstate New York.

Today, the maze of passages served a third purpose. The complex array of tunnels, work spaces and storage rooms offered the CEO of TitanX a hundred opportunities to hide—and eventually escape— from the people raiding his office a few floors above.

Nick skidded to a halt in the first hub and stopped. He looked at each passage, selected the second hall to his left, and took off again.

Asif's small radio headset crackled to life.

"Asif. The Americans are closing." one of the men from the fantail transmitted.

"How close?"

"Hard to tell. It's black as pitch out here." The voice paused. "Two thousand meters. Maybe less."

Asif paused before responding. "Just the ship?"

"What?"

"Is there a small craft yet?"

"Not that I can see."

Asif paused again. When the small craft became visible, that was the moment to use the phone. When the Americans were close enough to attempt the boarding, they'd be focused on maneuvering instead of speed. On the safety of their small boat. That's what he'd been told.

But the night is black. And the water is black. Would they see anything?

Asif swore. He was tempted to give the order. To use the cell phone and dial the number. But the American had been specific. He swore again and depressed the button on the mike. "When you see the small boat, let me know."

Mike Nixon could hear Lieutenant Lee yelling into his radio over the roar of the growling diesel. He turned to look and Lee flashed a thumbs up. Mike knew what came next and turned to face forward again, rifle at the ready and eyes scanning.

Lieutenant Lee's voice rang out. "Here we go."

Each man hunkered down in the boat, lowering their centers of gravity to absorb the boat's motion while keeping two hands on each rifle. The boat reared back and launched through the water, skipping like a rock as the driver slung the craft around the Williams and raced towards the target.

Nick DeGuerra made several more turns at the tunnel's various hubs before using a key card to enter an abandoned maintenance office. After ensuring the door locked behind him, Nick pulled the phone from his pocket and scrolled through the numbers programmed in.

★ ★ ★ ★ ★

Khan checked his watch and worked the numbers in his head. A few more hours. He raised the remote to change the channel. Every channel was football—a sport he'd never embraced. He kept flipping through the channels, hoping he'd find a cricket match. His phone buzzed. He reached for it, knowing who was calling. No one else had the number.

"Hello, Nicholas."

DeGuerra's voice was barely a whisper, an angry whisper. "Do you have contacts here?"

Khan laughed into the phone. "In New York? You have the wrong branch of my government. I can drop your name to a friend in ISI."

"Not fucking funny, Saeed. I'm in deep shit. The FBI just kicked in the front door."

Khan sat up. "Where the hell are you?"

"Never mind that. You stay put."

"Or what, Nicholas?" Khan roared. He'd had enough of this. "What can you do from whatever little hole you're hiding in? Nothing. I can make a single phone call now, disarm the weapon, and still disappear with your money. And there isn't a damn thing you can do about it." Khan stood and walked into the tiny backyard.

DeGuerra's voice came through, quiet, but threatening. "I wouldn't do that if I were you."

Khan wasn't impressed. "And why not? I have done everything you've asked for and now you have me babysitting one living person and two dead bodies you intend to frame as culprits. You're on the run already because of your own employee and I'm just supposed to sit here for the next two hours and hope nothing else goes wrong?"

"That's exactly what you're going to do, Saeed."

"No, Nicholas, it isn't. I'm leaving. Now."

The line went silent for almost thirty seconds before DeGuerra spoke again.

"Fine, Saeed. You can leave. I need a favor first."

Khan felt his face redden. "And what is that? Kill someone else? Phone for help? This operation of yours is over and I'm getting the hell out of here before you can screw me over."

"That's fine, Saeed. Really. Just one thing. There's a bag in the closet in the hallway. I need you to check that it's there before you hang up."

"What bag?"

"It's the shit I am using to set up Will and the others." DeGuerra snapped. "Just eyeball it for me before you leave. I'll take care of the rest."

Khan was confused. "What evidence? Besides bodies, what else is there?"

"Just check for me, Saeed. Check. And take off."

"Fine." Khan walked back inside and found the closet. Inside were piles of linens—some clean, some soiled—but no bag. He searched through the piles, using his free hand to move the sheets out of the way. "I don't see a bag in here, Nicholas."

"Top shelf, all the way in the back."

Khan looked up to the top shelf and pulled the piles of linens down, following them with his eyes. When he looked back up, his knees went weak.

"I'm sorry, friend." Nick's voice whispered.

The last thing Khan saw were the red, digital numbers of a timer blinking from one to zero. The explosion destroyed half the block and shattered windows five hundred meters away.

DeGuerra hung up both cell phones and let them fall from his hands. He picked the key cards and his pistol up from the desk and walked to the door. He made it halfway across the shop before he heard the beep and saw the door swinging open. His brain froze—half decided on fighting and half decided on surrender. As the first FBI agent swung through the door, decades of instinct took over.

Nick's left hand dropped the key cards and joined his right hand on the pistol. His body turned. His right foot eased backwards. The gun was not yet at eye level when he squeezed the trigger, sending a round low and into the thigh of the first person through the door. More individuals rushed in, yelling and firing as Nick squeezed off a second round that went high. He saw muted flashes and felt the hammering on his chest as he was thrown backwards.

Nick collided with the floor, the Colt skittering away as black-clad figures poured into the room. He tried to breathe, but his lungs didn't seem to work. The room was full of noise, but his brain refused to translate it. He could feel the wounds like fiery fingers in his chest. He could taste and smell the coppery blood filling his mouth and throat.

Nicholas DeGuerra lay on the floor of the workshop and stared at the dimming maze of pipes and ducts above him. Before his world went dark, he thought he recognized the face of Paul Burkhart.

★ ★ ★ ★ ★

The rigid hull inflatable boat from the Williams began its approach with each member of the boarding team watching for movement on the target's weather decks. Mike was the first to see movement and he shouted the warning to the rest of the crew moments before a pair of flashes erupted from the aft end of the cargo ship.

"Target! Fantail!"

Bullets snapped past the boarding team as the coxswain swung the wheel, slinging the boat into a sharp turn to starboard and up the cargo ship's right side. Mike was thrown sideways, but reset and resumed scanning as ocean spray peppered his face. He saw more flashes midships.

Bullets raked the water and peppered the boat's steering console as Mike screamed again. "Targets! Midships!"

Mike snapped off two rounds, flinching as an incoming round hit the handrail next to him. The coxswain swerved again, slinging the small craft around, back towards the rear of the ship. Mike continued firing, aiming for the flashes as the boat under him bounced through the larger ship's wake.

★ ★ ★ ★ ★

Asif Bukari huddled against a short steel wall. The man with him leaned over and fired at the retreating craft. Bukari's rifle lay on the deck and he clutched his arm. He'd been unlucky. He hadn't expected the attackers to come up the starboard side with such speed and he'd been switching hands to use the cell phone when a ricochet had nicked his right forearm.

He probed the wound with his fingers and decided it was nothing serious. He retrieved the phone from where he'd dropped it, ensured it wasn't broken, and opened the contact list. Asif Bukari grinned as he pressed the 'call' button.

38

EVANS

"MR. PRESIDENT?" It was SECDEF, pointing at one of the displays. "The Williams boarding team is taking fire from the Dorian."

Evans watched the display. "She engaging?"

"Commander Allen just ordered the use of the autocannons."

The trilling of a phone caught the president's attention. He looked over to see his Director of National Intelligence answer the phone, listen for a few moments, and disconnect the call. Evans raised an eyebrow at Adams.

"That was the AG. FBI entered the TitanX compound to arrest Nicholas DeGuerra. After a brief hunt, they found him holed up in an office down in the maintenance tunnels."

"They pick him up?"

Adams shook her head. "They executed a forced entry and DeGuerra opened fire. One agent took a round in the thigh. She's been taken to a nearby hospital. It's not serious."

"And DeGuerra?"

"He took six rounds in the chest. Died at the scene."

Evans nodded. "How about Khan and Patterson? We getting anywhere on that?"

"No on both, sir. Khan's last suspected location was Karachi, but we don't have any confirmation. No leads on Patterson. FBI found cell phones near DeGuerra. They're running down the calls he made. Shouldn't take long."

★ ★ ★ ★ ★

Brian was focused on his engines. The temps had cooled off a few degrees—getting within a few hundred yards of the target vessel had allowed the Williams to reduce speed—but now he had another problem. He was watching the oil temps drop slowly out of the allowable range—the analog system designed to control that item dated back to the Second World War and was failing badly. Brian picked up one of the mikes in front of him and ordered the space operator to manually adjust the controller.

★ ★ ★ ★ ★

Petty Officer Gearhart was trying to shut the non-watertight door that separated the USS James E. Williams' shaft alley from the sewage collection room and cursing about it. He'd usually be in a repair locker, ready to race around the ship and fight all sorts of damage. Fire. Flooding. Anything. He liked that job. It was exciting. This, he decided, was boring as hell. And that, Gearhart was certain, explained why MM1 Donaldson had liked it.

Gearhart swore again and shoved the door closed. The door's hinges had been damaged at some point and the resulting misalignment kept the lock from engaging. With the ship rocking and swerving to stay in position, the door was swinging around wildly. While it wasn't close enough to any equipment to cause problems, it had just caught the electrician square in the face. It hadn't drawn blood, but it had wounded his pride.

After several attempts, Gearhart got the door shut and tied it in place with a piece of wire he'd found in the bilge. He resumed his tour of the machinery room.

Gearhart rounded the air conditioning plant sitting in the room's center and looked aft. His eyes locked in on a blinking red light that shouldn't have been there. Gearhart's head cocked sideways seconds before an explosion ripped through the space.

★ ★ ★ ★ ★

Only the explosive charges built into the starboard inflatable shaft seal detonated—the port-side device had short-circuited just hours out of Seychelles as the near-constant spray of saltwater from the leaking shaft seal corroded the delicate electronics in the device's receiver.

Part of the device's explosive force was directed into the space where Petty Officer Gearhart stood, destroying nearly everything within a ten-foot radius. The shaft, leading through the hull to one of the vessel's bronze-manganese propellers was nearly severed. Thousands of gallons of hydraulic oil used to change propeller pitch poured into the space as the shaft continued to rotate, still forced to turn by two of the Williams' gas turbine engines. Some of the explosion's force drove the shaft forward. The thrust bearing, not designed to handle explosive damage, failed and transmitted the axial force to the ship's main reduction gears and engines. The vibration generated when the reduction gears were shoved out of alignment caused the starboard engines to, mercifully, trip offline.

Inboard of the blast's epicenter, a ten-inch section of piping running down the space's aft bulkhead—part of the ship's fuel transfer system—cracked and allowed the expanding fireball access to highly explosive fumes which ignited on the spot, creating a second explosion that ripped through the space.

Both explosions tore smaller items—storage boxes, tools, gages, and phone sets—loose from their fittings and flung them forward. That, plus the concussive force of the twin blasts, wrecked some of the piping on the aft end of the same air conditioning unit that had partially shielded Gearhart from the initial blast.

Two of the damaged lines on the air conditioner poured seawater into the space. A third line, a pressurized portion of the unit's refrigerant system, vented hundreds of pounds of gaseous refrigerant directly into the inferno already devouring the aft quarter of the space—instantly decomposing the cooling agent into the modern-day equivalent of phosgene gas.

The rest of the device's explosive force traveled aft, blowing out the shaft seal and ripping a hole in the fuel tank the seal penetrated. The force of the explosion created an air bubble within the tight confines where the seal had once been for a split second. When the bubble collapsed, ocean water and fuel began pouring into the space at over three hundred gallons per minute.

★ ★ ★ ★ ★

Mike Nixon and Miguel Jimenez were both reloading. In anticipation of the support from the Williams' remote cannons, Lieutenant Lee had ordered the coxswain to back off and tuck the small craft back behind the destroyer's starboard side bulk—allowing his team a reprieve from the volume of fire they'd been receiving.

Mike was looking up at the Williams and marveling at the fact that no one had been hit when he heard the muted boom of an explosion and saw the aft portion of the ship kick away from him. He had just enough time to realize that the destroyer shielding them from the cargo ship had slowed and exposed them. He got behind his sights, too far for an accurate shot, and screamed.

"Lee. What the fuck was that?"

★ ★ ★ ★ ★

Brian picked himself up off the deck in Central Control amid a cacophony of alarms and screaming. The lighting flickered and went out, replaced by the faint glow of mounted battle lanterns. Warning lights flashed and sirens wailed on the control panels as the consoles shifted to battery back-up power and announced a series of disasters.

Every sailor began yelling, listing the alarms sounding on their stations as they worked to silence each one.

"Top! Got flooding alarms in shaft alley. Both starboard GTMs tripped. Loss of starboard prop hydraulics. Fire alarm in shaft alley. Smoke alarm too." The propulsion console operator punched buttons on the console while another sailor at the damage control console listed more problems. "Central! Got a halocarbon alarm in shaft alley. Losing firemain pressure and seawater pressure. Isolating now."

Brian turned to examine the room and saw the electric plant operator lying on the floor. He stepped over debris to check on her.

Announcements flew through the space for a full five additional seconds before Brian yelled. "Quiet!" He turned to the DCA. "Flooding, fire, and toxic gas in shaft alley. And I need a damn corpsman in here."

Lieutenant junior grade Hunter was on the 1MC in seconds calling away the casualties and ordering response teams from the ship's repair lockers to the scene. It took twenty seconds for a corpsman to enter the space, Brian handed over care of the electrician to the medic and lifted a nearby phone. The call was answered immediately. "Captain."

"Captain. Got flooding, fire, and a gas leak in shaft alley. Lost the starboard shaft. Repair five is already moving to the scene."

"Got it, Chief. Electrical systems? Fire control just shut down."

"Wait one, sir." Thompson turned to the Electric Plant Control Console. The operator was back in the seat, a gash above her left eye being tended to while her hands were flying across the station's built-in keypad, dialing up readings for each piece of the ship's power generation equipment. "EPCC?"

The sailor held up a hand for a moment before answering. "Broke something, Chief. One generator is still online. Some of the bus transfers didn't flip. Gonna take a few minutes. Gotta do this manually. I need repair electricians now!"

Brian swore and relayed the information to the captain. He got a curt order to get the electric plant stable and place the starboard engines in battle override. He hung the phone up and called the order to the propulsion console operator. Brian watched as the operator reached up and depressed one button for each of the Williams' two remaining engines—placing each in a condition that would ignore every warning condition up to where the engines would just tear themselves apart.

Brian turned to the DCA. "Ma'am? I need repair electricians. Put 'em in flash gear and on air. Dial in on channel..." Thompson turned back to the EPCC controller who held up three fingers while the medic tried to get a bandage in place. Brian turned back to Hunter. "Channel three."

The DCA issued the appropriate orders and went back to work, carrying on seven conversations at once while the four sailors near her marked up a panel of ship's diagrams—each marking representing a casualty and the effort to save the ship. After nearly a minute, she turned. "Chief, space is electrically isolated and we've got one team accessing the space on air right now. One more at the scene and additional teams ready to go. I need the eductors running to control the flooding while they fight the fire!"

Brian cursed. He'd forgotten that. "On it." He grabbed a nearby mike and ordered his engine room operators to make the necessary plant alignments to dewater shaft alley. After receiving a pair of acknowledgements, he turned back to the DCA, holding up four fingers. "DCA. Four mikes on the dewatering."

She nodded and returned to her work. Brian found himself with nothing to do but wait. Without a mechanical task, his mind could dwell on the human side of this disaster. An explosion. Fire. Flooding. Toxic gas. Shit. He turned.

"DCA! Gearhart is down there."

Mike looked around as Lieutenant Lee yelled into his radio. To their left, the USS James E. Williams was still slowing, losing ground to the Dorian. Looking forward, he could see the gap between the two vessels opening.

Mike turned and looked at the boarding officer as the coxswain struggled to keep them hidden behind the decelerating warship. Lee finally turned to him.

"Something went wrong on the ship. Best speed right now is twelve knots. They're trying to bring the weapons systems back online. Lost power."

Mike looked at the ship and back at Lee. "Those twenty-fives aren't gonna stop that ship."

Lee shook his head. "Captain ain't gonna use the twenty-fives."

39

RANDOLPH

IT HAD TAKEN SEVEN MINUTES for Petty Officer Randolph to get his fire-fighting team into shaft alley. They'd had to crawl through, over, and under wrecked gear and a spinning shaft one-by-one while dragging the fire hose behind them.

The space, poorly lit under normal circumstances, was nothing more than a collection of wrecked machinery, thick black smoke, and searing heat that enveloped Randolph and his team. They were all standing in an ankle-deep mix of fuel, oil, and water and Randolph reported that information to his repair locker. He couldn't see much and only knew where his nozzleman, Petty Officer Allen Brooks, was because he had a firm grasp on the collar of the other sailor's turnout gear.

Randolph tried to look around as the rest of the team found their way to the hose and picked it up. He patted Brooks on the back and felt the man move forward under his direction.

Randolph patted Brooks again, a signal to open the bail and dump foam on the roaring inferno visible behind the burnt carcass of the air conditioning plant.

The team worked its way forward, inch by inch, Randolph directing and Brooks swinging the nozzle back and forth to knock the flames down. As they advanced on the roaring furnace, Randolph yelled reports into his radio and rotated his team through the nozzleman position every few minutes. They'd moved to the edge of the air conditioning unit when Randolph felt his mask vibrate.

Fuck. Running out of air. Randolph was lifting his radio when he felt a hand on his shoulder.

★ ★ ★ ★ ★

"Central, Repair Five. Scene Leader reports attack team two fighting the fire. Attack team one egressing the space."

The DCA acknowledged the report and ordered the entry on her boards before calling for another repair locker to deploy their next team to the scene and giving them an appropriate route.

Brian watched and listened to everything going on around him. DCA was controlling and directing damage control efforts and the ship's repair electricians were out shifting power to alternate sources under the careful direction of the EPCC Operator. The ship was moving through the water at just under twelve knots with a shudder that was strong enough to be felt in Central.

Commotion to Brian's right got his attention and he looked over to see a pair of legs dangling through the hatch above the DCA's head. Brian watched as the figure dropped down the ladder tucked into the corner.

"XO?"

Lieutenant Commander John Polian pulled the hatch shut behind him and spun the locking wheel before crossing the space to where Brian and the Chief Engineer stood. "Gents. Where are we on the plant?"

Brian nodded at the electric plant console. "Two minutes."

The XO pulled a phone off of its cradle. He dialed a number and put the phone on speaker.

"Captain."

"XO, sir. Chief says two mikes."

"Very well."

Brian turned to the XO as the electrician continued directing her plant alignment. "Where's the boarding team?"

"Hiding beside us. Starboard side. Gap between us and that ship is too far for them to try anything. And it's getting bigger. Fire?"

Brian pointed to the DCA. "Just got word. Second team is fighting the fire. First team is still trying to get out."

Randolph watched as his last man was relieved and backed out of the space before beginning his own egress. The heat, even through the turnout gear, was like sitting on the surface of the sun and he'd already sweat through everything he was wearing. Forcing himself to be patient, Randolph backed out of the space step-by-step. Between the smoke and the fogging in his mask, it was difficult to see where he was going. Walking out backwards was an added complication, but he had no intention of turning his back on a raging inferno. He made it four paces before tripping and falling.

Randolph caught himself by reaching out and latching onto a pair of nearby pipes before he looked down. The roiling smoke in the space made it difficult to see much past his own knees, so Randolph squatted and felt around, patting here and in the darkness until his hand grabbed what looked like a uniform.

"Sixty seconds, Chief" The EPCC operator reported.

The XO pressed the transmit button on the phone. "Sixty seconds, Captain."

"Very well." The CO sounded inhumanly calm through the speaker. "Combat, sixty more seconds on the electric plant. I want the Mark 45 ready as soon as possible. High explosive rounds."

"Combat, aye."

Miguel was splitting his time—half of it spent looking down range through his own weapon's sight and half spent keeping a wary eye on the massive gun sitting on the Williams' foredeck. It was barely visible from where he sat and that made him nervous. He was familiar with artillery but he'd never sat right next to a 127-millimeter cannon belching twenty high-explosive rounds per minute.

He spoke over his shoulder. "That thing able to take down a cargo ship?"

Above the wind and the roaring diesel, he heard Lieutenant Lee yell. "Just watch."

★ ★ ★ ★ ★

"Done, Chief. Plant is stable. Combat should have power." The EPCC operator announced, blood running down her face and the front of her uniform.

The XO depressed the transmit button. "Plant is stable, Captain."

"Very well." A pause. "Weps, get me online."

"Weps, aye."

★ ★ ★ ★ ★

Four members of Randolph's team entered the ship's medical office carrying the limp body of Petty Officer Gearhart on a stretcher. They placed him on the exam table and left the ship's medics to their business. Master Chief Carrillo was there thirty seconds later.

★ ★ ★ ★ ★

"Attack team three is engaging the fire. Team two is egressing the space. Reports that the flooding is two inches above the deck plates and holding." DCA finished her announcement and ordered up the next attack team.

Brian nodded. "The fire?"

DCA turned back. "Team three reports the fire under control."

The speaker phone behind Brian crackled back to life. "Captain, Weps. Fire control systems online. Mark 45 coming online in thirty seconds."

"Captain, aye." A pause. "XO, Captain."

"Go for XO."

"Make damn sure the boat crew stays behind us."

"Aye, aye, Captain." The XO keyed the mike clipped to his collar and passed the word to Lieutenant Lee.

★ ★ ★ ★ ★

Mike Nixon heard the crackling of Lee's radio and felt the boat slow beneath his feet. To his left, the Williams surged ahead until the coxswain pulled the small assault craft over into the blackness of the destroyer's wake.

★ ★ ★ ★ ★

"Captain, Weps! Mark 45 is online. Ready in all respects!"

Brian turned to the speaker phone, unconsciously bracing against the seat in front of him as the captain's voice broke over the net.

"Commence firing. Put that fucker on the bottom!"

★ ★ ★ ★ ★

The first round caught everyone on the boarding team by surprise— an explosion of flame and a concussive blast wave rocked the destroyer as the USS James E. Williams' 127-millimeter deck gun flung its first seventy-pound shell downrange. With a muzzle velocity of over two thousand feet per second and an effective range of nearly thirteen miles, the cargo vessel less than two miles ahead was little more than a sitting duck.

★ ★ ★ ★ ★

Asif Bukari, arm wrapped with a makeshift bandage, was watching the American warship fall further and further behind. It was nothing more than a shadow now. A black dot on the black water that could not hurt him or stop him. The warship was wounded. Possibly mortally. He smiled at that thought and the idea that his own vessel would make its escape. He smiled at the men around him on the fantail and raised the binoculars to his eyes just in time to see a massive orange and yellow flame erupt from the dot on the horizon.

★ ★ ★ ★ ★

The first shell struck just below the Dorian's bridge, penetrated six feet beyond the steel skin of the superstructure and exploded. It sheared the superstructure almost completely off.

★ ★ ★ ★ ★

Asif Bukari survived the first explosion, despite it happening directly above his head. He'd thrown himself into a passage built into the superstructure and had escaped with a few minor scrapes and bruises.

He was not smiling now. His orders had been clear on this point. If the Americans somehow jeopardized the end goal, he was to use the radio detonator and activate the device secured to the Dorian's foredeck.

Asif Bukari prayed as he reached for the device in his pocket.

He never made it.

★ ★ ★ ★ ★

The following rounds from the Williams' main gun—ten to be exact— followed every three seconds with only one miss, the tenth and final round hitting nothing but the open water that Dorian had just vacated when the ninth round hit low on the stern and blew the entire aft end of the cargo vessel to port in a devastating primary and secondary explosion.

The holes punched in and through the Dorian were already proving fatal to the merchant hauler. Poorly maintained by a crew that earned little and cared less, the damage control systems designed to protect the ship from fires and flooding were overcome within ninety seconds.

The sea poured into the cargo ship through three holes—the largest of which was over twenty feet in diameter.

Within two minutes of the last hit, the bow of the Dorian rose, throwing cargo and crew aft towards a dark, watery grave highlighted by growing puddles of burning oil.

★ ★ ★ ★ ★

Against orders, the coxswain had swung the boat outside of the Williams' wake to watch the explosions downrange. Mike looked at Miguel.

"Holy fuck, boss."

Mike sat down on the boat's rubber sponson and leaned his head on the handrail. "Yeah."

★ ★ ★ ★ ★

DCA turned away from her boards and walked over to where Brian, Lieutenant Walker, and the XO were monitoring the plant. "Team three reports fire is out. Reflash watch set. Flooding is four inches from deck plates and dropping. Team four is entering the space to relieve team three."

"Gearhart?"

The DCA lowered her eyes to the deck, shook her head once and returned to her work.

Brian sat heavily in his chair and leaned forward, letting his head rest on the open casualty control manual on the desk in front of him.

★ ★ ★ ★ ★

"Mr. President?" SECDEF was replacing a handset in a cradle. "The fire on the Williams is out and they've reduced the flooding as much as they can. Commander Allen is driving the ship to Chennai on one screw."

Evans nodded. "Survivors from the Dorian?"

"Two crew members, apparently unassociated with this mess. Both engineers. Ophelia's folks will run that down. The Williams' boat crew pulled them out of the water a few minutes ago."

"How's the crew of the Williams?"

SECDEF's eyes lowered. "Commander Allen reports one casualty. Petty Officer Richard Gearhart, an electrician, was killed in the fire."

"We know what caused the explosion?"

"Not yet, sir."

Evans turned to his chief of staff. "Get me a call sheet for the sailor's family."

"Yes, Mr. President."

"Leslie?"

"Yes, Mr. President?"

"What do we do about Pakistan?"

The chief of staff rose. "That's the million-dollar question, Daniel."

40

ROBINSON

CALVIN HAD THOUGHT ABOUT QUITTING his job and hauling ass before disregarding the move as premature. He'd seen a brief news report three weeks earlier about a collision between the USS James E. Williams and a cargo ship called the Dorian in the strait between India and Sri Lanka, but he'd not heard anything else.

He should have been nervous, but he wasn't. After thinking about the situation logically—an ability he prided himself on—he decided there wasn't really a danger. He'd not heard any mention of an explosion aboard the destroyer. That, he concluded, meant one of two things. Either the devices had not been used or they'd been discovered and disarmed. If the latter was true, he'd have woken up to the sight of armed federal agents crashing through his door. But that hadn't happened. That decided the engineer in favor of the former scenario and his course of action was simple. The ship would be transported back stateside and he would be part of the repairs. He would, when the time was right, manufacture some excuse for removing the unused explosive devices from the Williams and replace the inflatable shaft seals with unaltered units.

As sat on his couch and flipped through the channels he considered the fact that he hadn't seen pictures of the damage to be something that was slightly out of the ordinary before dismissing the notion. The people on that ship had bigger things to worry about than sending photos back to the repair facilities and a collection of GS-9 government mechanics.

After cycling through the available channels twice, Calvin turned the television off and dropped the remote on the couch beside him. He yawned and stood and decided that heading into the kitchen to make himself lunch was preferable to ordering out.

Calvin was halfway there when his front and back doors were thrown open and a dozen figures in black body armor charged into the small townhouse.

★ ★ ★ ★ ★

Evans sat at his desk and signed the last of a stack of commendations and awards for the crew of the USS James E. Williams. The Navy had done its part to recognize the men and women onboard, but he had insisted that a little something extra was in order. Besides, he told his staff, it was a welcome duty considering that he'd spend the next four hours in another series of economic briefings.

A knock on the door got his attention. He looked up to see Leslie Barnes escorting Ophelia Adams into the room.

"Good morning, Ophelia. Leslie." Evans nodded at both. "What's up?"

"An update, Mr. President." Adams said.

Evans gestured to seats nearby. "Khan?"

Adams nodded. "And Patterson. There was an explosion in Bhuj, India on the same day as the interdiction. When firefighters got in there, they found four bodies. DNA tests just came back. Khan and Patterson both died in the explosion."

"You said four bodies. Who were the other two?" Evans asked.

Barnes answered. "The missing operators from TitanX. Andrew Cook and Dave Fogarty. We notified the folks at TitanX before we came here. They're contacting the families right now."

Evans nodded. "Get me a call sheet, Leslie?"

"Yes, Mr. President."

★ ★ ★ ★ ★

Brian stumbled into the USS James E. Williams' Chief's Mess, still half asleep. The ship had been in Chennai for three weeks, shut down and with a complement of replacement sailors to cover for the exhausted crew. They still didn't have an official word on how the ship would get home—under her own power, towed, or carried on another ship designed for the purpose—but that didn't matter at the moment.

Brian pulled his coffee mug from its peg, nodded at the new and old faces, and poured fresh, black coffee into the dirty cup. He looked around and took a seat across from the men who'd replaced him on the boarding.

A nod. "Mr. Nixon. Mr. Jimenez. How are you two holding up?"

Nixon leaned back. "We're good. Agency is flying the two of us home tomorrow."

"And Mr. Raza."

Miguel nodded. "Him too. How's your crew?"

Brian leaned back in his own seat. "Losing a sailor is always tough."

Both men nodded. "You know," Nixon began. "It's not something you think about 'til it happens. Got a buddy back home. His nephew is in the ICU out at Balboa after that shit at BUD/S. He said he never thought about this until the kid got caught in the blast."

Brian took a sip of coffee. "How's the kid?"

"He's gonna live. Breathing on his own. He's never gonna be a SEAL with the injuries and all, but..."

"But he's alive," Brian pointed out. "That beats the alternative. What's next for you guys?"

Miguel grinned. "I'm going home. Maybe open a food truck or something."

Brian laughed. "You cook?"

Another grin, this one from Nixon. "No. He can't."

Miguel punched Nixon in the shoulder. "Hey. How hard can it be?"

Brian was about to say something about his own poor cooking skills when the 1MC crackled to life.

"Chief Petty Officer Thompson. Captain's Cabin."

Brian left Nixon and Jimenez to their coffee and began the trek up three decks to where Commander Allen lived. When he arrived, he looked down at his uniform, decided there wasn't much to be done about it. Brian knocked on the door and entered when directed. The captain was wiping shaving cream off of his face and motioned Brian to a nearby couch.

"Chief, you look better."

Brian sat. "Thank you, sir."

"Get some sleep?"

Brian nodded. "A little. Spending some time getting caught up on everything else. You know, actually doing my job instead of turning wrenches."

The captain sat heavily into his own chair. "Bored yet?"

Brian took a sip of coffee before speaking. "I've been on board, what? Ninety days? Something like that? I don't know if I'll ever complain about being bored again."

"I thought so." Commander Allen rubbed his face. "I just wanted to see how you're doing. I saw the letter you sent to Gearhart's family."

Brian nodded and let his eyes fall to the floor. "Yeah."

"That letter made it sound like you felt responsible for Gearhart."

Brian looked up. "I kicked Donaldson off the ship and wrote the watch bill. I put Gearhart down there."

"Chief. You didn't kick anyone off the ship and you didn't send Petty Officer Gearhart to shaft alley. You may have recommended both actions, but they're my responsibility. I made those calls. I signed the orders."

"Legally, maybe. But I can't think like that. They're my sailors before they're yours."

Commander Allen leaned his head back for a moment. "We're not gonna see eye to eye on this, are we?" He smiled.

Brian smiled back. "No, sir."

"I figured as much."

Brian stood. "Anything else, sir?"

The captain stood. "Yeah. It's gonna be a bit before they work out how we get home. We'll be rotating people out on leave, starting with you and Guillory. Fifteen days to get home and get your heads on straight. We're gonna need you two to help put this ship back together."

Brian nodded and opened the stateroom door. "Understood, sir. Anything else?"

"Just think about what I said."

"Yes, sir." Brian stepped into the passage and shut the door. He walked aft and made his way up to the bridge, gaining permission to venture out onto the starboard bridge wing. Brian looked at the busy port—watching the gulls spiral around the cranes in the bright sunlight while he sipped his coffee. He closed his eyes for a minute and took a deep breath. When he opened his eyes, he checked his watch and did some quick math before deciding that it was a good time to call home.

Acknowledgments

To the staff at Double Dagger Books, I offer my sincere thanks for this opportunity and the professional direction they have provided during the process.

To the professors and students from Johns Hopkins University's Writing Program, I am appreciative of the lessons and valuable insights that aided me in crafting this tale.

To the Sailors, Chiefs, and Officers of the United States Navy, especially those who served on USS James E. Williams from 2014 to 2016, I want to say that I am forever indebted to you. You are living proof of the strength and resiliency of the human spirit.

DOUBLE†DAGGER

Double Dagger Books is Canada's newest military-focused publisher. Conflict and warfare have shaped human history since before we began to record it. The earliest stories that we know of, passed on as oral tradition, speak of war, and more importantly, the essential elements of the human condition that are revealed under its pressure. We are dedicated to publishing material that, while rooted in conflict, transcend the idea of "war" as merely a genre. Fiction, non-fiction, and stuff that defies categorization, we want to read it all.

Because if you want peace, study war.

www.doubledagger.ca

CONFIDENTIAL
NOT RELEASABLE TO THE PUBLIC
RECEIVED
11 / 3 / 11
A novel
by A E MERRICK
THE TRUTH WILL SET YOU FREE

11 / 3 / 11

9/11 was an inside job.

The moon landings were faked.

JFK is alive and well and spends his days with Elvis.

Everyone knows what happened on 11/3/11. But do they really know the truth?

John Doe – JD to his friends – knows for a fact that things are not as they seem. The world is wearing blinders, but he has his eyes wide open. And the more you truly know, the crazier you seem.

Dive into a rabbit hole of conspiracy theories and see the world through JD's eyes. AE Merrick's debut novel is a wild ride through mind control, paranoia and isolation in search of the ever-elusive truth.

Available January, 2022.

Matt Hardman is a retired U.S. Navy Chief Petty Officer who currently works as a marine engineering consultant to the Navy's DDG 51 Shipbuilding Program Office. While on active duty, he served onboard a submarine, two aircraft carriers, two amphibious transports, one submarine tender, and one destroyer. During his final tour of duty, he served as the Engineering Department Chief, or "Top Snipe," for the USS James E. Williams (DDG 95). He holds a bachelor's in Intelligence Studies and Counterintelligence from American Military University and a Master's in Writing from Johns Hopkins University.

Matt Hardman is also a husband and father of six children and currently resides in Calvert County, Maryland.